NOMAD
DIARIES

A Novel

Yasmeen Maxamuud

WHAT PEOPLE ARE SAYING ABOUT NOMAD DIARIES:

NOMAD DIARIES, which follows a Somali refugee family from war-torn Mogadishu to resettlement in the U.S., is a trenchant critique of the social prejudices and inequalities that have marked Somali society in the past and have caused so much suffering, hypocrisy, and rage. Through the unfolding lives of this family's members (young and old), the author depicts the grueling impact of sexual (as well as class-, clan- and race-based) discrimination as inflected by the traumatic events of civil war, flight, and resettlement. The novel also draws a compelling picture of how tragically dysfunctional 'the old ways' can become in the Diaspora setting. Though one may object that the author has little eye for those Diaspora Somalis who have successfully combined the best of both worlds, it is also true that the deeply flawed characters she has created are fully realistic and, in the end, not completely irredeemable. Perhaps it takes the voice of a Somali woman writer such as Yasmeen Maxamuud – a critical, strong, indignant voice – to cut through nuance, ambiguity, and silence to address certain ugly realities that characterize Somali society at this junction of history: violence against women, male chauvinism and women's implication in it, and male and female ignorance, prejudice, and greed. Whether Somali or non-Somali, the reader will be moved by this novel's cry for justice and respect for all Somalis.

LIDWIEN KAPTEIJNS
WELLESLEY COLLEGE

A must-read first-and-only novel by and for the post-civil war generation of Somalis coming of age in the United States, NOMAD DIARIES is a treasure chest—a Pandora's box of drama, trauma, and elation bubbling just beneath the quizzical refugee grin, and Yasmeen Maxamuud is a master narrator of the entwined intergenerational fates of Somalis who fled catastrophe for a Pyrrhic dream. Bordering non-fiction, Maxamuud's work provides an expose on hot-topic taboo issues plaguing the community, lays a trail of breadcrumbs for young Somali Americans seeking a more wholesome relationship to their past, and turns the casual reader into an intimate confidante of one of the richest and most enigmatic strands of the American social fabric.

JESSE MILLS, PH.D.
UNIVERSITY OF SAN DIEGO

NOMAD DIARIES is a captivating narrative that recounts the horrors of the Somali civil war and the onerous, often dehumanizing burden of trying to construct a second life in a new culture where one is not understood. This story explodes clichés and instead forces the reader to experience the horrors of war as the home of Nadifo, the wife of a Somali foreign minister, is attacked in Hamar, Somalia's capital city. The experience will haunt her daughter Henna for the rest of her life. We come to care deeply about Nadifo, Henna and Henna's son Shirwac, as they expose us to an America only refugees can see. This is a compelling life story that anyone interested in a diversified America should read.

DOUG RUTLEDGE, PH.D.
WRITER, SOMALI DOCUMENTARY PROJECT

In *NOMAD DIARIES*, Yasmeen Maxamuud beautifully threads together a tapestry of a nomadic Somali narrative and its journey from African refugee camps to the more complex cosmopolitan cities of America. Rich with details, entrancing and moving, "Nomadic Diaries" tells the harrowing account of the destruction of a Somali family that once was a tranquil middle class household, then suddenly found itself embroiled in tribal conflicts at the height of Somalia's civil war.

The story is brilliantly constructed, describing as it does the unbearable stresses a Somali refugee family faces in its struggle to remake itself in melting-pot America. In the end, Nadifo, the protagonist and her family, are more defined by the pathologies of urban America than by their traditional tribal mores. This is a terrific tale told in lambent prose.

SAID S. SAMATAR, PH.D.
PROFESSOR OF HISTORY RUTGERS UNIVERSITY

NOMAD DIARIES
by Yasmeen Maxamuud

NOMAD DIARIES © 2009 by *Yasmeen Maxamuud*

Soft Cover ISBN: 0-9708587-3-6
Hard Cover ISBN: 0-9708587-4-4

Library of Congress Control Number: 2009936845

NomadHouse Publishing
ENCINITAS, CA

DEDICATED TO SOMALI WOMEN,
FOR THEIR STRUGGLE
AND ENDURANCE.

DISCLAIMER:

This story about a Somali immigrant family in America is fictional. The characters, settings, names and storylines are all purely fictional creations of the author.

TO THE READER:

To maintain context and flow of events, many words, terms and sayings are written in Arabic or Somali. You will find a Glossary on page 471 to help you with definitions and pronunciations.

ACKNOWLEDGMENTS:

First and foremost all praises are to Allah (SWT), who gave me the strength and patience to see this project through.

This book would not have been possible without the selfless efforts of many individuals. In particular I am grateful to those who have believed in this project even before I realized it was a possibility.

I am deeply indebted to Jesse Mills for your incessant support and for using the book in your class even before it was complete. Exceptional thanks to Professor Jesse Mills students at University of San Diego and University of California, San Diego for giving the book an audience at such an early stage. Darlene Bauer for being an inspiration throughout the writing process. Monique Gaffney for agreeing to help out in such a short notice. Mike Norris for your utmost professionalism and creative mind. Doug Rutledge and Abdi Roble of the Somali Documentary Project for your earnest dedication to the Somali community at large and for being available to lend a hand. And Lidwien Kapteijns of Wellesley College for your heartfelt devotion and many contributions to Somali literature. I am beholden to professor Said Samatar whose prolific writing, books, articles and essays were a great resource, and for being available amid a busy schedule.

I am appreciative to Adan Adar, Fiasal Robleh and Ahmed Hamud for your careful eye and useful insights and for reviewing early drafts. Ali Artan, for helping with all sorts of computer issues and assisting with many aspects of this book. Ahmed Hassan for your God-given talent in the Somali language and exceptional expressions. Jamad Suryan, Amal Dalmar and Idil Dalmar for cheering me on and being available at moment's notice. And my husband Abdikarim for never yielding and always being supportive. For your sense of humor which saw us through and your patience and endless revisions and editing. My father and siblings for always being loyal.

ABOUT THE BOOK

The corridors of Cedar Springs Luxury Apartments hold many secrets. If you were to peek into the lives of Somali refugees who call this notorious run-down high-rise home, you will find all that eighteen years of civil war has produced. Strong-willed women dealing with language barriers, hardships, and a new country called America where everything is vastly different from what they were used to, Americanized children and polygamous husbands.

Nadifo Cafi is one of these women. Nadifo's emigration to America is not one of choice but one forced on her by war. She is unable to reconcile her new life with the one she lost. She was the most glamorous woman in Hamar, a trend-setter, a fashion icon, and the wife of the prominent and influential Foreign Minister until heart-wrenching violence interrupted the life she shared with her husband and their five children. Her leap into her new American life comes with mixed feelings. It's where her children begin to defy her, and where a tragic secret past she thought she had purposely left behind on the shores of Africa trails her.

She finds herself at the helm of a family on the brink of life when Henna, her youngest daughter, decides to marry the American Brian Shields, not only to defy her mother but to escape a judgmental, unforgiving culture. Warsan, her eldest daughter had fled the new refugee life her family inherited, lured into a criminal life of greed. Ceebla's love for Haybe is forbidden by a culture that doesn't see beyond tribal lines, and Cartan, the former Minister of Foreign Affairs turned refugee, elopes with a younger woman after thirty-five years of marriage to Nadifo.

Come and eavesdrop on the lives of these colorful refugees to get a slice of American immigrant life with strong willed women, rebellious teens and a rare taste of American immigrant life with a twist.

Nomad Diaries is an endearing, heartbreaking story of loss, despair, and family bonds tested by the destruction of a country. *Nomad Diaries* examines the human condition at its weakest. It's the epitome of life and loss at the crossroads of a new beginning. Somali refugees stagger through American immigrant life with their vibrant, colorful, unique culture, making their mark on the melting pot called America.

PROLOGUE
HAMAR: FEAST OR FAMINE

DECEMBER, 1989

The streets of Hamar hum with commotion. The sour aroma of the beach and the glare of pristine white villas accompany the bustle of pedestrian traffic, made up of people from other regions, each bringing their distinct mores to the capital city. Young and old alike accomplish their daily errands, greeting each other enthusiastically in a diversity of local dialects, catching up on the day's news. The men wear their sarongs gracefully, while the women flaunt their *guntiino*, *diric* or *cabaaya*. Most of the youth perch defiantly in Western attire, desperately striving for an effortless cool look. The clothes tell many stories: a family's position in society is made apparent by the attire of its members. The villagers look homely, and not up to par with the latest fashions, while city dwellers exhibit their struggle for sophistication and status.

Hamar, named for its sandy chestnut beaches and the sour-sweetness of tamarind. The most cosmopolitan city—if ever there was one—in Africa, where the Catholic Cathedral sits less than a mile from the Cabdul Caziz Mosque, built in the 12th century at the gate of the old port. The diversity the city offers to people from other regions, countries, and even religions was once unparalleled.

The tranquility of the turquoise-blue Indian Ocean created hope for the people who remembered Hamar's grandiose, peaceful days. People remember with nostalgia the days when a Barawaani designer, an Arab gold smith, lost young peasant girls from the countryside, Northern merchants with their loud accents, exiled Eritreans and South African students could assimilate into the melting pot of Hamar, which attracted people from all walks of life for the possibilities it offered, where even youth with regional dialects faked their way into the Hamari dialect to make their perceived primitive tongues disappear. Hamar was the city of night life, countless bakeries, restaurants, storefronts and cinemas, where one could snack on xalwo, cookies, sambuusa with bur and bajiye all at once, after eating finger-licking muufo with suqaar and isbar-muuto on a lazy hot afternoon. It was only in Hamar where one could end the evening with Hema Malini as a young sad widow in Andaaz and an action-filled western like "The Good, the Bad, and the Ugly". Hamar was to the average Somali-Milan, New York, and Los Angeles rolled into one, where entertainment, fashion and business collided. It had sophistication, style and an openness which welcomed everyone into its bosom.

But there came a time when the dream city of red sandy beaches bloated with fear, and the air filled with stifling tension. People's faces weary with worry as they wonder, is it today, has the day finally arrived? The long-awaited day when a dictator will be ousted? This wish may indeed be granted soon, as rumors the government is countering opposition forces that have in recent days become particularly strong, swim in the tight, anxious air. A coup d'état is eminent, if one heeds these rumors.

People carry on hushed conversations, looking over their shoulders. If they are caught discussing political affairs, it results in the suspicious and deadly disappearance of the culprit. Mothers urge their sons to avoid all political activity and to keep any negative thoughts about the government to themselves; better that such thoughts are kept at bay altogether. Instead they encourage them to praise their leader, *"Noolow, noolow, noolow Siyaad noolow"*— as no mother can stomach the task of digging a son out of a shallow grave.

Cartan and Nadifo's home in Hamar had been a destination for the villagers of Gobwanaag. The guests from Gobwanaag embarked on long journeys to Hamar in order to obtain birth certificates, passports, and any other government documents which they cannot get in their local municipalities. These documents are obtained with false information: to acquire their legal documents, the villagers hailing from the North of the country would have to present a fake birth certificate boasting their birth place to be anywhere in the Southern part of the country, with this the current government would deliver passports and birth certificates. If you were born in Hargeysa you would claim to have been born in Kismaayo and if you hailed from Gobwanaag you professed to be a local reer hamar. The falsification is part of the system created by the people who feared marginalization

In private, people refer to the president as *Afweyne*—it is as if they got their revenge by repeating *Afweyne* in every disastrous situation, *Afweynaa maanta xidhay rag inagga ah! Afweynaa halkaa ka nacnac lahaa, Afweyne ha dhaco!* He ruled the country for over twenty years with an iron fist. Cartan is the Foreign Minister, and as such he is able to address the needs of relatives from the village with ease, even if their birthdates, birthplaces and places of residence are falsified on their documents. They may dislike having to travel with documents that have false information, but they count their blessings for having documents at all. They sometimes travel two, three, or four days to reach Hamar, just to obtain an identity card with false information. No matter what part of Somalia one is from, one had to travel to Hamar to obtain the documentation; even a simple identity card required such a journey.

The mansion Nadifo had built took six years to complete. She had refused to live in the government housing provided to them rent-free: it was too modest by Nadifo's standards by now. A five-bedroom house that came with a chef, guard, and a driver was too modest for a peasant girl from Gobwanaag who only a few years earlier shared a crowded run-down apartment with three other families.

When she moved into a small government home after her descent into Hamar, Nadifo appreciated its advantages: at least she did not have to share the bathroom with other roommates as she previously did when she left Gobwanaag and moved to Hamar. Then, she had to share the common areas such as the washroom, hallways, and kitchen. For privacy she retreated to the single cement room she shared with her husband and two kids. In her hometown, Gobwanaag, the impoverished Nadifo had lived in a small mud house with twelve, sometimes fourteen, relatives; so the cramped apartment was a blessing away from the mud house where her movements were restricted by the tightly-packed bodies surrounding her. In Hamar the bathroom proved particularly difficult for a village girl like Nadifo; she waited to use the toilet until everyone else had gone to sleep. The culture in Hamar was so different from Gobwanaag: in the city, women went to use the toilet in clear view of men who were not relatives. Nadifo walked around for hours at a time with a full bladder until everyone vacated the entire common area, then she would sneak and relieve herself.

It took some getting used to for Nadifo to go from sharing space to having an entire house to herself; but soon Cartan was promoted to the prestigious, influential position of Foreign Minster, and she immediately prepared for the change. This time she was not modest about it: Nadifo was by now so far removed from the humble beginnings of Gobwanaag that change meant a mansion, a new lifestyle, and becoming the trendsetter for the whole city.

As she began the search for a house suitable for a woman with the title "Wife of Foreign Minister" she came across a mansion built by the renowned and award-winning international architect Marissa Piatzaz. The mansion she eventually chose was modeled after a palace she had seen in Milan when her husband was in Italy for a political trip, a 110-room palace belonging to a fashion designer. She hired Mrs. Piatzaz immediately to build a replica of it, and then hired the world-famous interior designing company Piera Renzo International to decorate it. The only instruction she gave was to have various themes of Moroccan, Turkish, Japanese and European ambiance in the new mansion. She wanted to harmonize Europe, Islam and Asia in her house, a unique design never seen in the elite houses of the ruling party in Hamar.

Nadifo vainly scheduled the completion of the mansion to coincide with her son Geele's wedding; she planned the wedding ceremony to showcase the various extravagant themes of her new home. She was particularly excited to invite the wife of the president, whom she often competed with for popularity. The garden of the mansion was so massive they hired three gardeners to care for it, and it grew enough guava, papaya, and mango to serve all their guests and neighbors. There were three different kitchens, four living rooms, ten bedrooms, and six bathrooms, each espousing a different style. There were guest quarters, maid quarters, a swimming pool, and the first Jacuzzi to ever grace a house in the tropical city.

Nadifo's children looked forward to the legends and village practices of the visitors from Gobwanaag. This time the villagers got lost in the new mansion: they marveled at the bathrooms, not understanding why such a massive elegant room was used to do the most unsightly human act. Some were found looking for a forest to do their private business— others accepted the use of the room, with huge reservations and much guilt, sometimes leaving the entire bathroom in a horrid mess. It was so complex that no amount of instruction could adequately express the different uses of the sink, the tub, the commode and the bidet. They mistook the area to relieve themselves for the area to shower, sometimes creating undue work for mansion staff.

When they were not worrying over where to wash or urinate, they animated the children with tales vivid with lions, frogs, turtles, and giraffes. They told endless tales of their encounter with lions, foxes, giraffes, and hyenas that roamed the village, which apparently lived harmoniously with them. The children lost themselves in the stories, staying up late every night, hungry for a new story every time. It reconnected them to the basics of culture. City life forged a forgetful self, a self in which their heritage escaped like air from a balloon and was replaced by Western emulations. The humble peasants brought the family much-needed reality and simplicity. Their odd smoke smell, crocodile skin, bloodshot eyes and loud voices brimmed with culture and love the children had not seen in city dwellers.

Mako the chef tired of them when they refused to eat at the family dining room table, would find empty glasses discarded in the yard where she would sometimes catch one or two of the villagers eating. She marveled at their odd behavior despite the irritation at the extra work it created for her.

The streets of Hamar erupted with blasting revolutionary slogans from Radio Hamar which broadcasts kacaan songs, speeches by the president, plays about the president, and news handpicked by the president—a reassuring impetus to remind every citizen of his greatness. Legendary poets, composers, songwriters, playwrights and talented singers part-take in the praise of *Afweyne*, corrupting innocent ears with lies and propaganda. He single-handedly and effectively brainwashed a people to the point where they praised him endlessly, sometimes believing in the empty slogans themselves. Every other song on the radio was a kacaan song that was tattooed into the psyche of the people, to keep them in line.

The immense talent of composers, poets and broadcasters are used to condition the people to fear the state. Gigantic posters of Afweyne line the streets. On every corner one could find him in a different pose: he policed the streets with an agonizing gaze which followed people everywhere, hovering over them. Even God-fearing adults would look over their shoulders to assure themselves Afweyne and his henchmen were not following.

People would curse him under their breath, unable to trust their voices, as if their own words would betray them, leaping out of their mouths to the ears of a callous few called *guulwadayaal* (victory pioneers)—who were rural drifters handpicked by Afweyne and recruited to spy on the bewildered citizenry. Scientific Socialism (SS) is the slogan one heard every time Afweyne gave a speech, and he gave speeches every day to propagate fear. Fear is part of everyday living like eating, praying and breathing, used to create timid, frightened, willing people to follow his laws in order to simply survive his brutality. Composers composed, singers sang and dancers danced in the name of Afweyne while Hargeysa and Burco were besieged, as Cartan, Nadifo and other elite rulers of the country enjoyed their wealth and extravagant lives.

He stashed citizenry funds in fat Swiss bank accounts in the name of SS. Poor peasants and informal business women gave their hard earned change in the name of SS. His family lived lavishly around the globe as a result of SS. Farmers saw their farms taken by SS. Poor women who labored for hours to feed their families saw nothing of their hard-earned income in the name of SS.

Inequality and brutal dictatorship have fatigued the people. Everyone is a willing participant in this new experiment, anything to get rid of the thief, brutal, cruel, evil SS.

SS put young educated men from Garowe in shallow graves, SS delivered widows and children who now had to call SS father and mother. SS hanged Kaahin, Nadifo's brother, while Nadifo built her mansion, travelled the world and in the name of SS lavished her family with the most extravagant life possible. A guulwade took Kaahin, a businessman, from his home one afternoon at siesta as he slept next to his pregnant wife, and his three children slept in the next room. Three weeks later, his body was found, beaten, shot, and hanged. The reason given for his murder, he was part of the opposition and a threat to the government. After years of the elusive SS, Somalis became suspicious of each other; every tribe held abhorrence for the next, and people just about had enough. War was looming in the shadows as Nadifo and Cartan prepared for Geele's over-elaborate wedding.

NOMAD

DIARIES

GLORY & GORE

Die here!" the assassin said, slapping and throwing her to the floor all at once. "Where is your husband? Where are you hiding the honorable minister? Where the hell is he?" He barked with a mocking voice. There was a smirk on his face, and he glared with hate.

The entire episode came back rushing into her mind, vigorous and merciless as if it were new. Nadifo kept fighting to erase the ugly words, but she remembered that day as clearly as the messy spaghetti and sauce with banana she had for lunch.

The day did not start as horrifically as it ended: it had been an otherwise pleasant day until the assassin and his compatriots had shown up fully prepared, in his words, to annihilate them. The pleasant breeze outside contradicted the terror that ensued in the brand new mansion, the first of its kind in Hamar. The sky flared with hues of copper, merging with the deep blue of the Indian Ocean, yielding a shimmering fire colored with hints of deep purple. Melodic summons of the *mu'addin* Sheikh Cali Harun awoke the sleepy city to devotion. Drops of sweet rain melted with the purity of morning mist. The Cartan family, who occupied the West quarters of the mansion, had danced into the wee hours of the morning celebrating Geele's final wedding festivities.

Geele had returned to Hamar from America, having left three years earlier to study chemical engineering. He came back to marry Sagal, the girl Nadifo had handpicked for him. He only had two weeks before returning to Washington to start his first job as an associate Engineer with Banner and McGinnis, a prestigious engineering firm in Washington D.C. It was a proud moment for Cartan and Nadifo: they boasted of Geele's quick accomplishments, proudly showing off the degree bearing his name and educational accomplishments from Georgetown University. She made sure a framed copy of it adorned the living room wall, and that everyone got an ear full of Geele's success whether they wanted to or not.

They had taken him out of the last year of high school to groom him for Carter Kennedy Prep, the private school he would attend in the outskirts of Washington D.C. Privileged kids like Geele went to the US and Europe to study, while children of families who found themselves on the wrong side of politics were expected to complete a grueling mandatory national service after high school. They only dreamed about traveling overseas to study, a dream that often never materialized.

Geele arrived in D.C. with excitement and a commitment to study hard. It was tempting to follow other elite kids to parties and chase American girls, but he knew his father's position in government had afforded him this rare chance to travel abroad while his friends lined the passport office with false identifications to escape the cruel dictatorship. He did not have to do much to gain this spot, but he had promised his parents to study hard and earn a degree, and study hard he did, earning a degree in chemical engineering in three years, summa cum laude. He was now back to marry the beautiful eighteen-year-old Sagal, hand-picked by Nadifo for her complexion, light-skinned like an Arab, and the noble blood that ran through her veins. Every mother wanted such a girl for her son, pretty, shy and obedient, and above all conservative. Sagal had another role to play, and if she was perceived to be unable to play that role well she would not be selected by a meticulous mother-in-law like Nadifo: to put it bluntly, her job was to convince the world that she adored her mother-in-law, even if she detested her. Sagal was obligated Nadifo's de facto slave. She was to give birth to children with fine features whom Nadifo approved of, and to raise them to be well-mannered. Another important role that came with being a good Somali wife was to keep family secrets, to never ever complain and no matter how bad things were to always pretend. That meant if Sagal was being abused, beaten or mishandled by Geele in any way, she would have to suffer in silence and take it in stride like a good wife—such things were not abuse but more like minor snags that came with the territory; or, more likely, any abuse from husband to wife was abuse the wife invited in some way or another.

When Nadifo started searching for Geele's wife, she encountered all types of girls. Some were merely interested in the opportunity to travel to America and get a taste of the American dream; some made their intentions known that they would not allow a mother-in-law to run the show; others were nearing spinsterhood and sought to avoid that stigma through Geele. Nadifo searched high and low until she found the jewel that would make her son Geele, the apple of her eye, happy and prosperous.

Sagal did exactly what was expected of her. She kept her light skin tone glowing with bleaching creams; she straightened her fine hair to give it sleeker lustrous look. She kept quiet and to herself, only speaking when spoken to. Women from the neighborhood came to envy Geele's luck. Some came to murmur praises for the young couple—*Ilaahay nabad iyo caano ha ka yeelo*—and some came out of jealousy of Sagal's luck—*naa way is caddeysaye sidaana uma qurux badna*. Few came as genuine well wishers, congratulating Sagal on her luck in marrying a fine young man from a prominent noble family.

Nadifo traveled with Suad, her personal shopper and assistant, to purchase gifts for Sagal. They went to Dubai for rare gold jewelry, to Milan for the wedding dress, to China to find the rarest of silk. Nadifo spared no expense in preparing Sagal for each of the ten nights they would celebrate the wedding ceremony. It was a cultural duty for the groom's family to provide the bride with all of these frills and embellishments; Nadifo was thrilled to be at the helm, splurging the details of the extravagant purchases at every female gathering.

After the wedding, Geele and Sagal were to travel back to America where Sagal would be expected to perform her wifely duties in the new townhouse, bought and paid for them, in Georgetown.

It was the last evening of celebration, the last night of ten eventful, elegant parties each filled with food fun and glamour. The house was full of guests from all over the world. Geele was the first born, and as such his wedding would be remembered by everyone who attended, and anyone who heard about it. The guests and house servants nestled in the east quarters of the villa, resting from the drawn-out celebration. For ten days they danced, ate, socialized and fatigued themselves, witnessing what was, to them, the wedding of the century.

On the tenth and final day of the wedding festivities, the adults awoke to the torpid peacefulness of a sleeping house while youngsters continued their envied sleep. The *mu'addin's* summons marked the defiled final day. In unity, spiritually devoted adults assumed a fine line of bowing: they prayed the habitual morning processions concluding their final prayers with wishes of health and prosperity for the newlyweds. Nadifo folded her mauve velvet prayer mat under her feet, her face still dampened from the ablution she had performed only minutes earlier. A shining spiritual dark mark graced her forehead. She remained on the floor beating the rosary in her hand ever so gently; her lips moving rhythmically with each rosary beat as she prayed silently. The exquisite smell of *canjeero* and *suqaar* lingered while a golden tray brimming with cups of spiced tea, sugar, milk, honey and a mixture of cinnamon, cardamom and ginger waited for the guests in the family room. Mako, the great chef whose delicacies have fattened the bellies of the Cartan children, filled the dining table with a variety of breakfast items according to Nadifo's orders. Nadifo, who habitually busied herself with the presentation of things, overwhelmed Mako with directions to prepare varied types of the freshest food, and how it should be arranged. Homemade pita bread sat neatly next to the kidney beans and humus. The *sabaayad* piled on top of each other next to the *suqaar* it was intended to accompany. Wheat *canjeero* sat next to a plate brimming with *beer,* a delicacy of sautéed liver, onions, tomatoes and green peppers. Mako attempted to maneuver around Nadifo, setting out a mahogany tray of papaya, mango, pineapple and guava. Various imported drinks, fruit shakes, and fresh orange juice hugged the table in one corner.

Nadifo was grateful to Mako, who labored endlessly with very little sleep for the entire ten days to ensure guests were fully fed with the best food and drink Hamar could offer. The guests ate to their hearts' content, stories from the previous evening's celebration overtook the dining room and loud chatter and joyous laughter engulfed the house as guests discussed in detail their awe of the planning committee for having assembled such an array of entertainers, including a Sudanese band Ya Ba'ed, Egyptian singer Raheel, and the Indian duo TurDan Troupe with their intricate colorful dance routine.

Guests disappeared into their rooms after breakfast still discussing the elaborate five-course meal presented by Chef François Herme of Paris the previous night. Some of the guests rested as others prepared for an outing organized by Nadifo's event coordinator to visit Bakaraha market and then Jazeera beach before attending the final evening of wedding activities. Everyone wanted to look their best on the last evening—it was a great opportunity to indulge and show off a little.

Nadifo was on the phone with Suad, checking on the details of the dress she planned to wear for the final gala. A few months earlier Suad had made a special shopping trip to Paris to buy Nadifo's clothes for the entire ten days. All the dresses were custom made; this evening, she was to wear a silk cream-colored strapless gown with purple beads, but the dress turned out to be too revealing and Suad, who was ever so attentive to Nadifo's sporadic—sometimes impossible—taste, discussed the matching shawl she found the last minute. Nadifo chuckled over something Suad had said as she held the cordless phone to her ear when she heard gunshots, loud wails and the roar of men. The uproar originated from the main living room at the front of the house. The noise grew overwhelmingly wilder and louder, as it overtook the festive house.

"Kill them. Finish the dirty bastards!" The voice was angry. Nadifo rose abruptly and ran in the direction of the noise, throwing the cordless phone to the floor.

"What is going on, people? Who is it, who...? Where are the gun-shots coming from? *Bismillaahi Raxmaani Raxiim!*" She screamed aimlessly, unable to understand the rowdiness.

"Who is it?!" Reaching the living room she found several men with guns and AK-47s drawn.

"What the hell do you think you are doing?" The spiritual aura of minutes earlier was replaced with a rage the slight woman did not know she possessed.

"*Waryaa Ugaas Faruur*, where are you? Get these dirty low lives out of here!" she called the watchman, who mysteriously disappeared as the house was being attacked. She turned, trying to maneuver around a stocky man with a midnight-blue complexion and eerie blood shot eyes. His stocky assassin's stature appeared benign next to the massive AK-47 which hid his qat-smeared lips.

"Hey, hey, why are you going through our house like this?!" she yelled, bewildered by the angry face that stared back at her with violent intent in the middle of her living room. The armed men entrusted loot-ers of all ages to empty the house.

A familiar yet distant face approached her. He was the one issuing the orders; he appeared to be the mastermind behind the chaos. Nadifo was dumfounded: only six hours earlier this same man had celebrated with them, eating and dancing into the wee hours of the morning. He was Geele's best man, and a great one at that. Hideously giddy, he bus-ied himself snapping photos, dancing and greeting guests. He had done a better job than Geele's first cousin Onkod, who was also acting as one of Geele's attendants. He had pushed Geele onto the dance floor while mocking his dance; he had danced with Sagal, Nadifo and little Henna. They had treated him as one of their own: now he stood in the middle of their living room, ordering their deaths.

"Kill her! Now!" he barked, waving a machete dripping with fresh blood in her face. Nadifo wondered wildly if the words were meant for her—maybe he had come into their house by mistake. Nothing made sense to her. Surely he did not intend to kill them? What had changed him in minutes from a happy well-wisher to a killer? When he sat next to Geele the previous evening, he'd betrayed no hint of hate; he'd been funny and cheerful. Why had he then led this militia into their house? He did not look like the man who had danced with Geele the night before—now he looked every inch the murderer he'd suddenly become.

"Geele! Where is Geele?! *Bismillahi Raxmaani Raxiim*, Ugaas Faruur, where is everyone? What is going on, please help?" Nadifo was frantic: It finally occurred to her they were under attack, but her perplexed mind could not decide on a course of action.

"Where is Henna?" he asked, looking to see if she were among the queue of people he gathered. He shoved aside the horrified guests who plead for mercy.

"Where is your little princess, the red one, huh?" He stood jauntily, chewing qat and spitting the juices in the faces of the frightened people before him.

"I will make you pay. You and your family will pay a price. *Waryaa*, find Henna, look for that girl and bring her to me, now!" He turned back to Nadifo.

"Is she still too pretty and pure for me and my cousins, Nadifo, huh?" He said, spitting again on her face. "I will show you who is pure and victorious today! Bring that pampered little bitch over here!"

"Show her what all that pampering has gotten her!"

"Please stop this craziness and leave now." Nadifo begged, abruptly changing her tone and attitude. Wailing, she attempted to hold on to his massive booted leg to stop him from going further into Henna's room. Throwing her aggressively onto the floor again, he proceeded to bark orders at the militia readily waiting in the roofless Land Cruiser with heavy weapons in the garage, just steps away from the living room. The young men, high on narcotics, were eager to slaughter as many people as they could in the shortest amount of time possible. Murdering the people was their next fix.

She continued running after him as he headed towards Henna's room to stop him, all the while pleading with him, crying hysterically.

The thin diric she wore was tattered by now, revealing parts of her body she would otherwise hide; unbeknownst to her she had a huge gash on the back of her head.

He pushed her to the floor again, thumping her small body brutally against the ground. He held the AK-47 to her neck while others rummaged through the house looking for Henna. As the killing carried on, once-trusted neighbors looted the house, emptying it of abundant valuables in few hours. It was not clear who was looting and who was killing—the traffic in the house made it difficult to separate the two; the speed at which the looters quickly filled the family's Land Rover, Jeep Cherokee and Toyota Pickup Truck with furniture, clothes, kitchen appliances, paintings, electronics, food and rugs amid the killings clarified their intent. They were not there only to kill but also to loot.

"Are you ready to pay for the sins of your people, ugly old crone?" he continuously shouted the same words at her, pinning her to the floor with one gigantic booted foot. She heard the cries of a child coming from her bedroom. It was Bile; she remembered the youngest of her five kids. He was fast sleep in her bed when she left to join the others for morning prayers: now he was terrified and alone, woken up by the clamor.

She ran in his direction forcing him inside the room. "Bile, stay quiet in here," she said, pushing him under the bed. Then she headed to Geele's room.

"Geele, run, please run, they are here to kill you!" Geele stretched his tired body, not fully awake or aware of the murderers in the house. In the next room Samatar slept soundlessly, Mahad, Geele and Samatar grew up together.

"*Hooyo*, what is all that noise, tell them to keep it down," he said, letting his feet stretch to the floor.

"Shush, Geele, they are here to kill you! Run, my son, run!"

"Who is here to kill me? Hooyo, what are you talking about?" Questions creased his sleepy forehead as he tried to make sense of the frantic Nadifo.

"I don't have time to explain, just run, come, come with me, maybe the back door is open—or just go in the attic, no one will look for you there. Hurry!"

"Mr. Groom, oh Geele, where are you?" In a split second, Geele went from a carefree groom to a hunter's confused prey. Of all the things Geele did well, preparing for disaster was not one of them. He could hear the uproar near his room: his mother was no longer there to direct him, she had gone to warn others. He looked around his room to escape, but all the windows in his room had solid metal bars, so he could not escape that way. He just had to brave a run towards the back door as his mother had suggested. Still in his pajamas, he opened his bedroom door and tiptoed to see where the killers she warned him about were. He could see two coming towards his room. He quickly ran the opposite direction, looking for an opened door. Reaching the rear of the house, he found the back door wide open. He looked behind him to see the two men approaching him fast—he had little time to get outside and close the door on them. As soon as he stepped outside he was confronted with three more men. Bullets came from all sides and he was shot in the hip, but he continued running. They allowed him to continue running, sniggering at his limp, bloody trail. More shots were fired at his back: Geele fell, and lay still for a few minutes, covered with blood but alive. *Alive.* He could hear them arguing over who to kill next while he gasped for air.

"Did you find Henna?! Kill her!" He heard one say. He tried to get up, still wheezing. His voice faint, he said,

"Henna—please don't kill her, she is only fourteen..." Before he could finish the sentence, three more bullets to his heart silenced him permanently.

Inside the house, the intruders, armed with guns and machetes, continued their murderous spree.

"Oh Allah, please have mercy! Bile don't come here! Stay in your room!" Nadifo cried in desperation, unaware that Geele was already dead.

"Geele, Geele!" she yelled, leaving Bile in her room and running towards Geele's room again. By now she was soaked in her own and other victims' blood.

"Hooyo, hooyo, I want you to come here," the little boy whined, peeking out of the master bedroom. "Come here, mommy, I'm scared." His pleas caught the attention of some of the armed men. When he heard Nadifo outside his room he would peek out of the room calling for her, then return behind a huge wood coffer, then scoot under the bed, terrified.

"Shut that kid up! Whose kid is he?" They followed Nadifo. "Kill the little bastard!"

They were too busy killing others to look for the child whose cries annoyed them.

Bodies began to pile up. Corpses of men, armless corpses of women, children's lifeless bodies, and adults with horrified expressions lay alongside bullets and discarded machetes that had delivered their ends. Warfaa's limbs, fond of dancing, now rested next to a little boy whose vibrant face, white shirt and khaki pants were damp with blood. Warfaa Badhnaag's titillating tongue had twisted words of praise the previous evening, unaware of his fate; he had danced and twirled alongside women, the only male proud to flaunt female abilities amongst women. Leaving earthly labels such as *badhnaag* behind, he appeared ready to embrace his fate. He lay parallel to a golden frame displaying a deep blue Chinese silk mosaic. Perfectly elegant in death, he celebrated something beyond.

Pristine Persian rugs had lost their luster—like so much else in the house, they too were now defiled with blood. The smell of death joined potent sandalwood, amber, and musk *attar* from Persia and Arabia.

The noise reached Henna's room. Delirious from the exhaustion of the previous evening, Henna instinctively crawled, trembling, under the bed. She was not fully alert to witness the ugly turmoil in the house but was paralyzed with fear, and felt numb: she heard gunshots, howling women, and what sounded like a forceful struggle. The roaring voices of men neared her room. She collected her small body in her arms, rolling into a fetus position. Wet and sweaty, her face dripped teardrops that arrived painfully at her mouth mixing with welling saliva. Wet and scared, she struggled to stay still, but every organ in her body was in overdrive. Her heart beat raucously against her chest, sweat glands enlarged, and her bladder leaked against her will. The overwhelming fear made her feel as if her head was something separate from her body...at a loss, she felt disassociated.

JINX DOWRY

Nadifo Cafi, a small-framed woman in her early fifties with severe high cheekbones and a sternly confident presence, sat in a corner of the firm burgundy and gold divan majlis. The Middle-Eastern oblong divan cushions covered the carpeted living room floor in the traditional Bedouin style.

She fervently glared at the black folder that sat on the table in front of her. Half an hour of glaring had not made the task at hand easier. The words she scowled at scowled back at her, with intense reluctance, offering no ease of mind. The title on the paper read:

WRITING ASSIGNMENT #74:
Use the present continuous tense to answer each question. For example: She/take/shower: "She has been taking a shower."

Her delicate henna-tattooed fingers flipped through the untidy notes. She gripped the pen tightly, attempting to follow the writing assignment. A lock of soft, henna-tinted hair looped around the fold of her headscarf. The elegance of her face sparkled with mystique. A small, straight nose nestled between evenly-spaced oval eyes with dark pupils and long thick lashes. Her eyes are sad and distant. Her vanilla-nutmeg complexion glowed without a single wrinkle, making Nadifo look ten years younger than she was.

Looking at Nadifo, one would never catch a trace of the tragic death she so narrowly escaped when armed militia overtook her home. One would never know simply from looking that she had witnessed brutal murders; that she had once embraced a shivering fourteen-year-old lying in a pool of her own blood, minutes after the girl had been savagely attacked. That she had covered corpses with her bare hands more than she cares to admit, and that she had walked away from a life of luxury, abundance and variety just to keep her family safe. No, there were no signs of her time in the torturous refugee camp, the daily fear of assault and violence. No sign of the anxiousness that engulfed her graceful poise while waiting for resettlement to America. Her former life of luxury is evident in her glowing beauty, something even the harshest conditions have not managed to erase.

Nadifo prays daily: she asks God to forgive her if she ever catches herself questioning the unending pain and destruction she witnessed. She accepts her fate, as only *Allah* knows the reasons for her delivery to a foreign land where disorientation had became part of her fabric. Often found kneeling facing Mecca, Nadifo praises *Allah* asking the Almighty for his mercy. She concludes each of her five daily prayers with a plea, a plea to witness a pleasant dawn in Hamar—the beautiful familiar town of her ancestors, the only place she will ever call home, the mere thought of which causes a drift into nostalgia.

As a child, Nadifo's family had constantly reminded her that she was a child born with ill fortune: that her life was marked by the evil eye and her birth was the end of her mother Ardo's life. The day Nadifo graced this world with infant cries, the mist of death visited the family's dwelling and took Ardo away into the next life.

Faal had been placed in their house by a resentful, poor, jealous neighbor, Nadifo's aunt explained. Every morning when they awoke from the peace of sleep, they found eggs, coins, and candy scattered throughout their yard. These objects were said to be the result of a jinx put on the family by evil supernatural powers. As such, anyone who ate the candy or eggs or even touched the coins would forever be plagued by ill luck and evil will. It was a trap for the children of the house. The adults would remove the objects every morning before the children awoke. The children were instructed to never touch the cursed items if they ever came across them. All the children in the house began to wear leather amulets inscribed with verses from the Quran to guard them against the evil eye. Nadifo's charm became cursed when she unknowingly munched on some chocolate-filled green candy mixed with dates and popcorn. The same jealous neighbor waited for Nadifo as she herded young sheep in the countryside one evening. She was delighted and surprised by the woman's generosity after a long day of shepherding. She consumed the entire bag of goodies, one gulp after another until she finished it all, not wanting to share it with her siblings.

Ever since the incident she was continuously reminded of her ill fortune. She tired of the legend that detailed her arrival on earth: Cusubo, her maternal aunt, repeated the tale at every opportunity, enjoying the reaction the tale received. According to Cusubo, after three days of difficult labor, Ardo's fatigued body became limp before the baby passed through the birth canal. Cusubo claimed to have extracted baby Nadifo alive from the birth canal; it was a miracle of *Allah* that she was able to pull the breathless baby from the mother's still body, she would say proudly, as if she herself breathed life into the baby. Nadifo would forever carry the stigma of birth, which according to Cusubo eventually led to her ill fortune. Cusubo began branding Nadifo with a burning knife until she was eleven; her chest and back were branded for life to rid off the evil.

Nadifo had never been treated normally ever since the munching incident. The evil curse intended for the family transferred to her, when she ate the munchies. From then on she was handled with caution, but people were not exactly discreet about their fears: they said she had brought demons that caused all sorts of evil for the family. Visitors would stop her from whatever task she was performing, abruptly reading Quran verses over her. Some would not enter their house until she drank from a jar of blessed water, and others stayed away altogether, fearing the curse would "rub off" on them.

The family had waited for her to wane with the ill fortune. Her father Cafi knew Nadifo was not admired for cleverness like her sister

Hawo, but mostly for her beauty, quietness and tractability: he waited with anxious patience for the day some wretched man would come and assume responsibility for her. He flaunted his daughter to would-be suitors, and actually gave her away in marriage to one man in his fifties who rudely declined his proposal. Cafi then promised Nadifo in marriage to his best friend Hirad Ahmed's son Yasin. Hirad also rejected the proposition, which raised eyebrows as to why Cafi desired such a speedy marriage for Nadifo. Cafi's lucky day came when Cartan, a distant relative unaware of Nadifo's ill fortune, came into town to visit an aging parent. Cafi seized the moment, hastily giving Nadifo to Cartan in marriage: after a rushed celebration, Cartan took Nadifo with him to the city, assuming responsibility for her and whatever woe that plagued her.

Nadifo's father Cafi did not ask Cartan for the traditional *gabbaati*. He had to forgo the customary bride price, which would be one hundred camels. Not only did he not secure a bridal price for Nadifo, she was the only girl in Gobwanaag who came with twenty camels, three cows and fifty sheep.

It was quite a scandal when neighbors found out Cafi gave away his precious daughter without receiving even one camel for her. What kind of father would give away his daughter without receiving gabbaati? Utterly scandalous indeed, it had marred the Cafi family for life, especially when news came Cafi gave away some of his own animals to accompany Nadifo in order to get rid of her. Other bachelors who admired Cafi for his wealth and status would not ask for the remaining three daughters' hands, fearing Cafi was giving away his daughter for a disgraceful reason. Maybe his daughters were not virgins, or maybe they were flawed with some unfortunate disease—or worse, maybe they were potential *qumayo* wives who would have uninhibited insulting mouths.

Cafi was happy to let Cartan take Nadifo away—he wanted to safeguard the rest of his household against the evil that accompanied her—but he was mortified about the scandal that he was giving away his daughter away for free. He reasoned he had enough camels of his own, and did not need to get more camels from Cartan, who was a poor government worker without the benefit of animal wealth. Cafi would show off his two hundred camels roaming around town, and his three hundred sheep, six horses and twenty cows to quiet the rumors. He reasoned he could afford to give away his own animals and did not need any from a poor relative.

Nadifo was sixteen, Cartan twenty-nine. Nadifo's family became prosperous after her departure; she had temporarily escaped bad luck herself after her marriage to Cartan when they moved to the capital city, Hamar. She eluded the evil curse, bearing children for Cartan and witnessing his success in politics. Evil had halted for the Cafi family ever since she moved away to Hamar with Cartan, yet she awoke every dawn to burn spiritually blessed incense. Her family awoke to the intoxicating aroma of frankincense and myrrh each morning. She would chant the *jin* farewell prayer *"Acuudu Billaahi Mina Shaydaani Rajiim"* asking Allah to cast away *shaydaan* from her household. She thought she could banish the evil that way. She believed her prosperity was due to the hounding of the *jins* every morning. The ritual followed the family to America, where she continued burning and casting away evil in their apartment in Minneapolis.

VAGUE IN BLISS

Nadifo spread herself out on the hardwood floor of the tiny living room, finding comfort in the air that wafted from the cracks in the floor beneath her. She sought comfort in even the slightest breeze: sweat dripped from her forehead as she scattered the varied purchases on the couch. Normally she would stay still and lazy on such a hot June day, but Nadifo is naturally an anxious woman, and she couldn't sit still. She prepared the suitcase that sat empty next to the shoes and blanket that would eventually end up inside it. A task others would find trivial made Nadifo tremble with worry.

Only eight months earlier, the very same Samsonite Silhouette caramel suitcase with its battered old top and crumbling lock had contained her own meager belongings as she immigrated to America. Sadness came over her as she tried to pack the various items into the suitcase. *Their needs are massive, far more than can fit into this small suitcase,* she thought in Somali, the language she usually thought in, the language that transmitted confusion and clarity while at the same time fretting her head with worries. She has become a sad woman: sadness that will not allow a smile, a grin or anything resembling happiness to visit her face. Neither has she seen her own tears for years, her tear ducts have dried up by now. She is no longer able to cry or smile, as if she purposefully left human feelings such as laughter, crying, smiling and sobbing behind to a time and place where happy, normal life existed.

This is the first time she has had the chance to send anything back home since her arrival. Cilmi, her cousin Salaado's husband, is traveling this week to Gobwanaag, their hometown. She collected all her energy to buy the necessary items, unsure if the little money she had saved would be enough for all the things she needed to send.

Earlier in the day when she set out to buy the items, the heavy stillness of the Midwest humidity suffocated her. The wet air weighed down her *jilbaabed* body; and every shrouded limb protested movement. The blazing June sun rested heavily on top of her head. She attempted a brisk walk to catch bus J218 to the Somali *souq*. She did not realize when the bus passed her stop: she was looking down, avoiding the stares of the people on the bus.

A small prayer and some boldness encouraged her to remain on the bus, thinking it would eventually turn around and take her back to her stop. It continued on, zigzagging behind a slope and some mosquito-ridden water ponds. Under different circumstances, she might have enjoyed the tranquility of her surroundings. Large elaborate houses with huge lush front yards were separated from the wide streets by guards of shady trees. Tranquil neighborhoods unlike anything she had witnessed since her arrival. She knew not where she was, only that she was very far, away from the humming cars and congested streets of the city, where every breath was shared. The bus emptied itself of all passengers, and there Nadifo stood, in the middle of the affluent *Eden Prairie Lakes.* The immaculate lawns and constant sprinklers left a cool sparkle suspended in the suburban air. Jogging mothers pushed baby strollers, and elderly couples sauntered hand in hand. Nadifo began to inspect her surroundings, to see if there were any bus stops around. She noticed a pack of countless little puppies bearing down her way. Without checking for oncoming traffic, she bolted into the street. No one could tell whether she fainted or fell: either way, she halted traffic, lying smack in the middle of the road. The owner of the dogs, a young man in his early twenties wearing a grey jogging suit and dark reflective sun glasses ushered his dogs toward her, thinking to help: she lay shaking in the middle of the street, repeating "Somali *souq*, Somali *souq*, Somali *souq*." She repeated it countless times in every accent her tongue could handle. The young man bent over her, letting his numerous dogs invade her space. He took off his glasses and kept repeating "Pardon me". He was too close: his garlic breath made her feel nauseous, and she began yelling "Somali *Souq*" over and over, thinking he must be hard of hearing while staring fearfully at the dogs.

She rose unsteadily, refusing help, and was directed by the man with the many dogs to the right bus stop. She barely heard him, avoiding the little puppies crowding in around her while he pointed to the bus stop. Their dirty little nostrils looked ready to defile her. They barked incessantly, licking their jowls and fighting to catch a taste of her. She could not be bothered to wash seven times to erase the filth of the dogs as required by religious obligation, so she showed her discomfort by standing a long distance from the man, who continued repeating the bus information hoping desperately for a look of recognition to cross her panicked face.

"You need bus number J18, not J218," he continued repeating almost as many times as she repeated Somali *souq*. Her fear of getting lost in the vast streets of America had finally come true. Her family dismissed her fear, asserting that if she got lost, she would somehow find her way back. If she ever found her way home today, she would not tell them of her misadventure, fearing further ridicule—or worse, being seen as a dependent unable to do things on her own.

Nadifo's eldest daughter, Warsan, who has lived here with her husband and kids for a long time, promised to take the newcomer to purchase all of the items. Nadifo waited and waited, but Warsan failed to fulfill her promise, as usual; so Nadifo decided to go alone. She even missed her ESL class, which the loud, angry social worker, Brenda Gayle, had warned against. The expression on the woman's face still loomed in her memory, the way she twisted her tongue and kept shaking her index finger, as if she were dealing with a juvenile delinquent who had broken yet another law. Ms. Gayle, as she preferred to be addressed, made her dislike of immigrants like Nadifo quite obvious. Whether it was their heavy accents, their lack of American knowhow, their general un-acclimated appearance that announced their novelty, or just general dislike for the unfamiliar, Ms. Gayle did not hide her loathing for them.

"I would not miss class if I was you, girl, they may take away your benefits all together," she had said when Nadifo picked her benefit check up the day before. Her thick lips moved with the rhythm of her words. "Make sure she understands, hear?" she articulated the instruction gloatingly, making sure the needy in her office felt the humiliation of each word for receiving welfare. "Learning English is the only way she can free herself! Hear?" This time she pulled a pen from where she'd jabbed it into the roots of her curly orange hair as she came back to her desk. She wiggled it in Diriye's face as she eased her rather large rear end into the chair. "Tell her what I said. Does she understand what I'm sayin'?" She instructed Diriye the interpreter. Poor Diriye looked petrified by the waggling pen and the rest of the woman's jiggling flesh. Whether he clearly understood or not, he shook his head in affirmation, then mumbled something nervously in broken Somali to Nadifo about never missing class.

A week earlier Nadifo stumbled into Ms. Gayle's office without an appointment. Nadifo anticipated Ms. Gayle to be rude and obnoxious for coming into the office when she did not have an appointment; after all, the woman appeared to enjoy reprimanding Nadifo at every opportunity. She was prepared for the humiliation that came with seeking answers as to the reason her monthly check was missing. Nadifo was highly suspicious of Ms. Gayle, often fearing the woman's dislike for her would halt the $800 cash and $350 in food stamps she received each month. Ms. Gayle wore a see-through black shirt and a cream colored chiffon mini skirt which exaggerated her voluptuous figure. Her breasts looked bigger than Nadifo remembered, and her hips looked ready to explode through the thin material that covered them. Her mid section looked as though she were preparing to deliver twins. As usual, Ms. Gayle had an air of exaggerated confidence and arrogance, popping her signature pink bubble gum. Nadifo waited behind a young woman in her mid twenties with a colicky infant hugging her bosom and a crying toddler strapped in a stroller. This particular morning Ms. Gayle appeared more malicious than usual. The young woman waved a letter in her face, annoyed.

"I don't got no goddamn income to report to you!" she roared. "Nothing in my life's changed since the last time I was here, but you been tellin' all kinds of lies in your records, no I don't got no man supporting me, you know damn well I don't have no man supporting my kids!"

"Keep it down, Sabrina, you don't have to yell," said Ms. Gayle, smoothing her red-tipped nails with a pink handled nail file. She did not look Sabrina in the eye once, unfazed by the rage.

"Now they cut off my food stamps and cash benefits! What am I gonna do with these kids, woman?" continued Sabrina, shaking the crying toddler's shoulder to make a point.

"Get a damn job, Sabrina, and stop having all these babies!" Ms. Gayle said, viciously calm.

"It ain't your damn business how many babies I got! What gives you the right to speak to me that way?!"

"I'm only stating the obvious, Sabrina." Her cool demeanor only egged the young woman further.

"I'm going to report your ass, you over-grown sloppy bitch!"

"Oh, look who's is talking sloppy, honey—you and your brats are so filthy, you need to be quarantined, put somewhere far from human life!" Pointing to the door with her nail file, Miss Gayle gazed from behind her leopard-print glasses and popped her bubble gum loudly, but before she'd reached the end of the sentence, Sabrina was taking off her earrings, ready to jump her; the two security officers nearby moved in to break up the scuffle. Sabrina, who was a much smaller woman, was on top of Ms. Gayle, wrestling her to the ground which was now covered with slime from the whiney toddler's puke. Sabrina tore out several braids from Ms. Gayle's braided blond weave, victorious.

"I told you not to mess with me, fatso!" Sabrina gloated. Ms. Gayle, very much the humiliated bully, was led to a back room. Nadifo watched in silence, but cheered the young woman privately, pleased that Gayle had finally met her match. All the poor refugees she had been harassing threw a damming curse on her. She re-emerged half an hour later, reserved and somber. She wore a purple leather jacket to conceal the torn shirt and hesitantly collected some more braids from the floor and tossed them into the trash. Finally she said "Next!" She would not look directly at the waiting public, witnesses to her defeat. Nadifo jumped running toward her cubicle. She went right to the point, avoiding any eye contact.

"Miss Gayle, me no check, me mail today, me no see check and me—"

"What the hell are you talkin' bout, woman?" The belligerent woman Nadifo knew too well re-surfaced.

"Me no check, me mail...."

"I heard that, 'me no check, me mail' is not English, lady. I don't know what the hell you're trying to say, I can't help you unless you speak English! Got it?" she said, struggling with the bandana she had covered her head with, to hide what was left of her braids.

"Yes, me English, Miss Gayle."

"Look go and bring that skinny dude to translate for you, I don't have all day."

"Me check only, please you look me check where, me long way me come, please—snow outside," Nadifo focused on the falling snow outside, pointing a finger at it.

"Next, I think you should go and get someone to interpret all that babble. I don't know what the hell you're sayin'!" and with that she sat down to help the next person. Nadifo's evil side wished that Sabrina would re-emerge to give Ms. Gayle another good beating. She stood there for a minute, thinking what to say. Something in her gave way, and then she said it, albeit in Somali.

"Foolxumada waxaad ku darsatay fulaynimo, fulay yahay fulaydu dhashay."

"What the hell is this woman sayin'?" Ms. Gayle looked back at her and then at the rest of the room to see if anyone could translate, when Nadifo shocked her with the next sentence. "I say you ugly fat and *fulay.* You fat *sangadhuudhi!*"

"What? Oh no she didn't. Did she say fat something?"

"She said fat nigger," said a young woman waiting in the lobby with three kids.

"She called me a ni—no she did not just call me the n word! Girl, where is her file, she just messed with the wrong bitch!" Ms. Gayle was coming around the cubicle, but by the time she reached the waiting area, Nadifo was long gone, hurriedly crossing the snowy street. She never returned to Ms. Gayle's office without an appointment and some-one to interpret.

Nadifo had no choice but to send these items to Hawo, the sister who remained in Gobwanaag. She had been collecting all sorts of things for the past eight months, and now everything would not fit into the small suit case. It was unfortunate she could not send a bigger suitcase. Even Ms. Gayle, with her bubble gum and rolling eyes, would not halt Nadifo from going to the market to purchase items Hawo needed desperately.

Clothes and other things mysteriously disappeared from her kids' closets, destined for the suitcase. She took a pair of fading jeans from a shelf in Bile's closet, turned them inside out and made a hidden pocket in the pant leg. She stashed three crisp hundred-dollar bills borrowed from Salaado inside the newly shaped pocket and stitched the pocket shut, turning the jeans the right way out and purposefully forcing the jeans to the bottom of the suitcase. Shoes, candy, Tylenol, lotion, cereal and toys camouflaged the jeans. An eighth grade algebra book, a U.S. history book, some used pens, pencils and spiral notebooks also made it to the suitcase.

Next, she tucked a cassette, safely resting in its plastic case, on the side of the suitcase. The cassette contained a recorded message addressed to her sister. She had finally perfected the art of the little tape recorder. She would set the tape recorder in front of her, press the red and black "record" and "play" buttons at the same time, and begin speaking freely as if her sister had really been there. In mid-sentence, she would wipe her eyes, as if to clear away the sadness that had poured into the little tape recorder. Sadness consumed the conversation. She would hit the "pause" button to collect her strength, and then continue with her sad story. It seemed surreal to Nadifo the way her life had taken such a tragic detour. Talking to her sister for the first time since her arrival in Minneapolis had brought back so many horrible, vivid memories unwilling to dissipate.

Free and candid, she conversed with the tape recorder as if Hawo was right there, cheering her on. The two women exchanged news through the tape recorded messages: Nadifo could not call her sister, since Hawo did not have a phone in her modest shack in Gobwanaag. Neither of them could read nor write, so they could not write letters to each other. In the rare case Nadifo was able to coerce one of her kids to write a letter, word got back the letter that was sent was illegible, asking if she wrote the letters herself. She would scold and reprimand the writer, asking to take great care the next time, but to no avail. They wrote letters that were neither Somali nor English. They wrote letters with confusing combined sentences of English and Somali. "Somenglish" was not a language which Hawo was familiar with. Their messages got lost somewhere between the writer and the orator.

Now all she had to do was press record and speak. As she sat down to tape the massage, her thoughts reverted back to the long, arduous journey she had undertaken five months earlier to make it to Minneapolis. She carefully hit the red and black buttons at the same time. She made sure the volume was low; she checked the electric cord to make sure it was plugged in. After she assured the tape recorder was ready for a message she proceeded to pour out emotional words only Hawo could decipher:

JUNE 26, 1994, MINNEAPOLIS.

Bismillaahi Raxmaani Raxiim, Salaamu Calaykum: My esteemed sister, I am talking to you from Minneapolis. It is Ramadan, and the sun had finally set. Allah has blessed us with a prosperous Ramadan, our first here.

I washed away years of anguish, dirt, despair and waiting, my sister. Time eternity of not knowing where my fate lay. Ever since the destruction of home, my existence has depended on a red-faced, suit-wearing man, whose eyes traveled up and down my body so as to find faults that could keep me behind. I washed away months of queuing at dawn in front of the blue and gray warehouse whose wall held the answers for millions of war-ravaged, torn, empty desperate people, the depressing warehouse wall where the American Embassy chose to post our fate. The mile long listing on that wall my dear would announce our luck to emigrate to America, or sadness to remain in the refugee camp. I would squint my eyes to go along with the person reading the tiny letters to see if we were among the chosen. I hoped for our name to be highlighted in red. Red announced you were lucky and blue unlucky.

The mighty pompous people in the American Embassy, "case workers" they call themselves, must have won these spots through the triumph of their mean spirited, inhumane ways. It is as if they were instructed to break our spirit, or what little is left of it. They acted as though they were mightier than God. It satisfied them to grill all of the black distressed faces that begged them for mercy. Their accusations abounded, "you barbaric lot, you destroyed your land, now what do you want with ours? You want to emigrate and become a refugee pest!" They enjoyed forcing you to repeat your horrendous ordeal, careless of the immense pain it causes to recall it. They asked questions over and over to try to catch fabrications; to see if you lied here or there. They hoped you would get a name wrong or that you

49

would change a detail so that they could cancel your spot and send you back to the hopelessness of the refugee camp.

Hope mingled with despair on our faces as we searched for our names amongst those lining the wall. My sister, only if you know how much I prayed to Allah to make our name appear in red. Allah only knows the private conversations I have had with myself about the wall. Now it appears a far distant insane conversation, but then it was real, I was close to insanity.

They picked a distant wall called the Green Wall located on an entirely different street on which to post our names. They wanted us far, far away from them when euphoric or despaired. As a result, it took another two hours to go back to their office to get clarification to why your name did not appear on the wall. Many left without finding out, not being able to come up with the money to pay for the taxi fare back to the Embassy. Others walked in the severe heat back to the office only to be turned away because the time in which they would answer such questions had passed.

We smiled nervously as if our snow-white teeth and massive grins could somehow change the verdict. Each of us silently whispered simple prayers, asking God to soften the hearts of those who determined our destiny. I borrowed clothes to appear presentable, shoes to brave the long, hot walk. I was the hope for the entire camp. Everyone would gather to meet me upon my return, hoping I would deliver good news. When I did not, they all felt the sordid slap. Endless days of scarce food, and persistent pain in a dangerous camp where thugs and rapists feasted on the agony of violated bodies, grated me. We desired to escape our realities. A reality of cavernous bellies, open sores leeching yellow fluid, flies excitedly buzzing in swarms, vultures circling, and brokenness with no boundaries. We told lies, to give hope to the young that their lives would soon change upon our immigration to America. America. It held all the answers. America. It was home to all our dreams.

Once a week at dawn I tried to beat the crowds that flocked to the Green Wall seeking answers. I left right after the dawn prayer when it was still dark outside. Vultures of all types lined my way. If not a rapist, the corrupt Kenyan police would try to extract bribes from me. I would sometimes get to the wall, beaten by them, exhausted.

The promise of the Green Wall was worth my life, even if I were violated by thugs. The wall held the dreams of a new life, a life without plastic covered shacks and the dizzying smell of hunger, a life without the constant worry of how to feed the young and keep the old and weak safe. A life where we could feel safe and somewhat stable. Until today, my dear sister, I am unable to shake the reeking smell of hunger, death and despair. My memory of the wall, camp and the desperation we once called life is as strong as the reality of my life today.

In the middle of the message Nadifo was interrupted by a loud knock. "Who is knocking? I am recording a message for Hawo."

"Hooyo, have you seen my hat? I can't find my hat."

"Hold on Bile, I am coming."

"That is little Bile interrupting my conversation, where is that stop button—hold it Bile I am coming! Oh, there it is, here is the button, there!"

"Hooyo, where is my hat?" Bile said outside the door.

"Waryaa, come and talk to your *habaryar*, say hi *Habo*"

"Hi *Habo*."

"Wait, wait where is that on button, ok here it is, now talk.

"Tell your Habo about your school."

"Hooyo, I just need my hat, I want to go outside and play with Jason!"

"Waryaa, stop being rude talk, to your Habo."

"Oh, hooyo please let go of me, Jason is waiting."

"Go, you stupid boy, here is your hat!"

Where was I my dear sister? Oh yes, I was telling you about our journey here! I prayed so much, my dear sister, not to witness another corpse in my yard, not to shelter yet another female body whose dignity was taken sadistically.

I washed it all away with my first real bath in a long time. But so much cannot be scoured away with a surge of hot water and the delicate, flowery suds of raspberry vanilla. I sat in a massive tub for hours to absolve myself of the sins of war. I sat there long enough to realize the showerhead hardly ejected enough water to scratch the surface. The jaded soil of disorder shall remain with me forever!"

JULY 2, 1994. MINNEAPOLIS.

Hawo, it is now after midnight, I must finish this message or Cilmi will leave without it tomorrow. To continue with our saga, sister, we arrived together with other refugees. We were finally here, in America. In the airport, I am not sure which city it was, we were herded like animals forced into one line so as not to stray into the refined American crowds. It was as if big yellow neon signs that said "NEW REFUGEES" hung from our chests announcing our plight to all passers-by.

We were disoriented at the airport, unable to comprehend the numerous large signs that hovered over us. We travelled from Nairobi's Jomo Kenyatta Airport, to Amsterdam airport, and some other airport in America. I am not sure if it were Atlanta or Chicago. Finally three days later we arrived in Minneapolis. We were going between planes, being moved here and there, adding confusion to fatigue. We were perplexed at the speed of people. Travelers sidled around us frenetically. We halted the airport's efficient flow as we roamed like a lost herd from some place to another. I found only hurried, anxious, sometimes angry faces. They appeared in deep thought, busy reading, eating and unfriendly! The way people sat around spread out, I could immediately sense personal space was something revered here.

The few among us that spoke English became tongue-tied, unable to understand the fluency of American English. Their way of speaking English sounded odd to us, and, in turn, we sounded odd to them.

When we finally boarded the airplane to our final destination, Minneapolis, we clogged the boarding process, misunderstanding our seats and scattering about the tightly packed
plane at will. The passengers shook their heads in frustration.
Take-off was delayed for one hour, to help us in the appropriate
seats. Delayed, I have come to understand, is a word Americans
do not like to hear.

'Ladies and gentlemen, take off will not be for another hour.
As you are all aware, the new refugees among us need assistance
to be seated. We would like to apologize for any inconvenience,
please be patient.' It was as if we did not come with instruction and someone had to figure out how to assemble us. This
marked the beginning of my misfit life.

Those who met us at the airport, an organization tasked
with our migration to America called People to People (PTP)
enjoyed what they perceived as our primitiveness. I caught
them laughing with each other in a self-congratulatory manner, ready to receive awards for their charity. I watched them
with detestation. It pleased them to think that we were beneath
them. Or was I imaging things because lately I have become
very mistrustful.

Three tiny bedrooms much smaller than the maid quarters
in our previous home have become home to all of us.

The PTP staff appointed to decipher America for us, a
pompous Somali who spoke a dialect none of us understood,
pointed to the stove, fridge, and bathroom as if this was our first
encounter with such things. He appeared proud to be the first
to show us such things.

They refused to let Cartan interpret for us, even though
he speaks their language flawlessly. Instead, they brought this
person who spoke neither good English nor good Somali well
enough to decode our new life.

"This is where you will be cooking your food," he said with
a smug smile. "You no longer have to employ a *girgire* with firewood to cook your food. No need to take daily trips to gather
wood." He said it with distaste. He took us for nothing, as if we
are people who have never witnessed refinement. "This is where

you store your food. It is called "refrigerator". It is a cool place that keeps everything fresh. You must clean it often. Make sure it does not stay open for a long period of time, or it will spoil the food. You must clean your apartment or else it will attract unwanted roaches and bugs. Make sure to wash regularly; you must use this deodorant. Here in America, personal hygiene is very important."

He had no shame to utter such words! Even if the people at PTP were judgmental, thinking all Africans are village people who have not had the benefits of city life, he should know better. Did America make him forget that it is our culture to be clean, that it is a religious obligation to keep clean?

This was the beginning of my new life, my dear sister, the beginning of confusion and the continuation of destruction in my heart.

"*Naayaa* Henna, what is that noise? "*Naayaa* Henna, come here!"

Sorry, sister, I cannot manage to finish one message without the interruption of these kids.

"*Naayaa* Henna, come and turn this thing off for me."

"Yes, hooyo, what is going on, why are you angry?"

"*Naayaa*—go put something decent on, you look like a slut."

"Hooyo, I'm busy. What do you want?"

"Turn this thing off, I can't find the off button. Did you finish cooking dinner?"

"No, hooyo, I have homework to do."

"Naayaa, go make *suqaar* and *laxoox* for Haybe, that is what he asked me to cook for him today."

"Then you cook. I have an English test tomorrow."

"Naayaa, go cook before you do that stupid homework of yours, I swear Henna I will take you out off this stupid school. I am tired of your excuses, homework, homework! Why don't you finish your homework before you come home?"

"Why do I have to do everything? You cook!"

Hear, sister, how she answers me back!

"Naayaa come here, you stupid..."

"Ouch! Get off me, *wallaahi* it hurts, hooyo!"

"Didn't I tell you not to answer me back like white kids? I will finish you off *wallaahi*."

"Hooyo, stop! God, I hate this."

"You better go and cook, spoiled girl, you are the girl in this house and that is what girls do, they cook for their family, that is the only thing they are good for!"

"I hate you! I hate all of you, I am not cooking!"

"Naayaa, come back here and talk to your habo."

"I don't wanna talk to anyone! Leave me alone!"

"I better see some food when I am done with this, or else, today is the last day you find air in your lungs!"

"I don't care! Kill me if you want! I am not cooking!"

"Naayaa!"

No one listens to me anymore, sister—this is how they turned out, they are already *gaalo*-like, and they talk to me the way white kids talk to their parents, disrespectful. I don't know why these stupid kids keep interrupting me!

What was I saying, yes, sister I expected America to free me from the feeling of ruin, guilt and civil war. Although carnage and destruction are behind me, my mind is tattooed with every detail of my loss. I want to feel free my dear sister, I want to absolve the self, but my mind seems stubborn to do so. My future seems vague.

And so, America met us with its enormity and we finally met her complexities, diversity, vagueness, opportunity, and vastness. We met our destiny.

PURITY DEBT

They were now in the confines of their new lives in America; indeed they were beyond the refugee camp and the ugliness of the day their lives changed forever. Yet, neither Henna nor Nadifo could escape the reminders of that day. The events of that day haunted Henna, forcing her to pull into full view details she longed to forget:

"Kill them all, don't leave any alive!" That message kept ringing in Henna's ears. The struggle next door added to her fear: she heard shots and a moan with an accompanying thud. Now they were in her room. One of them immediately instructed the others to look under the bed. She flinched, closing her eyes tight, praying silently. But they never lifted the sheet that veiled her under the bed. She did not feel the lift. Suddenly, stillness broke in the room.

"She is not under here!" one of the men said, infuriated. *Thank God, maybe Allah has blinded them.* She kept her eyes shut and prayed more silent prayers. She was cold with fear, paralyzed by their ashtray smell and the appalling sweat of *qat*. *Bismillah, Allah, I am at your mercy, please save my family,* Henna prayed faintly. She tried to recall the prayers she learned at *dugsi,* but none came to mind.

"Look under the other bed, you idiot! Find her and bring her here, hurry!" She felt the lift of the sheets and clutched her body tight. She closed her eyes as if that would make them go away.

"Not here either, where is she? *Waryaa,* you fool, look closely! Why are you in a hurry? Let me look!" the assassin said lifting the sheets himself; it was his sigh of relief that announced to Henna she was now under their mercy. At fourteen years of age, she was now in the hands of men she knew very well.

The sewn skin, once the pride of her family, viciously came apart. Her dear mother Nadifo prepared her cautiously to care for the area that met with violent cutting when she was six. But this is not how it was intended to come apart. She was packaged proudly to satisfy a culture that admired her ritual excision. After the carving of her skin, she was instructed to sit a certain way, walk a certain way, and assure the sliced area ample care. The carefully packaged purity had quickly disappeared through a callous violation, stinking of revenge.

Nadifo attempted to offer herself in place of the teen as the attacks ensued. Nadifo's mind was fully aware of the severe consequences this would have on the entire family. So she took off her clothes and pleaded with callous men whose enormous arms were at odds with their minuscule frames. They were familiar yet distant, their vacant faces set on destruction.

"Take me, please!" Nadifo screamed. "She is innocent, don't destroy her life!" by this time her arid tear ducts felt sore.

"Stupid old woman, what good are you?" Mahad sneered. "Your daughter is enough to teach your whole tribe a lesson!" He turned to the other thugs. "Kill them. I do not want to see them alive—start with this old woman, and finish them off quickly! We have too many houses to cover, be quick! Use whatever force you need, make sure this whole neighborhood is rid of the scum! Bring back empty guns! Look he is escaping, kill him! *Waryaa* why did you let him go? Was that Cartan? I told you to finish the scum!"

How did this massive planning right under Nadifo's nose go unnoticed? Her neighbors had been planning to attack them for a long time, but they acted otherwise. These hardened men who were here to kill her family had visited their house every day, drinking milky spiced tea, or sharing a meal or two every day. Nadifo ran a household that fed the entire neighborhood at least once or twice a week. There was plenty to eat in her home, and these young men and their families were at times there, enjoying some good old Somali chit chat and food. How could they be so complacent, not to notice the plan to wipe them out? Why didn't they pay a little more attention? Nadifo and her family were complacent, thinking they would remain the elite that ruled the masses endlessly as if it were a given right, as if the divide between them and their neighbors was not noticed. As if their neighbors enjoyed the poverty, limitations and inequality that existed. As if they enjoyed seeing Nadifo hop from one country to another, and hear names of countries they could only associate with her. As if they consented to the lavish lifestyle Nadifo and her family lived. They too wished better schools for their children, they wanted to build houses, buy Japanese cars and throw lavish weddings. But they were limited to the remnants that were thrown their way. Even the food Nadifo fed them was an afterthought, leftover food that was supposed to make them adulate their generous neighbors.

Nadifo did not take note of this developing abhorrence; it was not gradual, but rapid and prompt.

She remembered one specific conversation she had with Khadija, Mahad's mother. The two women were at Milano Salon getting ready for a dinner party Nadifo had arranged for a family who wanted to ask for Warsan's hand; it was two months to the day. The potential groom was from a prominent family and he had just returned from London after finishing a law degree. Warsan was home for the summer after completing her junior year at Saint Maria of the Immaculate College; she was due back to Missouri soon. Nadifo wanted to throw an engagement party for the pair before the end of the summer. Khadija, who had frequently accompanied Nadifo on such occasions, appeared distant and subdued about the dinner party.

"Mahad likes Warsan, she has been his dream all his life, he will be devastated when he finds out someone else is coming to ask for her hand!" The woman was obviously distraught by the event.

"Khadija, Mahad is like a son to me. Warsan does not see him that way, I am sure," Nadifo said, unmindful of Khadija's awkward demeanor.

"Why? Is he less, because he is not from your tribe? Is that why he cannot marry Warsan?" Khadija said, looking so curiously at Nadifo that the stylist relaxing her hair noticed.

"No, sister, it is not like that at all, it is just that..." Nadifo was tongue-tied, unsure how to explain the situation—how could she explain that she would never allow any of her kids to marry the likes of Mahad? They were good enough for friendship and as neighbors, but not to marry.

"He knows his place in society. He knows he cannot marry a girl like Warsan from an elite family like yours, is that it," Khadija interrupted Nadifo in mid-sentence, abruptly leaving the salon with unwashed, relaxed hair.

"Don't worry. He will get over her—he must!" Khadija said as she walked out of the salon; she never attended the dinner party. It ended disastrously anyway; the man was a show-off and the mother an overbearing, nosy snob. But Nadifo was concerned, knowing how Khadija felt about the situation. She realized, through no fault of their own, these hardened men knew they did not possess the proper lineage to be a suitor for Warsan or Henna. They knew Nadifo's girls were being preserved for someone outside their kin. This did not sit well with them. Now, Henna, the pride and joy of the whole neighborhood, was within their grasp. Without permission, they were able to take the delicate forbidden beauty they had desired.

———

"Bismillah, Bismillah, Bismillah!" Henna murmured with her eyes closed.

"Here she is! Oh, Henna, you can't hide from me!" shrieked Mahad.

She covered her eyes with trembling palms, refusing to recognize their presence, hiding in a darkness she hoped would remain. Her mind began to clear, and calm with lucid thoughts, maybe even brave thoughts. *I am not going to beg. I need to be strong. I will keep my dignity intact…*but what dignity? The fear edged back in. She had stared, looked right at them as they took turns with one of their neighbors, a fourteen-year old girl, a friend, very much like a sister. She was confused. Why would Mahad bring all these men to violate her? Wasn't he her best friend's brother?

The first attack came from the eldest of them, Liban Culusow. His appalling hands everywhere, after Liban, one by one, they emptied their hatred into her. They wanted to destroy their enemies through her body. They wanted to permanently mark her, impregnate her with a hateful reminder, a vendetta. Her body would become a casualty of war, a pillage of virtues, and a place to hold an enemy child until birth.

With the first, pain ripped through Henna, but by the time the others had finished taking their turns she felt nothing. Her tears gave way to silence. The groaning ravaged her. They were friends, neighbors, and respected Elders, yet they chose to violate her. She did not plead with them: she kept the pleas for herself. Even in the midst of it all, she wanted to keep some dignity for herself, something besides the confusion and revulsion, something besides the hurt.

Adeer Adan, their neighbor since her birth, Barwaqo's father, aunt Canood's husband, stood by with a slew of other neighbors to watch the ordeal in silence, apparently satisfied with the torture. He had played chess with her father as long as she can remember; he was also among the guests the previous evening.

Henna could hear Nadifo wailing, far away like everything else.

"God I beg you, Allah, please help me! Please stop this! Oh God, no no no!" As Nadifo attempted to pray, her prayers were somehow trapped inside her, the words would not pass her lips. Why now of all the times for the words to entrap in her throat?

"You are foul and dirty! That is what you all are!" shouted one man as he finished violating Henna.

"I swear we will make you remember this moment for years to come!"

"You will not forget us. Our sons will be in your bellies, we will multiply through you—your men are cowards who cannot protect you!" with that they left Henna in a pool of blood, naked, shivering and frail.

A nation that had fermented with loathing, poverty and mistrust finally met an opportunity to spill its rage. People like Nadifo and her family, who lived lives of luxury, had no knowledge whatsoever of the hate that brewed all around them. They lived fearlessly, unprepared, never imagining that one day they would awake to the destruction that ensued in the entire city. They lived lavishly, as if their wealth was of their own making; as if everyone around the country lived the same lives. How could they know what was going on underground when they were busy chasing life and the finer things in it? When Nadifo built a mansion that cost a million dollars, her neighbors hid their hunger shamefully. They may have eaten a meal a day if at all, when Nadifo's food was imported from Europe and the Middle East. But they were shocked when it was all taken away: call it naiveté or self-indulgence, but they expected their magnificent lives to remain undisturbed, while their neighbors ate, smelled and lived poverty.

Corpses—young, old, big, small—covered every floor of the mansion. Henna lay in a pool of blood and human waste. Nadifo's attempt to console her, to clothe the trembling naked body of the youthful girl, were refused. Henna desired no touch or embrace: she wished for death instead. She turned her face in shame, struggling against Nadifo as she tried to cradle her. After some time, Henna let out an excruciating cry; the cry soon turned to the soft, heavy sobs of a defenseless child.

Days before, Henna had giggled with Mahad's sister Intisar as they poked fun at the village visitors who had come for the wedding. Mahad's mother Khadija had combed Henna's hair, ironed her clothes, and even patted a bit of lipstick onto Henna's cute, full lips, saying it would make her pretty skin vibrant. Only twenty four hours latter Mahad seemed to enjoy her pain.

That day Henna inherited her ruined fate. Since childhood she had been instructed to shield her purity: it was the veracity of honor, she was told. No other topic as important as her purity was ever discussed with her. *Keep your purity and you honor your family. Your male relatives will walk tall, knowing you are a pure girl. Revered families will compete for your purity.* These were the words that swirled in her mind in the aftermath of the violence.

Her purity seemed to have held so much of the family pride, but in minutes everything she had grown up safeguarding was violently snatched. The velocity of the change was astounding. Henna's ears buzzed with the chaos in the room—the immense debt she owed her family for losing her purity. Violence, guilt, weakness and pain clamored in her head: the tearing of the skin, the loud obnoxious hilarity, the casual conversations, the sobs, the moans, the loathing and the stench, each left anguish in it's wake.

INFAMY BUNKER

In minutes the mansion was ransacked, bodies piled everywhere. The ghastly sight of slit throats and dismembered bodies decorated the mansion. The violated were many; women of all ages became the victims of raging bullies. With fresh wounds, Nadifo ordered Henna to go with a group of escapees who were fleeing the city to safety. It had only been a few hours after the attack and her fresh wounds hampered her movement. The group cut through dark alleys, running to evade the militia. Henna limped, leaving a trail of blood that attracted a wild cat to stalk them, hungrily slurping the blood. She tried to run fast, to evade her pain and push away the sorrow of the events that just took place, but the wounds were excruciating and she began to feel cold. Confused and short of breath, she stopped, only to begin vomiting excessively. She could not keep up with the others; finally one of the men in the group picked her up carrying her on his shoulder. Just before they entered Fadhi Xun, thirty miles beyond Hamar, they came across three militiamen, injured and close to death, lying next to each other. One of the men in her group took his shotgun and finished them off.

She escaped with people who limped with all sorts of injuries. Some held hands over gaping cuts; others dragged their hanging limbs attempting to brave the trip. If nothing else, their pain was much more visible than hers.

Fadhi Xun was nothing more than a makeshift camp for the now-displaced elite. They left behind all their wealth and comforts for a bare land filled with embittered people forced into their new deprived lives.

The inspection that began few weeks after they arrived was something Henna found cruel and inhumane. She could not figure out the mysterious thing Nadifo kept searching for in her body: the pushing on the stomach and the aggressive pat-downs did not reveal to Nadifo what she sought. Henna decided Nadifo was inspecting her for some horrible thing she had brought with her from the attackers.

That thing which Nadifo examined Henna's body for seeped through the sullied girl's body seamlessly. Henna was too immature to understand what was happening to her body. She would throw up, be nauseated, weak with splitting headaches. The evil Nadifo talked about, certainly caused sickness and discomfort. It was not until she was three months along, after she could no longer stand the constant vomiting, that she was told what was going on with her body. If Henna expected to find any sympathizers, there were none; only hateful stares and blame. She was the last to be informed of her fate. After much mourning, Nadifo instructed her on how to proceed. It was ugly, she would say to Henna. In six more months you will shame the family even further, people will whisper about us once again. She kept repeating this, adding worry to the sickness she felt. Nadifo's detest for Henna grew.

They had no choice but to hide it, but how could they hide such a horrendous shame? After all they did not have their own privacy. They shared a flimsy shack with another family. Their lives were suddenly interlaced with others, they mourned together, threatened together, but each family kept the secrets of their defeat hidden. Revenge, provocations and settling scores became the language of the day.

At night the aristocrats turned refugees would sit around a bonfire and recount their unfortunate tragedies. The most recurring regret was the lost of wealth. Various scenarios of how the wealth should have been protected were discussed. The men were asked to risk themselves and win back the looted wealth. While lost possessions occupied most of these nightly discussions, no one wanted to touch the issue of the violated women and the victims who were killed. They could not believe that their Land-Cruisers had been turned into militia trucks, their lavish homes, bunkers. Their spotless wall-marbled toilets into cess-pools where the rag-tag militia relieved themselves and quipped "these people must shit a lot; otherwise why would one house need six toilets!" But there was no sympathy for the dishonored women and girls.

Henna grew suspicious of any congregation. She assumed all conversations were about her, to disparage, and lament her situation. She grew wary of any hushed talk. Any misplaced glance confirmed her worse fears. Elderly women in the camp would recount the poor girls dilemmas, only to defile their reputations. They would bemoan the loss of cultural values in them. The militia had violated mothers, wives, grandmothers, even pregnant women, indiscriminately, yet it was the adolescent victims who were blamed, shamed for not fighting harder. The stomachs of pregnant women were gutted to eliminate future enemies, yet it was the girls who did not show firm resistance. For all sides it was the women's bodies which provided excellent vehicles for revenge. The women accepted it as the kind of injustice that came with war. They simply moved on, never speaking of their ruin. Henna like other females in the camp would suffer in silence, never complaining for fear it would exacerbate the dishonor she tired of hearing.

A haphazardly-constructed, small, flimsy shack became Henna's holding place. Nadifo instructed the slew of ego-ridden boyish males who without warning became cousins to keep a close watch over her daughter as Henna spent the better part of each day in the stinky, dusty, blazingly hot shack. It was bare, save for a few sectioned cardboard boxes which functioned as a mattress and a jug of water: The shack had suddenly appeared behind a slope near the family shack after Nadifo heard of an incident where Henna met with some girls at the camp. Of the six girls around her age, three confirmed they were pregnant; word got back to Nadifo that Henna had shared the family secret with the girls.

The sudden cousins, who wanted to prove their manhood, took the job very seriously; the family's honor and their own masculinity were on the line. They lost the war once, they were not about to lose it again with

Henna's disgrace. So they watched her every move—not that she had much room to maneuver beyond the camp. It was a struggle to get her into the shack which she called a bunker: she wailed to attract attention, often ending up going in bloody after a beating or two from Nadifo and the men. Her screams and the diligence of the boys made some passersby, who had no business walking there in the first place, suspicious.

This shack was to imprison Henna until she gave birth. Even simple talk was forbidden in this camp: after the nightly bonfire where news was exchanged, threats were made and revenge promised, Henna reluctantly retreated to her imprisonment, feeling as if time stood still inside her little shack where she was shielded even from her family. She saw her family only at meal times, which were once a day, if that.

She eventually lost herself in a new world by writing about her ordeal. The lone cardboard mattress that was to support her head and some charcoal she gathered from the nightly bonfire became a solace. She busied herself with the cutting of the cardboard, sectioning it into perfect small squares, and then the writing began.

It was Cartan's insistence that all his kids keep a daily journal. They all kept journals: it was one of those things that made her family appear more sophisticated when they were in Hamar. Henna had been writing her own stories ever since she was able to write. She kept a journal about every trip they took—but now she began writing the ugliest episode of her life. Nothing made sense to her anymore; she was too unprepared to comprehend the sudden change in their lifestyle.

She wrote whenever she could sneak a small kerosene lamp into the solitary shack. She wrote quietly so that those guarding the bunker would not hear and take away her journal. Writing with charcoal made her temporarily escape her situation:

DAY 1 IN THE PIT

I am veiled away from other people in the camp, my family and I live a lie. They stigmatized me. My mother began to talk differently, walk with shame. When she is alone, she sheds tears of anguish every night. She carries the burden of a lost son and a daughter who is expecting an enemy child. It's her sudden devoutness that makes her accept this unwanted child of war, a stray implantation. My father seems to handle it better. Each of his merciful glances is filled with sympathy and regret. The injustice of the violence against me is ever present in his eyes. He is the only one able to make me feel safe. He assures me that I am not at fault, that he was to blame for it all. His silence nurses my wounds. Even these stupid boys who think they are men are encouraged to hate me. They are told they will no longer be respected because of the child inside me.

DAY 61 IN THE PIT

The smell of poverty is overwhelming. Flies gather on my face, as though we share a destiny. The air is still, sour, and thick with the aroma of death. My hair, often admired for its lustrous thickness, is now dirty and limp. It has proven to be a nuisance as of late. Hooyo has chopped it away, as if to cut away any reminders of the past months. However nature seems to defy her order, growing longer, faster, as if it is nourished by the dirt and little animals crawling all over my scalp. Lice congregate on my body, holding meetings of destruction selfishly living of my blood when I am weak and malnourished.

Sweat collects in the crooks of my arms and the back of my knees and red ants bite at the damp parts. I want to scratch my whole body with a sharp knife, scratch everything away. The folds of my eyelids become too heavy, my tear ducts dry and itchy. My uncut nails collect blackened, gooey slime; I let it be, what point is there in cleaning them when dirt is all it seems to attract? Pus collects in my cracked, ashy feet. I pick thorns from my feet, ankles, and calves. I don't feel the pain though; I don't possess the ability to feel pain any longer. I don't recognize my ankles or my feet or my arms. If a cracked glass or mirror reveals my face, I must make much effort to remember who the girl staring back is, I don't recognize myself, we are all growing old much too quickly.

DAY 122 IN THE PIT

The life I am carrying reminds me of the hate that my family holds for me. I am consumed by the pain I feel inside, but my mother gives much to the entire ordeal. I have nothing but contempt for those who did this to me. No one ever acknowledged my pain. No one asks how I am. How painful it was? That it was not my fault. It is as if people forgot the attack and now only remember my disgracing stomach. My life disappeared with their attack, this child does not change me. I don't care what Nadifo says, it is not my fault. No, it is not my fault!

Allah has bestowed this body on me; it has long been admired, loved, and cared for. It was to become a special prize for my family one day. My mother admired my beauty for so long that she would sometimes boast to the point of embarrassment but now her wandering eyes say that my beauty is nothing but a vessel of shame...She began to despise me. They, the dirty men responsible for this delivered my early death. I am an empty shell, barely existing.

DESIRE DOOM

Many months of grief at Fadhi Xun had passed. The awaited journey to Kenya had finally arrived. Henna was now in her ninth month. The family gathered to plan for the journey. They planned that if she went into labor during the treacherous expedition, she would be isolated from public view and left behind for a few days so that her labor would not hamper the rest. In reality it was so that people in journey with them would not see her go into labor.

Nadifo and an aunt would remain with her at all times and help handle the situation. She anxiously waited for her body to vomit out the hated sin. What her family did to it after its arrival was of no concern to her. After nine months, she was still detached from the baby inside her: she viewed her body as nothing more than a temporary host. She kept counting the days, dreaming to see her normal body, back to the way it used to be, small, petite and endearing. She wanted her body back.

In the middle of the night without any notice, Henna was awakened abruptly from deep sleep. It was a rough night, she was not sure what was going on, but she knew her family was up to something. Whenever they held mysterious gatherings in the middle of the night, and when Nadifo threw wicked stares at her she knew they were up to something. So she stayed up all night, to ready herself for whatever they were planning to do to her. She felt they would do something horrible to her. She feared the pain, and so whenever she noticed their irrational gatherings she prepared for the horrendous pain they would put her through. She drifted to a fraught sleep a little before dawn, finally resting her protruding belly in a calming position. And then there he was, Laangadhe, the most calculating of her cousins, a few years older than her and the one who had orchestrated the plan to escape Fadhi Xun. He startled her, roaring "get up, naayaa", forcefully pulling her to her feet, and then pushing her towards the door where the rest of her family anxiously stood. His severe limp which is the reason he abruptly acquired the nickname Laangadhe—it appeared would limit him in the planned journey. He was to stay and wait for another means of travel to the refugee camp, since walking such a great distance would prove dangerous for him. He would not be alone at Fadhi Xun. Faroole, Lugbuur, Gacanlow and Filsan Jiis would remain with him. Maimed by war and with new nicknames that announced their disability, they were all hesitant to stay behind, but had no other alternative.

Silence and fear plagued the trip. They were now on their way to a more stable refugee camp in Kenya. But there were all sorts of horror stories: people got killed on their way to Kenya; members of the same militia that chased them from Hamar knew people would be crossing over, so they waited for them. Animals feasted on the starving refugees, and bandits stole what meager belongings they had possessed.

They had waited almost nine months for this day. For nine months they planned and concocted the safest plan to cross over to Kenya. They were four hundred people including elders, children and woman. Many elders came along, understanding the danger. They too were too proud to just remain and wait for death; they preferred an attempt to escape to freedom while risking death to being left behind in the camp to be killed by the militia. The sickly and weak tagged along knowing that the terrain ahead posed treacherous challenges. Anyone unable to catch up was swiftly left behind. Hunger, thirst, exhaustion, and fear characterized the expedition. Vomiting shakes, and fevers were ignored. Loved ones were left behind if they proved too slow for the rest. The stakes were too high for emotions. Fear creased the faces of people.

The lush green pasture they crossed over deceived them. The path to their destination was punctuated by thorns of death. Pouring rain and deepening mud hid dangerous insects, poisonous lizards, toads and snakes. Multi-colored berries which appeared inviting and nutritious at first poisoned the hungry refugees. Some met their demise unwittingly; others took to it purposefully after witnessing the fallen. Flying insects attacked immune systems, causing flu-like symptoms and diarrhea that discharged the entire insides of some. Healthy, able-bodied people would go limp and soon fall. Nature impudently attacked them. The skies wept; the ground bled a constant stream of carnage. It was as if nature was condemning them for committing sins against the motherland. Heavy floods and heavy rains restricted them one day, blistering heat and humidity the next. Blood and earth appeared rebelliously unified.

A lion chased the staggering group, snatching a three-year-old girl and dragging her behind a bush to break her flesh. The mother of the girl collected the other four children and walked on as if the flesh in the lion's fangs was not her daughter. Not even a tear.

Ordinary people temporarily transformed to midwives, nurses, and corpse handlers. Corpses marked the path. People had to maneuver around the bodies to advance. There was no room for error; the shadows of the militia lurked everywhere. Henna witnessed the violent murder of two of her camp mates after masked men attacked them. The lingering smell of death and rotten corpses caused the acid in her starved stomach to spill. The relentless death made bereavement void. For the fallen quick prayers were enough to send them home.

DAY 268 IN THE PIT

I sit in a simple tarred shack in Iffo. We arrived two days ago; I almost did not make the trip. The labor was painful, but it's over now. I was walking with everybody when I was overcome with an excruciating pain—a surge unlike the other pain went through me. It was unbearable and made movement impossible. I leaned against a tree for support, unable to continue. My mother kept shooting back evil stares, urging me to catch up. I wish she could have felt my pain. I wished for her to leave me alone, her stares and scrutiny were as unbearable as the pain. I was unable to walk, as the pain became persistent. Her displeasure was the least of my worries; she pretended not to know my dilemma. I collapsed in agony on the heat-cracked ground; pain tore up my insides. If I knew nothing else, I knew that the moment I have been awaiting for the longest nine months of my life was imminent. I empowered my soul to be strong and eject it, finally. Hot, painful water shot out of me. It hit me with such strength and force that I lost consciousness. Coming in and out of consciousness I could see my mother rushing back to me, annoyed, as if she were saying *wait, not now, don't give birth now*. She looked scared and annoyed. She was terrified; I was relieved. It was the first time that I saw any humanity in her, as though she temporarily discarded her rejection of me.

DAY 269 IN THE PIT

All the pain in the world did not make the labor easier. My presence in Iffo, free from the ordeal of labor seems surreal.

The second day of the labor I drift in and out of consciousness, groaning, moaning and hollering for help. My moans invited unwanted stares; my mother was overwhelmed but still resolute, urging me to shut my mouth and endure the pain. She left me under a tree as she raced back to the caravan to collect more help. I lay next to a woman, I exerted energy to shake her to ask for her help; her skin was cold, clammy, and rough. The more I shook her, groaning loudly the more her body felt cold. I was in pain and the woman was unresponsive. Then I came to a full sitting position to wake her. In so much pain I was too blind to see the woman whom I sought help from was herself dead.

The massive trunk of an acacia tree concealed me, veiling me from the merciless view of the people. Engrossed in pain, I lay at its base with the corpse next to me, seeking any compassion, any reprieve.

"Naayaa, stop making loud noises, don't let these people see you," mother said sternly, scaring me. She was concerned with how it would make her look?

72

I was concentrated on relief, a much-awaited, much-deserved relief. And then I found myself behind a hilly slope of trees. I am not sure how I got there perhaps, I was carried there; the details are murky. I was no longer under the tree with the corpse. All I wanted to do was to expel the repulsive child.

DAY 270 IN THE PIT

On the third day of labor my aunt Qorsho, an experienced midwife who has been delivering babies for decades, came along to help. She was a beast of a woman, stiff, merciless, and very pestering. You would think she would have offered some pragmatic advice, as the dozens of babies she has delivered in her lifetime are now grown, healthy adults. Instead, she attacked me with her cruel, rough hands, inflicting more pain. I protested her touch and that is when she began roaring at me to stop crying. She chastised me for being the most embarrassing person she has ever helped deliver. She began beating me with a stick to make me quiet, but I hollered louder. Her blows provided the chorus to my screams as she reprimanded me for humiliating them and inviting shameful stares.

A herd gathered to witness the labor, attracted by the commotion.

"Shut up Henna, do you think you are the first woman who has ever given birth?" she berated me.

"I am not a woman, I am only fifteen, stop screaming at me!"

"Stupid girl, I was fifteen when I had my first baby and God knows I did not roar like that."

"Were you violated at fourteen? Of course not, stupid old woman!" Every time I cried she was more belligerent. "I don't care! Take this thing out of me! Aaaah!"

"Stop this nonsense! Your mother has had enough; stop this stupidity!" she would scream alongside me.

I was appalled by their cruelty. The alleviation of shame was above all else for these women: pain, fear, danger, and all the other potentially deadly elements to our journey were ignored but shame had no place even when in danger. They were living a lie; I detested her just as I did my mother. How can they think of disgrace and honor when my entire life was in danger of slipping through their hateful hands? Their only objective was to preserve appearances.

DAY 271 IN THE PIT

After the throbbing labor, she took it out. I lay there recovering from the anguish. They cut me with a razor and tied the umbilical cord with a strip of fabric from my own diric. After the delivery they remained silent. I guess they had not planned for this moment. Unsure of the next step, the women stared vacantly at each other.

No one told me what it was. It was not even inspected for signs of life, nor the customary prayers whispered in its ears. Instead, it was wrapped in a piece of faded rag from my diric and put aside. But, to their great chagrin the dense, unrelenting silence suddenly rang with a thunderous shriek from the baby everyone present wanted to dispose of.

Henna's sleek bare midriff, which Nadifo fiercely opposes, does not reveal any signs of the hardship, pain, or the birthing of a baby in the middle of a jungle at fifteen. She is a sleek twenty-three year old who had begun her life in America with a burst of positive energy. She had embraced her new life with a promise to never blame herself or scar her future with the past. She is in college, had made friends, and began to appreciate her new freedom, promising herself that she would achieve success by educating herself and working hard. She desires a life alone, away from the constant reminder of the past, away from Nadifo. The woman is relentless: Just one look from her speaks volumes, but Henna has no place for negativity. She is busy now with a second chance, a beautiful life given to her by *Allah* after such a tragedy.

The beauty that is apparent to other people began to emerge in her own mind, to the point of vanity. She ignored Nadifo's reminders that her body was the host for the greatest dishonor for the family. Henna had had enough. She would shake off the blame and the curse that had befallen the family because of her.

Her relationship with Nadifo remains cold. Instead, she seeks attention from others, usually men. Anyone who admires her beauty and praises her womanhood is acceptable to her. Strange men simply desire her and she craves the attention. Her ears longed to hear nothing but how alluring she is. The body which is rejected by the Somalis, who by now began their ugly rumors that she is the mother of a bastard child, is a jewel to men in America, every kind of men—except Somalis. Among them is a manhole digger, a barber, a bus driver, a dot com CEO and a doctor. They come from every spectrum and hue in American society and had one thing in common: their desire for Henna. The solace she needed came from them.

"She is the mother of a bastard," is replaced with "You're breathtaking, baby!"

While she moonlights as a love junkie, the events of the past are never far away. Every time she comes across a Somali man she wonders if he were one of the beasts that assaulted her. Every face held an agonizing mystery, Henna is sentenced to a lifetime of doubt. She wondered what would become of her if she had not endured such appalling violence. The more Nadifo badgered her, the more Henna lost herself to some strange man whom she had just met at some club, or while walking home. She would come home drunk with tousled hair and Nadifo would cry, beating her with a baseball bat she bought for the job. There would be a week of quiet without drinking until her wounds healed, then the cycle would begin again until her culturally unacceptable behavior created tension in all her family relationships. Cartan never took part, but her brothers and mother kept beating her, kicking her out of the apartment and sometimes imprisoning her in her own room. This would only make her addictions more vulgar and wild.

MYSTERY MAIL

Henna arrived at the apartment hauling her heavy backpack, visibly exhausted from a long day at school. This has been their home since their arrival in Minneapolis. It is not the vibrant, elegant, open space she had envisioned when she dreamed about her life in America; but this is home. It is the dizzying stenches of Tide which Nadifo uses to clean everything from dishes to clothes and everything in between, *uunsi* the Somali incense used as air freshener, body freshener, and aromatherapy for depressing, stressful days, and decaying after-smells of strong spices that remind her she is home.

She snuck through the living room to avoid Nadifo in the kitchen, and dashed to her room, which occupied a tiny space at the end of the hallway. The living room, kitchen, and dining area were Nadifo's domain. Henna's self-conscious insecurity was fully realized in these areas: she felt judged, despised, and underappreciated. Henna scheduled her arrival to coincide with her mother's absence. She would arrive when Nadifo was at school or work: if she was home when Henna came home, Henna quietly slipped into her room to avoid being seen by her at all.

Her brothers and father who also shared the apartment seemed to disappear at will. In the event that her father was present, he could be found in his usual spot, a lone corner at the foot of the couch, a tiny space on the floor where he was usually on the phone or listening to his short-wave radio, chewing qat.

Henna threw her hefty backpack to the floor upon entering her room. A sigh of relief escaped her lips as she welcomed the idea of relaxing for the rest of the day. She wouldn't have to study for her history exam for another hour or so. She would spend the better part of the afternoon on catnaps, phone conversations, and watching her favorite show 90210. Henna came alive in her room; it was the only place she felt herself. An imitation version of Eternity which she had purchased the day before awoke her tired senses.

———⌒∞⌒———

She threw her slender body across her twin-sized bed, settling into a nest of clothes, books, and other knick-knacks after changing into a bulky pink sweatshirt that splashed "Wu-Tang Clan" across her chest. The upper half of her petite frame is shrouded by the boxy sweatshirt, which also manages to hide her Daisy Duke shorts, leaving only bare skinny legs to poke out uncovered.

The pink walls sport life-size posters of Tupac. She opened the cover of "What's the 411" which she had bought on her way home from school. She peeked at the images of Mary J. Blige, who looked pretty and daring. Lavender down comforter with matching pillows covered the floor. She hugged her snow-white teddy bear, while covering her bare parts with a pastel purple throw blanket. Dim green and red lights hung from the ceiling, and swirls of smoke escaped the incense burner adding to an aura of serenity. Earlier in the year, she had begged to move out of the apartment and into a dorm on campus at the University of Minnesota. Her parents, however, denied her request citing the necessity of cultural and religious adherence.

"It is not our culture to allow a daughter to roam the streets of a strange country!" Nadifo barked from the kitchen where she was either cooking or cleaning. "You will only leave when a young man asks for your hand; do you want to disgrace me?" Her father races to be heard behind a stuffed cheek of qat.

"A single girl should be in her father's house or the grave, nothing in between" he continued, emphasizing the grave.

She was forced to give up on the idea. Henna admired her American friends who seemed to be at the helm of their lives, living on their own, with roommates—or with whomever they chose—experiencing life without the smothering presence of parents. She simply had too many people in her life claiming the same air and space. The apartment held too many bodies. Soothing music from Sade played in the background. All her friends liked this song because it said something great about a Somali woman, but they did not really understand the song and they did not care. It was enough someone had paid tribute to some Somali woman. Henna immersed herself in the book resting in her immaculately manicured hands, *The Lovely Ms.Webster.* Henna relaxed as she read, immensely enjoying the ambiance that she had crafted for herself to dodge life as it existed in her parent's apartment.

A few minutes later, she heard a slight jolt, but she ignored it and continued reading. There was continuous noise coming from the living room when Nadifo was home. She would either be bossing Bile, forcing him to pray, read Quran, or stop watching TV. Or she would be quarreling with Cartan, recalling hurtful moments in their life or accusing him of something or another. Or she would be scolding Haybe for his baggy clothes, his late comings and goings, or something about school. The woman was constantly raising her voice to an inane pitch to shame someone. Henna had perfected a way to ignore her: she would pretend the attacks were directed toward others and refuse to respond. Unfortunately, however, Henna found Nadifo standing directly above her own bed, angry as usual. Nadifo was saying something to get Henna's attention. This was typically the way it went. She would barge in, ignoring the "RULES" that adorn the door (the first of which is to knock before entering). Nadifo found the rules absurd:

"Why should I knock to enter a room in my own house?" Nadifo complained about her to one of her friends. "Can you believe her audacity? She took a whole room for herself and then she wants to transport American ideas like privacy and re-decorating your room your own way and "the RULES" to this immigrant home. No one knows why she pretends, she knows perfectly well that having your own privacy and things of that nature will not work in here. She knows very well how her business is everyone else's business. And yet she continues the charade."

Henna continued reading as if Nadifo was not there. She found the romance books she read so profound, so consuming. It was as though the words pounced from the pages directly into her soul. She often dreamt of an existence similar to the women in these books. Their lives appeared perfect. She inhaled the fabricated lines and carefully orchestrated scenes of each engrossing tale.

Dipping into the Doritos that sat indolently on the mahogany-colored nightstand, she lifted her gaze for a split second to grant the fuming woman pressed at the foot of her bed recognition. Immediately, however, she returned to the book, causing Nadifo to shriek loudly to alert her to a pressing need. Nadifo just received a letter from the post office and she wanted Henna to read it. Henna dismissed her, annoyed.

"I don't need this BS, hooyo, God! This is insane!" Henna was interrupted by a sharp smack against her leg. "Ouch! What is the matter with you?" Nadifo's fuss accused her of inappropriately revealing her body, of reading nonsense novels, and of losing her culture, proclaiming that Allah will curse her if she continues to expose her naked body to the angels. Nadifo picked a sheet from the floor and draped Henna's skinny bare legs, entreating her not to show her ugliness.

"Yeah, yeah whatever!"

Nadifo ordered her to read the letter, irate that she is forced to ask Henna for anything. She used the opportunity to attempt to shame Henna for her hopelessly indecent ways.

"Oh God, not again, please," Henna shrieked sarcastically, dragging out the "p" as if to emphasize her anger. She spoke more to herself, knowing Nadifo would not understand English. She reluctantly obeyed Nadifo's command to read the letter. She sat up, sighing audibly. She had tired of reading letters for her. Nadifo never allowed anyone else to open the mail: she had decided that the entire family was careless and would not pay attention to important mail, such as immigration papers and letters from the welfare office. So, she made the rule that only she could open the mail. Unfortunately, she was also illiterate and was dependent on the very careless indolent family members to read the mail.

Henna had offered Nadifo complete fabrications of the content of these letters more times than even she was willing to admit. Some of the letters Nadifo brought to her for interpretation contained potentially damaging information, information that was better left unsaid.

A letter had arrived from the District Attorney's Office one time. Apparently, Bile, her younger brother, had had some mix-up with the police. A car he was riding in was stopped by the police, who found some illegal drugs. Henna knew that sharing such information with her would probably cause Nadifo chronic insomnia and endless worry, throwing her deeper into regret for her children's abandoned culture and tradition. Not only would it haunt Nadifo, but all of her friends and relatives around the world would be notified. They too would wallow in the misery of raising children in America. The endless chatter would go on for weeks. Other Somali parents would call Nadifo when they heard of Bile's situation to compare notes, asserting that their own children were also losers, shameless alcoholics, and drug addicts, even when this was often not true. They would collectively agree on a solution, which would usually include how Nadifo must trick the offending Bile into a grandiose vacation to Dubai, but instead discard him on the lawless shores of Somalia for *dhaqan celis*, amid the chaos and the civil unrest they fled, to teach him a lesson. They would all swap stories of how so-and-so sent her son back home, and when he returned, he became a model child, continuing with his studies, respecting his elders, and adhering to religious obligations. This would go on endlessly, polluting the ears of any poor soul who happened to visit or call.

Henna had therefore decided to spare Nadifo the agony of the whole ordeal. Instead, Henna had consulted with Bile and Warsan, her eldest sister. The lie they fed to their mother had varied from how the letter contained excellent grades Bile earned in school to how some high schools were extending the middle school student a spot to attend their school. She did not have to find out about the mess of a police arrest and jail time when such things gave her heart perpetration. A pro bono lawyer Warsan knew settled the entire matter: Bile narrowly escaped jail time, performing community service instead.

Nadifo was frequently suspicious of Henna; according to her there was nothing trustworthy about the girl, who shamelessly dropped her culture for the American one. Sometimes Nadifo would go to two, even three, people to read the same letter. She would occasionally even ask strangers in her community center to read the letters instead of Henna.

POSTCARDS FROM
THE BRINK

The ESL class Nadifo attends daily, albeit reluctantly, is held at a community center which sits on a lonely snow-covered street. It is as though traffic laws do not apply here: Somali refugees willingly ignore traffic laws and parking signs, parking wherever they desire, running over anyone unfortunate enough to be in the way. Unruly refugees as rebellious as the homeland they fled resist the laws of the land in this lonely corner where they come to escape their new miserable lives.

Chipping paint in shiny yellow and bright baby-blue coat the hallways reeking of stale air. Poor attempts to brighten the chronic unpleasantness end in uneven discolored walls. A group of rowdy Somali men converse in a room too small to fit them comfortably.

Unfazed by personal space and breathing each other's air, they down hot, sweet milk tea while swapping the latest political stories. A radio blasts in the background with news, music and English lessons, but loud conversation makes it difficult to hear the radio. Children play in a computer room, mimicking their elders who don't speak one at the time but all at once to be heard. Case workers and students attempt to maneuver through a group of women who purposefully congregate on the hallway to catch up with gossip or tales of tragedy, clogging the throughway for those whose job depends on passing through.

This particular center prefers to show off its success and the refugees they have helped by displaying smiling faces of ever-so-grateful refugees detailing their ugly pasts on small postcards. The postcards adorn the oddly colored hallway walls. It is as though the center could not find decent looking refugees to depict. The pictures appear staged, as if the families are photographed right after they dusted their faces with sand. The shock factor of dirt, misery and poverty in the eyes of the desperate refugees is well portrayed.

Amy Tucker, the ESL teacher, sat on top of a puny yellow desk, ready to begin class. She waits patiently as her students waste time catching up outside the class room. She is normally the only calm person in the class. She speaks with ease and enthusiasm, never exerting any undue effort to be heard, remaining tranquil despite the chaos around her. Somehow she has never succeeded in transferring her placid mannerisms to her students. Instead, they receive the lesson haphazardly, eager for a quick gain and instant gratification. They are ready to leave class as soon as they enter it: if it were not compelled by the department of Social Services where the majority of women in this particular class receive food stamps and cash benefits, they would be elsewhere, preferably in a warm bed under some cozy comforters instead of this freezing class where the only eager person is Amy.

Amy is often giddy with pride as she attempts to speak Somali to them. Their culture seems to please her; she goes out of her way to learn it. Nadifo wished she could be that excited learning English: the whole ordeal causes her fatigue. It is a combination of reservation, mistrust and stubborn old mind that cause Nadifo the anxiety she feels when she is in class.

"Morning, ladies! How is everyone this morning? Are you all ready to begin class?" *No, indeed, we are not ready to begin class. We would much rather continue our repetitive saga of sorrow, recounting why we have inherited this! No we rather be home eating some fattening foods to bring us comfort or be on the phone gossiping, anything to forget our miserable lives here!*

The women conclude Amy must be escaping something amazingly boring in her life—why else would she try to leap into their misery? They further conclude only a person with no life, or one with a very miserable, wretched one would want to be with them, a group of illiterate refugee women who rarely discuss anything positive. Maybe she is also forced by the government. Whatever the reasons, Amy is eager to teach them, patiently ready to transfer her American know-how onto them whether they received it willingly or not.

But the women in her class struggle with their mere existence in their new world, let alone learn. Learning is the furthest thing from their unpacked mental state. They make themselves believe their inhabitance here is fleeting, that soon things would turn around for them. Soon their beloved country, the place that never leaves their thoughts, will accept them back. They tell each other tales where the motherland is awaiting their return. They resentfully put up with Amy and her like, hoping she will soon be a distant memory, yet they are still here, some more than five years, others longer, still planning to return.

Nadifo was never schooled in her own language and arrived in America an illiterate woman. Refining this foreign language seems an unfeasible task for her, yet she complies. What other choice does she have? Whatever it takes to make the boisterous Ms. Gayle disappear from her life is a good enough reason to learn English.

Maybe Amy knows some magic; perhaps there is some American magic to teach English to an illiterate middle-aged woman like Nadifo, a woman whose fingers have never graced a pencil, let alone a pen. Wasn't America the land that made everything possible? She would just have to force her stubborn mind to believe it was a possibility, no matter how gibberish and foreign it sounded. It's difficult for Nadifo to follow Amy's delicate thin lips move with unfamiliar words, and equally challenging to race with Amy's graceful fingers, which turned pink when she held the chalk to the board. This was the first time Nadifo had struggled with a pen: it rested between her fingers as she attempted to do homework, entirely awkward. She had assumed pen holding was an art left to the well informed, people like her husband and children who had the good fortune of schooling. Her fingers would not wrap gracefully around a pen the way she has seen other people do.

"I never thought I would hold a pen like this," she confessed to Cambaro as the women swapped stories about their new setting. "It appeared so smooth in their fingers, but in mine the pen resists, it is deviant." Her fine fingers, which had accomplished so much over time, refused to become comfortable with the pencil she held as she tried to do her home work. Her kids laughed at her; Cartan simply ignored her.

"It is silly to think you are going to pick up this language all of a sudden, Nadifo," he would say. "You better pick up another hobby."

A hobby, that is what they thought she was doing, picking up a hobby. It became a challenge for Nadifo to learn English, to learn to write: the competitive side of her wanted to learn so she could show her family she was capable. As difficult as it was, she no longer wanted to ask them to write a telephone number for her, or read a letter. She wanted to end the bewildered life of never knowing what is on a page. She knew her only way out of the vague life depended entirely on the difficult tasks of reading and writing; she just had to push herself harder.

She would try to write: A, B, C, D, over and over again. She sometimes copied them upside down, bewildering Amy, who thought it must be harder to copy the letters upside down—but try and telling that to fifty-some-year-old fingers with a mind which functions in a totally different sphere. She was ashamed of the work she handed to Amy, knowing it looked like chicken scribble.

"Oh Nadifo, don't give up so easily! You will soon get it right! Remember, practice makes perfect" Amy would reassure her, eternally optimistic.

GRUDGE BEARING

Amy Tucker chattered eagerly for two hours every day; Nadifo and the other women never understood what she was saying, but they pretended otherwise. When Amy was not running her mouth, she would examine Nadifo's clothes. Amy would touch her *garbasaar*, the traditional shawl she used to cover her upper body. She would stroke Nadifo's *diric* with her pale fingers, admiring the colorful *henna* designs decorating Nadifo's hands. Amy would murmur, something then return to her desk with a silly smile all over her face. What made Amy so happy about Nadifo's clothes, Nadifo would never know. Amy showered her with what she assumed were words of praise; she wished that she could tell Amy to stop touching her clothes, but she did not want to seem rude, so she said nothing. Nadifo thought that maybe it was part of the class. How would she know what the norm was—everything here was awkward for her. Nadifo would nod her head as Amy approached and plaster a fake smile on her face.

Nadifo had been pleasing the Americans with her practiced smiles since her arrival—it was all she could do since she could not speak directly to them. She would nod and smile, and they in turn would nod and smile back, adding some odd words. It was strange at first, this mute life where her gestures replaced her voice. She had flawlessly refined this new language. She had even figured out when to place a slightly crooked large "X" next to some murky words which happen to be her name. That is the way she signed her name. When she went grocery shopping, she allowed the cashier to pick from her wallet whatever the register's screen displayed. Sometimes she would hand the cashier the entire wallet. That was how she handled most tasks, unless the issues at hand required language decoding—in which case one of her kids would be forced to come along. She reserved such assistance for very serious occasions in which her gestures would not suffice. Nadifo despised this sudden role reversal in which her children were able to assume the position of authority: she was suspicious when her kids spoke that foreign language in her presence. Why would they choose to speak with each other in such a manner unless they were hiding something? They did it to alienate her, and she told them so. They could easily speak their own language to each other, but, no, they chose English to exclude her.

It was not how she envisioned her life would conclude.

A whisper from her soul gave Nadifo the strength to go on. She needed courage to sail through this vague life, where nothing resembled life as it once existed. How did this happen? Now she was an alien, like a creature from outer space —that is what her brand new green card number N35963974 said, that she was an alien, and she felt it too. Nadifo stayed awake many nights, wondering. The images of her former life forced themselves into her enraged mind, furious, refusing to let go. It played back memories: Paris, Rome, Beijing, Dubai, trips of luxury shopping and fun travel. She had the best assistants to help ease her life—Suad had normally traveled with her to the finest cities to shop, all she had to do was pick her items and Suad handled negotiating and paying for things. Nadifo longed for Suad, and the worry-free life she once had. She felt naked, as if she was stripped of life's comforts. In her former life she had been, capable and worldly. People even mistook her for someone knowledgeable. That is what money does: it makes you appear more than you are. But without the money, and the status and all that came with it, she felt exposed, unable to tell a dollar from five and a nickel from a dime. Humiliated, even signing her name became a chore.

Nadifo shoved the letter in Henna's face, commanding her to read it. Henna made feeble attempts to dissuade her determined, aggressive mother. She had noticed the letter sitting on the dining room table earlier that day and had hoped almost desperately that Nadifo would not ask her to read it.

"Hooyo, let Warsan read it, you know I cannot read Somali!" she said, trying to get out of it.

"Who told you it is in Somali? Are you a mind reader? Naayaa, read it right this minute!" Nadifo hissed as rudely as she often had when dealing with Henna.

"I am not going to read it; I don't know how to read Somali!" Henna huffed, annoyed.

"Since when, Naayaa!" Nadifo belligerently pulled the comforter Henna was hugging. "Since when don't you read Somali, you just got here yesterday?" All the years they had been here amounted to yesterday in Nadifo's mind, especially when she was trying to make a point. She shoved the letter into Henna's face.

Every encounter with her ended up in some un-winnable fight. Henna thought she might have had a better relationship if Nadifo had not been so stubborn and relentless. Nadifo washed her hands of her a long time ago. It had something to do with how the girl had changed since the war. Suffice it to say mother and daughter were not best of friends; yet they were forced to deal with each other. Nadifo did not enjoy being reliant on Henna and her other kids to read these letters, but what other choice did she have?

Henna begged not to read the letter because it contained news she did not wish to share with Nadifo. Why would she put herself in a situation where Nadifo would put one of her helpless episodes when all of a sudden the world was conspiring against her? Henna was not stupid to do herself in to Nadifo's ever blameful world. Least of all she did not want to deliver bad news to Nadifo, less she be blamed once more for bringing nothing but bad luck and bad news to the family. No, indeed she would avoid reading the letter all together.

Plus Henna knew that the letter contained bad news that would revive a painful episode her family had tried to bury for the longest time; a past Nadifo had willingly and shamelessly left on the shores of Africa.

Henna realized Nadifo waited anxiously at the foot of the bed. She was as blatant as ever, forcing Henna to read the letter. The letter was now practically shoved between her nose and upper lip. She was now breathing on the letter, and Nadifo it seemed was intent on getting the information that was inside the blue and red striped envelope with a handful of out of the country stamps. Henna scrutinized the letter, wondering why Nadifo was so jittery. Nadifo nervously chewed her lower lip, she was visibly on edge. She must have figured out the letter was from the refugee camp in Kenya, the tattered look and the striped envelope gave it away. She also knew by now that letters from America were mostly white and very neat looking. Even the postage was an ink stamp, not a glued-on one. So she asked Henna for the second time to read it: this time there was something extremely meek about her. She looked vulnerable to Henna, who nearly never sympathized with her.

Henna decided to read the letter quickly and truthfully. She would tell Nadifo what the letter was about, and then she would leave fast, leaving her to mourn and blame her with all the names in the book, alone. She was not going to be a witness yet again to an ugly episode of name calling. So she practiced in her head how she was going to deliver the bad news—but her Somali was shabby at best, she would not be able to read the entire letter, only give her the gist of it:

"Hooyo, this letter came from Tusmo Xashi," she said, not looking up from the letter, afraid to meet her pained eyes.

"Tusmo who?" Nadifo asked, shaken, hoping Henna would not repeat the name.

"Mother, you know which Tusmo I am talking about. The one we left in Kenya," Henna wished she would just leave now. She reached for the CD player and increased the volume to create some noise between them, but Nadifo unplugged it. "The letter says they were coming, so they must already be here, I think she is here with the kid. She has immigrated here—that is what the letter says. This is her address if you are interested," Henna said, carefully gathering the CD player's electric cord from the trash can where Nadifo had just thrown it. "Please don't do that again, hooyo." She tried to change the topic.

"What did you say?"

"Nothing!" Henna wished Nadifo would just leave. *Just leave me the hell alone!* She said in the safety of her mind.

Nadifo's thoughts stalled. She realized that the day she had long dreaded had arrived. She was not ready for it. She had hoped that Tusmo and her family would never win a spot to immigrate to America. She had hoped that she could keep them far away, in Africa, with many oceans separating their realities. Somehow she trusted her belief, positive it would prove difficult for Tusmo to follow them; after all, Tusmo did not have any family members who could sponsor her in America, and she would not be able to afford the expensive trip on her own.

"Why are they here?" somehow Henna expected a different response. "Was the monthly stipend we sent every month not enough? Is he here too? When did they arrive? How? Why?"

"I don't know, mother! I do not know!" Henna said frantically. "Please stop asking me all these questions, I don't give a damn! I really don't care about these people, they are not my problem!" Henna got up and left the room. Paralyzed by fear, Nadifo stood perfectly still, her mind racing, searching. How could she withstand any further tarnish of the family's name? How could she stop Tusmo from spoiling their new American lives? How would they explain the child? What will her friends say? Everything would be revealed. Why did they decide to come after seven years?

"I am out of here!" Henna grabbed her backpack, throwing it across her back she dashed out of the room, leaving Nadifo in a mystified state. Henna was about to open the front door, trying to avoid Nadifo who was now following her down the hallway when the door bell rang. As the door opened, Bile and Jason, horsing around on their skate boards, came into full view.

"Hey guys, are you coming in," asked Henna, relieved, holding the door for them. Before the boys responded Nadifo called from the living room.

"Naayaa, call Haybe for me, he will know what to do!"

"Is she mad? Can we come in?" asked sweaty and out of breathe Bile, looking timid as he heard Nadifo's voice.

"Hooyo, I'm going to the library! I don't know where Haybe is, I can't call him and I honestly don't care!" Henna said, letting go of the door. She turned back to the boys. "Sure, you guys can come in—what do I care?" she said disdainfully.

"Call him and tell him to stop Tusmo from coming to America!" Nadifo responded as if she had not heard Henna.

"Look, Jason, don't say anything to my mum, she—" Before Bile finished his sentence Nadifo was out the door, still pursuing Henna.

"Hi Mrs. Gedi," Jason said, he stood between Nadifo and Henna, interrupting their exchange; he hid his skateboard behind his thin little body, unsure what to do next. Nadifo stared at the colorful freckles on his face; she'd never been this close to him before. *What an odd-looking kid*, she thought, he looked weird. His eyes were like glass, so transparent she could almost see through them, and his hair was messy and bright red—*is it henna that made his hair this red*? She wondered. He broke her chain of thought.

"Call Haybe," Nadifo extended the phone to Henna. Henna looked annoyed, Jason scared.

While the two argued outside the front door, the boys slipped into the apartment and quickly raced towards the kitchen.

"I am not going to call Haybe or anyone else, ok!" Henna began crying, while Jason and Bile nervously downed apple juice in the kitchen.

"This is not my problem! This kid you keep talking about is not my problem!"

"Please call Haybe, he knows some people at immigration! Please help me!" Nadifo was now sobbing, wiping her tears with the ends of her scarf.

"It is not my problem! I am not calling Haybe or anyone else, just leave me out of this!"

Nadifo sat down on the front door step, with the phone in her hand, still palpably distressed. Henna walked away, putting on her earphones and ignoring her; Nadifo watched until Henna disappeared from view, deep in thought until she was interrupted by the boys. Bile and Jason were in the kitchen opening and closing the refrigerator door; Nadifo was too preoccupied with the situation at hand to worry about Jason, whom she would normally not allow in her kitchen. Bile knew better than to allow that boy in their apartment, but he seemed to defy her as well.

She sat at the front door step for good five minutes longer, staring at the phone in her hand. Fresh tears stormed from her left eye, dripping into her shawl. She was motionless, as if paralyzed by her predicament. They were in America, where she had already met her defeat. Her daughter left her standing there, totally ignoring her pleas, and her youngest son was already beginning to show the American bad habit of disrespecting parents. *Tears of defeat are more painful than those of pain*, she thought.

She was about to dial a number, when Bile came out of the apartment, with his shoes still on.

"*Waryaa* take off those filthy shoes you stupid boy," she said, throwing the phone at him.

"What did I do? Ouch, *eeyaa* stop that," Bile said, ducking.

"Didn't I tell you a million times not to wear your filthy shoes inside the house?"

"Get this white kid out of my house!" She ordered him, looking incensed.

"No, we are going upstairs to play games!—and his name is Jason, not white boy."

"*Waar magaciisa wax igama geline ee iga soo saar saan caddaalaha, haddii kale wallaahi waan ku gowracayaa!*" Enraged, she asked again for him to make the kid leave the apartment.

"Wait for me upstairs, Jason," Bile said to Jason, who was standing outside the kitchen holding a glass of milk. Jason quietly went upstairs. Bile took off his shoes and was about to follow Jason upstairs, when he turned to Nadifo and said: "That is not fair! Why are you mad at me, what did I—" Before he finished his sentence she grabbed him by his shirt, pushed him towards the sofa and kicked him.

"*Waryaa* Jason, you go your home this *miridh*!" She said loud enough so that Jason who was now in Bile's room upstairs could hear.

"No, Jason, don't come down, stay where you are!" Bile cried behind the sofa, crying.

"Waryaa, tell him to go home," she said with one hand on her hip and the forefinger of the other wagging in the direction of the stairs.

"Jason, don't come down, she is going to hit you too!"

By the time Jason came down clutching his skate board, Nadifo sat on the base of the sofa, varying between hysterical sob and quiet whimpering. Jason tiptoed to the front door with his shoes and skateboard in hand. Bile stayed behind the sofa crying.

PLANNER 101

The precise ways things were done in America amazed Nadifo. For a while, she wondered why gigantic blue and grey plastic cans popped up every Tuesday morning, lining the street. These cans were not there the rest of the week, but every Tuesday there they were, in exactly the same spot at the same time. It was not until they had been in America for over half a year when she found out this was "trash day." For months she had been transporting their trash to the dumpster at the corner restaurant.

How did everyone remember to put the cans out on Monday nights? How did the trash company succeed in creating this system? She was mesmerized by the order. She was not used to systems or directives—in her country, there were none. She began to notice that procedures existed everywhere in America. It was not only the trash collecting that had a specific schedule, but everything else too. There were certain times to pay bills, attend appointments, and wait for the bus—which, if you were a minute late, would leave without you.

She found out the hard way that if you did not pay your bills on time, your services were cut off. If you were late for an appointment, you were not seen. And if you did not pay your taxes every year, you would end up in trouble with the IRS.

Nadifo was even further surprised by the amount of instruction people received. For people who were so orderly and precise, there was so much instruction to follow. Everything came with instructions. She felt people here were spoiled; they expected to have their hands held constantly, like children. When she saw signs like "watch your step" or "beware of this or that," She tired of the instructions that came with every little box. The manufacturers spent a lot of time telling people how to use their products. Her community, however, never fully adjusted to the orderly systems, schedules, and instructions. They forgot to put their trash out on time, didn't pay bills on time and didn't realize the penalty until their electricity or phone services were cut off. And they followed only the major laws, ignoring polite reminders, recommendations, and instructions. It was not out of stupidity, but rather out of unfamiliarity and sometimes stubbornness. They did ignore some laws out of rebellion and would try to create and enforce their own laws, trying to outsmart a system that had been put in place for centuries. They learned the danger of doing this when they lost their driver's licenses or green cards or other important documents because they ignored notices. They eventually began to understand that in America, the rule of law rules. They learned to become part of the existing system.

They even learned to prepare for the weather forecast. That is all Nadifo ever heard: weather this and weather that. Americans loved chit chatting about the weather. She marveled at them when they would not leave their home until they had checked the weather and gathered tools to fight its predictions. She often met blizzards and rainstorms without as much as a newspaper to hold over her head. In some ways, she regretted not listening to the weather like them, but she simply could not. It was sometimes guilt; she did not want to listen to some weather man who would predict the weather as if he were God. How did they know it was going to rain? Who told them it would snow?

She noticed women at the grocery store held checklists that contained all their grocery needs. They patiently ticked off the item they purchased, by the end of the trip all the items were either checked off or circled. How did they have so much patience and time to organize their day like that? Of all the ways Americans planned their day to manage their time better, it was the grocery list which she emulated. Before she employed the list, scribbling it in her own illegible handwriting, she would make multiple trips to the grocery store. Now she made a list before she went to the grocery store, although it appeared fake to her at times. Even family visits were scheduled into the planner: nothing ever took place without it being put into some kind of planner, she doubted if she could ever catch up to the over prepared Americans.

~~~

And it was altogether scary at first, taking the bus or walking through these streets without any of her family members. Eventually, however, Nadifo gained enough courage to do it on her own. It was better alone; she had grown tired of her children's undisguised embarrassment. Bile had taken to calling himself Bill and sat far away on the bus when he accompanied her; it was as if they were not together at all. For the first time in her life she felt like a pest, whom even the youngest children would reject. She noticed how elders were not respected, not taken care of and simply treated as an afterthought in this foreign place: her children began to treat her the same way, and she felt as if she was crowding their lives. They made her feel she was adding stress to their already hectic American lives. So she accustomed herself to lone errands and long, sometimes confusing bus rides. Loneliness was better than dependency—but her self-reliance came with a hefty price. She got lost often, finding herself on the wrong bus, and sometimes on the wrong side of the city. She came home late at times because of one mishap or another, but her husband and children were oblivious. They never seemed to care, so she kept things to herself.

It was with that recently acquired pride and self-reliance that Nadifo left home one morning. Nothing could have prepared her for the predicament that would entangle her jilbaab on a bicycle, and would bring busy downtown Minneapolis to a halt. She left home that morning like any other morning after her ritual morning prayers. An hour after she prepared breakfast for the family: *Canjeero* for Haybe and Bile, oatmeal with milk, honey and *timir* for finicky Cartan. Henna, who had stopped eating breakfast to lose weight in order to achieve "the look" (as she attempted in vain to explain to Nadifo), had nothing. In order to have "the look", she had said some days earlier, she would only consume light snacks—of which breakfast was not one. After Nadifo had a slice of bread and a cup of tea with milk and sugar, she set out for the ESL class she had attended since her arrival in Minneapolis. She got off the bus, right in front of the Convention Center on Nicholas Avenue.

She crossed Second Avenue, where the usual overdressed professional crowd with blank expressions hurried past her without so much as a glance or a simple smile. A homeless man lugged two shopping carts brimming with black trash bags; he appeared overwhelmed by the day's velocity just as she was. In silence, along with her prayers which were never far from her mind, she tried to remember the lesson Amy asked them to study the day before. She fretted about the lesson, unable to prepare her tense mind to remember the lessons. She repeated the question multiple times, trying to recall the difference between verbs and adverbs.

"Lovely ends with ly, words that end with ly are adverbs, or were they verbs?" she repeated that question over and over since she had reluctantly boarded the bus.

And it was at that moment she heard "Get out of my way, lady! Coming through, coming through!"

Unable to understand, she turned around to look; and that is when Nadifo found herself tangled with a young man in spandex on a bike with a bag strapped to his chest. Before she could respond, she was on the ground; her jilbaab covering the bike that was now resting on her ankle. Her backpack, rosary and scarf were next to some color-coded manila folders which were now soggy with old grey snow.

"Dude, I am screwed! How the hell am I going to explain this one?!" the young man was saying. The accident did manage to provoke some humanity from the expressionless professionals, who endlessly hovered over her.

"Call 911! Ma'am, are you hurt?" A man in a grey suit and an elegant black overcoat was giving orders while another in a brown sweater and denim removed the bike from Nadifo's ankle.

"Oh God, I'm fu—d, these are important government documents, my ass is—"

"Hey, this poor lady is hurt and all you can think about is your damn documents, has someone called 911?!" Asked the man in the grey suit.

"What the hell is she doing in the middle of downtown with this shitty outfit anyway?"

"You prick, get out of my way, this poor woman broke her ankle!"

"What kinda misfit is she anyway? She doesn't belong here! And I am toast!"

Somehow, Nadifo had managed to keep all her bones intact throughout her life. The violence of the war, the harshness of the refugee camp and all the other horrible things she had witnessed could have done it, but somehow, in an amazing coincidence, a spandex-wearing young man with tattoos and piercings all over his body managed to break her narrow ashy ankle; and yet he wasn't remorseful—he was mad. A clean white bone jutted through her flesh, which was soaked in blood, but the spandex-clad courier was fretting about some documents he was going to get fired for. Her mind was not even on the broken bone as much as it was on the guy who broke her ankle, who carried on as though he was the injured party. His outburst continued while she sat in the snow-soaked sidewalk, calm, not scared, suspicious or uncomfortable as she usually is when amid strangers; she didn't realize that she was in shock. Another man came, not only wrapping his expensive-looking scarf around her ankle, but also accompanying her on the ambulance to the hospital until he located an interpreter, not trusting the hospital staff with her. *What an angel*, Nadifo thought. She later found out he was a doctor at the hospital.

After the incident she learned quickly that there was a method to the madness. Keep to one side, preferably close to the wall on a busy street; on an escalator, stay to the right, otherwise you risk being run over by those unable to wait for the speed of the escalator to deliver them to the bottom. Simply stay out of the way of people in a hurry or else you risk being run over by unremorseful, incensed people who throw a fit because their day has been slowed.

⁓

Nadifo had an increasing suspicion of American men, although she accepted American women: she would eventually find friendship with a few. But American men made her stumble and fall, breaking an ankle, or have painful fumbles that would cause an inevitable injury. So why was Nadifo so adamant on finding Dr. Logan Clayton if she was so apprehensive about American men? Her pleas to invite him into their home fell on deaf ears. For the first time since their arrival, there were no home cooked meals. The few times Henna was asked to cook, she made inedible salty, oily food that made Cartan resort to the equally inedible greasy, cold food from Mirimiri restaurant. He would sit the Styrofoam container in front him, forcing himself to swallow, his adam's apple moving up and down as if it too were rejecting the food. His facial expressions said it all, that he missed the fine home-cooked meals Nadifo vigilantly made. Haybe resorted to Chinese food, General Tso's chicken mostly. He was not as apprehensive as Cartan—he all but inhaled the food—but to Nadifo it looked greasy and unhealthy. No one knew if Bile ate at all: when Nadifo offered him leftovers from her own meals he grunted "I am ok, I already ate" and Henna continued her "the look" diet. Nadifo's meals for the time came from their neighbor Haajiya. Cartan would hang around to eat with Nadifo what little food Haajiya had brought her. Nadifo often felt underappreciated, but from the looks of things her family wished she would recover quickly to resume her duties in the kitchen and feed them. She had been limited to using crutches, her ankle was in a full cast and she was as uneasy about the mishap at home as they were. After all, nothing gave Nadifo pride the way her needy family did. Cooking and looking after their needs

99

was something she did with care. So for four weeks, her husband and children lost weight from eating nothing or gained weight from eating greasy foods. Others were just annoyed she could not resume her duties fast enough, but all in all Nadifo's satisfaction was justified, for they showed appreciation they had never shown before. Cartan was no match for the Hoover—it was actually a Bissell but all vacuum cleaners were called Hoover in Somali households no matter the brand. He wrestled with the thing creating more mess. The bathrooms were dirty, the kitchen full of clutter. Henna would arrive late and leave early, knowing she would have to pick up after the males. That is how it is with Somalis: only women do house chores, the males are served, their dirty laundry disappears and in it is place clean cloths appear. Their beds are made daily, bed sheets changed and rooms cleaned. Their food miraculously turns up before them and absolutely nothing is expected of them. For four weeks it pained her to watch them struggle, wishing Henna's female abilities would spring to use. She was glad when the cast came off, and although she was still limping, she found herself in the kitchen cooking and creating order. She had cooked as if she was making up for lost times, determined to fill their bellies again, and show her love through her cooking.

Dr. Logan Clayton would not leave her mind though; she wanted to see him again. He was the man who had taken her to the hospital that fateful day when an American boy broke her ankle. The day of the accident he was gracious, calling her family and making sure she was comfortable until Haybe and Cartan showed up in the hospital. She wanted to thank him, but Haybe refused to look for him. The more she insisted that he bring Dr. Clayton to her to thank him, the more Haybe resisted. His excuse was that he didn't have time, but Nadifo knew Haybe did not appreciate the magnitude of his help. Two months after her accident, Nadifo set out to find Dr. Clayton on her own. Before she found herself in front of a restless receptionist who was confused about the person the lady in blue and white garb wanted to see, Nadifo cooked up a storm, Sambuusa, tender lamb, chicken suqaar, canjeero and saffron rice. She cooked all morning that Saturday when she found out Dr. Clayton was going to be at Hennepin County Hospital. She knew Dr. Clayton would appreciate her food. Americans she met appreciated food: they were often thankful if you gave them the smallest amount. Even a simple cup of tea would bring a smile to their face. They took interest in the process, the ingredients and the recipe, which Nadifo could not recall. She cooked like her mother before her. They followed no recipe and no specific process. She had her own way of cooking; but could never repeat the process. Amy resorted to watching her and writing the process down and committing the recipe to paper when she wanted to learn how to cook Somali food. That is how she made her first canjeero and beef suqaar which Nadifo thought was a bit bland.

Food was to Nadifo something to nourish the body. She frowned on people who overate. She could not understand why Americans obsessed about food. Every occasion was an opportunity to eat. People made arrangements to meet and eat. That was odd to her. She would sometimes sit in front of the TV when there was a cooking show. How meticulous and orderly their cooking seemed. She could never cook that way, preparing ingredients before they went into the pan. There was no order to her cooking; she may miss an herb one day or substitute one spice for another, but the food often turned out tasting the same. At the hospital, the receptionist called a young Somali interpreter. The interpreter appeared apprehensive, and unwilling to call Dr. Clayton for Nadifo.

"He is in surgery. Do you have an appointment?" She asked, everything was so formal here. Even if you wanted to thank someone you had to make an appointment.

"He is busy and won't be able to see you today. Call his nurse on Monday." the Somali girl was as rude as the receptionist. Nadifo took the food and headed for the elevator. The interpreter followed, asking her to leave the premises. Nadifo looked at the girl, and that simple look, which was not so simple because it was laden with shame for not being helpful to an elderly woman, made the girl disappear. Nadifo did not know where Dr. Clayton worked, what floor or department. She stopped at the nurse station on the second floor and asked the nurse where Dr. Clayton's office was. "He is in. Wait a minute," said the heavily-accented Asian nurse. "Dr. Clayton is in pediatrics, fourth floor."

"You say four floor" Nadifo jolted four middle fingers, repeating what the nurse said.

"Yes ma'am, fourth floor."

"Tank you".

The fourth floor was decorated with clouds and angels in mostly pink and blue. A giant stuffed panda sat next to a white board with doctors' schedules. There were stuffed giraffes, lions, toy trains and trucks all over the floor.

The place was pretty quiet, with three nurses each facing one side of the circular nurse station. "May I help you?" said one cheery nurse with purple scrubs. "Are you visiting a patient" she asked as she shuffled through papers, but she was on the phone before Nadifo could conjure up a response. "Yes, what can I do for you? Oh you're Connor's mom in room 456, yes ma'am, I will send your nurse right away." Then she turned to Nadifo who stood nervously next to the various containers of food.

"I need see Dakhtar Calaton, blease," she said.

"Dr. Who? Oh, Dr. Clayton. Is there anything I can do for you? Dr. Clayton is in surgery. Ma'am, do you have a child here?"

"No, me friend" she said pointing to the food.

"Ok, ma'am please have a seat over there and I will ask Dr. Clayton to come and see you when he is done with surgery, but that is not for another two hours."

"It is ok, I wait".

So Nadifo waited and waited in the waiting area with parents, grandparents and young patients. She was alarmed by the scene. Sick children were being comforted by family members.

Her prayers were not far from her mouth, and after what seemed like ten hours, Dr. Clayton appeared in his blue scrubs, as handsome and kind as ever. He looked surprised to see her but took her to his office. Nadifo could tell he was awestruck to see all the food. As she predicted, he was sincerely happy, calling the nurses to share the food. She found comfort in naming the different foods for them and they in turn attempted to pronounce the odd-sounding but delicious food with full mouths.

Nadifo was now a little bit into her American life, taking precious time to send a plate or two of food to Dr. Clayton and his family. Every holiday she would labor over the food for the Claytons, and every ciid, Dr. and Mrs. Clayton would send Nadifo greeting cards and gifts, sometimes cash gifts which she would send to Hawo.

MARCH 2, 1996.

Sister, sometimes I can't help but drift into the past with nostalgia, other times with regret. Some events I don't remember, others I cannot forget.

Do you remember in 1984, when we decided to go to Europe by ourselves? We left the kids and the men and everyone said we should be stopped, for we were about to start a trend where mothers would abandon their families. It was me, you, Shukri *Buuro* and Tiriig *Belo*—they nicknamed us *Firqat Shaydaan.*

That is how we met with Chef Francois Herme in Paris. His restaurant Herme was our favorite restaurant: we used to eat so much, but never gained a pound. Remember the beautiful décor of the restaurant from the 1950s? The long counter made of pure mahogany, benches finished in purple velour, the monumental oak staircase and high ceilings. Remember everywhere we went we wanted to copy the décor? That restaurant ended up being the blueprint for my French kitchen in the mansion.

We weren't even able to pronounce the names of the dishes, yet it never dissuaded us from asking for them, even when Suad was not there. It was a beautiful time, but why do I feel guilty about it!

Remember the food kept coming, first drinks, then appetizers, then another dish and another, and finally the main course. We couldn't finish it and we started laughing at our primitiveness, not understanding why they were feeding us so much food. Every time a new dish came out we said that must be the main course, then when it wasn't we burst out laughing.

Remember how the waiter was so fed up with us because we kept retuning food? You ordered beef tongue when you just wanted chicken crêpes. Remember we would call the crepe *laxoox*, and that was all we would eat at the beginning because it was the only thing that looked familiar to us? Then we would ask the waiter if the food had *khansiir* to the point where even he became familiar with the word. All those French pastries and salads and cheese we feasted on. After that trip we introduced French manicures, French twists and Chanel handbags to Hamar. And after a few weeks everyone wanted to do French manicures and they wanted to twist their hair like us and carry Chanel bags. We were gone two weeks and we covered three countries, France, Italy and Spain, Suad was with us helping with the translation, she helped us with everything then, may Allah protect her. She was a good girl; I hear she is still in Hamar, struggling to raise ten kids, widowed by the war. I wish I knew her whereabouts, I would send her money. That was us then, and today we are paying for those sins.

UNHOLY PURSUIT

C artan glides through the brightly lit hallway into the bedroom to get ready for lunch. He dons his casual sarong and t-shirt, which he finds neatly folded atop the shiny blue bed cover.

After he performs his ablution for *duhur* prayers, he crosses the apartment swiftly. The dining table is adorned with colorful assortment of baryani rice, rich with floating pieces of lamb and potatoes. Sautéed red onions and raisins edged the plate. A shallow bowl full of tomato sauce with salmon and fresh cilantro, thickened with spices, sits next to a dish of crispy, warm *sabaayad* on the lacy, tan-colored tablecloth. The sight pleases Cartan. As he sits down to tackle the food, he pours a sugary orange drink from a silver pitcher into a red plastic glass.

"That which pleases the sight also pleases the soul, Nadifo," Cartan said, visibly satisfied with his wife's abilities and devotion.

"Yes, *xaaji*," responds Nadifo shyly, preserving the deference still present after thirty-four years of marriage.

Cartan dived into the delicious food with his bare hands. Nadifo decanted the various items, carefully arranging them on his plate, just the way he likes it; Cartan's finicky appetite requires small portions, equally distributed. He draws his hand to his mouth assuring equal amounts of meat, rice, and sauce.

"Nadifo," Cartan continues as he looks up from his plate to examine his hand for any straying juices, which he would then slurp loudly with his tongue. "There was a shooting at the community center today." His forehead creased at the thought.

"*Bismillahi Raxmaani Raxiim Cartan, Acuudu Billahi Mina Shaydaani Rajiim!*" Nadifo appears alarmed, and shaken by the news. She recites prayer chants to keep Satan at bay; her thoughts immediately drift to the whereabouts of her sons. Her thunderstruck voice cut through the gold and burgundy curtain that veils her from the dining room where her husband ate lunch alone, as the two conversed and ate separately. She pushes away the plate she nibbled from. "Who was shooting, Cartan? Did anyone die?" she asked, carefully choosing her words.

"It is those Cedar Spring kids, you know those hoodlums who act as though they are black," Cartan replied.

"Why do they emulate those black Americans who are always shooting and robbing innocent people? I will never know!" she said, her voice raspy from the piece of meat stuck between her back teeth. "No wonder they don't get anywhere," she continued, taking a sip from her glass. "These black people are bad, and those Somali kids who emulate them are just like them, they are all criminals." She pushed the plate she ate from aside, with most of the food still on it. She then began preparing the tea Cartan likes to wash his meals down with. The aroma of simmering cardamom, cinnamon, and cloves seeps through the tiny kitchen into the rest of the apartment.

Rarely does Nadifo finish a plate of food; she starves herself unconsciously. How could she eat so much delicious food when her family members back home are dying from starvation? Every bite she takes provokes the guilt she feels over all her relatives who passed away hungry.

"These kids are so lost—as if we have come here so they become killers and robbers! What a waste! I am so disappointed with them. They forget they have a rich culture of their own and don't need to imitate anyone. Instead, they dress like these black people, dragging their pants to the floor, they talk like them in broken English, and shoot like them as if they are criminals," Cartan said casually, pushing away his plate with its leftovers. He dunks his hands into the awaiting yellow bowl of warm water; Nadifo pours orange-colored dishwasher detergent into his hands to rinse off the grease, and then hands him a roll of toilet paper to dry his hands. In a meticulous order—she has done it many times before—she then swiftly clears the table and brings out a steaming cup of milk tea which Cartan instantly takes quick, hot mouthfuls, burning his tongue. He makes all kinds of satisfactory noises as he downs the tea, continuing the conversation between slurps: "I am afraid we have brought to this country hooligan who will sadly never amount to anything."

In the afternoon, after a relaxing siesta, Cartan gears up for his afternoon chewing session. Nadifo prepares the necessary items for him: a thermos of hot, spiced, weak black tea; a pitcher of water; and several bottles of soda. She also spreads out some old newspaper and a few plastic bags to gather his spit and stray bits of qat. All these items are prepared in the one corner of the apartment which he claims to carry out his qat chewing comfortably and without any interruptions.

He sits on the bare floor, removing the cushioned rug, which supposedly tires his behind after he sits in the same position from five to ten straight hours.

Cartan chews qat every day. He continuously alludes to being pushed to it by his much-despised new life; his right cheek, where he stores the leaves, swells up as if he were just stung by bees. He sucks the juices of cathinone from the stored leaves to a state of dissolution. His lips become the color of grass as he sucks small amounts of the bitter juices, sipping extra sweet tea to temper the bitterness. He excitedly rubs his hands, jumps around, and babbles gibberish to anyone who would listen. Of course those who share the apartment with him don't listen; they disperse as soon as they see his jittery self approaching.

His elated anticipation before the arrival of the qat is marked with various trips to the front door, energetically running in and out, greeting neighbors to whom he had never spoken before. He extends his long neck into the freezing rain, carefully inspecting the street for the delivery man. When his visits to the door do not yield the expected results, he resorts to the phone, keeping it busy, inquiring about the arrival of the qat. Nadifo wishes that the floor could open and swallow her whole. Cartan deserts his otherwise withdrawn, serious personality for a childlike one, sometimes chasing Nadifo playfully. She would shake her head, pushing him away to leave her alone; to her this is an unholy hour, which seems to visit their household more and more frequently. She is forced to participate, preparing all the items he needs. Then she offers two prayers to absolve herself from the sin he commits under her nose.

The unholy hour is filled with frivolous activities, none which help the struggling family in any way. Cartan preoccupies himself with politics, repeating the same stories all night long, forgetting that he had told the same tale before. Stories of the days he was an important official in government—stories his family and anyone in his company tire of.

His hallucinatory chewing often leads him to call the shepherd of his herd in Somalia, who usually neither hears him well nor understands the words of this stoned man who constantly calls in the middle of the night when the poor shepherd is resting. Cartan's calls to the shepherd never yield the answers he seeks.

If she ever complains about his addiction, he is unrelenting. "You are in America," he would tell her. "Tell these kids to get creative and make money. I am not here to worry about their food and shelter. That is their business. I am waiting for the day they contribute to my life." Shoving more dirty leaves into his cheek he would continue, "Remember they are my social security, *Allah* knows I have no other way of retiring except what they will contribute to me at my old age." At the height of his high, he is hyperactive and aggressive; then it would be downhill from there. When his high wears off, he becomes fatigued, dull, and sluggish.

Haybe walks in as his father is separating qat leaves, discarding small pieces of caked dirt. He does not notice Haybe's arrival.

A lanky, slim man, Cartan's clear bright skin makes him look much younger than his sixty-odd years. As stiff as a stick, his neatly-shaped graying beard shines with streaks of red and orange henna. Struggle and refugee life have made an otherwise happy man a suspicious sad one.

Cartan worked in Framer Freddie's Grocery Store for ten long years as a bagger and a security guard. Although he did not make enough to support his family, he was proud he could give his wife something every two weeks. Even if he spent most of what he made on his qat-chewing habit, at least he had a job to go to every day, until he got fired a year ago. He suspects Robert Fox, the store manager to be behind it. According to Cartan, Mr. Fox does not like Muslims. He ordered Cartan to stop praying on company premises the day of the firing, to which Cartan replied: "Never, not in my life time, will a person whose last name is Fox tell me how to worship my God."

"Pardon me!"

"You heard me, Mr. Fox. Who gave you such a name anyway? How can you assume any authority when your last name is *dawaco*? Go shake your big belly elsewhere. I am not taking orders from a person named after a fox!"

"What is wrong with my name? Is it too Christian for you? Which do you dislike more, Robert or Fox?"

"Fox, it means *dawaco* in my language."

"I don't care what it means in your language! You can't talk to your supervisor that way! Do you know I can fire you?!"

"Why? Because I am Muslim, or because I'm black? Or perhaps both?"

"Mr. Geedi, I am not going to bicker with you. This is not Somalia where—"

"Where we ran around like wild animals, is that it?'

"That is not what I was about to say, I was about to say that—"

"Where *dawaco* roam with *libaax*, and people roam around like animals, isn't that what you said the last time?" At that point Robert Fox left him standing answering his own questions, and half an hour later Cartan was fired.

He has not been able to find work since. He suspects his fate, like so many other Muslims in America, has changed after September 11th. It is as if everyone he interviews with has been talking to Robert Fox, who certainly would never say anything pleasant about Cartan.

A few days after the Twin Towers fell, he was told not to pray on the premises and then he was told not to come back to the store and was escorted out by a security guard. He felt like a criminal.

Unable to obtain gainful employment, he has been volunteering his time at the local community center where he teaches the Somali language to Somali youth. Cartan has reached the sad conclusion that this is a country for women, where he must hinge on his wife's welfare check for support. He describes his new life as undeniably unfavorable to an old refugee man. "Exactly what type of opportunities is there here for me, a former Foreign Minister of a country that no longer exists?" He would say to no one in particular. "I lost those impressive titles the day I became a refugee. She gets the welfare checks, food stamps, and I get nothing, absolutely nothing."

"Nacas!" Nadifo said as Bile entered the apartment. "I am doomed to have a nacas for a son!" By now Bile is used to all the words reserved for him. The Somali that he perfects are the insults used to describe him— nacas, doqon and dhaandhaan are variations on the theme idiot. He had heard these words so many times he could teach a class on Somali insults and clever put-downs. Bile, aka Bill, came to Nadifo and Cartan at a time when neither seemed ready for a baby; at the height of their material-collecting, mansion-building days. Nadifo hid the pregnancy until delivery day, and as soon as the baby passed through the birth canal. He was then put into the hands of Cartan's sister Kaaha, who raised him. For the better part of his childhood he did not know which of the women was the mother; Nadifo acknowledged him only in passing, rarely picking him up or playing with him.

The first time Nadifo was forced to interact with the boy was after they were ousted from their mansion—but by then she was too busy with other issues to pay him any mind. So when little Bile arrived in America at age ten he could not have predicted what the streets of Minneapolis had in store for him. One thing he was glad about was the fact that he did not have much interaction with his parents: school and teen life and their struggling immigrant life meant their day-to-day interaction was minimal. Bile functioned in two vastly diverse worlds: at home he was the elusive kid who dashed for the stairs to disappear into his room among his posters, music and video games. He would not initiate any conversation with his parents and would answer only when spoken to, and even then he answered hurriedly. At school he was a cool kid, popular with girls; no one would ever guess the aloof Bile was quite liked by everyone. His only interaction with his father was limited to the times when the elder Cartan ordered the boy around: "Waryaa go fetch my qat", "Waryaa make tea for me to chew qat", or "Waryaa turn down your music, I can't hear the radio!" Cartan's words were positive and loving compared to the venom Nadifo laid on him. Bile was one of the brightest in school, but that did not matter since neither of his parents nor his siblings ever inquired about his school work. Every weekend when he had homework to do, his backpack, filled to capacity, stayed in the same corner of the room next to his CD player; play station and messy cloths. The backpack stayed there till Monday morning when Bile fetched it, home work and assignments still untouched. On the rare occasion when he did turn in homework, Mrs. Steward, his English teacher, would praise him endlessly. She would try to encourage him to take his school work seriously, to no avail; she even suggested that he go to college. That is the way things were at Cedar Crest High—very few teachers and even fewer parents cared about kids' assignments.

He shared a room with Haybe, who was the only person Bile either admired or trusted in his family, but Haybe was too busy with his own activities to worry about his kid brother. Bile slept only five feet from Haybe, who would never know the secrets that made his younger brother

111

toss and turn every night. Haybe was busy keeping inner city kids out of jail, but had no time for Bile. Nadifo blamed everything on him, but little would ever pass between them to know the situation her little boy was in. Nadifo's interactions with Bile were limited to the basics. She endlessly forced food on him, looked for him in his hangouts, washed his clothes and assured all his needs were met; that is how she showed her love. And his mediocre Somali never missed a beat of chastisement.

Most of Bile's comforts in life are American, which of course adds to the tension. He loves hanging around his friends, playing basketball, video games, watching TV. When he finds his clothes in the trash, he knows how much trouble he is in.

Nadifo's dissatisfaction with him shows in the oddest places. She inspects his backpack for drugs and eavesdropped on his telephone conversations as if she understands what is said.

Another point of contention with Nadifo is Bile's best friend Jason. She is suspicious of Jason and his family; she would prefer it if he would befriend Somali kids. Jason's dog worries her too, since it is *haraam* to touch a dog. The dog barks at her every time she passes Jason's home. Nadifo tiptoes around the dog, sometimes walking on the opposite side of the street, but the dog often senses her, grunting and growling, causing an intense panic. Oh, her dislike for the dog! "Why do these people bother to keep one around anyway?" Bile would hear her say. He also got all kinds of warnings about Jason and his family and their dogs: "Don't eat their food—it has *khansiir* in it. Don't drink from their cups—they are coated with *khamri* remnants. Don't sit on their coach—it is laced with dog hairs and dog drool, which is *haram*." Don't, don't, don't—too may rules for Bile to remember.

Nadifo gave him a list of all the products that contain *halal* or *haram* ingredients, instructing him to watch out for these ingredients in food, drinks, toothpaste, deodorant and lotion:

HARAM INGREDIENT LIST
- *Derived from pork or other animals*
- *Bacon, ham, sausage, lard, fat, gelatin, shortening (animal)*
- *Avoid or doubtful (may be derived from animal or vegetable)*
- *Lecithin, emulsifier, dough conditioners, mono and*
   diglyceriders, enzymes or rennet in cheese

USABLE
- *Soy lecithin, soyabean lecithin, vegetable lecithin, vegetable*
   shortening

Nadifo took an early bus one Tuesday afternoon and noticed Bile sitting all the way in the back of the bus. Headphones hid his chilled ears, and his head was slightly bent, hidden behind a bulky hat. He was fidgeting with his phone. She pretended not to see him, knowing that is how he would prefer it. She took a seat next to an elderly woman and removed the brown glittery rosary that hangs from her neck. She settled her backpack on the floor and then began to move her lips harmonically to the rhythm of the beads that flicked between her fingers when, suddenly, a long-limbed figure rushed past her, hurriedly jumping off the bus. She peeked through the window, but Bile had quickly disappeared in the mix of the chilled crowd as the bus sped off.

Her thoughts rushed back to the day she had taken him to school when they first arrived. He was ten and assigned to fifth grade. While she waited in front of the school with him, he disappeared. She wanted to meet his teacher, and without him she did not know where his class was; after much search she found him in class comfortably listening to the teacher. He purposefully eluded her, leaving her standing in the corridor. She knew he was ashamed of her: her colorful cloths and odd look did not fit his desire to have a sophisticated, short-skirt-wearing, bob-haired mom who could negotiate his grades, praise his accomplishments and decide what books should be read by students in his class with the PTA while extracurricular activities were planned.

Unlike Bile, Haybe's life seemed on track. Tall and muscular, Haybe's dark hair curled delicately into a goatee and mustache that accentuated his handsome features. His baggy pants dragged from his hips. He wore a bulky black t-shirt which read "If X were here": it emphasized his well-built frame. Removing his "Injustice has many faces" cap, he walked into the apartment quietly, not wanting to invite any attention.

Reeking of cigarettes, he offered a faint hello, murmured in a low, mysterious voice. At twenty-three, Haybe is Nadifo's favorite. After the death of Geele in the clan conflict, she had become obsessed with him, spoiling him to the point of carelessness.

"Salaamu calaykum, hooyo," Haybe greeted Nadifo, hoping she would not press him about where he'd been. Sitting on the divan, Nadifo raised her head slightly from the Quran book in front of her. This is her usual spot in the evening, listening to Quran tapes. She was happy to see him, although she noticed his sagging pants and could smell cigarette smoke on him. Removing her gold-rimmed spectacles and admiring his handsome face, Nadifo saluted him grimly. She chose not to say anything about his clothes and the dreadful smell.

"I am glad to see that you are in one piece, son," she said, assuring he noticed her disapproval. He lowered himself to her level and placed a light kiss on her forehead; she reluctantly accepted, as if too guilty to receive such affection. She almost never reciprocated the gesture.

"What's shaking, hooyo?" Hoping to evade her questions and change the direction of the conversation, Haybe began joking. A sliver of a smile escaped her creased lips. Indeed, Haybe was the only one who could still make her smile, even if slightly.

"Why are you gone so long every night?" She sighed, not really expecting an answer. "You are wasting your time with people with whom you have nothing in common." She looked down at the holy book in front of her, resuming her silent prayer.

"Hooyo, you worry too much, I'm gone doing good things, believe me. I'm not wasting my time," he said, sipping the chilled water he had poured for himself. "It's all good. Where's Cartan?" He asked, as if to derail her worries and questions.

"Don't call your father Cartan—you are beginning to be disrespectful."

Haybe was away at boarding school in Switzerland when the war broke in Somalia. Guilt is all he felt ever since. He has not seen the inside of a refugee camp, and never witnessed any of the killings that took away his own brother. He is engulfed with guilt when around Nadifo because he knows he can never console her enough. There is an innate feeling of sadness that comes with not relating to his family's trauma. By the time they were all reunited in America, he met a family that was drastically different than the one he left before the war. But Haybe unlike Bile worked hard to overcome their new circumstance. He chose a path to educate his mind and stayed away from illegal issues that could limit his chances of success. He knew in America he was categorized as a young black man. That meant limitations. It meant an overwrought police system and a justice system willing to forget him in prison.

More fluent in Somali than Bile, Haybe found himself fitting in by fully immersing in his own culture. He embraced his heritage better than all his siblings, who were very impressed with American pop culture. He very carefully chose clothes with slogans that favored anti-establishment, anti-colonial mentality.

Cartan walked in holding a *caday*.

"You will send your mother to an early grave, Haybe," he said, scrubbing his teeth back and forth, collecting small pieces of the root inside his cheek.

"Salaamu calaykum, Aabo," Haybe walked over to Cartan and quickly kissed his father's hand.

"Do you know any of those hoodlums who were shooting at the community center today? Were any your friends?" Nadifo asked, still searching Haybe's face for hints. He found it ironic that they confused

his activism with criminal activity. Before he could answer, she continued "you have too many choices here, and you choose the wrong ones.
You could choose the right path, you know, these nice white people welcomed us here—follow their path, I am certain it will lead you to the
right place." She looked pained while Haybe groaned internally.

"I can't believe you just said "the nice white people."

"Yes, if it were not for them you will be rotting in some African
refugee camp."

"Oooh mother, I should be so grateful," he said mockingly, pitying
her misunderstanding— of the way things are.

"We did not come to this country for you to get lost in this 'melting pot.' I expect you to do something with your life, Haybe." Nadifo
got up to leave the room, but Haybe continued, one of his impassioned
lectures.

"Hooyo, you do not see things as they are. All that glitters is not
gold—these people you talk about as good people have caused so much
pain in the world." As Haybe tried to explain himself to Nadifo, he
became almost incoherent. He and Nadifo no longer spoke the same
language. Their experiences in America were so vastly different; they
lacked sympathy for each other. To him, America meant police brutality, unjustified suspicion, and rude stares. He was tired of being followed
in department stores, of being brought down to the "station" for "failing to signal" or for "speeding." Fluent in five languages, his childhood
was a rainbow of international travel, boarding schools, and exposure
to various cultures. He had received his acceptance letter to Columbia
University Law School a week earlier, and rejected three top Ivy League
schools. He planned to attend Columbia in the fall on a full scholarship,
but the issue of race was never far from his mind; and yet his parents
could never relate—how could they, when their world was one of refugee
immigrants trying to live in a country they did not choose? They came
here desperate, fleeing from despotism; if there had been a choice they
would have stayed in their homeland. They knew nothing about the civil
rights movement, the LA riots or the fuss about slavery. The war that

still raged in their homeland and their status as immigrants in America at the lowest possible position in society was part of their daily struggle. They could care less about the dilemma African-Americans faced in America: it is a struggle they could never understand and frankly they wanted Haybe to stop his activism and concentrate more on his education. So Haybe faced suspicion, not just from the outside world, but from his parents: Nadifo and Cartan insisted that he was confusing himself with African-Americans. Their complaints were of no use, however; Haybe had found his voice in the gloomy legacy of slavery. African-American history stung him. Every tree he passed dripped the blood of lynched men. African-American women saddened him, the violence and misogyny their ancestral grandmother went through was a reminder of their current status.

In fact, he toiled at reducing the plight of the entire underclass. He had been fighting for Native Indians, blacks, migrant workers, and Muslim immigrants since his arrival believing they all suffered from the same injustices, and this was the sole reason he was going to law school.

MRS. TRENDY AND
MR. PASSÉ

Warsan walked into her beautifully furnished gated community home, visibly shaken by the piece of paper she held in her hand. It was a bill with an envelope marked "Final Notice" She clutched her jaw and shook her head, throwing her purse into the dining room table where books, papers and dishes piled on top of each other. The clutter hid the elegance of the mahogany table. She was very upset—furious in fact. She forcefully threw her Claudia Cuiti Crocodile-Embossed Pumps and a pink and gold silk pashmina on the sofa. The shoes, which had come out of their box only hours earlier, came from the suggestions of In Style Magazine's trendy page. She wore a black Christian Dior suit, perfectly showing her curves and tall limbs. She sat on the sofa and turned on the TV. Her mind was not on the reporter emanating with excitement as he detailed the latest indiscretions of a supposedly prominent senator. She flipped through the channels which bustled with the exact same story. She vacantly stared at the slew of experts, the ones who come out of the woodwork when such sensational news replaces what is really important in the world. Warsan in deep thought, enjoyed the background noise for distraction. She sat there for what seemed an eternity flipping through the latest edition of Vogue, when a sudden outburst from the phone roused her. She carefully inspected the screen of the black cordless, her facial expression changing with the displayed number.

"Hello," she said reluctantly. Warsan appeared ready to lay ammunition, but kept quiet, as the person on the other end would not allow her an opportunity to speak.

"I am tired of you," she said finally, seething, cutting the other person off. "You are a sorry man, not even able to pay the bills of your own home, how can you respect yourself? Why did you not pay the mortgage this month? I am exhausted from this fiasco!" She slammed the phone while Hannad, her husband of thirteen years, attempted to explain himself.

Hannad walked into the house a couple of hours later, but was met with the same unwelcoming mood he encountered earlier. He ignored his wife, throwing his keys on the coffee table with a loud bang, which annoyed Warsan further. Hannad appeared occupied with the cell phone pinned on his ear, ignoring Warsan who looked ready to carry the fight they have had earlier. Hannad anticipated his arrival at home to coincide with one of Warsan's tirades. Her nagging arguments and relentless put-downs had become predictable.

"I am so tired of you wasting your time with this stupid job, if you are not making money to take care of your household, then go look for a decent job so you can at least take care of your family!" she said. He ignored her, engrossed in the phone conversation he carried on while she talked. She snatched the phone from him, throwing it against the wall.

"Naayaa, why the hell did you do that for!" he said holding her hand firmly.

"Waryaa, let go of my arm, you bastard!"

"You better behave, or else, *wallaahi*, you will get a good beating!"

"Oh really? I dare you! Come on, show me what a big man you are!"

"Don't make me do something I will regret, woman!" he said, letting go of her as he pushed her away.

"Wallaahi one of these days you will make me break one of your bones, I promise!" he said, leaving the room.

"You would not be behaving this way if I showed you who the man of this house is!" he continued while she cursed him.

"I promise, Warsan, one of these days, Allah will give me the strength to teach you manners!"

"What a loser you are!"

"Naayaa, stop disrespecting me, I don't need this nonsense from you!" Hannad came back to where she stood, waving his forefinger in her face as if to make a point.

"Don't call me naayaa, you are so disrespectful, it shows how small-minded you are!" Warsan said, moving to the dining area.

"Well welcome to real life, you married a small-minded cab driver, deal with it!"

"I am sick of you Hannad; you are a sorry excuse for a man!"

"Okay, so what are you going to do about it? Maybe you should be in search of someone more compatible!" he said, sarcastically. "Isn't that it? You need someone who can understand your complex world? Well, not this nomad, no ma'am you have made a mistake here, because this nomad is not going to pretend to be anything but!" Her eyes spoke for her mind as she gave him an all too familiar evil look he knew too well.

Warsan moved towards him ready to reply when Idil, grappling with a hefty backpack, barged in from the library.

"Hi aabo, hooyo," she said as she put the backpack onto the floor.

"Where are you coming from, Idil?" her father asked, glad to change the course of the conversation.

Idil rolled her eyes. "Dad, I told you, I was working on a project with Samantha, and her brother took us to the library, God!" She rolled her eyes again.

"Of course you know nothing about their school activities, why should you, you are busy with other nonsense!" Warsan took the opportunity to humiliate Hannad again, this time in front of their eight year old daughter. Hannad ignored the comment and turned to his daughter.

"Honey, are you done with all your work, do you need help with anything?"

"What, aabo? What did you say?" asked Idil, displaying her inept Somali.

"Idil, pay attention, did you finish your project now?" Hannad repeated.

"Yes, dad, I am finished now. Where is Hillac and Hogad?" Idil continued, somewhat annoyed by her father's questions.

"I think they are here, maybe upstairs. Warsan, where are they?"

"Do they look like they are here, on top of me?" she shot back, clearly still angry from their argument. At that point, Hannad ignoring his wife's nasty attitude went upstairs to change. Idil went to the kitchen, looking for a snack. She slumped into Warsan's lap with chips and a drink in her hand.

"Hooyo, are you okay? You look sad today. Mama, what is the matter?" she asked as she munched on the chips.

Warsan forced a smile. "I am okay, darling. How was school today?"

Idil started hugging and kissing her mother's perfumed cheeks.

"Do you really wanna know?"

"Yes, honey." Warsan appeared distant.

"Well I hate all my teachers, I hate all the students, I hate the food, I..."

"Okay, okay, I get the picture Idil," Warsan chuckled, pleased; she temporarily escaped her misery with Hannad and concentrated on the moment. She stared at Idil, admiring the delicate beauty of the eight year old—her elegant straight nose, fine features, slim little body and nice soft hair, messy from the day's activity. She envied her daughter's beauty: Idil had inherited the best features from Henna, Nadifo and Hannad. She had Hannad's high cheeks, his serious but companionate eyes, Nadifo's softness and Henna's refinement.

Warsan escaped her critics with her elegance, but even she knew she did not possess the beauty the women in her family where famous for. Her broad nose appeared hurriedly positioned between drowsy eyes that peeked from dark sunken sockets, and her lips were too large for her tiny teeth. A slender body with killer legs is all Warsan could ever boast. She invited double takes as a child. People asked if she were Nadifo's child or a loan child from elsewhere. *Naa Nadifo tani xagay idiinka timid,* a cruel country where one's flaws are on the tip of everyone's tongue, Nadifo defended the unattractive child by repeating her shrewdness. "Warsan is a smart girl, she doesn't need beauty to get along in life!"

Nadifo reasoned Warsan did not need beauty when she had quick mind and the creativity of Salugla Gedi, Cartan's great aunt. In the early nineteenth century, Salugla was elected the mayor of Gobwanaag. It was a first in the small town and the entire country. Salugla was elected for her wisdom and crafty mind. Legend has it the town had been under the evil eye of a neighboring town: three mayors mysteriously fell to horrific, bloody deaths in one year. The town fortune teller suggested the only cure for the curse to be erased was to allow Salugla to govern the town. The fortune teller—a close relative of Salugla—claimed the vision came to her in a dream, so Salugla was elected to run the city.

But town elders would not accept a woman to govern their town. They wanted one of her male relatives to assume the position instead. So Salugla had to find a solution to the dilemma.

She went to the family village and came back with her younger brother Samakab, who resembled her in stature and height. She agreed to inaugurate him into position with an elaborate celebration. For two decades Samakab came to the mayor office wearing elaborate traditional cloths. Since he was a rather large man, he preferred the loose fitting clothes instead of the western attire others wore. His shabby beard hid most of his face when people addressed him directly. He had the handy assistance of Saciid Fara Taag, who was the go-to person for Samakab and the people he represented in Gobwanaag. It was only on his death bed that Saciid revealed it was Salugla all along who dressed like Samakab to govern the town for two decades. Samakab was paid a generous sum to move to another village and assume a new identity. During her tenure, Salugla went to war with a neighboring town to win back looted animals, and used her quick wit to handle complex issues, settling land disputes, conflicts and carrying out traditional ceremonies. She ran Gobwanaag, all the while married with thirteen children. No one ever found out she was the one managing the city for the duration until sometime after her death. While people detailed Salugla's clever and sound mind people never failed to insert her bizarre look. She was a large woman with the features of a man, they said: if she was not as sharp as she were she would most likely not find a husband. Warsan grew up knowing she could achieve greatness like Salugla, but she also knew she would have to maneuver through her God-given looks in order to compensate for its harshness.

She may not have Nadifo's grace or Henna's beauty, but Warsan's entrance into a crowded room never failed to attract attention for her cosmopolitan look. It is how she compensated for the shortcomings nature bestowed upon her.

※

As Warsan reminisced, she could see the apparent signs she chose to ignore. She remembers how odd he appeared among her friends one evening. They were invited to attend the MinGuar museum of contemporary art, where ZiTre, the hottest new artist, had a rare short stint. Warsan bought the tickets months before without asking Hannad, that was how she ambushed him into joining her. He was watching a soccer game when she broke the news one evening.

"Honey, you know we are invited to attend the opening of "ZiTre Camouflage" tomorrow night," she said while she combed her hair in front of the vanity mirror.

"What camouflage, who is Zsit?" he asked, concentrating on the game.

"That is the name of the show, silly, ZiTre Camouflage."

"Ok, whatever you like sweetie."

"We have to go shopping for you," she said snatching the remote.

"Shopping for what?" Hannad wanted to know, wishing she would leave him so he could watch the game.

"Well, you need an outfit for the event," she said turning off the TV.

"Hey don't do that," he protested. "I'm watching the game."

"Well you're not paying attention."

"Ok, Warsan, what is it?"

"We are going to go to the MinGuar and you need an outfit."

"When?"

"Tomorrow night."

"But I am watching the game with the guys."

"Please, honey, this is really important, the museum is showing his art for only two nights. You know I've been waiting for it for a long time, and—"

"Ok, Warsan, I guess I have to go with you. Please let me watch my game now!"

The next day Warsan purchased a brand new suit for him. She appeared more excited about the designer name than the suit itself. "It is a Versace," he heard her saying. "It was practically a steal!" But he felt awkward in the suit, uncomfortable and out of place. Warsan wore one of her glamorous outfits. He no longer tried to pronounce the designer names: her taste seemed to be made up entirely of hard-to-pronounce designer names with hefty price tags. They joined a crowd gazing at a large, oddly-shaped canvas, nibbling on some minute hors d'oeuvres. Inside the multi colored canvas were tinted broken glass of various colors and rusted nails. The curator explained an elaborate tale of the canvas which the people were marveling at, while Hannad wandered off to the front of the museum where a receptionist watched the soccer game he'd been denied. He'd waited all week to watch the game. When they arrived home after an edgy, quiet ride, she lashed out at him:

"I can't believe you were caught watching TV at the MinGuar!" She said foaming at the mouth with anger.

"What is wrong with you?"

"What will people say?"

"Well, they will say 'he is not sophisticated like her, poor Warsan'! He is a town boy trying to imitate a city boy, and they are correct."

"I am not playing, Hannad! You really pissed me off tonight. I will be the laughing stock at work tomorrow!"

A week later he received a credit card bill that astounded him. Warsan slept like an angel next to him, unmindful of his dilemma. They spent $2,500 on that event alone. He could not build Canab, his dear aging mother, a cement house in the destitute town he'd grown up in, but he just paid $2,500 for an event to view what he thought was a use-less piece of art. Canab still lived in the same shack where he grew up, and he paid $1,500 for paintings which hang from a wall in the living room, another painting of odd objects of paper, trash and soda can tabs which Warsan personally requested as a birthday gift adorned their dining room wall; it was often the first point of conversation for both Americans and Somalis. Americans in admiration of the elaborate tale his wife told as she proudly pointed to the various objects. And Somalis in bewilderment as they asked the reason a canvas of trashed items was allowed to be inside the house.

The amount spent on the painting could feed his mother Canab for several months. An exhibition they went to six months earlier consisted of old rags that were curved along the wall of the museum. The sheets had holes which resembled an old tattered rag. It reminded him of the old rags Canab wrapped on her hollow body when she saw him off to America some fifteen years earlier.

He paid $1,000 for a dinner benefit to encourage new artists in their county, or was it to save wild life, or maybe it was to save the envi-ronment or whatever the benefit was for—he is a man who cannot adequately provide for his family or send monthly stipends to his starv-ing mother, yet his wife wants him to care about issues that at best go over his head, issues he does not regard as important in his life unless he pretends to care, like Warsan. Warsan is so absorbed in the life she had envisioned for herself, which happens to be a life she and her hus-band could not afford on their current income. But she ignores that fact, maxing out credit cards to continue an extravagant social life of her own making, as Hannad struggles to pay the mortgage. There is a sense of entitlement about Warsan, as if Hannad is obligated to provide for her the dream life she had been promised, even if that dream life in reality involves her cab-driving husband who can't deliver that lifestyle. That sense of entitlement is the one thing Warsan and Henna inherited from the façade life their parents provided before the war: they grew up thinking they would be taken care of forever, if not by parents then by spouses.

He went along so he is not perceived as unsophisticated, unhip or all the other "uns" his wife keeps warning him about—but he has had enough. Warsan dresses him up like a manikin for each occasion, but a cautionary tale accompanied each outfit. He was not to dress like a Somali, ever, "with your shirt hanging out of your pants while you walk around with miss-matched colorful outfits and some odd discounted imported sandals," she would remark. He submitted to her more expensive, apparently stylish taste, all the while suffocating and itching in the stiffness of the cloths. He longed for the days he could dress his way, with his shirt un-tucked. The entire pretense he had to perform as if he was some actor bothered him. He has had enough of the façade life, and felt as if he was drowning. He longed to live a normal Somali nomad life, with much haphazardness and simplicity, no planning or sophistication. He no longer wants to surround himself with that word "sophistication" which Warsan thinks sums up her life. He longed for what he was familiar with since infancy, the same things his wife rejects—the backwardness, unplanned events, untimely visits, and the never ending need from relatives, which in her own words causes "fatigue".

Things began to crumble, and Warsan was dumfounded. They were six years into their marriage and parents of two children when he lost interest and became her worst nightmare and inconceivable reality. A typical, slack, untrained, and unsystematic Somali man!

Hannad was deterministically relegated to cab driving after he was laid off from the engineering firm where he worked as an associate engineer. She remembers the exact moment he went from a respectable associate Engineer at a respectable engineering firm to a cabbie. It was their anniversary and she had planned dinner for them at Mansour Sa'ada Bistro. They were swimming in marriage bliss and Warsan was comfortable with how life turned out for them. She sat in their favorite table. Zubair, the waiter, knew exactly where to sit them. They'd frequented the restaurant so much that even their orders were predictable. He was late and would not answer his phone; finally, Hannad, sluggishly walked in, holding his jacket in his right elbow with his tie loose. He did not crack a smile and when he slumped next to her reeking of cigarettes she knew something was wrong. Zubair began piling the table with appetizers: humus, babaganouj, tabouli, pita bread and kibbeh.

"Hey, what is the matter, you're late," she inquired, nibbling on the appetizers

"It was the worst day of my life," he said, picking inattentively on the appetizers she put on his plate.

"What happened? Honey, are you okay?"

"The human resource manager, Mrs. Banes, asked that I bring a college transcript from my University."

"What does that mean?" she asked with a full mouth, staring at him.

"Well, apparently someone has submitted false credentials from—I am not sure if it's India or the Philippines—so now they want everyone to produce a transcript from their colleges"

"Everyone, or just the foreigners?"

"No, everyone, even the Americans."

"Well, you don't have to worry, your degree is legit, right?" the kibbeh in her hand dripped with the tahine white sauce she dipped it in. Zubair brought more food, kabobs, rice, soups.

"Well, yeah, but how am I going to get a transcript from a university that has vanished from the face of the earth?" He said, fidgeting with the food on his plate.

"Here, eat this, my God, it is delicious! It's your favorite" she stuffed salmon kabobs with green pepper and onions into his mouth.

"I don't remember— did you ever have a transcript? It seems logical to me?"

"No, I did not; it was a miracle that I brought my degree along with me when I fled Hamar."

"Well, then, find a way to get it; I am sure there is a way"

"I doubt it."

"Honey, don't worry— please don't spoil this moment for us, we will figure something out."

She was naïve to assume he would easily obtain the transcript and go back to his engineering job. But that is not what ended up happening; Hannad switched professions and was annoyed with her whenever she asked him to look seriously into authenticating his credentials. But it was not easy for him to authenticate a degree from a university that was now defunct.

When he was not able to produce the transcript, he was laid off, he looked for positions with other local engineering firms, but nothing materialized. Soon he tired of looking for a job and began driving a cab full time.

Warsan was so shocked by his switch, and terrified of the effect the change would have on their lives, or more bluntly her life. Imagine your life turning into the one thing you have always escaped. She was now officially a cab driver's wife.

How could she reconcile the separate lives she and her husband would lead after his professional mishap? Here she was a successful professional married to a cabbie. Their lives would not be the same, as she began to detest him and he began to defy her. His cab driving came with lazy schedule, odd hours and unpredictable income.

She felt as if that is all she did anymore, to reminisce and look for the signs she had missed. Did he find it too tedious to be part of their lives, as he had promised when they got married? After all, it was part of their marriage contract to tend to their family affairs first and foremost, no matter what life brought their way. She realized she had lost the battle after Hannad took up the same pattern of uncontrollable hours as the other Somali cabbies: their family began to deteriorate as he fell under the influence of other irresponsible men, cab driving ate up the time she expected him to spend with her and the kids.

Warsan was so wrapped in her depressed thoughts she almost did not hear Hogad and Hillac walk into the living room. Hannad was in the kitchen fixing dinner for the kids, which had become the norm of late; Warsan began a notorious protest to do little around the house. This was brought about by her continued frustration with her life. She knew the children suffered in the process, but she had to give him a taste of his own medicine. She hardly cooked, cleaned or did laundry any more. When he could no longer watch their filthy house and the continuous sickness of the kids, Hannad began to do it all. Warsan never knew she could be this careless about anything, but she was. She refused to be treated as if she were a maid. Hannad had begun to take her hard work and dedication for granted, and began to expect a hand to mouth service. When he was contributing to the household, and helping with the kids, Warsan did not mind doing all the household chores, even without the live-in nanny he refused to hire. But after he began working odd hours, bringing less and less to the household, she became a recluse and deteriorated into a severe depression. She no longer cared what her children ate, or how filthy the house was. She did not care if they ate junk food, or nothing at all. Her motherly instinct was still intact—at least she kept convincing herself it was—but she could no longer pull the weight of the whole household. She spend a lot of time watching mindless episodes of other people's lives on TV, or meet her girlfriend Hibaaq in one of the popular mall gatherings to catch up on some gossip. By the time she went home every night, it would be around midnight, and the vicious cycle began all over again the next day. When she got home, Hannad would be watching TV and the kids would be fast asleep. She would utter a faint "Hi" and proceed to the bedroom. He would later follow and slump next to her, making sure he kept a distance between them, drifting off to fast sleep almost as soon as he lay next to her. She envied him for falling asleep so fast and so callously; it meant he did not care about their crises, it meant life as she knew it was over and she had to face that alone.

⸎

The next day Warsan dashed out of the house as if being chased by the devil. Something extremely forceful and horrendous has just taken place, something repulsive and dangerous. She ran along Dakota Lane, on the north side of the street, unsure where she parked the Land Rover. Dr. Greason's pickup truck sped past her, startling her. She turned her face away, as if she did not want to be seen in this state.

"Hi, Mrs. Gedi," with her face still turned Warsan, waved to the speeding truck, recognizing Brandon's deepening adolescent voice. With fresh tears, she stopped for a moment to look around for the SUV, only to realize it was parked right in front of the house. She held the car key in her hand, but hesitated for a moment; she had originally run from the house to take the SUV, but the force of the encounter just few minutes earlier made her delirious, unsure what her next step should be. She could hear her pounding heart.

Warsan tiptoed past the front porch of the house and slipped quietly into the truck. She placed the keys into the ignition as soon as she was inside the SUV. She almost shouted as she pulled out of the garage, realizing she was safe. She had no idea if she was injured, or how badly: judging from the bloodstains all over her clothes and hands, she thought she might need medical attention. She kept wondering where the blood came from, as squeamish as she is about blood.

She was embarrassed by her appearance: she didn't want to be seen this way, but she had no choice. In fact, for the first time neighbors, relatives, and strangers alike would see her imperfect, not at all elegant and all made up. She will not look like herself today. She could see Mrs. Dunn peek through her living room window—the neighborhood nosy, she seemed to be in tune with everything that occurred in every home,

130

only to repeat it to other neighbors who in turn became suspicious or concerned.

Warsan was still wearing her work clothes, an otherwise beautiful pant suit that was now torn, splashed with the evidence of the severe assault she had just escaped. Her usually neat, silky honey-blonde high-lighted hair spilled messily over her face. She was barefoot, having run out of the house before she could slip on the Jimmy Choo pumps she wore to work that day.

She occupied her mind with the details of the fight she had minutes earlier with Hannad, she wanted to remember every little detail, so she would repeat it to Nadifo when she reached her house. She couldn't remember the route she took, or if she cut a red light or two, but now she was in front of Nadifo's apartment, and she dashed out of the SUV as fast as she had rushed into it, leaving it in the middle of the street with the ignition running. She was now more hysterical; as she ran into the house she began to cry loudly.

"Oh my God, hooyo, the bastard almost killed me!" She said it again and again, making the situation sound worse than it actually was, to cause alarm. "Hooyo, where are you, where is everyone?"

"Who is it, Bile? Is that you making all this noise?" Nadifo shrieked from the master bedroom, annoyed by the distraction. As she entered the living room, she saw Warsan's bloody face. "Who did this to you, *Subxaana Allaah, Istaqfurulah?*" Nadifo gasped, shocked and almost not wanting to hear the answer. Warsan did not answer; instead she cried loudly when she saw Nadifo.

"He beat me because he knows I have no one to protect me! Why do you think he was brave enough to touch me, huh?" she attempted to persuade Nadifo, looking for sympathy. Bile appeared from the stair-way, woken by Warsan's shouts.

"What is going on, why the hell are you crying? Warsan, who did this to you, oh my god, your face?" Bile asked.

Warsan continued, still shaking, unable to calm down enough to explain her predicament: she knew she was not making sense, but she couldn't help it.

"You and Haybe are good for nothing, look what he did to me!"

"Where is Haybe? Is Cartan in his room?"

"You are all weak; I wish I had brave brothers who would finish the idiot!"

"That motherffff!" Bile pounded on the wall, dragging the word "f" but not quite saying it.

"Did he do this to you?! Oh my God, I will kill him; I will blow his effing brains out!" Bile was ostensibly serious about his promise to finish off his brother-in-law.

"You stupid boy, stop your nonsense, you know you will do no such thing!" Nadifo exclaimed, as if frightened of her son's vile intent. "Warsan, calm down, hooyo, everything will be ok. Henna, *naayaa* Henna!"

Henna appeared reluctantly, hating Nadifo's continued disruption, rolling her eyes as she switched off the cordless phone. She was annoyed that Nadifo's favorite name to summon when she wanted something was hers. Never did she call on Haybe or Bile to do something; it was always Henna do this, Henna do that, she was tired of it. Her brothers got away with everything. They did not do chores around the apartment, they did not have curfew; yet she had to abide by all of Nadifo's rules. She was expected to cook, clean and do the laundry for the entire family. The minute she came home from school, there would be a list of chores waiting. Henna convinced herself that Nadifo did it out of spite, to make Henna fail in school. She spent most of her Saturdays doing chores; she had no personal time, not even a minute to spend with her friends. Now that Henna was among people who adored "me" time, she longed for "me" time of her own. She could not wait until she was done with college so she could rest from this never-ending cultural nonsense. She wanted to move out, like other American kids who put distance between them and their parents. '*That is it. I will just have to move out and create a distance between me and Nadifo,'* Henna thought to herself, privately, knowing full well it was more of a dream than a reality.

"Hi, *hooyo* what is going on?" Henna appeared lost for words when she saw Warsan, briefly forgetting all her problems as a young Somali female.

"Oh my god, Warsan, did you see your face? Who the hell did this to you?! Where the hell is this blood coming from?" she inspected Warsan's face and neck.

"*Naayaa*, shut up and get your sister a wet towel." Nadifo ordered. Henna left the room to fetch the towel annoyed by Nadifo's rudeness. She came back with the towel and more questions.

"Why don't you go to the hospital, Warsan?" Warsan was too busy crying to answer.

"*Naayaa* stop putting ideas into her head, no need for a hospital, there—it is a small cut that is all," Nadifo began dabbing the blood from Warsan's neck.

"There, it is a little cut in your neck; it is not a big wound."

"I think she should go to the emergency room and alert the police." As soon as Nadifo heard the word police, she flew into a rage, throwing a flip-flop at Henna. She made it clear the idea of involving the police and hospital in every little beating that occurred between a man and his wife had no place in their lives.

"Naayaa, get out of here, don't you have chores to do!?"

"Of course I have chores to do, I'm the maid, aren't I?" Henna fled as another shoe was thrown in her direction.

"Why do these police waste their time with things like this anyway?" Nadifo seemed uneasy. "Don't their police have more important things to tend to instead of concerning themselves with family matters? A man beats his wife; that is part of life."

Nadifo was concerned that if the police came to their home, they would probably arrest them for one reason or another; after all these big white men in uniform seemed busy breaking families and jailing men for taming their wives. She'd heard of all the immigrant families

133

deported as a result of a simple phone call to 911. 911 was the notorious number that, when called, led to kids disappearing into foster homes, parents ending up in jail, and close-knit families separated. There was no place for 911 in her home.

She never trusted anyone in authority anyway. Even back home, when she was a Minster's wife, she feared the police. They were very abusive, taking anyone they saw fit to jail. Stories of families, who met with unpredictable misfortune after they called 911, swam in the hallways of Cedar Springs where Nadifo lived. Imagine calling white men with guns to your apartment—the idea sent a chill of fear down her spine.

Warsan began to calm down, finding comfort in the tumultuous exchange between Nadifo and her feisty younger sister. While inspecting her bruises, Nadifo interrupted her thoughts: "No need to bring outsiders to our home, Warsan. Your wounds will heal and this will be forgotten soon enough. Husbands do this to bring order to their homes; be a good wife, do your duties and avoid quarrels. I know you are hard headed and you talk back to your husband—men don't like that." Warsan understood Nadifo's concern—she did not want her daughter divorced. She kept insisting that at least he was working hard to take care of his family—as if that alone should grant him the right to beat her. There were plenty of men in her community who did not take care of their families and yet beat their wives, even when the wives were the sole providers. "You are spoiled, Warsan. You need to be a good wife, don't compete with your husband."

SOMENGLISH

A few days after Hannad and Warsan's fight, a knock on the door startled Nadifo. She was dusting the furniture, but had been going over a stubborn sticky spot on the dining table for some time. Lost in thought, she scratched the spot without seeing it. She was in deep thought about the phone call she had received earlier from Hawo. Besides the usual struggles, Hawo had reported the death of their brother Saxardiid. The knock got louder.

"Okay, okay!" she said, searching for something with which to cover her head. She found an apple green *garbasar* on top of the drum in the corner. She quickly draped it over the transparent *diric* and uncovered hair. Hogad, Hilac and Idil, Warsan's children, stood at the door impatiently. Whoever had dropped them off sped away.

"Hi, *ayeeyo*" Hilac said. Idil went straight for the TV. Her little body shaking as she danced to the music on her mp3 player. Hogad threw his backpack on the sofa insolently; it lands with a soft thud which made Nadifo shake her head in displeasure.

"Waryaa, don't bring your dirty shoes into this apartment, leave them outside the door!" She leveled a piercing stare at Hogad; who obeyed her, reluctantly.

Hogad at eleven is the only boy. He is spoiled and angry, and seems to get away with much. He and Nadifo have little to say to each other: he detests coming to her apartment, preferring to stay at home, hanging out with his friends, or going to the mall. He never figured out why his parents choose to drop him off here when they know full well he dislikes the place.

"Snap, there is nothing to eat here! Ayeeyo, I am hungry, *gaajoon-ing*," he points to his stomach. "I need to eat," he raises his voice when Nadifo does not reply.

"Gajooning, gajooning!" Nadifo mocked his mediocre Americanized Somali with a smirk. "They are raising fools for children," she says, mainly to herself twisting her lips with frustration.

Hogad does not care for the traditional assortment of food that line the fridge. He searches for junk food, although he knows very well he will not find any here.

"Hilac, call your mother to bring some food for these two," Nadifo says, pacing back and forth between the living room and the kitchen. All three drew out their cell phones to make the call.

"I am going to call daddy first. I want pizza," Idil said. Hogad pushed her, wrestling her phone away to place the call himself.

"Little brat, I will call *aabo*, I want some burgers, fries, and a chocolate shake." He said licking his lips.

Hilac, the eldest at twelve, is reserved and quiet. She is often confused and angry with her neglectful parents, but would not say anything neither to them, nor Nadifo; she keeps her anger inside.

"Stop it, you two, stop all the noise, God!" Hilac exclaimed, rolling her eyes.

"Hello, Daddy? Could you bring us some pizza? I'm hungry. I want a cheese pizza, please don't put anything else on it." Idil's call got through; Hogad gave up, and busied himself with his cell phone.

"Dad I want three cheese burgers and fries and a chocolate shake." Hogad snatched the phone from Idil, slapping her around as she tried to get it back.

"I hate you, Hogad! Dad, he is hitting me—ouch, I hate you!"

"Ayeeyo, let me comb your pretty hair," Hilac purred as she stroked Nadifo's hair while they waited for the food to arrive. Nadifo pecked her on the cheek as Hilac assured her "*Aniga adiga ku jecel ayeeyo*," in the most disjointed Somali.

"Allah will bless you for helping your ayeeyo. I pray to see you married with a nice husband and children one day."

"Ayeeyo, *Cigaal Shiidaad*, please tell me that story."

"Straighten the living room, and I will tell you the one about *Cigaal* and the Lion."

"Cool, I love that one," Hillac said, very conscious of her accent. She is often the translator for her siblings, not because of superior language skills, but because she is the only one who makes an attempt.

Her favorite time with Nadifo is when she tells Somali stories. Nadifo tells the stories so well, adding animal roars and hilarious, colorful animal voices. Hillac pays homage to Nadifo's clever mind as she listens with childlike enthusiasm, anticipating the end as if it were her first time hearing the story. Although she is twelve, she never tires to hear them.

"*Alif laa miim daalika kitaabi....,*" the stereo blasted with Quran.

"Oh my god, gosh, wow I am wining, oooohh sweet, sweet, come' on come' on, snap, snap!" Hogad pounded on his laptop, playing a game.

"I am going to the mall tomorrow to get that cute outfit! Shoot, I am tired of this," Hilac complained, her cell phone on one ear, an mp3 player ear bud in the other, while she tidied up the living room.

"They toss us here every weekend while they run around, doing what I will never know." Hilac continued.

Idil's mp3 player played, "B...ch, b...ch, shake that thang, I wanna ...., shake your a..."

The children remained inside Nadifo's apartment the entire day, watching television, playing computer games, listening to earsplitting hip-hop music, and gabbing endlessly on their cell phones. No one knows with whom they converse on these calls: Nadifo does not understand their conversations, and even if she spoke perfect English, they employed the latest slang, a language unto itself. When they surf the net, she thought they were doing homework.

Nadifo shouted from her prayer mat, "Idil, stop shaking your hips!" The nine-year-old ignored Nadifo, totally consumed by the music video she is watching, full of gyrating bodies. She concentrated on creating the closest imitation possible with her own tiny hips, grinning in thoughtless admiration. The video ended as the channel broke into commercial; Idil shimmied her way into the kitchen to get some juice. She had not grasped what Nadifo had been saying and continued to dance audaciously, singing "shake that thang!" without having any idea what the words meant. Nadifo, frustrated, finally threw a shoe in Idil's direction, speaking in Somali as she launched the shoe into Idil, making the girl yelp as the shoe hit her ankle.

"I hate you, you stupid terrorist," All Nadifo understood is the word 'terrorist.'

"I hate you, you are so mean to me," Idil sobbed vindictively. "You are always hitting me, it's not fair," Whimpering, Idil attempted to launch threats at Nadifo in broken Somali, but was overcome with crying.

"Naayaa, who taught you that word?" Nadifo grabbed Idil, pinning her to the wall.

"That is what my teacher calls people who look like you. Now I know what she means, you are evil," she shrieked, all but spitting at her grandmother. "All my friends say that you are weird and that you are a terrorist." Nadifo let go of Idil, and the girl ran out of the room sobbing. Nadifo's arms dropped slowly to her sides; her eyes foggy—she was lost in thought.

"Mom, I hate this place, come pick me up! I wanna go home! Mom, pick up your stupid phone!" Idil howled at Warsan's voicemail.

"Idil, stop calling her every five seconds! God! I can't stand this. I hate you all! I hate this whiney little girl! Get off! Idil get off of me!" Hilac protested as Idil attempted to get a hug from her older sister.

"*Allahu Akbar, Allahu Akbar,*" The call to prayer filled the small apartment with a curious calm—making every movement still, the television was clicked off, Idil's sobs subsided, Hilac dropped to her knees—as the mosque-shaped clock fulfilled its purpose. Nadifo savored the quiet, her head grazing the prayer mat, reciting Quran. Beside her, the three children kneeled in the darkened room. The stillness immaculate.

"Idil turn the face of your shoes up, upside-down shoes bring bad luck." Nadifo says, calmly after they are all done with their prayers.

GLIMPSE AND AWE

All of the photos in the apartment are either turned face down or are totally out of sight. She did that for religious purposes, believing that angels will not enter a house where pictures are displayed. But once in while she peeks as if to steal back a moment from a far-gone time when there was some happiness in her life—although the peeking itself appears sinful.

Nadifo no longer recognizes herself in these photos. In them she appears happy, youthful, and full of life: whenever she sees herself in these old pictures, pictures she took with her family before the war, she wonders if it was possible to have had such a full life. How could she be the same person? The woman in those pictures looked so vibrant, and she was so sinfully clothed—all but naked. Nadifo does not remember dressing that way, revealing herself, standing next to men and other women wearing equally revealing clothes. She was ashamed of this former self, but she can't bring herself to get rid of the pictures. They are all she has left to remember the only semblance of happiness she had ever known. For some reason or another she liked the feeling looking at the pictures brought: moments of happiness and hope, which do not exist in her present life. There was one particular picture which would spring back to life memories she had endlessly tried to bury.

It was the summer of 88; Nadifo and Cartan were spending summer vacation in Geneva. In the picture she is laughing so blissfully she had thrown her head back. Cartan is sitting next to her holding a drink. She is wearing a long lace-neck black gown with a simple, elegant set of lavender pearls. She is holding something in her right hand, maybe a purse or a drink; it is unclear, and when she tries to remember, her mind fails her. In the picture they sit next to the Finance Minister and his wife. There are so many drinks on the table; the place looks like a nightclub. She remembers that trip more vividly than any other trip she had taken with Cartan.

The phone rang at about five thirty that morning, interrupting the dewy calm of Nadifo's luxurious sleep. Cartan took the phone call in the living room. When he came back, he began to go through the closet as if he was preparing to go out. She pretended not to hear him, and buried herself deeper among the velvety sheets, trying hard to fall asleep again.

"I need to leave for an emergency trip, *habibi*, could you prepare a bag for me?" She ignored him, hoping he would call the maid instead of bothering her in the wee hours of the morning. She was still jetlagged, though it had been two days since she had arrived.

"Nadifo, get up. I am traveling to *Masar* for an emergency trip." Nadifo stretched leisurely, fully extending her lean arms above her head. She sat up slowly, still confused as to why Cartan was disturbing her unruffled morning. She was not ready for the day to begin; she was not supposed to get out of bed for another three hours.

"Cartan, what are you doing, making all this noise so early?" She leaned out of bed, still stretching. "What is the emergency?" She ran her perfectly manicured hands through her gleaming copper hair. She looked exquisite, even so early in the morning.

"I am going to Masar. The president has been assassinated." Her eyes widened. *Is he talking about President Sacad?* "Are you talking about President Sacad?"

"Yes, he was assassinated,"

"What happened? When did this happen? *Allah*, I must call Najma, poor poor woman; should I come with you?" *Of course not*, she reasoned before he answered. The kids needed her here. After all, this is their summer vacation, and they have so many activities, French lessons, swimming lessons, tennis for Warsan, piano for Haybe.

"Cartan, we should have let Haboon come with us, she would be good with the kids," she said as she fidgeted with the suitcase. "This woman, what's her name, Michèle, she does not know their needs." Cartan had decided to hire only French-speaking help this year, he wanted the kids to learn the language. So they had a French nanny, a French maid, and a French driver (well, an Ivorian who'd lived in Paris and viewed himself more French than the French). She arranged several of his suits in the case. "I end up doing everything for them anyway." Nadifo did not mention that the reason she does not like the kids with her on these vacations is because she ends up missing shopping sprees with other Ministers' wives: she did not come all the way from Hamar to be worried all the time about their activities and safety. She actually wishes sometimes she could have separate vacations from them.

"You know I tried, but she got her visa too late, what can I do?" Cartan said. He looked handsome in his blue shirt and khaki slacks; and wore the dignity of his post well.

"Could we send for her while you are gone? I don't think I can handle the kids by myself."

"No, I don't think that is a good idea, dear. Warsan is old enough to help you." Cartan continued, splashing BOSS cologne.

"Warsan is selfish; she won't help with anything. She is busy being ungrateful and complaining I don't allow her to hang around with the president's kids. She is convinced she hates me because I don't allow her to do what she pleases. Give my best to Mrs. Sacad and her kids. Make sure to call! Oh, and Cartan, how are the arrangements for the new house coming along?" Nadifo hoped her new house would be ready by the time they got back.

"Marisa assured me everything will be done by the time you return; I will check on it when I arrive in Cairo." He called the new house "Nadifo's mansion." He suspected she was building it to start a trend— which she argued was not her intent. She didn't want homes like hers popping up all over Hamar. Her house must stand out from the rest.

The driver took Cartan to the airport. Nadifo went back to bed, ready to fall asleep again, only to feel Henna's little moving feet. This meant no more sleep for her. How will she cope with all the activities of the day, she wondered if she is this tired? It is times like these that she thinks she should take her own vacations.

The kids and Cartan had arrived in Geneva four days earlier. She had stopped over in Dubai for a wedding and, of course, some shopping. By the time she had joined them in Geneva, her husband had already signed a lease for a house. She was shocked to find the house he had picked. He said that it belonged to some famous American celebrity, but the place was too homely for her. It was too small and simple for all the prestigious guests who would visit them. She should probably lease another house for entertaining, she felt uptight. She would ask Cartan to handle it after he came back from the funeral. She did not know where she would entertain Princess Nisreen and her kids. Nadifo sighed; so many things to plan and so little time. There was a huge competition amongst the Minister's wives. Everything was fair game: looks, clothes, jewelry, even acquaintances. There was so much backstabbing on these trips and so Nadifo tried to vacation in places these women had yet to discover. Everyone came to Geneva in the summer, which is why she preferred Spain or Prague. But Cartan loved Geneva.

Nadifo was very popular and most of the women competed for her attention. Cartan joked that she was popular because she was so beautiful, but Nadifo shrugged at the thought. It was silly to think someone would like her because of her looks. Last year they had vacationed on the French Riviera with few other couples. She rented a magnificent house on the beach and sent the kids to Paris. She entertained the whole time. Princes Badriya of the Emirates and Princess Nisreen of Khuzaymah Saqr Island were among the people she vacationed with. The president's wife was jealous of her when she heard about it. She snubbed Nadifo for months after that, refusing to invite her to prestigious parties at the presidential palace. This year, no one would remember her, Nadifo thought, considering the house Cartan picked. Cartan would pay for ruining her summer, she brooded. She was so tense, the kid's music made every room vibrate. She was glad to have scheduled a three hour massage session with Pierre, her favorite masseuse; hopefully that would relax her little before she dove into the swing of things, she thought.

The photos depict a life that Nadifo no longer remembers. All the hardship that she had endured is ever present in her mind, but these pictures revealed a life which had been erased from memory.

In her present life, far from the nostalgia of building a mansion, the unseemly way Americans often say "I beg your pardon" made Nadifo go to lengths to get what they called "an education." She is determined to learn, learn and learn some more so that she does not seem brainless.

"Who is Dorothy, The Wizard of something or another, the Tin man?" She is tired of asking—the only response she ever gets is an astonished "You mean there are people who haven't seen the wizard of Oz? Wow, how do people live?" The determination to rid herself of ignorance made her register for Everything American for ESL students, a class offered to ESL students to learn, as the class says, "everything American". The class is held on Friday afternoons in a makeshift classroom in St. Louis Park. As she is leaving her regular ESL class one Friday afternoon a blanket of snow covered the entire street: she crossed to the entrance of the University to catch the number Y9 bus to St Louis Park. The bus waited to collect patrons, but as Nadifo approached, it hummed loudly, as if ready to accelerate into street traffic. After the new class she would visit a friend in the hospital, and then make her way home for the day-break prayers.

Backpacks ride on the backs of students like African children strapped to the backs of their mothers. She was busy observing the students when a sudden thump shocked her. She was too consumed with where she needed to be that she had missed a step, falling hard to the snow-packed ground. A hooded young man who was running to catch the same bus turned around to help her.

"Ma'am, are you ok?" he asked, removing his backpack to assist her. But Nadifo remained still, motioning for him not to come any closer.

"Ok, ok," she said with blank eyes, as if not seeing him.

"Are you sure? Should I call an ambulance, ma'am?" The man removed his cell phone from a side pocket. He appeared concerned, but she rose abruptly and shook her head.

"Okay, goot, goot, no *broblom*, no *broblom*."

"Are you sure you are not hurt?" he asked, his cell phone in his fingertips, ready to dial.

She dusted herself off. "Tanke yuu," she said in a final, polite way and walked away quickly, not waiting for a reply. The man dashed off, inserting his earphones back into his ears, but he kept looking back. The inconvenience of the fall annoyed her. She limped a little, but assured herself she was all right. The wetness of the snow on her jilbaab was more annoying than the pinch of pain in her leg.

She did not speak of the incident to anyone that night: she never whined about issues of health and things that required someone to accompany her. The hustle and drag to some doctor's office where her pain would wrongly be diagnosed became burdensome. A few days later the pain in her left leg restricted her prayers, but she endured it. Three days after her fall, she was unable to move, becoming totally bed-ridden. The painful throb in her leg persisted. For five days, she was silent about the fall, never mentioning to anyone the severity of it. She attributed the pain to her body's rejection of the alien Minnesotan climate. Many ailments such as this one had somehow healed themselves without any visit to a doctor in the past. When Warsan found out, she forced her to visit the doctor. She was reluctant, assuring Warsan her leg would heal on its own. Then Henna was asked to take her to the doctor when Haybe and Warsan became unavailable.

Henna grudgingly agreed. The trip to the doctor's office proved to be awkward. Nadifo appeared consumed with the visit; anxious and reticent, she sat in the car with Henna who seemed lost in the hip-hop station she listened to, fidgeting with the heavy scarf that weighed her hair down. She wore it only to reduce the constant squabble between them.

Otherwise, Nadifo would find an opportunity to label her with one of the unflattering descriptions she seemed to reserve only for her. That is the only reason she let sweat drip from her covered hair.

Henna stayed on the cell phone the entire time, speaking in English. Nadifo knew it was on purpose. Nadifo, uneasy with the whole trip and disgusted by the close proximity between the driver and herself, beat her rosary rigidly, praying. Soon they were both relieved to sit in the doctor's office with other patients.

"Hello, Mrs. Gedi," said Dr. Osborne, her internist.

"Tell him my name is not Mrs. Gedi, it is Nadifo Cafi." She snapped in Somali.

"Dr. Osborne, her last name is Cafi, not Gedi."

"Oh sorry, it's not Gedi?"

"Yes, she has a different last name."

"Okay. That is odd isn't it?" The doctor appeared puzzled, the chart he held in his hand said otherwise.

"Why does he assume I am not whole without Cartan's name? What does our marriage have to do with exchanging our names? He is his father's child and I mine. There is merely a marriage between us, not exchanging of names," she said frigidly, as if taking her anger on the Doctor for another matter.

"Okay, okay, hooyo, I got it," Henna snapped, looking at the doctor with sympathy, while ignoring the redundancy of the story she has heard ten million times.

Nadifo did not wait for Henna to explain the situation to Dr. Osborne; instead she forcefully interrupted Henna. "Dakhtar, me no Cartan sister, me wife—why me Gedi, me no Gedi!" her voice was loud and high-pitched.

"Is she ok?" the Doctor asked, noticing Nadifo's uneasy demeanor, and not understanding a word she said.

"It is nothing, Dr. Osborne; she's alright," Henna answered, embarrassed.

"Ask your mother to remove her scarf so I may examine her," the doctor urged quietly, his stethoscope at the ready, still unsure about the woman's uneasiness.

"Tell him I will not remove my garb. It's my leg that hurts, tell him to put a bandage there!" Nadifo instructed, edgy, and holding her leg where it hurt.

"Please ask her to kindly remove her clothes and put this robe on," the doctor repeated, clenching his jaws.

"I can only try, Doctor, no promises here," replied Henna, shaking her head in disbelief, all the while sliding her own scarf into position.

"Dakhtar, me only leg sik, why you me take off?" she pointed to her jilbaab, seething with anger. "You job this leg no me jilbaab, me no take off cloths," she repeated, knowing Henna would compromise the message.

"Hooyo, please listen to him, he needs to examine you!" Henna said in frustration.

"I am not going to take it off; tell him not to touch me. What does he want with my jilbaab? He needs to look at my leg, not my body!" she shouted, hanging her rosary across her neck as if to restrict access. "I did not want you to come with me; you never understand my needs. Where is Warsan? Take me back; Warsan will bring me here tomorrow," Nadifo said in a sad tone, shaking. Henna rolled her eyes. The doctor left the room, livid. He called his nurse to perform the exam instead.

"Ok, Miss Afi, let's try this again; I promise I will be gentle."

Nadifo was not happy she had to be naked in front of this woman either, but she obliged simply to avoid any further grief from Warsan. She was uncomfortable throughout the exam, flinching every time the nurse's chilly hands touched her body.

"Tell her to stay off her feet, ok?" The nurse entreated Henna, stroking Nadifo's back comfortingly. But Nadifo as stubborn as she is did not stay off her feet as instructed, and the prescribed medicine went in the trash. A week later she had to go back to the doctor.

ABYSS NESTLING

Nadifo reminisced back to an incident at the Somali *souq* a couple of days earlier—a woman she did not know kept pointing her finger at her. She was at the *souq* to purchase some *tiireh* roots to ease her unpredictable off-again, on-again menses. She had been in pain for two days, and had heard of a traditional healer in the mall that could provide the roots. As she waited alongside other women suffering from various ailments, she noticed one particular woman whose gaze followed her throughout her wait. Nadifo did not think much of it—she ignored the women who were at times looking for trouble.

Then the next afternoon Salaado, Cosob, Shacni, and Cawral's visited Nadifo at home. She had returned from class and drifted into a light sleep; the knock on the door made her heart skip a beat. She hesitated for a minute, wondering who it could be, since her husband and kids all had their keys. Door knocks terrified her—even Girl Scouts selling cookies raised her heart rate. She tiptoed to the door and peered through the peephole, deciding only then whether or not to open the door. The faces outside the door were familiar, but still she felt a knot in her stomach.

Something was amiss. They were living in a country where people busied themselves with work, kids, and responsibilities. The great distance between people, did not allow friendly visits. *What emergency or piece of bad news had initiated this visit from these women?* She wondered. They must have come here to deliver news too horrendous for the telephone. Only hours earlier, Nadifo had been on the phone with

Shacni, who complained of the difficulties she was facing in America. She talked of the endless bills and about visiting her son Soyan in jail. He had been in jail for two years: no one knew why, but no one dared ask or discuss the matter on the phone. The women had been warned that because they were Muslims their telephones were now wire-tapped. Sometimes they would speak in a locally concocted coded language so that the spies would not understand them. Nadifo stood at the door for what seemed like an eternity as they continued knocking.

"Nadifo, open the door! It is cold out here!" Cawrala's shout sounded sharp behind the solid brown door.

"I am coming, please wait." Nadifo found the courage to respond. She pulled the door open. The women filed in one by one, offering their greetings. Shacni's winter coat made her appear larger than usual. They settled into the Arabic divans while Nadifo's mind raced with worry. An incense burner sat on the table, emitting fresh Somali incense, slightly blurring Nadifo's languid face. After greeting the women she ran into the kitchen to fetch tea for them. Salaado eagerly followed, but Nadifo ignored her, methodically beginning to prepare the tea kettle. She began peeling fresh ginger which she threw into the kettle on the stove while eavesdropping on the conversation at hand in the living room.

"Nadifo, how are the kids?" Salaado asked. A sudden attack of creeping paralysis seeped through Nadifo's body when she heard the word "kids." She tried to show strength and patience, but she wanted it out of the way. She wanted to hear the horrible news that had made them come all the way here. The hum of the kettle agitated her, so she turned off the stove, took Salaado by the hand and came back to the living room where the rest of the women scattered comfortably but anxiously.

"Who is it? Which one of my kids is dead, Shacni? Please tell me quickly, is it Haybe or Bile?" Her throat felt as if it was unable to keep in the loud roaring of her mind. Shacni held an insulin syringe, which she had moments earlier injected Cawral'a with. She got up abruptly to where Nadifo stood with Salaado. Cawral'a purposefully fidgeted with the syringe case she held in her hand.

"*Bisinka, Bisinka,* Nadifo, no one is dead! *Alxamdulillah,* thank God, it is nothing like that," Salaado assured her. Hardship and foreign living had not claimed Salaado's cool confidence.

"*Alxamdulilah,* then what happened? Why are you here unannounced?" she demanded to know rudely.

"Why is Cawral'a making herself busy with her syringe, why does Shacni stare at me with guilt, what is going on? Your faces tell a long tale—please, out with it." The women looked at each other nervously; enjoying the distraction coming from the kitchen where Shacni had disappeared to and was now pounding cinnamon, cardamom and other spices in a black wooden mortar. If she made the tea she could avoid being the one to tell Nadifo the bad news they had assembled to deliver.

Each waited for the other to break the news. They envied Shacni, who had disappeared away for the hardest part of the visit. Cawral'a busied herself with the incense burner, allowing the smoke to scent her hair while a long silence consumed the room. It was obvious that they had not rehearsed this part of the visit. Then Cosob, who had appeared furious the entire time, found the courage to speak.

"My dear sister, we admire you. You are a woman of faith and bravery. You have shown great strength through difficulty—"

"Cosob, please, I can handle it; tell me what is wrong," Nadifo interrupted her hands shaking, with a twitch in her left eye.

"It happens to the best of us; it is culture and religion, and although we as women do not like it we must accept it and show heroism throughout," she continued. Nadifo's face went blank, now she was baffled.

"What is going on? What courage, culture, religion— are you talking about, common ladies all this prelude talk is killing me, what in Allah's world is going on?"

"Nadifo," Salaado took over, "we are women; in the eyes of most men we are transit stops and Allah has given them the right to marry four—" Salaado did not have to complete her sentence; Nadifo felt nauseated right then and there before another word left Salaado's mouth. She crumpled up like an old newspaper before their eyes.

"Dear sister," Shacni tried to offer comfort as she took large sips of the creamy sweet tea she had made earlier. "These men are dogs. They are nothing but full-grown animals. They are selfish and only care about their own comfort, happiness, and pleasure." She continued between sips of tea and bites of cookie.

"You and I know that it is unjust, when they choose a younger woman for no reason, you know Allah does not condone marrying for the simple reason of pleasure," Cosob said bluntly staring at the flowery mug in front of her. "Allah will punish a man who leaves his family for the reason of pleasure. Hell waits for Cartan," Cosob continued as she bit into a cookie.

"Who is she?" It was all Nadifo could think of. Her obsession with the other woman was in full swing now, as her mind swirled with sentiment. *"Have I seen her? Do I know her? How old is she? Is she pretty?" Is she tall?* Her attention went back to the women at the mall. Were they mocking her, was one of them her co-wife?

"Her name is Saxarla. She is a single mother with five kids, Warsan's age. He has been married for four months now." Shacni tried to think of adequate insults—would it suffice to call her a home wrecker, a slut, a cheap single mother who snatches other women's husbands? Would that bring Nadifo any consolation?

"It was done in secret, but she started talking to reveal herself. We found out yesterday after class," Cawral'a explained with lowered eyes.

"I hear she has been around, she is cheap and a slut," Shacni interjected, surprising the women.

"Shacni, shame on you, insulting her in God's eyes will not do you or Nadifo any good. We are not here to insult anyone, we are here to console our sister," Cosob said pushing the tea away.

"Look it is what I heard, okay, I was making calls before you came to fetch me, Samira my neighbor tells me the woman Cartan married is a slob and a…. a easy." Save for Cosob, the other women chuckled lightly.

"I am sorry it is not pleasant to the ear, it is what I heard, she has been through three men already, barely thirty and she has already been around the dirty block, Allah have mercy on my soul. Men do it because they can, they hop from one woman to the next, but how can women do that to themselves? Home wreckers like her are why many honorable women like you lose out Nadifo, may Allah cut his—"

"*Acuudu Billaah*, Shacni, take it easy, no need for the ugly talk," Cosob said, clearly bothered by Shacni's remarks.

"*Allahu Akbar Allahu Akbar*" sounded the glimmering green mosque shaped alarm. The women repeated in unison "*Allahu Akbar*"; a few minutes later the women formed one line and began praying, Cosob leading. Nadifo could not follow the prayers the way she diligently likes to. Her mind was consumed. "She is a single mother with kids, Warsan's age" kept interrupting her concentration. "Cartan took another wife secretly." She attempted to bring her thought back to the prayers but failed.

While the women were praying the bell rang. Bile, unaware of all the women in the living room, opened the door without checking who it was. A middle-aged African American woman stood outside the door in the frigid air.

"Yes, can I help you?" he said, keeping the door half closed.

"Good day, I mean, evening, young man. I am a Jehovah's Witness. My name is Darlene McCabe."

"A who?" Bile asked irritated with an afro comp sticking out of his hair.

"Is there an adult in the house? I need to speak to an adult if you don't mind, please."

"Look, my mom is busy praying over there. You are welcome to come inside and wait for her if you like," he said anxiously glimpsing behind her into the street.

"Are you sure it is okay?"

"I don't know. I guess you can wait there," he said pointing to a chair at the foyer before he hurriedly vanished into the dark, cold night.

Nadifo was surprised to find a woman in the foyer of the apartment after they finished the prayers. She could hear Bile talking to someone while she prayed with the other women, but she did not expect to see a woman waiting in her foyer.

"Who you are?" she asked rather rudely, wondering how the women got into the apartment. "*Waryaa* Bile, come here!" she cried while the woman attempted to explain herself.

"Good evening, madam, my name is Darlene McCabe. I am a Jehovah's Witness here to preach the good news to you. I am here to share the word of God, the truth."

"You sell something?" Nadifo interrupted, unable to understand the woman who kept going on, despite Nadifo's confusion.

"*Waryaa* Bile!" Nadifo called again, never once checking to see if Bile was in the apartment.

"Did you know God loves you and he...?"

"Lady, please, what you sell?"

"Madam I am not selling anything, just preaching the truth," By now the rest of the women circled the woman. Shacni opened the door.

"Get this weirdo out of here, she is probably sent by the FBI."Shacni looked furious. "Ma'am, you go, we no understand English!" She said, holding the door wide open.

"I'm sorry. I did not mean to interrupt you all. Please accept my apology—take these and read the word of God on your own." The woman handed them small leather green bibles with the words "The New Testament" engraved in cursive brown letters. She also tucked several copies of Awake! Magazine and leaflets with the message "What Does God Require of Us?" into a wooden foyer column.

"Oh, this dictionary, thank you," Cosob said, inspecting the bible.

"No, it is not a dictionary it is the—"

"Okay okay ma'am, bye, we no interest," Shacni held the door brusquely, interrupting in the woman's conversation. When the woman left they began to inspect the bibles she had given them.

"I needed a dictionary, *Allah* knows I could not afford to buy one, now here it is free," Salaado said, stuffing the bible into her purse.

"Isn't God great? These people are sometimes good," Cosob joined with the jubilation.

"How do you know it is a dictionary?" Shacni asked with an unfriendly face. "Maybe she came in here to spy on us, may be the CIA sent her here," she said tossing her copy into the trash. "Nadifo, how did this woman know we needed dictionaries? And who opened the door for her any way?" Shacni attempted to collect the bibles from all the other women, to throw in the trash.

"I don't know, Shacni, but you are right, we should not trust her," Nadifo said, distantly.

"I am going to take one," Cawral'a said, snatching one back from Shacni. "I need it."

"Me too," said Cosob, following suit. "It looks like the dictionary my kids use. I will take it to them," taking Shacni's copy out of the trash Cosob, shoved the bibles into her duffle bag.

"Ladies let us be on our way, we have a long way to go. Nadifo, look after yourself, Sister," Shacni said, intruding into the much needed distraction. "Cartan will get what is coming to him, may Allah have mercy on us."

Nadifo felt a range of emotions: numbness, sadness, rejection, betrayal. Her heart raced, her eyes ached. She had trouble speaking; when she tried, a fake coarse giggle leapt from her throat.

He had been in her presence only hours earlier; she had not felt any change in him. He had displayed no evidence of being shared. He was as quiet and pleasant as usual, as clumsy and forgetful as the day they married. She had been doing her duties as a wife, having absolutely no idea that she was now a first wife, a pitied second to a fresh, firmer, more vibrant woman. She felt debased, cheated, betrayed, and violated. And yet, one of the first images to come to her mind was that she would have to pretend, act as if she blessed the union, that all was normal in her household. Her anger would not be acceptable; she would be labeled as counter-traditional and weak. Was she really that unpleasant to Cartan now, too old to hold? Unattractive, the immediate anger and hate she felt for Cartan surprised her, as if she was waiting for him to err so she could release ammunition she had been collecting since the first day they married. Her mind went back past the problem at hand, recalling with clarity all the things he has done wrong, all the anger she talked herself out of for one reason or another or to simply keep the peace in her marriage. Her marriage appeared the only stability she had known, the only thing in her life she could hold onto: after they had lost every-thing, it was one of the rare things she still felt happy about when alone, and so she had taken it for granted that even it, the only permanence she had known would be taken away, snatched by a carless woman who would never comprehend the paralyzing trauma she had caused. A dou-ble-timing woman who would never appreciate that she had stolen the only thing an older woman called "her life". Saxarla the co-wife probably had many choices, but she chose to carelessly warm her bed with a man who is so much more than a bed warmer. To Nadifo he is more than a bed warmer, he is—was—her life.

"Nadifo!" the voice cut through her. She had forgotten the women were still standing in the foyer while she drifted into agonizing reality. She could not hide her sadness; and looked into their eyes with an ach-ing stare. She was grateful for their help. She would obviously prefer to hear this news from friends than have it sprung on her unexpectedly by someone else—but that did not mean she would adjust.

"*Insha Allah*, *Allah* shall give me the strength to handle it," she whis-pered. "I trust *Allah*; he has all the answers. *Insha Allah*, all is well," she said trying to sound convincing.

"Sister." Shacni's voice trembled with sympathetic sadness. "Be strong. "We need to go now, but we are here for you any time you need us. Minimize the talk, do not show any sign of *masayr*. Don't let the vile mark of weak female jealousy enter your house! Everyone will look for it. Defy it. Kill it. Do not offer it a space in your heart!" her words stabbed her as Nadifo shook her head affirmative for a promise she

156

knew she would not be able to keep. "Never allow a scorned woman into this blessed dwelling my sister, never do. Cawral'a where is your walking cane?" Shacni looked around to locate the cane.

"Nadifo, be grateful to Allah you are in full health. Look at me, a simple walk becomes a chore!" Cawrala got up, clenching her jaws, holding into the coffee table for support. "Even getting up hurts," she groaned. "They tell me I have something called diabetes, my blood pressure is high. Allah knows I didn't have anything like that when I came to this country, I was healthy! We have never heard of these things at home, now they tell me to stop eating goat meat, rice, and xalwo, instead they want me to graze on green things like lettuce as if I am a goat, and fruits—how can I live on salad and fruit alone? Qamar's husband had his leg cut off, they claimed the disease was the cause. May Allah take them I think these doctors bring the disease to the people—stay away from these doctors, Allah knows I was well when I went to him the first time, now I have all these prescriptions to take," she pointed to the ziplock bag of prescription drugs in her tote.

"Okay, Nadifo show courage and be strong! Ladies, let us be on our way!" Shacni summoned the others and they marched out one by one, disappearing into the damp night, leaving Nadifo alone with the shock they had brought with them.

⸘

The women left, as easily as they have arrived, abandoning Nadifo to herself. It was agonizing to be alone. She felt weak, unable to pull herself up from yet another let-down. Her knees shivered uncontrollably. She sought strength to walk to her bed and bury herself amongst the blankets. But she remembered it was no longer their bed—it was now her bed, the bed Cartan no longer wanted to share with her. Indeed, that bed had already let its rejection be known.

Henna's room proved more inviting, and less judgmental. She ignored the posters of big muscular naked men that adorned the walls.

157

She usually avoided her daughter's room, but now she found herself lying on the floor, awash a sea of the very items she considered sleazy and cheap. She curled up, her legs in her arms, with nothing else protecting her from the bare carpet. She lay there somberly, immersed in deep, painful self-doubt. What did she do wrong? Where did she err? Was it her constant criticism of his ways? Maybe she was too harsh with her words? He had finally given up on her, but why? She was an obedient wife, a spiritual, God-fearing woman. Her lips had never shared unflattering news of her family with outsiders.

Thinking back to their lives in Hamar, she and Cartan have drifted apart, he was busy stroking the president's ego, helping to run the country to the ground while doing things that came with being the foreign minister: such as nightly entertainment complete with all the vices she now viewed as unholy. And she busied herself as the famous wife of the foreign minister, going to nightly women-only parties, where the same immoral acts were committed. She may have never chewed qat or taken a drink, but being a willing witness to these indecencies was then the norm—part of being the elite.

After the war, when they became refugees, they were forced to deal with each other. *Maybe that's what Cartan fled: their daily dealings with each other may have become excessive, but where things so horrible that he had to abandon me?* Her head ached with painful thoughts.

The spark in his eyes had chased away her fears. Theirs was unconventional love: it defied the norm, it was affectionate and endearing in its own ways. She remembers their early life together, when without so many words they decided to be united in marriage—the unspoken ways they began to love each other, in a culture inundated with bitter, unhappy unions. In a culture where women were encouraged to never reveal their innermost feelings for their husbands, and husbands were expected to be tough on their wives and in the rare case a loving husband showed affection, he was perceived as weak. Her life was satisfying because of his weak sense of self. She cared for him, propped him up. She looked forward to serving his every need, to create comfort and love for him. Even if she never approved of his addicted ways, she put up with it. His happiness and needs completed her; it was one of the very few things she lived for. He was an excuse to hurry home.

Now her mind raced; she felt insane, betrayed, and used, a spent autumn leaf drifting aimlessly in the wind.

"Hooyo, why are you in my room?" A loud voice interrupted the quite throb, rather boorishly. "God, what is she doing in here?" Henna thumped the floor with her books, paining Nadifo's already throbbing head.

Nadifo opened her eyes to see her vulgar, half-naked daughter. With loud make up and even louder outfits Nadifo reluctantly realized how fully American culture had ingested Henna. The lewd smell of cheap perfume seeped from her body, a smell Nadifo had come to detest. Nadifo collected her lean body and attempted to stand up from the fetal position she had been curled in for hours. Eyes red, hair tousled, without the usual scarf. Nadifo's face showed signs of aging. She lost her balance moments after the visitors presented her with her new reality, ignorant that their short visit shred to pieces what was left of a once vibrant life.

"Hooyo, are you alright? What is going on?" Henna asked after she reluctantly grabbed Nadifo so she would not hit the floor. Henna did not remember the last time the two were this close, feeling Nadifo's thin, aging body. Nadifo did not resist the contact. She reached out for Henna, holding her close enough as if she was using her to balance her body. Then without warning she did the unthinkable, she hugged Henna, clutching her close like she has often done when she was a little girl. Before the war, when she was innocent and pure. She held her so close Henna found herself reciprocating the embrace, dumbfounded by the entire episode.

"Hooyo, what is wrong? Are you okay?" Henna asked, conflicted by the closeness. Nadifo did not say a word. Then the silence was cut with a razor-sharp wailing, which hurt Henna's ears. Nadifo began to shake and say things Henna did not comprehend.

"Why are all these bibles here? My god, what is happening to you?"

"Aabihii la gub, ma anuu halkaa igaga dhaqaaqaa! Awalba jidh xun buu ahaa! Ilaahow maanta maan dalkaygii joogo, wallee waan dooxi lahaa!"

"Hooyo, who are you talking about? Who are you going to kill, who are you cursing? Why do you have bibles everywhere, who the hell brought these here?" Nadifo did not answer; she released Henna from her tight grip, still crying vigorously. What happened next is what Henna had been trying to prevent from the start: Nadifo collapsed to the floor, but she was conscious, calling out curse words. Then she started pulling her hair; then she sat up and started ripping her clothes off. She began hitting herself, slapping her face, pulling her hair and hitting her chest with massive blows from her tight fist.

"Hey stop that," Henna leveled with Nadifo on the floor. She attempted to grasp Nadifo's hands to make her stop hitting herself. "Stop it hooyo!" she repeated, her shinny made-up face a mask of worry. "What the hell is going on?"

"I can't believe this is my end, *L&R* did this to me!" Nadifo continued the loud mourning as she continued saying unflattering words about Cartan. Henna left the room abruptly, going to the living room. Nadifo heard Henna's pleas to Haybe.

"I don't know what the hell is going on, hooyo is hysterical, and then there are bibles and Christian magazines everywhere!" Henna was now weeping too. Nadifo continued the assault on herself: she was in the living room throwing table lamps, bringing down curtains with force, throwing furniture around. She was full of energy, going into the kitchen and grabbing a large knife.

"Why keep an orderly home, if the cheat does not care anymore?"

"Haybe, I don't know what is going on please come as soon as you can! Oh my God, she has a knife—I think she is going to kill herself! Give me that," Henna forced the knife out of Nadifo's hand. Nadifo did not resist.

"We are doomed, your father left us!" Nadifo rhythmically assaulted different parts of her body, her face, chest, pulling hair, stomping the floor. She tortured her body, letting each hit coincide with the words. Words one uses when one's marriage has unexpectedly melted into the abyss. Words one uses when one blames the world and the universe for the things that go wrong in one's life. She used words that had lain dormant, words waiting to be pulled out from the most excruciating place. She felt as if Cartan reached behind her ear and physically inflicted the most aggravating assault.

"Stop this craziness hooyo, what the hell is wrong with you? Here, talk to Haybe!" Henna handed the phone to Nadifo, who was still throwing curses around as she pulled her hair.

"I can't believe my life is over, I am doomed!" she threw the phone across the room.

"Hello, hooyo," Haybe's voice cut off on the other side.

"Hello, hello? Haybe? Shoot! Thanks a lot, you broke the phone! Hello?! Hello?!"

Polygamy visits noble, holy homes and ravages strong, courageous women. Its indignity makes leftovers of majestic, beautiful women. Their walk begins to stoop. They avoid eye contact, fearing exposure and reminder. Nadifo hoped to move through the streets without any mention of the ugly truth. Yes, the truth was acute: she no longer attended events that had elated her when she felt whole. No more wedding ceremonies to numb the feeling of being a refugee, no more spiritual gatherings to revive the soul; from here on out she would worship in the privacy of her own home. She needed to stay secluded for a while, to dull her senses against the massive rejection of being a first wife. Every time she got used to one bad thing in her life, another bad thing revealed itself. She avoided human contact all together, and sulked alone in silence. In the apartment, the reminders of rejection lingered in every corner. No matter how much she attempted, she could not escape it. People's stares confirmed she had erred—that maybe she deserved it for some reason or another.

Glorious women visited and offered their condolences. For, indeed the night Cartan took another wife Nadifo's old carefree soul was buried, welcoming in it is place a miserable doubtful one, one that had lost her strength and pride to adjust to a baffled life of accepting husband-sharing and bed-swapping. Others came to watch her recede into the emptiness of polygamy. Yet others arrived to receive some wisdom when their own husbands greedily broke their marriage vows.

Women often prayed to God to shield them from the *minyaro* vile— the horrendous ordeal of becoming a first wife.

Nadifo's feet hit the surface below the bed she had been lying on for the past few hours. She felt disconnected from her body, somewhat delirious. She attempted to move, but her feet defied her, refusing the load. All the attempts to keep her family together were failing. Cartan had discarded their life. The noise and commotion that had transpired only hours earlier kept ringing in her head. She was bloated with rage. How could he walk away from the wrinkled life she had so meticulously ironed?

Cartan walked into the apartment, unaware of the news that awaited him in the apartment.

"Naa Nadifo, where are you, what in God's name is going on? Who did this to the place?" he said as he moved about the ransacked apartment, picking the broken lamp off the floor. "Hello, Henna, Bile, where is your mother?" he said, not noticing their shaken demeanor he picked up the broken pieces of a bulb carefully. "Ouch, ouch, what the hell is—" he didn't get to finish his sentence; but run quickly to duck under the dining room table, avoiding the knives, pots and pans that were headed his way. Bile helped Nadifo as she threw all sorts of things at Cartan.

"What is going on? Allah! Naayaa, stop throwing things at me! Ouch! Ouch! Ouch! What is the matter? Waryaa, stop you mother, don't let me beat this woman!"

162

"Stupid skinny Cartan, I hope you rot in hell!" Her speed petrified Henna.

"Oh my God, hooyo, stop it, oh my God you are going to kill him!" Henna said as she tried to restrain Nadifo.

"Ouch! Please, Nadifo stop!" he said, still crouching under the table. She went after him and tried to pull him out, ready to beat on him. She assaulted him with eggs and threw hot water at him. He began to kick her. "Woman, don't touch me again, I swear to Allah you will die by my hands if you don't let go of my leg!" Nadifo tried to pull him out from under the table; she bit his hand while he tried to kick her out of the way. "Akh, uf, naayaa Henna stop her, what is this mess? Bile, waryaa Bile, stop her at once! Waryaa, call Haybe, your mother is gone mad!" she scuffled with Cartan under the table.

"Hello, Haybe? She is acting crazy again, she is beating on him—oh God, they are going to kill him!"

"Hey, I can't hear you the stupid phone is broken."

"Hello? Henna, what the hell is going on?"

"Can you speak up?"

"Hooyo and Bile are beating on Cartan, oh my God!"

"Stop that you asshole!"

"What did she ever do to you, making her cry like this?" Bile said, not understanding the magnitude of the problem.

"Haybe, where the hell are you?"

"Get out you cheater!"

"Haybe, hurry—what? Okay, I will call 911."

"Yeah, get out you cheater!" Bile repeated after Nadifo.

"Bile get the telephone from her, she will call the white people!"

"Give me that, you stupid bitch!"

"Get off me, moron!"

"Allah! My God! My arm is broken! Henna where are you, help, help!" Cartan lay on the floor, giving up as Bile broke his skateboard on him. Bile wrestled him to the floor as he tried to find refuge in the bathroom. Nadifo used a rolling pin to attack whatever part of his body she could. Henna was struggling to free herself from the bed Bile and Nadifo had tied her to when she attempted to call 911. Nadifo went into the kitchen to fetch more things to use on Cartan: it was only after she heard the knock on the door that she changed her mind and headed for the bathroom room instead.

"Look what you made me do aabo!" Bile sat in a corner, crying. "I hate you all, I wish I was dead" Bile looked pitiful as Haybe entered the apartment to calm things down.

Nadifo was glad she created the fear of God in Cartan. Cartan did not brave any visits after Nadifo broke his arm. They threatened each other back and forth for couple of months. Each threatening the other with a justice system neither understood. She said she would report his polygamy and he threatened to press charges. But the threats remained threats. Nadifo never asked for divorce either, fearing the stigma that would accompany such a crude act at her advanced age. They remained married in name only.

Cartan gathered his legs on the floor in front of the plastic covered rustic low table with a colorful plate of spaghetti and lamb stew. He rested his right arm draped in a cast on a pillow on his lap. Large white gauze with dots of blood covered his forehead. He peeled a banana, holding one side of it in his mouth to ease the peel with his left hand. He mixed the banana with the food as Henna and Shirwac entered the apartment.

Clothes and toys were scattered all over the floor. Children of all ages rummaged through the apartment. The place resembled a day-care center, not a home. A tall, attractive female with a fat protruding stomach emerged from the corridor. Draped in a blue glimmering diric, Saxarla offered polite greetings to the visitors. Five children roamed around the overcrowded apartment. Some of the children cried; some smeared food meant for their mouths on the carpet and walls and yet others lay lazily next to a loud TV set in one corner of the living room. Their mother continually asked them to be quiet between phone conversations, which lasted the entire visit. Cartan ignored the uproar; his attention on the plate of food. He was not particularly enjoying it, as much as he was trying to avoid the little floating bodies of dirty, loud children.

The apartment reeked of soggy diapers, puke, and old food. Snot and phlegm found its way from the children's noses onto their upper lips and hands, and cheeks, not to mention the furniture and walls. Shirwac was determined not to touch any of them; he leaned against an empty wall, as far away from the children as possible.

Noise blasted from a small radio pressed against Cartan's ear. Once every so often he would ask at the children to calm down so that he could hear the radio better. When they continued the noise, he put aside the radio to shovel more food into his mouth and press his ear more firmly against the speaker.

"How are you feeling, aabo?" Henna asked as she inspected his face, lightly touching the gauzed area. He moved his head to avoid the touch, then ignored her, appearing bothered to see her. "*Aabo*, this is Shirwac," Henna began introducing her son, aware that she was disturbing Cartan's routine.

"Hmm." was all she got in return. Perhaps his full mouth restricted conversation. Shirwac received no acknowledgment from his grandfather, but Saxarla, with her expanding belly, kindly spoke welcoming words to him. Cartan continued eating, never looking at Shirwac.

"Shirwac, say hello to your *awoowe*," Henna beckoned. As Shirwac was about to speak, Cartan purposefully turned away and increased the volume on the radio.

"*Awoowe*," Shirwac said without moving toward the old man, to show his respect.

"Hello, Shirwac," Cartan mumbled in an offhand way while shaking his left hand free of food remains, not even looking up.

"*Aabo*, I came here to ask you for a favor."

"What do you want? Did she send you here?"

"No, *Aabo*. Can we go into the other room?"

"No, I don't need to hear anything any of you have to say!" he said while chewing his food loudly.

"*Aabo*, I think you shouldn't press charges against her, you made her angry," Henna said speaking quietly so Saxarla would not hear their conversation.

"*Naayaa*, you came here to tell me what to do? Who the hell you think you are?!" he said pushing the plate away from him. "Did that crazy woman send you here?"

"No, *Aabo*, she does not know I am here. I just think you should go on with your life and leave her alone—the last thing she needs is a police record or to go to jail."

"She deserves to go to jail! That crazed woman—do you see what she did to me?" he got up to show Henna his wounds.

"I know, Dad, she shouldn't have done that, if—"

"If nothing! I am glad we are in a country where there are laws against assault!"

"But if you press charges she will tell the authorities you are married to two women."

"She can never prove it."

"Yes, she can. Your wife is pregnant."

"So what? People here have children without being married all the time."

"But you are a Muslim, you are not supposed to have a child out of wedlock."

"The authorities don't care about our customs; I will tell them Saxarla is my girlfriend."

"What? That is disgusting! God, how demented!"

"Naayaa, I have my plans. Go and tell your mother I will press charges against her."

"Great, just what I need, both of my parents in jail. Just great, Dad, go on and press charges! You will both end up in jail!" As Saxarla poured sugary Mango Tang into dirty glasses for Henna and Shirwac, a little girl ran against Shirwac's leg, her bare bottom dripping. Shirwac decided not to drink the juice. Maybe Cartan had confused Shirwac for one of the rowdy kids in the apartment, he reasoned, or maybe he simply did not care to meet him.

Cartan signaled to Saxarla that he had finished, prompting her to bring a bowl of warm water to wash his greasy hand. He submerged his greasy hand, covered with little flecks of food, into the bowl as she poured dishwashing detergent directly onto it. He lifted his greased hand out of the oily, stained bowl. She toweled off his bony hand, splashed cologne from a bottle that read "if you like Obsession you will love Possession" and handed him a toothpick to pluck the remains in his teeth. Cartan extended his gangly legs comfortably on the floor and indicated that he was ready to listen to his daughter.

A naked little boy, about four, knocked the drinks off the table. Cartan barely seemed to notice. The spill remained on the table and floor while Saxarla continued her phone call and Cartan listened to the radio absent-mindedly. Henna was forced to attend to the spill, gathering up the broken glasses. Henna pretended to be similarly indifferent to the scene—the weary old man, the overwhelmed laid-back woman who appeared to have given up any hope of control in her life, the disgusting apartment—silently she wondered why everyone put up with this life.

Shirwac wondered why Cartan, with an obedient strong wife who kept her home straight and orderly, would stay in Saxarla's disgusting apartment. He learned later, however, that Nadifo had refused to allow Cartan to return home, and threatened to inform the authorities of his polygamy. Cartan had been hiding out at Saxarla's apartment ever since.

Saxarla, which means "the flawless one", had five children from two previous marriages. She was twenty-nine, thirty-nine years Cartan's junior, and looked more like a daughter to him than a wife. Although young, her body already displayed signs of fatigue. She was now pregnant with her sixth child, her first with Cartan.

She was kept busy with various female visitors and phone calls, neither attending to the children nor acknowledging Cartan's discomfort. It seemed that Cartan and Saxarla made decisions based not on their desire for a certain kind of life, but on the various cultural pressures, although neither appeared to accept the life that came of these decisions. No one had really noticed when Henna and Shirwac left. The apartment held many antagonistic worlds together, each determined to exist independently.

CLEMENCY FOR
THE BAFFLED

The grey Minneapolis skies bloated with stubborn rain. The dull day made the already miserable-looking streets intense. The skies promised a wet day, while humidity and still air made walking a chore.

Amy summoned her class to meet in a new location on Lake Street. The busy intersection of Lake and Lyndale sizzled with men at work, pedestrians and cars alike. Old brick buildings erected with a beat up and weary aura made the otherwise friendly city unreceptive. Amy selected this location, the main city library, to expose her student to the concept of library research. It took Nadifo an hour to find the location. She flipped through highlighted bus schedules and city maps. She could never understand these bus schedules; there was no point in wasting her time to deciphering them, so Haybe had come over the previous night to explain the route she was to take the next morning. He spent what seemed like hours to explain bus schedules and routes. Amy purposefully chose this location an area out of ways so Nadifo and other students in the class would embark on finding the location on their own. Haybe offered to drive Nadifo to the library but she refused, opting instead for three bus rides. It was an attempt to prove to Amy and others who doubted her that she could find any location in the city if she so chose. Nadifo sat at the end of a massive gleaming white table where three other women sat detailing their frustration at getting to come to class. The vibrant city library burst with fresh gold and orchid colors. Contemporary art hung from the walls, ceilings and virtually any space that would support it. Perspiring pedestrians came in off the hot humid street to the cool air-conditioned library. The onlookers passed Nadifo without a glance, except today they appeared at ease, gazing at art canvases, statues, exhibits and woven baskets in the lobby. The sound coming from an elusive saxophone player in the lobby distracted Nadifo; she almost passed the assigned room, The Mandela Renaissance room. The library had rooms named after great world leaders. Nadifo passed the Gandhi Tolerance Room, The Carter Peace Room and Malcolm X Technology Center to get to the assigned location.

Amy wore a white blouse with a red and white flared embroidered skirt. Her white sandals revealed delicate, well-cared-for, French manicured feet. Her flawless appearance blended well with the well lit room of purple desks and white chairs. Amy's succulent feminine scent of jasmine flowers, strawberry and lime overtook the room, inviting Nadifo's otherwise dull senses.

Amy held a book in her hand explaining to the ten women present (there were usually twenty) methods of research. As they listened to the lecture which mostly went over their heads, they noticed Amy's demeanor. She was not her usual animated self: she moved lethargically, contradictory to her unblemished exterior and alluring smell. Over all she appeared as if she was forced to be with them.

"Okay, ladies, if we were to look up, for example, George Bush on the internet, what would we—" Chatter overtook her attempt to explain internet research. Aasho, a stylish woman not much older than her, was the loudest.

"Aasho did you want to answer that?" Amy asked.

"He kill women and children." Asho said with a raspy voice.

"Who killed woman and—?"

"He, your Bush."

"Okay, Aasho, but we are only discussing methods of research in the internet, not our political opinions about Bush."

"Yes, but he is killer, racist, right?" The usually timid Amina surprised Amy with the comment. "He hate Muslim people, like us."

"Amina, Aasho, ladies I am not here to discuss George Bush."

"But he kill innocent people!"

"Okay, okay, ladies I understand that was not a good topic for research. Let us pick a different topic." Amy bewildered her students; they found her to be a paradoxical figure. On one hand she had given up so much of her life to teach English to these illiterate refugee women—she'd given up a six figure salary as Vice President for Market Research at Wellner and McGuire, an advertising agency, she took an extended leave to teach women like Nadifo the ins and outs of American culture. Amy would receive only half her usual salary; the rest went to fund various programs, such as the ESL class Nadifo attended, administered by The African in US, a nonprofit organization which raised funds to teach English to African women and girls around the world. The NGO also installed latrines in rural villages in Africa.

She picked this charity after she read an article in the New York Times where female students in Mali would miss a week of school every month when they were on their menses. The schools were not equipped with latrines where these girls could change and clean themselves, so they were kept at home where such things could be done. Female teachers also missed a week of school a month for the same reason. Amy organized volunteers and involved big corporations to donate school supplies, pads, and building materials for the latrines. Every summer she visited Nopti and Mara, the two villages she chose to support. She even had pictures of her initiation ceremony in room 32C at the community center along with other pictures of students in her class. In the ceremony Amy appeared pale among the girls that danced around her. She sat in the middle of the group with a deep green Erykah Badu head wrap and a bright brown and cream *Bogolan*.

She knew all their names, and repeated them to Nadifo every opportunity she got: Kady Mousa, Tata Yacouba, Rokia Trore, Fatou Diarra, Aicha Cheick, and Aissata Fode, who was graduating from high school this year. She had plans to stay in touch with these girls and assure their success in college. Every summer she traveled to the village to teach them English.

She had developed close relationships with her students in this class as well; she knew virtually everything about their lives, their family situations, their needs and constantly sought ways to make their lives easier. When Nadifo first came to America it was Amy who bought the first tape recorder so Nadifo could send taped messages to her sister Hawo. She made sure each of her students had a computer at home. Amy made their difficult refugee lives easier.

The way Amy took her time to get involved with people who were so far removed from her upbringing and daily life astounded Nadifo. Why would anyone spend so much precious time on people they knew nothing about? Was it out of self importance to feel good about themselves—Americans sometimes wanted to feel good about something—or was it genuine? And yet Amy is an unhappy woman. Some days she is gloomy, depressed, and talks about killing herself. She hates the way she looks, and how she feels. Amy often plans hiking and camping trips to escape the bustle of the city. She would go to Indian Breeze, way up in the mountains to get in touch with nature. She would take the bare minimum with her and stay on the campground for the entire weekend. This Nadifo could not relate to—of all the things she found odd with Amy, planning a trip to go to the wilderness for an entire weekend by herself seemed altogether pointless. Nadifo grew up in the kind of environment Amy escaped to, the place where she sought solace. Being a village girl she remembers wanting to escape nature and it is surrounds. She wanted to see the lights of the city, the stir of city life. She was glad when Cartan rescued her from Gobwanaag: it was one of the best things that had ever happened to her. Hunger, the limitation of endless laboring and animal husbandry is all she remembered of her youth in the countryside. Now Amy plans elaborate schemes of escaping to a place Nadifo would not want to be found dead in, let alone visit—the countryside. Amy often talked about the burden of society that she wished to strip everything that society has saddled on her. Amy wanted to lose "Amy" and find in her place another person less fraught with expectations, tittles and status. She wanted to strip away society's pressures.

Nadifo could not understand exactly what Amy meant when she said "I am trying to find myself." What part of her was lost? Nadifo dismissed all of Amy's ways as spoiled people's ways of justifying an abundant life. They had so much, and yet wanted less—sometimes they wanted to have nothing, rejecting families, assets, friends to find themselves. It was mystifying, and Nadifo had stopped trying to make sense of it.

On depressed, blue days when Amy simply wanted to end her struggle with life, she spent the entire class period talking of things the women could not relate to. Amy's blue days coincided with the visits she would latter have with her shrink.

Her problems consisted mainly of her disappointment with her life. While Nadifo and other women in the class stumbled on life never knowing where they were, why they were there and what would become of their lives, Amy was concerned with her fattening belly which to them looked extremely malnourished, and her disappointment with men. Through her constant chatter the women felt as though they had met every man Amy has ever dated. After every date she would come to class announcing how Elijah, Ian, or Skyler did not call after their first date, or how one or another of these men stood her up, or that they feared the word "commitment". The women actually formed opinions about Amy's dates.

She lived with Cornell, her boyfriend of three years—a concept her students did not understand—she had complained that he had a problem binding to her in marriage. Sometimes after class she went into long drawn details of the reason Cornell was afraid of marriage: he said he was not sure she was the one he would want to spend an entire life with, he simply wanted to wait. She sobbed as she told the story, patting away tears from her red cheeks. Nadifo burst out, saying something Amy could not understand. Nadifo made the comments to the other women in Somali, appearing displeased.

"Nadifo, did you say something?" Amy asked, blowing her discoloring nose.

"No, nothing." Nadifo said, writing something on the book in front of her.

"Please share your ideas with the class." Amy sat up at the edge of her desk, as she dropped the tissue into the waste basket.

"Amy, Cornell no marry you, ever," Nadifo startled Amy with her quick response.

"What does that mean?" Amy tried to hide her surprise. "Why? Nadifo, why do you say that?"

"Why he buy milk when he has cow?" Nadifo said, frowning.

"What are you talking about, Nadifo?" Amy's demeanor changed.

"You free, Amy—men, they don't like free woman." The other women chuckled.

"He touch you, another man touch you, then no money for you when marry."

"What money? What touch are you talking about?"

"When men touch you too much, no money for your family"

"Nadifo, in this country we do not value a woman that way." Amy was angry, but tried to contain her anger.

"Amy, woman is cheap and no *meher* for her if she cheap with many men."

"What is *Meher*?"

"You know, the money for girl family when marry."

"Oh, you mean dowry."

'Yes when girl pure, no man touch, money a lot. But when girl go with this and that one, no money for her family and everybody say she bitch."

"But we don't have dowries here."

"That is why women here cheap." Amy went quiet for a long moment. Her face was blank; the women could not read her expression, whether she was in deep muddled thought or ignoring the insult. She paced back and forth as if trying to choose her words carefully. The room went quiet, the women fretful. Nadifo flipped her journal, making the only noise in the room.

"Nadifo, did you leave your feelings in Hamar or something?" The outburst from Amy was quick, and unexpected. "You know what? I don't even see you as 'them', no, no, no—I see you as Aamina, Aasho, Nadifo." Her pace quickened; she was looking directly at them. "Why the accusatory look, Nadifo? All of you, what you dislike my skirt! Is it too short for your taste? Do I look like Bush's keeper, must we all share the sins of his actions? Come on, ladies, what does one have to do to prove to you we are trying? I get it, I know—whatever the hell my government is doing is inhumane. But I try, God knows I try. It isn't fair, give me a break. Your eyes, Nadifo—I don't like that look. Do I look like a slut to you huh?" She went over to her, imposing her petite figure over Nadifo.

"Amy, take easy" Nadifo felt obliged to say something. Amy's reaction came as a shock.

"I can't help it if I like men to sleep with me." She was now next to Amina, who looked the other way. "It was never a sin for me before, but nowadays I am actually trying to curb my desires for men a little, because of the way you guys look at me, every time I talk about my dates."

"No Amy, we no like that, please me no...." Nadifo got up and attempted to sit Amy down. She could hear Amy's intense breathing; she knew she was very angry.

"Actually Nadifo, Amina, Ha-ha-amilmo or however the hell you say your name, my virginity is not all that special, it doesn't deserve all that freaking money yours is worth" Amy moved Nadifo's hand away. "Good for you, yours is worth a million freaking bucks. Good for you!"

"Amy please, I am sorry like that." The other woman were now surrounding Amy, who sat at the head desk, sobbing.

"Why does it matter anyway—the one who paid a million bucks for yours left with another woman who didn't get a penny for hers, didn't he, Nadifo?" Nadifo looked at the other women, surprised Amy made her case public —some of the other women did not know Cartan had taken a wife.

"Sit ladies, sit, Amy calm." Nadifo tried to disburse the women, hoping to make them forget what they just heard.

"Jesus!" Amy was now collecting all her books from the desk. "After all, we are the same—eventually all men leave, eventually they all do! I know you find my books odd." She threw the books to the floor. "Yes Nadifo, this one tells me how to handle my relationships." She kicked one of the books. "This one how to be happy with my body; this one how to handle my anxiety—and yes, don't forget the one that tells me how to stay calm. I need them to actually survive this shitty life!" Some of the women started leaving, whispering something to Nadifo.

"Making fun of Mr. Wiener, my shrink. You pay that man all that money to feel good? Yes, yeeees I do. I am actually under a lot of pressure from you, from these brainless books, and magazines, from society. And Mr. Wiener, he is a blessing." She began screaming as if to get the point across. "This freaking best seller tells me I am too fat. "5 foot 8, 125 pounds, and yes I am ten pounds too fat, according to this book" she threw a book entitled *Achieve Your Ideal Weight In Ten Days* on Nadifo's desk. "Unacceptable, too fat, too pale, too this and too that." She erased the board and picked up her handbag. Before she dashed out of the room she had one more thing to share with them. Amy pulled some prescription drugs out of her bag. "Look, these are my downers, these, my uppers and those I take in between when I am not exactly sure if I am up or down. "Okay, happy? That is my pathetic life—nothing without all these" she threw the prescriptions into her bag. "I have enough judgment around me; I certainly don't need any from you." And with that Amy left the room, still sobbing. She left all her books scattered on the floor.

ANCHOR OF ASSEMBLY

At ten, Shirwac's dark glowing complexion is already handsome, but his delicate face is distorted by a thick scar on his cheek. He approached the apartment gingerly. The dry winter day outside exaggerated the dots of ice that graced the apartment's living room window.

Burgundy and gold fabric hangs over every window, creating a shadowy ambiance. The sweet burnt-sugar scent of *bukhuur* competed with the aromas of agar wood, amber, sandalwood and attar oils. The familiar, heavenly aromas captured his imagination. The incense smoke from the burner lingered, sending up circular swirls of scent. Trendy furniture joined various colors and shapes in a fluid rhythm creating a *gaari* sensation. The entire apartment shined with pristine neatness. Calligraphic renditions of Quran verses covered a black canvas with gold trimmings; red, yellow and pink plastic flowers are mounted on the dining room walls between two large golden portraits of the al-Aqsa Mosque. Fluffy deep green rugs blanket the floors of the apartment.

Shirwac often wondered why he had spent years away from the family who had unexpectedly reclaimed him. He did not ask any questions when asked to join them, but he wondered as he obediently accepted their sudden invitation. Tusmo told him that he had a mother, grandmother, uncles, an aunt and cousins in America. A slew of new family members came into his life somewhat abruptly, ready to claim him.

He was incredibly excited, having just arrived a few months earlier from the refugee camp, and then finding a family of his own. Shirwac felt the burden of newness. From the second he stepped on that enormous plane in Jomo Kenyatta Airport, life had become surreal. As he entered the apartment, his new family sat right in front of him. Many faces appeared before him, some bewildered, some elated, some expressionless.

Nadifo waited anxiously for this living painful memory to re-emerge. Memories she had forced away now clouded her throbbing head. His presence brought confusion and the memory of horror: the loss of her son, the destruction of her country, the violence against her daughter, the obliteration of family honor. He embodied everything that she so desperately wanted to bury. She could not now reject his arrival, however; not because she did not want to but out of fear of Allah. Refusing a human being, especially a blood relation, would be unacceptable to *Allah*. Nadifo was in deep thinking the entire time.

Shirwac, an anchor of assembly, this is what his adoptive family had named him, she pondered privately. *But he is far from that.* She wondered why they had called him that. He was the mediator of extremes— love and hate, sorrow and opportunity. To Nadifo he is an immaculate myth, a faulty beginning, a seed of pollutants; a child of mystery, his name should be Shirwac *Qahar*, or Shirwac *Shar*.

She examined him warily, searching for imperfections, any marks he might have carried from the night he was violently brought into existence. She scrutinized him, showing her repulsion. If she was not being scolded, she would have searched for the ugly marks herself.

Instead of the ugly remnants of the assault her daughter suffered at fourteen, Nadifo noticed his resemblance to Cartan and Geele. She tried to accept both his familiarity and his otherness, although it proved impossible. His ghostly presence provided a constant reminder of what she had lost. *He is a bad luck child*, she murmured in the safety of her own mind, but the words passed her lips inadvertently.

Shirwac did not understand the constant scrutiny from his new family. He decided that perhaps it was the way of families who have been parted by war. He took the excitement, cold looks and continues examination as a warm gesture, a welcome for a child who has rejoined a lost family. That is how Tusmo would explain the situation. She fed him the fabrication he needed to hear, that his family lost him. But in reality Shirwac would come to find out the reality of his life was much more tragic than just getting lost.

He would miss the family he'd grown up with, the only people who had ever loved him, but he understood that he had to merge with his blood family. People had spoken in hushed voices around him, now it all made sense to him. He was a lost child, not an abandoned one, as his neighbor Cambaro once confessed. She said harsh words to him, saying that at birth he had never received the welcoming Quranic prayers, that he had never had any family members to celebrate the *gardaadis* ritual ceremony. She told him that was the reason he was all alone, that he was a bastard!

He was a child of Satan, she had told him once. It was too cumbersome for his mystified mind to comprehend what it meant. He simply rejected it all. He believed if he pushed it away from his mind, it would not become him.

Finally, his lost family was here to proudly count him among them. They could finally do all the things that he had missed at birth, maybe even his gardaadis ritual could now resume.

No longer would *garac* refer to him, he supposed. These were terms reserved for him as he was growing up in the refugee camp. Tusmo relentlessly assured other children who called him these names that he was *Alle keen*. Tusmo admitted that he was indeed an extraordinary child. He never saw anyone ask about him and so in private, he knew this was because he was an unwanted child. He had witnessed too much in his short life, and now he was happy to finally meet the long lost family who wanted him back.

Haybe appeared the most happy to see him. He extended his long arms tenderly to receive the boy. "Shirwac, welcome home, *abti*, look at you!" Haybe exclaimed going over his face. "You are a handsome young man."

"Hello abti," Shirwac eagerly returned the embrace, much as a boy would with his father, finally resting his cheeks against Haybe's muscular stomach. Shirwac felt at home. Haybe hugged the boy very tightly, inspecting his face, kissing his soft cheeks and running his hands along the deep scar. The smell of sweet musk cologne filled Shirwac's nose, calming him. Haybe's chin was rough and scratchy, but comforting. His wet, smoky lips graced Shirwac's forehead and cheeks repeatedly.

Shirwac looked around the room. There were many people smiling, welcoming him, but the elderly woman, she is his grandmother he is told, rebuked him with her stare, her face lined with misery and sadness. She looked at him as if she wished he would melt away. He looked away from her uneasy piercing.

She did not seek his embrace and kept mumbling Quran in a soft tone, moving her lips from side to side, as if to keep Satan at bay, asking *Allah* to bless their household as if Satan had entered it. Her henna-colored fingers vigorously beat the rosary in her hand.

"Allah please forgive me for asking, but if this child is bad luck, please take him back. Forgive me of my sins, Allah; I must have angered you enormously. I beg to pay the price here and spare my soul in the hereafter. I shall offer two protestation of sin forgiveness, bowing to you. Allah take him away, I beg of you!" She wanted to say it out loud, but kept it in the silence of her mind.

Henna stood there admiring him, although this was not their first encounter. She gave him room to meet the rest of the family, reserving her embraces for later. Her gaze towards him appeared empathetic. The overwhelming anguish that she had experienced at their first meeting had by now receded. She regretted she had not met him sooner. Suddenly she felt the loss he felt: they were both victims of a horrible crime. They would have to learn to face their challenges together, she thought as she marveled at his eagerness to meet the family.

Even in his joy, Shirwac felt tense. He doubted the reality of his new-found luck, thinking grudgingly that any second this would all cease to exist. Nothing was permanent in his avant-garde life. He knew only destruction. Good things in his life eventually ceased.

Shirwac had been in the same refugee camp as his own mother, but Nadifo made sure they never crossed paths. They stayed in Iffo for three years waiting to come to America, and for three years Nadifo made sure her family members would never cross paths with him.

⟊⟊⟊

His earliest recollections of life were at Iffo refugee camp. His onset of life was set deep within the carnage of war and marked by extraordinary shame. He was left under a tree in the middle of war, abandoned by a girl running away from the stains of shame.

He lay cold and untouched, suckling grief. He longed for a mother's touch. Awoken daily by the constant growl of hunger, he sought warmth in the bosom of dusty cold floors, his usual resting place every night. He felt nothing but sorrow and numbness. Shirwac's first steps were punctuated by the violation of thorns piercing his bare feet around the camp. All he knew about his life was that people spoke around him in whispers and that he lived with people who were not his parents. Shirwac learned the flight instinct early on in the refugee camp. He was named after Shirwac Madoobe, a hundred-and-one-year old elder who survived the war after he was stabbed but passed away at the refugee camp. Shirwac was the first to find the old man dead, and so he was named after him.

His blistered feet traveled many miles to search for food and water. He would gather wood to sell so that he could buy food. He constantly begged for food, and often he went for days without. Many called him *agoon.* He never understood what that meant, but he took advantage of it when people he did not know gave him food or took care of him. He witnessed violence, beatings and killings. This was the only life he knew.

As he walked home one day, he came upon the bodies of his neighbors Cali, Siciid, and Axmed Xareed under a tree. They lay in fresh wet pools of their own blood. They had not been dead long. He did not cry, or get scared; he went through their clothes to search for money or anything else of value. He found some cash that fed his distended belly for a few days, a watch which he sold, and a leather wallet. "Their luck had run out" he said to himself. That is what everyone said when someone died, it was their time to go and face Allah. He wondered who would go next, and how they would meet their end. He had a callous view of death and enjoyed being the first to report it. He loved seeing the reaction of adults when they heard someone had just passed: The fear in their eyes delighted him. Tusmo warned him to stop reporting bad news, but he wanted to be the first, it was the only time he had gotten attention.

One sunny afternoon Sulekha asked that he accompany her to gather wood from *Dhuxul Cad*. Sulekha was his favorite *eeddo*, although he knew they were not related by blood. She took a keen interest in him, caring for him as much as her own children. He hopped behind her, excitement and nervous anticipation widening his large brown eyes.

Sulekha forged ahead, saluting friends, halting briefly to gather tales and on occasion to catch up on the latest gossip. Along the way, others joined the expedition. The dusty bare gravel road erupted with excited children who would chase anything that moved. Graceful women and girls steadied buckets of water on their heads. One woman pushed a wheelbarrow with heavy sacks of grain. She balanced the baby on her back with the load, appearing at ease as if she settled her fate. Men stood around talking, uninterested. Shirwac lumbered behind the women, playing as he listened to their stories and gossip. He may have to repeat some of it later, he thought to himself. Information was gold at the camp. Often, it was his only means of survival.

They came upon *Dhuxul Cad*, but it was sparse, almost barren. Only discarded, spoiled wood remained, not enough to heat an evening meal, so they walked another three miles or so to *Qudhac Dheer*, which had more wood. Notorious for its predators, most women did their best to avoid it. It had caused the tragic end of many at the camp. He helped the best he could, gathering little scattered pieces on the ground while the women went deep into the bush to heap more sturdy wood that would last for a few days. With uncanny speed, six men emerged with their weapons drawn. Chaos broke out as the women scattered to save themselves. They forgot about him.

One very homely man attacked Sulekha with great cruelty. She did not give in easily, as she had done so many times before. This time she ran as fast as she could, throwing the firewood behind her to impede the attacker's progress. Shirwac hid behind a bush. Another man ran from the opposite direction and wrestled Sulekha to the ground; she knew at that point that it was the end. The man salivated with excitement as he violently tore her clothes off, revealing her willowy, shivering frame. He violated her with the speed only much practice can bring. Shirwac's eyes filled with painful water; disgust moved his gut to compress, expelling thick slime from his mouth into his own legs. Other men caught up with the homely man and took their turns. Three men had raped Sulekha when her wide-open eyes fogged with death, her unrelenting body went stiff, and a trickle of bloody vomit escaped from her screaming jaws. She had ducked similar death before; they finally took her the way she had prayed not to go. Shirwac's entire soul seemed to have passed through him at the sight. He tried to shout, but no sound came from his throat; he fell to his knees trembling and shaking hysterically.

By the time Shirwac had the strength to stand, the men were gone, leaving Sulekha's unclothed corpse. Shirwac shook her body, begging her to not go. He was not ready. Her's were the only familiar hands that had touched his infected feet, the ones that healed the discolored lesions, still on his body.

Sulekha would never go to the bushes without him; she even said that he was her man. She stroked his juvenile male ego, telling him that she felt safe with him, that he would protect her from the evil maniacs in the bushes: but now he had failed her.

He was still laying, his head on her stomach, when he felt hard drops. The sky, dressed in its bluest blue, darkened, bled sour drops that pounded him like thousands of tiny fists. His exhausted spirit died with hers. When people arrived to collect her body, they mistook him for yet another heavenly soul that had departed this earth. They were lowering the two into a shallow grave when his frail sobs broke the somber silence.

Shirwac's face had run against the sharp edges of the bush when he fell to his knees in disgust as he watched Sulekha take her last breath. The trunk he fell against had ripped his face open, although he had not noticed it at the time. Tusmo alerted him to the wound, telling him that he was marked for life. "What exactly does that mean, *eeddo*—marked for life?" he would ask her. She pretended not to hear him and he pretended not to care. He was six years old.

That week fever and pain threw him into convulsions. He found lesions on his stomach. Tusmo awaited his death as his little body shook violently as if to vomit his soul. She confessed that she did not think his fragile body would handle the deadly attacks. It did. The wounds somehow healed themselves. He awoke from every violent shake.

———

Shirwac smiled, revealing the elation he felt in his heart through his gleaming, toothy smile. When Henna had first visited him in Tusmo's home, he was unmoved. After all, there were too many new additions in his life—a new country, a new language, new peoples who looked so different, and now a new mother. Frankly, Shirwac was overwhelmed. The woman who Tusmo introduced as his mother was not much older than him. She looked very similar to Tusmo's teenage daughters, although she dressed much more provocatively. How could anyone so youthful have birthed a boy his age? It was all too surreal. But Shirwac received her well; it would have been rude not to. She was pleasant, loving; their first embrace was filled with tears, hugs, and sniffles. She seemed consumed with grief. She sat him on her lap and made so many promises. He knew it was her emotion talking, she promised too much. She promised not to leave him ever again. He was confused; did she leave him on purpose the first time?

The following visits were much easier to handle. By this time, they were more familiar with each other, and Shirwac was no longer shy. Actually, he looked forward to seeing her. She would take him to fun places and teach him how to play video games. They spent two Saturdays by themselves, well almost by themselves, except there was a man, a foreigner, with them. Shirwac was apathetic toward him, a white man named Brian. Shirwac ignored him, not understanding his presence. It was just as well that they did not understand to each other. The man looked like Mr. Mathew in the refugee camp. Mr. Matt, as he liked to be called was the nicest white person Shirwac has ever seen. Mr. Matt was responsible for bringing food to them. He brought toys and candy. Brian looked like the people at the camp who came to visit them and then left them with their misery—the people who brought hope for them and then vanished with it. He did not have to pretend to understand this person; he was confused as to why Henna was with him. Maybe he was her teacher or co-worker. Brian said things that went past him like a fast wind.

Now Henna stood there sheepishly, grinning. Her eyes followed him across the room, as if she were proud to present him to her family. She was beautifully put together, not the type of mother Shirwac was used to seeing. He was used to the diric-wearing type that looked old, like a grandmother, the kind that ordered kids around and spanked them when they caused mischief. Henna was a kid herself. She would not discipline him or reprimand him. They were more like a brother and a sister, not a mother and a son. On this visit the stranger, Brian, was not with Henna.

Shirwac noticed a small person like himself in the room, Idil; she was around his age, but she was a girl. He could not play with her; she would not know how to do boy things. She said "hi." He has been told to say "Hi" back so he did. Other than this greeting, they did not exchange much. She was eager to show him something outside; he was confused and did not want to follow her, but Henna said it was ok to go with her, so he did.

She said so much in English that he could not understand. He only shook his head to demonstrate that he had heard what she was saying.

"Do you want to go to the park?" Idil asked anxiously, looking inquisitively at her new cousin. Shirwac looked confused and finally said,

"I do not wish to play with a girl; you are a girl. Let me go back inside; you find some girls to play with. I am a boy." Now she was confused.

"Are you coming or not? Mom, he is not playing with me!"

"Where is your brother? I hear that you have a brother. I want to play with your brother. Shame on you running in the streets; you are a girl. Go back inside and call your brother to play with me," Shirwac ordered her sternly.

"Mom, he is saying something weird!" Idil said confused, when Warsan asked Henna to the rescue,

"Shirwac, she wants to play with you and take you to the playground," she broke it to him slowly.

"I do not wish to play with a girl! Where is her brother?" snapped Shirwac. Shirwac could not understand a place where girls played boy games. Everything here was strange. Even the people were odd looking, like cold, white ice.

RELENTLESS AND DEVIOUS

Nadifo found less and less time to send taped messages to Hawo, and their communication became sporadic. Like Americans she found time a precious commodity. It was the only way she could get stuff off her chest, although she would not share everything with Hawo. Details of her kids, such as Henna's break with tradition and Warsan's problems with her husband, remained secret. Even between sisters there must remain some secrets. This is how she began her message on this particular day:

APRIL 6, 2002.

Dear sister Hawo: I embrace you with the most delicate love and best regards. We all send greetings as sweet as honey. I hope that Allah will sprinkle abundance on you and your family.

My life has become a surreal saga of self-denigration. I reside among the vain—a nation obsessed with its appearance. My bewilderment is justified, as I am bombarded with loud ads, displaying undignified women who are used by all to advertise products. Advertisements fill all types of spaces, it is constant and cleverly done and it works. After seeing them on TV I find myself buying the products, only to find out they do not perform as well as they do on TV. They even convinced me although you and I both know I am not fooled that easily. It happened when I saw an ad on TV about a magic mop which the advertisement promised would magically lift all the dirt from the kitchen and bathroom floors. I hurried to the store to assure a magic mop for my house. I dragged little Bile along, although he was reluctant to come with me.

After I brought it home the magic mop was nothing more than few flimsy materials thrown together in haste. It did not lift anything from the floors. I still had to bend down and lift the dirt myself while the magic mop lazily sat on the exact same corner I put it, not once moving itself and doing the magic like the TV ad promised it would.

Sister, I witness as my children willingly emulate the people here. The children here in America are confused, selfish, and materialistic. Parents no longer discipline their children because of something called 911. This number, which the children have memorized, scares parents away from parenting. Once children has called this number, people from the government come and take all the children in the family away. Because of this number children talk back to their parents, do whatever they like and are untamed.

I am disgusted by how selfish my children have become. Indeed, we are doomed. This generation will never look after us and take care of their extended family. They will squander their money purchasing the latest of everything and pretend to be American.

As I emerge from my home into the larger world, my world, as I know it begins to fade away. Sister, I stumble through blank streets, pass vague faces. Nobody knows my name. I walk wondering, do they think I am a terrorist? Do they think I keep bombs under this hijab? Do they hate me? If I were in danger, would they help me, or would they walk past me?

I hope the little money that I sent was helpful for the ciid celebration. Please sacrifice a lamb for me, may be Allah will bless this house once again. Pray for my children. I think I have lost them; I no longer recognize them. Also pray for our people who are wandering aimlessly in Gaalo-lands. They came looking for paradise but ended up doing menial work which the Gaalo do not want to do. They pretend to be alive, but in reality they are dead inside. A walking dead if you ask me!

CORRIDOR CANDOR

Ceebla means the perfect one, one without faults. She is proportionate and slim; her skin glows a deep honey brown, and her dark, straight hair glitters with the redness of careful highlights. Her straight, pointy nose fits perfectly between prominent hazel brown eyes, which give an aura of mixed mystery and innocence when gazed. She is medium height and voluptuous in all the right places and slim and soft in others. Her long legs extend to the most proportionate waist, and flat tummy. But the most amazing beauty Ceebla possesses is her neck—it is as smooth and straight as a swan's. Modest but sophisticated, she carries herself with pride, piety, and confidence.

The phone rang as she walked into the living room of her meticulously kept house, deep in thought. Burnt copper sunlight streamed into the room through the elaborate patio door, which swung open to allow fresh breeze to dilute the intoxicating smell of incense. She slouched into the stylish floor divans as she answered the phone.

"Hello?" She took her right earring out, so that she could pin the phone comfortably between shoulder and ear.

"Ceebla."

"Yes, this is Ceebla." Her eyes widened animatedly as she recognized the voice on the other end. "Hi, Raaxo!" Her face was elated, her shoulders shrugging down in ease.

"Hey girl, how is it going?" Raaxo asked jokingly, "What's happening, my sista?" Parting her lips with a wide smile, Ceebla replied, "Girl, all is well, *Alxamdulillah,* Allah has been good to me. I thought you were on a business trip, are you already in Dubai?"

"Girl I am at the airport, but I met the most amazing person and I wanted to hook you up." Raaxo gushed hysterically, "I think this is the right one for you, Ceebla." Raaxo's voice brimmed with hope. Ceebla was not paying much attention. She grinned as she watched her favorite show, Sex and the City. "Hey are you listening?" Raaxo demanded.

"Huh, what did you say?" Ceebla stuttered.

"Hey, are you in the middle of something?"

"Oh no girl, nothing important, what is going on?"

"Did you not hear me?"

"Yeah girl, I heard you."

"Well?"

"Oh God, Raaxo, no, not again. I am done. You know I am tired of this fake stuff girl, please spare me the headache. I am done. I have decided to concentrate on the positive things in my life; no more of that marriage mess which ultimately will lead to some crazy tribal mess. Forget it. I will not do it." Ceebla glided from the living room to her bedroom, slipping out of her clothes piece by piece. She slid out of her black pants, replacing them with a pair of tight jeans. Next her blouse, a pink, silky, voluminous creation, came off. She looked around the over-flowing closet for what to wear. She then picked a white sweatshirt and pulled it on, as she juggled with the phone.

"Ceebla, please, *walaal*, this is your man! He is an activist, idealistic not to mention highly educated, so unlike the others," Raaxo continued, oblivious to Ceebla's prolonged silence as she struggled with the cloths.

"Raaxo, give me a break. I just divorced a wife beater. Does it look like I will take a chance on someone else?" She was now back in the living room, looking around the neatly kept room, shuffling through precisely stacked glossy magazines as Carrie, Miranda, Samantha, and Charlotte sat comfortably in a New York bistro picking at hors d'oeuvres. "I am not going to expose myself to another blow," Ceebla said, still sorting through the piles of magazines. She slumped onto the floor, collecting her feet in a yogic pose. She picked dates from a plate of assorted dates, baklava, and nuts, aiming them for her mouth as she savored the delicate, tender taste

"Hello, are you still there, Raaxo?" She said attempting an interest in the conversation.

"Ceebla, trust me this time, I am certain it will work out. I know this guy. Haybe is your man, he is an attorney and a fabulous guy with a great heart, not to mention sophisticated and—" Ceebla rolled her eyes, revealing only the white part.

"Wow, what did this guy give you to talk him up like this, he sounds amazing."

"I am serious. I am not just talking him up, he is amazing! Please meet him for lunch and I promise to go with you if you don't want to be alone with him." Ceebla reluctantly agreed to a meeting, if only to shake Raaxo's persistent pleas.

"Ok, Raaxo, let me sleep on it, although I am not sure why you insist!" She located her keys on the brown and white drum that sat next to an oddly-placed giraffe. "I have to go meet Hodman; I'm late. We will talk when you return."

"Who is Hodman?"

"The girl I mentor, remember the *dhaqan celis thing*—"

"Oh yeah, that messed up girl with the baby."

"Don't say that. She is not messed up, she is a sweet girl with lots of potential."

"Is her grandma keeping the baby?"

"No, girl that is why I am going to see her, she kicked her out of her apartment with the baby."

"Poor thing! Ceebla, promise you won't disappoint me. Please consider it; I have already gotten Haybe excited about you." Ceebla rolled her eyes again.

"*Allahu Akbar*, okay, Raaxo, I will." Hanging up the phone, Ceebla took a quick look in the foyer mirror. She patted lip gloss on the edges of her full lips and brushed her hair into place.

Faint blue skies scattered pockets of cottony clouds as Ceebla's difficult day drew to conclusion. She had almost forgotten that she needed to pick a few items for the party at Raaxo's apartment. She loved stopping over at Raaxo's, and had done it so often it was now a habit. Raaxo, a former child bride and a single mother of four, was Ceebla's best friend. After purchasing her American dream, a three bedroom single family home in an upscale part of town, it began to echo with loneliness. She had spent a year decorating it, choosing a different theme for each of the two living rooms. The African room represented her multifaceted African heritage; there were decorations from Uganda, South Africa, Kenya, Djibouti, and Tanzania, places she had visited throughout her lifetime. Drums, masks, and other art crafts hugged each other in this room, truly representing the spirit of mother Africa. The Middle Eastern room reflected the Islamic and Middle Eastern influences in her culture. Adorned with Arabic divans, this room was finished with banners and tapestries demonstrating the abundantly colorful and elaborate beauty of Muslim calligraphy. Many in the community emulated the uniqueness and splendor of her house; her home was a conversation piece.

Ceebla thought the house would make her happy, but it actually confirmed her loneliness. Decorating the house no longer comforted her, which meant she had much spare time to get lost in the restless, ever-grueling 'Single woman in search of a man' world. The house began to remind her of her failures. She had no partner with whom to share all of her successes. She longed to meet a decent man who would share her beautiful life. The threat of spinsterhood loomed in every corner, and it seemed as if the world was conspiring against her. She would see nothing but happy families everywhere, parents with children, happily licking each other's ice cream cones. The mood in America seemed to turn to celebrity kids, marriage and families. Every magazine cover splashed dolled-up women with tight bellies filled with much loved babies whom the world celebrated even before their arrival. After decades of telling women they did not need men or children to complete them, without any notice and no warning at all, they were now expected to be with babies and husbands to join the ranks of happily—or not so happily—married women. What a disaster. Nothing could prepare her for the loneliness they made her feel. She celebrated the freedom she chose through the single lifestyle she shared with other American women: after all, they were all professional women, furthering their careers and having a family was not a priority. What a fool she was, having fallen for it. Astoundingly all those single free women became part of some joyful family, leaving her in the dust.

She would avoid the tabloids and their sturdy-bellied stars, filling her shopping cart with comfort food instead. To hell with your happy family BS, here's to you, Ben & Jerry's Chubby Hubby! Ceebla wanted to share her bed with the happy fat cow and the cheerful chubby clouds. She would momentarily escape to Ben & Jerry's happy, happy land, where everything was fat and soothing.

To add to her fears, her own community appeared to be one miracle baby-popping factory that burst out children with ease and speed. It must be true what they say; poor people just produce children. Ceebla noticed the speed at which lonely refugees with vague lives numbed their war wounds with plenty of baby-producing activities. She had to remind herself that it was the only thing these refugees could have plenty of without paying a hefty price.

The piercing noise of unruly children arrived in her ear as the most harmonic music strings composed with tender love and ease. She began to detest anyone who was married whether they were happy or not. She began to wish she had the pot belly and love handles only content married people could flaunt without guilt.

And of course the harsh critics in the community, those that made sure everyone's most private issues were outed without permission, were on the attack. The corridors of the noisy, dirty, deteriorating Cedar

Springs where Somali refugees roamed as if they were in their African villages chimed with remarks that she was approaching spinsterhood, crushing her to the point of despair.

"Ceebla, what are you waiting for? A decent, respectful girl is one who is in her father or husband's house." They left out the part of the proverb that said "a decent, respectful girl is one who is in her father's house, husband's house or the grave."

"*Eeddo*, don't waste those delicious eggs, give someone a chance to rescue the last few eggs before they spoil, you know you could produce some pretty choppy babies with your pretty complexion."

"A bad marriage and few kids are better than spinsterhood!"

It is not that they cared about her situation; they just wanted to remind her that they had one over her. While they read the sermon of shame, their bad-mannered children would stray, causing mishap, while their clumsy husbands picked their noses and gazed at any passing female who would make a suitable second wife.

It is not as though these women witnessed anything pleasant in their marriages; but they somehow perceived their lives as stellar simply because they had live bodies next to them in the dark of night. A single woman living alone without any relatives ran utterly counter to –tradition; Ceebla would shrug, smile faintly, and say *"Insha Allah,"* hoping it would end the conversation, all the while seething inside *"May Allah curse you and your children and may Allah make you weep as you run after every woman your husband has been sleeping with as a second, third or fourth wife, also may you burn in...."*

Not only did they recommend she settle for anyone, but they would shamelessly point out a homely-looking man, who could be the neighborhood molester, right to her face when she least expected. They claimed it was their duty as Muslims to arrange marriage for a single woman; it would bring them endless *ajar. May Allah bring you endless pain and misery*, she would latter gripe in private.

In their eyes, she led an empty life—no husband, no children, no family. Sometimes she felt their brutal criticisms were in fact the horrible, painful truth. She was alone, and as the saying goes, loneliness kills. But in their eyes, it is not a choice to be husbandless, but a curse. She thought they were seriously advising her because they wanted what was best for her, until she got to know her culture and its people. No Somali ever wants good fortune for another Somali: the idea is nonexistent, and if it exists you better run before you are lured to disaster. As much as she felt outrage at their invasiveness, they continued the attack.

The word privacy means nothing to a Somali: your business is simply everyone else's business. She began to admire the individualistic, lonesome lives of some of her American colleagues. Raaxo's apartment, located in Cedar Springs, the most notorious Somali high-rise—2046 Cedar Avenue, overlooking the main campus of the university—was home to a group of newcomers. Families chose it for its cheap rent and its proximity to everything Somali. In this cold, foreign land most Somalis valued this small familiarity. It is as if they traveled for days over the Red Sea, Indian Ocean and the Atlantic to join other Somalis in a place that was run down and dismal where the weather was harsh, the people white and the community unkind.

Ceebla jumped into her sleek black Lexus. Somali music blasted from the stereo. She murmured the lyrics, her head moving to the melody as she turned onto Goose Landing Road, *"Noloshaydiiyey adaa najmaay, nuur caashaqee neecow da'daa..."* A sky-blue flag with white five-sided star in the middle hung from the rearview mirror alongside several Quran charms.

Aging snow that had lost its vibrant whiteness, now turning to brown slush collected along the street. Ceebla found herself in evening traffic. A slim woman cloaked from head to toe in a bright pumpkin jilbaab resembling a giraffe walked passed Ceebla's car: she had four little similarly-garbed girls with pink- and violet-cartooned backpacks gathered around her, walking forward, cautious not to wet the hems of their *jilbaabs*. A little fellow in a black North Face jacket with a matching scarf and gloves trailed behind them, hopping along, conducting a private conversation with the slush that swooshed around his booted feet. The mother chatted animatedly on her metallic blue cell phone; a baby buckled to her back peeked from the cloak that covered her upper body.

Ceebla turned onto a poorly lit, unpaved road. She flashed the high beams, blinding a herd of black, brown, and copper-toned men. Their stares shamed her, even though she garbed her hair with a heavy scarf for approval only. She proceeded feeling each agonizing stare pierce her carefully built confidence. As she parked, she contemplated how to best cut through the crowd of men that had collected directly in front of the door. She tightened her headscarf, assuring that no stray hair or patch of skin was visible, and marched forward, avoiding eye contact and dismissing their remarks. It was all a façade: they would condemn her as a shameless slut if she came to the mall in her elegant work attire, a pant suit, yet even with a long flimsy skirt, big baggy shirt and a huge scarf, they checked her out, hoping to get lucky. This was what she found pathetic in her community: hypocrisy, lies, and plenty of promiscuity. Scattered in front of her were the only potential bachelors available for her and her ilk, losers, deadbeat dads, political junkies—all qat addicts with no jobs. These are the men they recommended to escape solitude and spinsterhood.

Ceebla pulled open the door to the Somali mall, Fifty-Fifty, a makeshift strip mall that housed scores of look-alike stores with identical merchandise. At the entrance she encountered a flock of cheering children celebrating their luck with an out-of-order candy dispenser. They filled their tiny palms with rainbow-colored candy, competing to see who could collect the most. Ceebla stomped the slush off her boots and cut around a corner, maneuvering around another pack of men outside an all-male sports bar, where the tables spilled into the area in front of the entrance. The men sat around pointing fingers, throwing their hands in the air, while speaking vibrantly. Self-conscious and constantly pulling her head scarf into place, Ceebla was elated to reach her destination, Istanbul Clothing and Jewelry. The store was packed to the gills with fabric and cheap trinkets imported from Asian and Middle-Eastern countries. Istanbul was a replica of all the other stores in the mall. She looked around only to find the exact same goods from the same supplier—flimsy cheap skirts, scarves and other copy-cat merchandise.

"Variety, people, variety," Ceebla said, frustrated. "I don't want to go to an event and find ten other women wearing the same *diric*. Someone needs to recue this mall. Think outside the box people."

"Ceebla, you said the same thing the last time you were here. If this mall does not meet your needs then go somewhere else," Istanbul snapped, knowing full well that Ceebla had no other choices when it came to purchasing Somali merchandise.

"Has it ever occur to you to sell merchandise that differs from your neighbors?" she said in a half-joking tone, noticing how mad Istanbul looked.

"We are doing fine, Ceebla. Don't come in here with your superior 'I am more educated than you' attitude!" Istanbul said handing her the clothes she came to pick up.

She picked up her neatly tailored diric, slid some money across the counter, and left the poorly lit strip mall. She crossed the street and entered a bustling area which was home to countless *halal* stores. Hamar, Berbera, Markah, Daalo, Bosaso, and Sanaag sat snug next to each other, each proudly named after a once peaceful and thriving city.

She marched through Daalo where her senses awoke to the sharp and familiar smell of spices. She passed the crowd queued at the back of the store for a butcher who pointed his sharp bloody knife to customers to get orders. Next to him sat brown, chewy, oily, cardamom-scented *xalwo* on a massive round metal dish. Ceebla's taste buds danced inside her mouth at the sight of the freshly made *xalwo*. She ordered ten pounds of it, thinking if the sweet she loved so much would send her elevated cholesterol sky high. She greeted the goateed creamy white storeowner sitting at the cashier stand. He saluted her back, asking politely about her family, liberally sprinkling praises and blessings throughout the conversation. They dodged each other's eyes and exchanged the money on the stand to avoid any physical contact.

Next Ceebla entered Badbaad restaurant to pick rice and meat for the event. Every time she came to these stores, her longing was affirmed: she felt homesick for a peaceful time, when people who now detest each other loved one another, when people were patriots and their country was calm and beautiful. A time when a Somali death was mourned by all, and Somali children were not the ugly stamps of Africa. The blend of basmati rice, lamb, and spices stirred her stomach, which growled; she hadn't realized she was hungry until she entered the restaurant.

A number of men stood around the entrance, picking their teeth with toothpicks. Some surrounded an elderly gentleman who held their undivided attention. She walked around them and waited for the cashier, who was engrossed in a story being told by another energetic man in competition with the elderly man. He kept moving around, with excitement as he told the story: the movements alone could serve as a day's exercise. Everywhere she looked in the gloomy dark restaurant, men collected in one corner or another. She chuckled when she recalled the seriousness of a reporter on TV earlier in the week:

Local police has committed time and funds to investigate the reason recent immigrants from the East African country of Somalia in the twin cities block entry ways, bathroom entrances, coffee shop doorways, hotel lobbies and any wall or corner they can claim to congregate. These recent immigrants are known to congregate for reasons that are making city authorities shake their heads with bewilderment. In three separate cases, the men from the war torn country of Somalia were banned from local coffee shops. The three coffee shops which banned the practice have invested heavily in security guards to dissuade these congregations. The general public is warned that this uncanny trend which has plagued cities across America in recent times is not harmful to the general public and that the men are only suffering from what the police chief refers to as FDK—*fadhi ku dirir*, for the lack of a better acronym or arm chair politicking. Attempts to interview some of the men in the ban were unsuccessful.

Ceebla looked around as she waited for her order to an area of the restaurant designated for families. The area crammed together in uncomfortable proximity families with children who opted to eat away from the gazes of men in the large common area. Families in this make-shift area tolerate each other, sometimes becoming privy to private talk. As hands dive into one big plate that sits in the middle of the table, mothers feed their children by hand while attentively listening to sto-ries told by other, equally busy mothers. Children run around the small space, occasionally finding themselves in unavoidable accidents. Soon they find themselves in their mothers' arms to be fed or spanked, or both.

Juices drip from hands that had perfected the art of simultaneous eating, feeding, and socializing as gossip swirls the room. It becomes natural to eavesdrop and it is where one hears uncanny stories of women she knew to be respectable citizens of the community.

Raaxo, a single mother of four in her early thirties, is a couple of years older than Ceebla. Ceebla had become suspicious of Somali women, and for a good reason. As a naïve new comer to Minneapolis she befriended a group of women to re-introduce herself into the mix after a long hiatus from the community, living in the suburbs of Boston. She was excited to be amid a culture and people she loved, but that was precisely the problem—her enthusiasm. She did not ease into the community she had been away from for over ten years; but rather rushed into it without any reservation. The sudden eagerness to help and hang around them caused great resentment and mistrust. Within a short period of time her private business was everywhere, all types of rumors were invented about her and vast amounts of cash loans, bor-rowed clothes and jewelry were not returned. Somehow her generosity was interpreted as gullibility. She was even threatened when she asked for her stuff back. To save herself embarrassment she just withdrew from the community as fast as she rushed into it. Jealousy, backbiting, revenge, gossip and pure resentment from women as young as she and as old as her mother left nothing but a bitter taste. She vowed to be cautious and so when she first met Raaxo she was wary. The longevity of their friendship may be due to the unlikely collision that brought them to the same emergency room one fateful winter night.

Ceebla waited clutching a broken arm in the Hennepin Hospital ER when Raaxo's raucous rush into the emergency room angered the security guard, who instructed her to wait like everyone else. Three month old Cusayb was running a dangerously high fever, and Raaxo was hysterical.

Ceebla avoided Raaxo, immediately worried that some concocted rumors would float in the hallways of Cedar Springs. Ceebla hurriedly got up and sat in another section of the ER, but to Ceebla's panic Raaxo followed her and sat the feverish child next to her, unaware of Ceebla's discomfort. She greeted her with a faint "*Salaamu Calaykum,*" but her attention was on her son. Ceebla returned the greeting and then rose abruptly to move again to a secluded side of the waiting area, dragging her arm along with her. After her arm was set in a cast, she left the emergency room with some speed. A few minutes later, after picking up some pain medication from the pharmacy, Ceebla sat in the passenger seat of her neighbor Jade Mackenzie's jeep when she noticed Raaxo sitting at a corner bus stop with the child. It was in the dead of winter, and Ceebla was conflicted: she didn't want to associate with the poorly-dressed woman and the little boy resting on her lap, but she couldn't bear leaving a sick child sitting out in the cold. When Jade pulled to the bus stop Ceebla let her arm rest on her lap, concealing the cast with the shawl that draped her shoulders. Unlike the curious women Ceebla was used to, who would ask all types of questions about her broken arm, Raaxo was a free spirit. She began talking about her life as a single mother raising four children almost as soon as she set foot in the jeep.

She was so engrossed in telling them her story she never gave them a chance to interrupt or acknowledge her. Ceebla realized that Raaxo was not interested in her broken arm or her business: the woman was on a marathon to finish her life story in the twenty minutes it took to drop her off.

Ceebla's visits to Raaxo's apartment offered an escape from her mundane life, and she had plenty to run away from: the horrible marriage that ended only a year earlier, the boredom and fatigue, the loneliness, and the daunting pressure at work to outsell other publishing houses. It was an escape for her to witness the simple lives of refugees in Cedar Springs. Growing up in the Middle East and America; Ceebla knew little about her home country, and had not experienced much of her own culture firsthand. Her parents had moved her from boarding school to boarding school in multiple foreign countries in search of the best education and better opportunity for her and her siblings, and so Ceebla genuinely appreciated being surrounded by other Somalis for the first time in her adult life. She immigrated to America from Paris right after college, after the civil war broke in Somalia. Refugees from her country who were casualities of war with nothing but hope in America simply touched her heart.

Cedar Springs was where Ceebla experienced the typical Somali refugee life. It was a welcome change for her; she escaped the rigidity of her own life for the spontaneous, easy-going sometimes dizzying life of these refugees who laughed, prayed, shared and ate, genuinely giving thanks to Allah. "Americans would pay millions to get the secret to their happiness," she often thought to herself. Losing everything to war had made them resilient, optimistic, and grateful. These refugees had no time for victimhood to ask "why us": they accepted their fate and quickly learned to be happy with what God had given them in their new lives. Maybe it's the reason Ceebla chose to be among them, to catch some infectious optimism.

Allah knows she needed optimism in her life. Sure, her first experience with them was not acceptable, and still jealousy and backbiting existed, and yes she has had more than her share of challenges with them, but in the end it was worth it: in a way they coached her in how to count her blessings. She had so many material possessions, yet she felt empty. They had nothing more than the basics in their American refugee lives, and yet they were rich spiritually and mentally. They had to walk away from everything that mattered to them, and yet she hardly ever saw them regret it. She looked forward to walking through the hallways of Cedar Springs to witness rowdy children, gossipy mothers, and nosy neighbors. The aroma of Somali food filled the air, and *uunsi* and *foox* incenses wafted throughout the hallway. En route to her destination, Ceebla had to prepare to provide her clan affiliation, the name of the person whom she was visiting, and her place of residence. These questions led only to more questions, which led to a full out inquisition they almost required an identity card just to allow her through. If there was anything she disliked it is this furious inquisitiveness which was constant, and never yielding. It is these inquisitions that alerted her to the emptiness of her life. Her visits were often delayed by the insistence of one neighbor or another to have a cup of tea in an attempt to drill her further.

She knew she was at Raaxo's door by the volume of boisterous noise that emanated from the door. Children ran around and Raaxo's mother Barako was having a loud conversation on the phone; women laughed and reprimanded children, and there were ear-splitting clamor from both children and adults. Not even the heavy drapery that adorned the tiny apartment could contain the rising noise. But Ceebla was used to the loudness of the place: it was as typical a Somali dwelling as any, except Raaxo and her family were louder than the loudest people in the building. One could hear laughter, castigation, bickering and any sort of tongue-lashing awash with curses and acidity.

The door swung open and Ceebla walked in, slamming the door on the snooping woman who had followed her from the elevator to witness firsthand the disarray inside the apartment. A woman was bellowing on her cell phone, attempting to be heard above the roar. Ceebla wondered how Raaxo fit so many distinct people, each with a catalog of problems, under one roof. The tiny, three-bedroom, low-income apartment was home to Raaxo and her four children, a brother, and a sister and her ailing mother. Every time Ceebla visited, she left wondering how anyone could live in such a disorderly, cramped apartment. Somehow, Raaxo, a single mother, not only handled her exhaustingly busy home life but was also a successful business woman. Although Raaxo's life was neither melodious nor typical, there was something harmonious about her life, which began with a severe trauma and if you could ever catch her bad mouth her kids to remind them of their good-for-nothing father *ma wax lagu dhalay i daa iyo diiday baa khayr yeelanaya, wallee ilma Kaarshe ayaan dad noqon* you would understand why.

Raaxo came to America when she was fifteen, not as a refugee girl with her family, nor a minor with some relatives, but as a bride. The girl was engaged to Kaarshe, who was forty-two when he asked for her hand—she had been only five. She was promised in marriage to a horny forty-two year old man from America by a desperate hungry father of twelve in an insane qat joint. Neither was rational when her father's desperate petition ended in Kaarshe exploiting the situation and asking for Raaxo's hand in marriage. Raaxo was not watching TV or attending pre-k at the time; she was a barefoot African child roaming the village amid her eleven siblings. That day she accompanied her elder sister to herd young sheep her family kept for another family while her delirious father bartered her away in marriage to a married man with children. When her mother came to fetch her, the five year old awoke from a delicious nap under the shade of an acacia tree where the girls rested from the blazing sun. She was weary and hungry but knew there was no food to eat until night, so she defied the growling stomach on the comfort of her mother's back.

When they made it back to the modest mud house they shared with the rest of the family, a truck full of stuff was being unloaded. Raaxo ran to her father, who was standing with a tall bearded man. The man shamelessly gazed at her and gave her candy, and a duffle bag full of new clothes. After she was dressed in the clothes, her mother fed the family a very elaborate meal of meat and rice. That meal was reserved for celebrations. May be it was *ciid*, or maybe someone was getting married; either way she feasted with the family. She did not ask questions but was happy to receive the nice gifts and all the attention. For ten years his name shadowed hers, "Kaarshe and Raaxo", 'Raaxo and Kaarshe", "Kaarshe sends us money, isn't Raaxo lucky." She would plug her ears so she would not hear his name. As soon as stuff came she would disappear to spare her ears, because he was the only person who ever sent stuff. His name became synonymous with pain in the pit of her stomach; his name was the reason she shed tears at night, fearful to close her eyes.

At thirteen, her mother insisted that she speak to him whenever he called. His throaty voice caused her to shiver but by then she understood who he was and why she had to speak to him. The fifty dollars he sent every month was to assure the promise, the price of Raaxo to him. Raaxo dreaded reaching that age, but before fifteen arrived came all types of restrictions. She was instructed to dress like a married woman, could not go with her friends outside, and she was constantly watched because her parents feared she might run away. They had moved to the city, and the money Kaarshe sent had elevated them to better living conditions where the children could attend regular school. When she reached fifteen her family performed a religious ceremony to tie her to Kaarshe, and then she was given a one way ticket to go to America and join her husband.

But her life in America started miserably. As soon as she arrived she tasted the sweetness of American life, but the delicious possibility of ever obtaining that life was shattered by the ugly, now fat and old Kaarshe, and his meek dull wife Shamis, who actually groomed Raaxo for her husband. It was her duty as a co-wife, she claimed. Her mind played an ugly trick on her when they picked her up from the airport: Caydiid, Kaarshe's first born, picked her up from the airport and she was so elated to meet him. She thought that maybe old man Kaarshe had changed his mind and wanted his son to marry her instead; but

Caydiid was picking Raaxo up because his father was in the hospital recovering from a stroke. Raaxo prayed so much she began to believe her own lies. She was certain that Allah would not let the man wake up from the stroke. Not only did he wake up from it, he seemed to have gained strength to chase her around the living room he shared with his wife and five children. Every night before bed time, they would play catch-me-if-you-can: Shamis and Kaarshe would chase her around the apartment, his oldest three kids Caydiid, Muna and Sabaax would try to free her from the beastly father and then attempt to call the police. They would all be beaten by both Kaarshe and his wife with a belt for trying to involve the police in their lives, and then she would be carried to his room bawling. The episode was repeated every night until Caydiid left home, Muna eloped with a Mexican man and Raaxo was transferred to another apartment where Kaarshe could chase her alone. She burned down the apartment, ran away three times, and threw bleach at him twice. She then ran away few months short of her eighteenth birthday. By then she had two kids and a third on the way. Her fourth boy, Cusayb, was a love child between her and her married good-for-nothing second husband Farah, although some claim he is a byproduct of one of the many love affairs Raaxo has had since her divorce from Kaarshe.

NOTORIOUS WELFARE QUEENS

The signpost at the entrance read 2046 Cedar Springs Luxury Apartments. Cedar Springs is notorious for its deafening weekend parties organized by welfare queens called single mothers who have recently overtaken the building. There is nothing luxurious about Cedar Springs; it is an old high rise of low income apartments which has seen better days. Dirty hallways, unkempt lobbies and piles of trash have replaced whatever luxury Cedar Springs has ever known; it's dubbed Crack Towers.

It attracts newcomers, while those who know better flee from the constant gang activity, lead ridden walls and unsanitary conditions. For Somali refugees who have witnessed all sorts of disasters in their lives, Cedar Springs is nothing short of a miracle. Its proximity to everything Somali adds to the allure.

So women in Cedar Springs throw parties every weekend to indulge and escape something in their Minnesotan lives which they have not yet come to terms with. Raaxo's apartment, number 6835, is a magnet for these loud, boisterous single mothers and their louder mischievous children. Trying to erase whatever in their lives that make them alien, these women take every fleeting opportunity to celebrate. When there are no big events to celebrate, they create an occasion: going away parties, coming back to town parties, getting rid of those no-good-husband parties, getting married for the sixth time parties, winning a fight against an arch enemy parties, and winning back those not-so-bad-after-all-husband parties. Whatever the occasion, these parties are a sure way to relieve some of the constant ache these women have encountered in their refugee lives.

Ceebla handed the trays of rice and *xalwo* she had picked for the occasion to Raaxo as she walked into the apartment. She was not sure what the women were celebrating today, but she had made sure not to miss the occasion, where welfare queens who have perfected the art of being on welfare, mothers who knew the nuts and bolts of section eight, cash benefits, food stamp and low income housing, whose minds caught the smallest fine print came to escape the grimness of their lives. Women who have multiple roles in the community as mothers, wives, interpreters, singers, poets and ad hoc wedding planners. Being a refugee in America meant you wore whatever hat thrown your way, and the welfare queens of Cedar Springs did not shy away from their self declared areas of expertise.

In the living room, gossipy women nibbled on delicate homemade pastries while sipping sweet milky tea, talking over one another excitedly and gesticulating wildly. Periodically, a group of them would burst into laughter. Very few sat quietly, unmoved and contemplative. In the next room, their children watch blaringly rowdy TV, while others beat at the keyboard of the one and only play station in the entire building, taking turns forcefully to play Grand Theft Auto with vengeance. The dissonant sounds in the apartment fused with the bright, layered, clashing colors of deep green, maroon and gold fabric covering the walls and floors. The women had assembled in the cramped apartment to perform *taraara,* a blessing ceremony for the humungous Saxarla. The twenty-something wobbling woman is pregnant with her sixth child, while the youngest of her children lay on her lap sucking milk from a bottle while she chattered away with others, periodically jolting and scaring the baby with jerky laughter.

Incenses burn in off-white cylinder shaped clay burner to rid the room of the smells of food; the smoke burns the eyes of the children, mixing with the aroma of the food and the various scents of the many bodies, forming a funk only a refugee Somali can appreciate.

The women either obese or pregnant (no one knows) overindulge on the loads and loads of food which they mostly prepared themselves. There are multiple trays of biryani rice, cubed beef in sauces, *canjeero*, Alfredo pasta, lamb chops, lasagna and fried chicken, as well as humus, sambuusa and three salad platters which remain untouched. After they are done overdosing on the food they get in line for the sweets—*xalwo*, butter cookies, devil cakes, baklava and fruit topped custard lined one corner of a table next to a variety of sodas. The women, who may not be thoroughly acquainted with each other to follow the details of one story or another, are content to occupy a space in this celebration to break away from the reality of refugee life.

To outsiders, those not used to the way Somalis do things, the gathering may be loud and intolerable, but for these women the louder the exchange the better; after all they did not come here to exchange civility, but to be belligerent and flamboyant to tell as many stories as possible, trying to attract the entire party to their part of the room. In order to accomplish this, they talk over each other, forcing one to listen to two, three and sometimes four stories at a time.

They came to bless the wobbling Saxarla, who appeared ready to deliver the baby right there and then while she changed her infant daughter. After eating and dancing and between story telling the women take turns to scent their hair and skin with sweet exotic incense smoke and oily perfumes from decoratively shaped bottles sitting on a golden vanity tray. Their elegance and opulence is a far cry from the women who line social service offices during the day, looking clumsy and wretched. Ceebla marvels at them, admiring the transformation.

Ceebla, who would usually prepare smart acidic comebacks for their nasty personal comments, was engrossed with one woman's story to ready a defense for the agonizing assault they took turns to lay on her.

"Ceebla, when will we eat your *xalwo*? Still no Mr. Right?" asked Saxarla, huffing laboriously as she moved her fat belly from place to place.

"No Saxarla, no such luck yet, but *Alxamdulilah*—Allah will deliver," Ceebla said, attempting to shed her distaste for these unrelenting remarks. In private her thoughts are not so forgiving: *fatso, shouldn't you be worried about your four baby daddies and dwindling benefits instead of worrying about my affairs!*

"Stop lying to yourself, Ceebla, you are a woman; time is passing you by." This cruel remark comes from Basra aka Erica Badu, a woman Ceebla hardly even knew. She declared her persona through her outfit: meticulously chosen colors announce her style, to show her narcissism. She visited many stores to assemble it, sometimes buying pieces directly from a merchant in Dubai. To stand out, be emulated and become a conversation starter, lilac blue is the color she preferred today—lilac to sweeten the sour conclusion to her life. She lives in apartment 5323, and her secret has been floating the hallways lately. Rumor has it Basra's husband mysteriously disappeared three months ago. He is in jail for doing something illegal, the rumor said. Basra is aware of the whispers; it is precisely the reason she picked lilac blue, to disappear in the midst of the beautiful colors of her diric and grabasaar. The bleaching cream on her face did not do justice for her otherwise striking nutmeg skin, giving way to bulging skin where the coverage failed. Dubbed Erica Badu for her signature head wear, Basra should seek advice from Raaxo, who has lost her vibrant glowing dark complexion to an elegant and equally glowing lighter one, where no traces of the old complexion existed. But women from Cedar Spring prided themselves on the best kept secrets of bleaching, never sharing tips with anyone so as not be outdone.

"Ceebla, honey, go give someone a chance; soon the eggs will spoil," said another woman, moving her big hips from side to side as if proud of the pounds childbearing had bestowed on her.

"Surely you can find a man amid the millions that hang around the mall looking for a woman like you—or just tell us and we will fix you up, please let the next celebration be yours!" added another, Istaahil *CNN*, while stylishly trailing her turquoise garbasaar from her left shoulder to the floor instead of its usual resting place atop her head. It is a scrupulous deliberate vogue to gracefully drag the scarf behind her ostrich body so it shadows behind the emerald green guntiino she wore, keeping her polished shoulders bare to flaunt her figure as well as to be different from the rest of the women. Istaahil's girlish figure showed no signs of the thirteen kids she'd birthed, thanks to excessive exercise. She stayed away from fatty foods and the bulky dirics other women wore to flaunt her runway figure in a vain self obsessed manner.

Istaahil *CNN*, whose name means "one who deserves", who was nicknamed CNN for her none stop inquiry into people's lives has never met a man she did not like. Her womb has carried enough ethnicities to adorn any United Colors of Benetton poster. She had birthed children on four continents and said "I do" in six different languages. That same stunning body, the envy of all the other women in the room (who had fat cells in places where fat cells had no business forming), had also been infected with what the building gossip troupe referred to as *cudurkii xumaa.*

This is the only place she feels admired, and the only attention she will ever get. Two of her sons are in jail—one for killing a police officer, the other for stabbing his stepfather. Istaahil's Louis Vuitton handbag was attracting as much attention as the rumors leveled against her. She would insert the $2000 she paid for the bag in every conversation, allowing others a mere touch of the bag—after all, what's the point of purchasing an expensive handbag with child support payments if others were not privy to the price she paid?

Their attacks on Ceebla halted temporarily as they all got up with a roar to dance to the ongoing song about the pain of revealing one's love: *Hadaan bogsadoon ka raysto sidaan uga booday caashaqa, jacayl ba hadaan u oyoo hadaan nin danbe u baroorto hadaan baxsanow idhaahdo ala belaayoba ha iga raacdo....* The women sing along in unison, swaying to the melody of a song the meaning of which some find shrilly literal. The children look annoyed by the sudden chorus. "Oh, my god, they are dancing again," "They are so annoying, we can't hear anything!"

"Mom, stop yelling!" yelled one kid, for yelling is the only way to be heard. Children yelled alongside the elated dancing women.

"You guys, we can't hear the TV, stop all that noise!" the children demanded, attempting to teach their mothers some of the etiquette they picked up as first generation Americans. The children watch Madagascar and do not look as if they belong in the same world as their mothers.

These women find their way through each day by recreating the good past while discarding their present, keeping only a sheer reflection of the refugee life they inherited for the purpose of appearances only. So they take their time to outdo each other, to occupy the minds and hearts of their peers for a few weeks. Surely what transpires in apartment #6835 will be headline news and will be broadcasted across the country via telephone lines. Glamour has its rewards; admired women are sought out to be part of the in crowd. The children and other family members of these refugee women are an afterthought forced on them: they would rather forgo their needs and stay in the moment. To feel alive, needed and admired. They invite favorable gazes from like women, indulging themselves while starving their dependents of everything but the basics. They keep up their self-care as if they are making up for old times when as girls they did not matter and their needs fell by the wayside. Having been a minor detail in the lives of their families, they seem intent to have vengeance, to erase the old with the present. They are welfare refugees who have crowned themselves reigning queens of Cedar Springs.

Their Sunday night lineup does not include the latest episode of Desperate Housewives, but rather true stories of betrayal, divorce, polygamy and children killed or in jail. They raise autistic children as single mothers, take care of aging parents, send back money to starving relatives in Somalia, and yet they find time to enjoy and forget all that is expected of them.

THE HOSTILE ONE

Ceebla met Colaad, her first husband, at a wedding which had recently became the only place where Somali singles could meet. His name, which meant 'the hostile one', should have been enough warning—but naiveté has often been Ceebla's weakness.

She was dancing with a friend when a stocky short man with a protruding belly approached her, ignoring her companion. He was bold and relentless from the start. She looked him up and down, her facial expressions changing with the hideous man that blocked her air. He asked her to dance, and then without missing a beat asked for her phone number. She found herself saying "No, creep, go and stalk someone else." She felt it was rude, and she felt guilty. His eyes followed her around the massive ballroom the entire night and by the time she came home to shower and sleep she could not help shake the scene off her mind. She finally fell asleep thinking "what a creep!"

She had totally forgotten about him until he showed up at her workplace two weeks later. There he was sitting in the reception area, as if he had an appointment with her. His rigid features looked angry even when he was happy; he rarely smiled, and it was better that way as his closed lips hid badly stained teeth. After the incident at her office she threatened to call the police on him, but that made him pursue her persistently. She kept seeing him around, at the gym, the grocery store and other public places. Then late one evening, she had left work late and stopped at the grocery store to purchase some Ben &Jerry's Cherry Garcia ice cream to erase the lengthy week she thought would never end. She approached the cash register, her hands clasped around the little indulgence, when she saw him standing right in front of her. She had been avoiding his phone calls; she tried to pretend she did not see him and left the cash register fast, but there he was, stalking her on the other side of the store. He wasted no time, immediately inviting her to dinner. She refused.

For months she refused to see him and she refused. She couldn't say why, but there was something humble about him. She knew perfectly well that a marriage between someone of her tribe, *Gobaad*, and his tribe, *Laan yar*, would be taboo. All she heard growing up was how her tribe is the lowest tribe and that it is the reason they marry from within. That meant if he proposed to her in marriage and she accepted it would be taboo.

And then one Sunday afternoon as she lay comfortably watching American Beauty her doorbell rang. She had turned the phones off, and was glad to enjoy a lazy day of nothing but sleep and TV. She hesitated before opening the door—Kevin Spacey and Annette Benning captured her full attention as they stood in their massive living room shouting at one another. She wanted to know what happened next, so she stood in the foyer her attention still on the story, a massive apple-green bed sheet draped around her. The doorbell kept ringing, and so without checking, she swung the door open. And there he was, standing on her stoop like a guilty child who was scared to be found out after doing something mischievous. Before she could say anything, he shoved a dozen yellow roses into her hand, as though he were just delivering the flowers rather than the one giving them. She could tell it was something he thought she would enjoy, or a tip he'd heard on TV. There was nothing genuine or endearing about the clumsily bought and oddly wrapped flowers. He acted as if he did not even want to be seen with them.

"Hi, can I come in?" he asked, hardly greeting her.

"What? What are you doing here?" she asked unable to hide her displeasure, and not knowing what to say.

"I came here to talk to you," he replied, matter-of-factly.

"How did you get my address?"

"Is that how you welcome all your guests?"

"Look, Colaad, I am sorry, I am rea—"

"Please come with me; I need to tell you something!"

"No, but you just cannot barge in here and—" he continued interrupting her, never allowing her to finish a sentence. He appeared nervous and anxious.

He would be embarrassed for being rejected for a few days and she would be relieved only to find him in the least likely places. After six months she agreed to meet with him, but only if she could bring a friend along. They were engaged a year later. It was his persistence and seeming attentiveness that convinced her to consider the marriage, but it was a failure right from the start.

Ceebla did not know much about him, yet she'd agreed to marry him. Some frowned on her eagerness to marry, but there were so many urgent issues in her life that made her rush into it. Regret later persuaded her that it was the cultural pressure, she should have avoided. Now she concedes it was all the corridor advice and the unrelenting cruelty of the women in her community that made her rush into it. After all, Ceebla kept standing out from their mix. No matter how much she humbled herself, she was different in many ways. She wanted to blend in, be one of the notorious queens of Cedar Springs. She knew perfectly well there was a huge divide between them, that she would never have to collect welfare or have multiple children just to stay on welfare, that while they collected welfare she labored at her job earning a six figure salary, yet she did not want her upper class status to marginalize her. She figured one way she could be one of them was if she got married: then she could at least have that in common with them. So she went along with the marriage. Talk about doomed marriage. The first violent blow came on their honeymoon when he was unable to consummate the marriage. Somehow that was her fault, just as not having a good job and driving a cab was her fault.

She lay in bed many nights wondering why she agreed to something she knew would be a disaster. Here she was, an educated, intelligent woman who fell into the trap of cultural pressure: now there was no difference between her and the women she ridiculed when she watched Jerry Springer. How had she turned into one of these women? Every attempt to fix the marriage was a disaster. Wasn't that her job, to fix her marriage, no matter how wrong Colaad was for her? Wasn't the whole idea of marriage to make the best of a very bad situation?

The only positive thing that came out of the marriage—if one could claim there was anything positive about living with Colaad—she was welcome in the midst of the women who had pushed her into the marriage, the Cedar Spring women. Now that she had a husband, they began to ask if she were barren. They wanted to see babies nine months after the marriage. But they were almost kind to her now, because they knew she suffered like them in the less than acceptable marriages they all settled for.

She thought a baby might improve things, and so she got pregnant, but that pregnancy ended in miscarriage. She spent a lonely, cold night in the hospital by herself, in a city where she had no family except him. She drove herself to the hospital for the DNC and drove herself back. On weekends, he hung around his buddies drinking himself sick. He would come home reeking of alcohol and demanded she feed him. She would spend endless weekends alone, watching TV and soothing her broken soul with more Ben & Jerry's. By the time Colaad was done with her, he had wiped out her savings, given her a concussion, several broken bones, bruised soul and self esteem. Ceebla, quite the survivor, moved on with life, never looked back, taking a mental not of the marriage she should have been careful to pursue.

PERCEIVED ASCENDANCY

Haybe had seen Nadifo chose her acquaintances and affiliations based on tribe. He found tribalism sickening and contagious. He found it quite ironic when his best friend and colleague Marcus Oliver, an African-American, marched into his office one day to announce his recently found lineage. After an extensive (and expensive) round of DNA testing and lengthy analysis, he was finally told where his ancestors hailed from.

He was told that he was now an esteemed member of the proud Ashanti tribe of Ghana. His jubilation was overwhelming. Marcus felt that he finally had roots. He could finally escape a lifetime of not knowing who he was. "The only legacy this country had given me is racism and marginalization—now I belong to a proud tribe in the motherland!" he repeated, elated. Finally he could be part of a proud lineage which had existed for centuries. He now had an identity beyond being a black man in America. He was now an Ashanti. Euphoric tears streamed down his cheeks as he proudly told his children that they were Ashanti.

Ironically Haybe could recite his lineage going back at least two hundred years. His forefathers were impressive men, he was told, tracing their roots to the proud people of Basra. Yes, his grandmother claimed they had blood lines with the Iraqi people. Haybe viewed this knowledge as a curse. It was a curse that had created the civil war—the brutal murder of his brother, the dismemberment of innocent people, the skinning, severing, and chopping of children, and violating women. And now this lineage which had caused his family so much pain was her obsession. She hugged the knife that had slain her family, destroyed her daughter, and pillaged her homeland.

Haybe was impressed with Ceebla on their first meeting. She was strikingly beautiful, well-mannered, and very cultured. Raaxo, whose brother was a client, introduced them. When Raaxo spoke of Ceebla, Haybe was intrigued. He wanted to meet this strong, beautiful, sophisticated woman. He never asked what tribe she belonged to. Tribalism was something he had shunned; Raaxo's description of her friend was enough to animate him.

He was smitten on their first encounter. She picked a Moroccan restaurant in Nicolette Island, complete with flickering incense lights, comfy Moroccan love seats and a dining room with understated Mediterranean elegance against the dramatic background of the Mississippi and St. Anthony Main. The Moroccan theme of lavish colors of maroon and gold and brilliant blue textures, brocade pillows, rustic hardwood furnishings, and Moroccan tiles added to the ambiance, while the elegant gold and copper interior added to his anxiety. Raaxo sat alone at a table, talking on the phone, when Haybe tapped her on the shoulder.

"God, what is with the sweaty hands," she said into the phone she held against her ear.

"Shhhh. Where is she? I am so nervous," he said, not noticing Ceebla returning from the bathroom behind him. Raaxo chuckled loudly, winking at him to look behind him. That was the beginning of an entire evening filed with embarrassment and awe.

"Hi, I'm Haybe," he said, timidly extending one sweaty palm.

"Yeh, I know who you are!" Ceebla said casually.

"Nice to meet you. Shall we?" he said, pointing to her seat. He would usually flaunt his fine manners and help a lady to her seat, but she intimidated him, making him short on good manners. Unlike him she appeared calm and collected.

He was surprised that she wore complete Islamic garb. He had never before been with a woman who dressed this way, nor even who was particularly religious; and yet, he found himself drawn to her sincerity, confidence and beauty. He stared at her face, infatuated, humiliating himself. He imagined touching the silkiness of it. He shunned the eagerness to touch her hand or face or any part of her body, everything about her glowed with confidence. She wore modest make up and yet looked radiant. She wore her garb elegantly and Haybe found her to be self-assured, eloquent and sincere.

She refused to see him after their first meeting. Escaping her community's gossip, she did not want to be seen with a man without knowing where the courtship would lead. It was not Islamic, she assured him. She was dignified following the religious tradition throughout the courtship. How ironic, she was exactly the type of woman Nadifo would have picked, had she been a member of the chosen tribe.

"If your intentions are pure, ask for my hand. Otherwise, we should not waste our time on "dating." That is a borrowed concept, and one on which I am not willing to embark" she said on the phone few weeks after they met. He admired her strength and candid nature. The few times they met, she brought along Raaxo and encouraged him to bring a friend along as well. "If two people are interested in marriage in Islam, then they should meet each other only in the presence of others," he remembered her saying. He did not even know there were such details about courtship in Islam, but he went along with her wishes, obeying all the rules she laid out for him. He proposed to her after three chaperoned meetings. She accepted, and they were married seven months later in a small religious ceremony held at the local mosque. Haybe was not particularly religious, but he went along with her desires, knowing well she was the one for him.

She sent money to her relatives in Somalia to hold a religious ceremony at the local mosque to bless her new life with Haybe. Haybe admired her simplicity. Women he had courted in the past all wanted big, lavish weddings they could ill afford. They wanted to show off, to splash their insecurity all over the scene for a few days. Ceebla, on the other hand, had nothing to prove to anyone. Nadifo fled to Hamar two months before the ceremony. Haybe and Ceebla both knew why Nadifo had left Minneapolis, but they kept the ugly truth inside, never talking about it. The thousand dollars Haybe sent to Nadifo to do a similar blessing ceremony in Hamar was returned.

Three weeks before she fled to Hamar to escape his wedding, Nadifo urged him to come over one night. It was nearly five months after he met Ceebla. He had not yet made his intentions known to his family; he lived in Eden Paradise, some thirty miles away, and was busy with his new law firm. He preferred to visit Nadifo on weekends when he had more time, but she insisted that he come as she had a pressing matter to discuss with him. Haybe was never the topic of grievance with Nadifo; he naturally reckoned she would be complaining about Henna or Bile who were proving adept at keeping their mother awake at night. When he entered the apartment, Nadifo was frazzled. The redness in her eyes assured him she was crying. He took a seat next to her after she reluctantly accepted a respectable peck on the hand. He felt the resistance, which he was used to, but today she held her hand at her side firmly refusing his touch.

"*Salaamu Caleykum, hooyo*, are you well?" he asked before he settled into the seat.

"My affairs should not concern you!" came the boorish answer. Haybe was tongue-tied, unsure of what to say next. All sorts of problems presented themselves in his mind. Before he could formulate a response she wailed loudly, beating her chest and assaulting her head with her fists.

"She is a Gobaad! Why would you marry a Gobaad?! She is lower than you; she is not your equal! May Allah stress you the way you have stressed me! May Allah punish you with severe punishments, Haybe! May you never witness prosperity with her!"

"*Hooyo*, calm down, what are you talking about—"

"Don't you know we don't marry her kind?! How many times have I told you that! You have angered me and distressed your family!" she said, not allowing him a word. "Could you not find a fine noble girl in the streets of America? I will bring countless such girls to you! Professional ones, pretty ones, and girls who will obey you and serve you! Here, right next door is Mecca's daughter Raqiya, a pretty girl from a good family! Why are you so blind?! A lucky man took her older sister Ebyan since you refused her, but the younger one is still here! Why must you dirty my blood line?" She continued wailing, sternly staring at him. He has never seen her upset this way. He could not explain his decision to marry Ceebla, even though he did not know her tribe: every time he said he did not care about tribalism she threw a shoe at him, like she had when he were a little boy. He responded to her firmly when she personally attacked Ceebla. "She is trying to cleanse herself through your blood!"

"*Hooyo,* she is an honorable woman, she is religious."

"What does her type know about religion? They ate unholy meat, she is using you!"

"I will not allow you to talk negatively about her, okay? You don't know her!"

"Yes, but I know her type, you naïve bastard! Did you also know she is a divorcée, older than you, she just wants to make a life for herself with you because she has no other choices?"

"She has plenty of choices—and by the way, she is not older than me! Even if she were, it wouldn't matter!"

"How is she not older than you when she is a divorcee?"

"What does her divorce have to do with her age?"

"Of course it does, it is your stupidity that is blinding you!"

"Haven't we gone over this before? Why are you repeating yourself?!"

He has known Ceebla for five months and never once asked her what tribe she belonged to or about her divorce. Now Nadifo revealed a part of Ceebla he did not know, a part of her which has no importance in their courtship. Nadifo's revelation changed nothing about his feelings for Ceebla. *She is the one, whether Nadifo approves of it or not,* he reasoned as he drove back, dazed.

POUTS AND PIETY

L eave the one in jilbaab kill the other one!"

"No man, don't kill them! Just take their money!"

"Look, if these bitches survive, our asses are in jail, man."

"Man! What the hell was that?"

"Did you kill her?"

"Oh man, you killed her, man! What did she do? Oh my God, why did you kill her?"

"Did you get it?'

"Yeah man, I got it. Let's go! Get out the back door."

"What is going on, guys? What is she saying? What y'all sayin?"

"Why did I bring this stupid gaal? Come on, Jason I'll explain later!"

"Come on, *waryaa*, what the hell are you looking for?"

"Man, you know these bitches have lots of gold! Maybe we'll get lucky!"

"Hey come on, this way, Jason, come this way."

"*Walahi*, I think they are both dead!"

The bodies lay side by side. One fully garbed in *jilbaab*; the other modestly dressed in jeans and a blue turtleneck sweater. The metallic warm smell of blood lingered in the room, splashed on the walls and carpet. The woman in jeans lay in an expanding pool of blood, originating from her head. She lay face down in a pile of junk, magazines, plates, cloths and cushions from a divan in the living room. The other woman stirred, sticky with blood; her jilbaab stripped and bits of old newspaper and other junk stuck to the clumps of blood and skin on her back, she lay there gasping for air.

Moments after the two women were shot a man knocked on the door. Receiving no answer, he cracked the door open. He peeked in before entering. The gruesome scene shocked him; he murmured the prayer of death quietly, *"Innaa Lillaahi wa innaa Ilayhi raajicuun"* He then closed the door hastily and found himself vomiting outside the building. Confused and delirious, he paced to the corner gas station unable to locate his car which was parked a few steps away.

Shivering and throwing up all the way, he rested his head against the gas station door. He pulled out his cell phone but quickly put it back into his pocket, remembering it had no credit. Then he looked around to locate a pay phone, and was sick one more time. Unable to locate a pay phone he entered the gas station to use the phone inside, but the attendant was not behind the counter, so he went around it and grabbed the phone to dial 911. He detailed the horrific scene he had witnessed moments earlier, giving the address and other pertinent information. He turned around to leave the area to find a hefty middle aged woman with limp greasy hair directly behind him. He tried to maneuver around her, not noticing the gun she held on his back.

"Oh my God, please don't kill me" he said shaking.

"Who the hell told you to come behind the counter? What did you steal?"

"Nothing I swear, I was just using the phone, please don't!" he said emptying his pockets onto the floor.

"Why don't you use your damn cell phone, moron!" she said, snatching his cell phone from the stuff he emptied onto the floor.

"It's not working, it's broken—I mean it has no credit!" he said, trying to hide his fear.

"There were some people shot in that building, I was just calling 911, I swear," The hefty woman went through his pockets, still holding the gun on him. When she did not find anything she pushed him towards the door.

"Don't ever do that again, you loser!" she said putting the gun inside her pants and throwing the cell phone at him.

When the paramedics and police arrived, they found two women in their thirties, one already dead, the other barely alive.

———⊗———

Haybe had not heard from Ceebla all day. He repeatedly called her cell phone, to no avail. He had lost track of time visiting a client in jail. Court days were usually cumbersome, particularly when he appeared in front of Judge Harrison.

The pompous, self-righteous, bigoted Judge had never accepted Haybe's achievements as an attorney. He often deliberately mistook him for one of his defendants. When he encountered Haybe in the court-room, Harrison's eyes protruded from their pale red sockets, past the thick-framed silver glasses. He acted surprised, as if he had not seen Haybe in his court room only hours earlier. Wonder, astonishment, and dismay creased the flabby pouches that composed his face; his foaming lips pouted sourly. For the longest time Haybe assumed that maybe all black people looked alike to Judge Harrison. As much as he wanted to make excuses for the Judge, he knew he would rather not hear cases with men of color at the helm—so Haybe began to look forward to days he appeared before the Judge, just to spite him. He wondered —with little remorse—that he would probably give the old man a heart attack.

"Honey, I'm not sure what is going on, this is my fifth message. It's ten o'clock. I just got home. Please call me back to let me know what you're up to."

"Honey, it's me again. It is past midnight, where are you?"

"Ok, Ceebla, I am beginning to worry now. What is going on? Please pick up the phone." Haybe fell asleep on the couch watching American Justice.

———⊗———

"Hello?" Haybe fumbled with the phone, awoken from a deep sleep by its screech.

"Hay-babe? Are you Hay-babe?" asked the voice on the other end, mutilating his name.

"Yes this is Haybe, what can I do for you?" Haybe asked still sleepy, wiping his eyes from sleep while moistening his dry lips with the wet tip of the tongue. He sat up rather quickly, still delirious from sleep. The clock radio next to the sofa said it was three-thirty in the morning. Still in his suit, he drew his stiff limbs into a seated position.

"Sir, we have a young lady here at the hospital, we found her—"

"What! Ceebla! Oh God, what happened?" He stood up straight as a board, his heart racing, not waiting for the man to finish his sentence. "Where is she? What happened? Where is she? Oh my God! No please, God NO!"

"Sir, calm down; you need to calm down—"

Haybe was at the scene shortly. He was not sure how he had arrived at the hospital. Not certain where he was. He recited the few Quran verses he knew, sobbing the entire way. He snapped at the receptionist who directed him to the ICU on the fourth floor. Unable to wait for the elevator, he rushed up the stairs to the ICU ward, pinning a hospital worker, who was pushing a cart full of hospital food to the wall. He finally reached the room. He halted for a minute, almost unable to go, closing his eyes, nervously licking his lips before entering.

Inside, he saw the ghastly scene. After eight hours of surgery, Ceebla was unrecognizable. Her face was swollen and bruised, her eyes sunken and blackened. Her head had been shaved. He wasn't permitted to touch her.

"Oh my God! Who did this? Sir answer me! Who did this to her?" he demanded the officer in the room to explain, then started to pound the wall with massive fists. The police officer attempted to restrain him.

"Sir, you need to calm down."

"Hey stop that, you need to get out of here," two nurses and a doctor sped toward him. Haybe began crying and shaking. The policeman seized both his hands, pulling him towards the door.

"Stop that shit, what the hell are you doing?" he resisted the policeman.

"Sir, let us talk outside—she is unconscious. How are you related to her?"

"Who did this? Did you catch him, did you—?"

"Sir, sit down here; we need to—"

"No way! I am not going to sit down!" He proceeded towards the room again but found his way barred by a security guard who stood in front of the door. Haybe let forth a stream of curses.

"Sir, we need to talk to you." It surprised him how compassionate the police man sounded. He returned to the waiting area dazed. The policeman sat next to him, unsure what to do. Slowly, he began giving the details of the crime. He alluded to finding Ceebla with another woman, "Jameela." Haybe had never heard of a Jameela. *Who is she*, he wondered. He ran to the bathroom to vomit as the police officer described the frightening murder of Jameela and the near-fatal shooting of Ceebla.

What was Ceebla doing in this woman's apartment? Who has done this? He sat next to her bed as she staggered back and forth between life and death holding her hand.

A surveillance camera in the same gas station where the man reported the crime had captured six adolescent men high-fiving each other as they bought beer with their new-found fortune an hour after the crime.

The next day all six were arrested—five Somalis and one American, all in their late teens: Shire Samatar, Bile Gedi, Guleed Dafle, Sugule Casayr aka *Faruur*, Mire Jeenyo, and Jason Martin. One of the young men later revealed how they followed the women from Fifty-Fifty mall. Faruur knew Jameela fairly well, they said; she'd been his qat supplier. He wanted to rob her and get some free *qat*.

They all agreed that Faruur was the mastermind behind the crime, that he had specifically targeted the victims because he realized they would have some money on them. The others had come along for the joy ride. Bile had brought Jason, his neighbor, along for some fun. The motive behind the gruesome murder was not so simple. Finger pointing began as soon as the culprits were offered deals to snitch on each other. The police heard several different versions of the same story.

When their fresh dusty feet hit the clean, cold concrete of first grade, the hopes of their fatigued parents were falsely raised. How was it that they had strayed from the path to greatness? Why had these refugee kids fallen? Their families endless recount of how they raised them with sweat and blood, performing the harshest of menial jobs—driving taxi-cabs, plucking chickens, picking up the wasteful leftovers of exuberant Americans in massive shopping malls.

The refugee parents, growing older by the day, dreamed of the day they would retire in Somalia, while their rich, educated American kids would send them monthly stipends so that they could live lavishly among their destitute relatives in Somalia. The sacrifice was well worth the futures they were to have as returned parents of American educated children.

At home in tribal warfare, the parents had taken up arms in the name of tribal cleansing, and yet they hated their children for the horrendous crime, killing one of their own in a foreign land. In this alien culture, the refugees had somehow stumbled on righteousness. Somewhere between the monstrous war they waged against each other, tearing apart their lives and devastating their homeland, and their emigration to America, they had acquired a sudden morality.

They overlooked the fact that these are children of violence, that their childlike pouts had witnessed the desecration of human flesh. That they were children of war, the product of reviled days—that even as fetuses in the solace of their mothers' protruding bellies they heard nothing but guns, artillery, killing and the massacre of innocence. These children lived a legacy of hate, bequeathed to them by the very parents who sought their piety. Even in exile they hear endless conversations about fundraising for arms, constant hate talk against one tribe or another. They are privy to the constant hypocrisy of their parents boasting religious piety outside the home while they plan the massacre of innocent civilians in the name of tribal warfare. Their fathers consumed qat daily and yet forbade them a joint.

How different is a drag of a joint from a chew of qat? They argued in the privacy of their American minds. *How much more criminal is shooting a rival gang member than its shooting a rival tribesman? Isn't it all the same? Aren't drugs still drugs, no matter what name you give them, and killing, killing?*

Their poor parents mistook the streets of America for those of the nurturing villages they grew up in. They believed that the streets were raising their kids just as their own villages did in Africa, oblivious to the violence of the home country which had merged with that of the host country, simply and seamlessly. They were flabbergasted by the actions of their kids, never questioning their own.

Ceebla had stopped at the mall earlier that evening to arrange a meeting with the tailor to sew some outfits for her upcoming wedding. She had bumped into Jameela, whom she had met through Raaxo, at the mall. Jameela had asked her for a ride and Ceebla had agreed. As they approached her apartment, Jameela had invited Ceebla to come in and look at some new merchandise she had just received from Dubai, including some unique jewelry sets. Ceebla accepted, curious about the new stuff. As they entered the apartment, Ceebla heard uproar behind them. She did not think too much of it until the noise got louder. Jameela was busy with a phone conversation and did not hear the fuss behind them. Ceebla tapped Jameela on the shoulder to get her attention. When Jameela noticed the young men behind them, she smiled recognizing their faces—some of them were her customers.

When they entered the apartment together, Faruur asked Jameela to hand him the qat money that she had in the apartment. She protested, arguing with him. That is when he shot her carelessly, as if her life did not matter.

Ceebla begged them not to kill her, handing over her purse willingly, hoping they would spare her life. That was the last thing she remembered. One bullet went through her shoulder and one through the leg. Another bullet went through her stomach, barely missing her spinal cord. It was the bullet that skimmed her head that knocked her unconscious.

She remained in the hospital for six months, learning to walk again through physical therapy. Her speech was impaired. Haybe witnessed her daily ordeal and felt guilty. He could not help but think that she had been targeted for her boldness to marry him. As their wedding day drew closer, she had received many threatening phone calls jamming up her voicemail.

"Your kind doesn't marry our sons, leave him alone! Do you think Haybe will marry you? He is only enjoying himself with you! You better find your own kind! Nobility does not mix with your blood!" Every time she received an obscene message, she would go to Haybe, distressed. She had actually considered leaving him at one point when the pressure had gotten unbearable, but his steadfast support and assurance that the women who called her were simply jealous made Ceebla change her mind. But he wondered if she was targeted because she was marrying him? Or did she stumble on a bout of bad luck? Something in Ceebla's gut told her his family was behind it. Bile, Haybe's brother, was among the men in custody. The incident created a rift between Ceebla and Haybe for a while. She was suspicious of Nadifo—wouldn't it serve her purpose to get her out of the way, so she could marry her son to a desirable bride from her tribe? But Haybe unwaveringly disagreed; no matter how cruel Nadifo could be, he could not believe her capable of committing such a horrendous crime. But the buzz in his mind created all sorts of scenarios. Why was Bile involved, could it be a coincidence? Why

Ceebla? He could not help but be angry with Nadifo and her refusal to accept his wife-to-be. Although he convinced himself Nadifo was not behind Ceebla's fatal shooting, he wondered even if slightly that Nadifo's obsession with blood lines and family nobility could make her do such a thing—but killing a human being? Was that a possible action from his devout mother who seemed to put Allah and his prophets above all else? Would she put her own son to commit a crime such as this? Nothing made sense and Ceebla's nagging to get to the bottom of it dissuaded Haybe from sharing his inner opinion. For the first time he saw Ceebla's angelic soul soured by a need for revenge. She wanted to use the legal system to the fullest extent possible to bring whoever was involved in the matter to justice. Meetings with Ceebla became remorse-ridden. She was struggling to regain her strength and speech, and yet it was the contempt she held for the young men who attempted to kill her that consumed her energy. He felt conflicted. He wanted to support her but he was unable to find the same amount of revenge inside him to pursue the matter the way she wanted. For the first time Haybe began to question their courtship. Maybe Nadifo was correct to say he could not undo centuries-old traditions. He put Ceebla in such great danger he began to worry what was next. He began to worry about the future. What would they do after he married her? Would they try to kill her again? But who were they?

MAY 15, 2002.

Dear Hawo: The most powerful nation on earth is home to some disconsolate people willing to believe anything to feel good. I am illiterate, as you know, sister, and as such I can only fathom the empty slogans behind the lies that tell women it will make them youthful and more beautiful. Yet I admire the relentless nature, the cleverness of the messages. They come on at all odd hours of the day, never relenting. They want to deliver happiness in a bottle and suck away badness. Body parts are sliced away in the hope of reinvention. How can one feel good when one tampers with God's natural creation? I do not know.

The end must be near, dear sister, these people live so lavishly. Their shops are massive; one single shop could be the size of Gobwanaag. I cannot grasp the sheer size of one store! There is a whole section for dog food. While humans waste away in utter despair in Gobwanaag, dogs here have hospitals, hotels, and special foods. Imagine the world where a dog lives a better life than a human being.

I am sorry sister; I am taping this message the next day, I am not sure what I was saying? I just came from a man who has gone mad. They say he has something called depression, the doctors here prescribe pills that create an atmosphere of eternal rest—happy pills. The natural climate of life is forsaken for a temporary relief. And yet, constant desire for heaven on earth continues.

Depression, anxiety, and stress are diseases diagnosed easily by doctors here. They prescribe pills for them. They tell me I have PTSD, I don't know what these letters mean, but I throw away these pills. What I feel is the natural discomfort of life. I am homesick, I am lonely, I feel I don't belong here, there is nothing depressing about it, it is only facts! I have many pills lining the bathroom cupboards. I take none. I feel fine without them. Did you ever hear of someone suffering from depression at home? These are rich peoples' illnesses, known only to people who have achieved so much, people who now have free time to analyze their psyche, while many others are busy trying to survive.

INAPT WHOLESOMENESS

Somali children, like other African children, are tossed at one relative or another when parents deem it necessary. Shirwac has by now gotten used to being tossed: it was in essence a big part of who he was. When Henna claimed him back she was still living at home, but that changed when she abruptly got married and left, tossing the boy once again, this time to Nadifo. No one really frowned on the idea of parents leaving their children abruptly. The children are not notified or given an opportunity to discuss the matter. On the contrary, the kids are expected to appreciate the gesture that some relative is willing to put up with them and so they are told to be grateful. And so Shirwac ended up living with Nadifo. He would accompany Nadifo every morning on the J18 bus. People at the bus stop showed up everyday looking fatigued, as if they were brought to the stop against their wishes. Nadifo dropped Shirwac at school on her way to ESL class. Shirwac got an earful every morning that Henna claimed her busy schedule did not permit her to care for him. Nadifo would have one-way conversations making sure the boy heard the entire tale whether he wanted to or not.

"Why would she take you away from Tusmo if she was not up to the challenge? I don't understand her selfishness, she is so self indulgent, 'Oh hooyo I am travelling with my husband,' 'How is Shirwac, I wish I had time to come by and see you all', well then why don't you, instead of travelling so much with that white man? She should come and take care of her responsibilities, but no, of course not, she is too busy with herself and that American man. And who else did she think will take care of you—Cartan, Warsan or Haybe? No one has time for you, but me, just remember that Shirwac."

Shirwac was ready for a diversion every morning, and this particular morning as they approached the bus stop Shirwac's eyes widened when he noticed a couple embracing affectionately. He gawked at them: they held each other so close they were breathing each other's air. The girl giggled while the boy traveled all over her body with whispers and kisses. Shirwac turned to Nadifo, glad the conversation about Henna halted.

"Why are they doing this in public?" he asked timidly, ashamed for them.

"Be quiet, stop asking stupid questions! Turn your eyes away, waryaa!" *How does one discuss such issues with a child?* She struggled to explain the situation to herself, let alone the boy. *Everything is in public view here*, she contended. *Whatever happened to doing such things behind closed doors?*

Mrs. Bailey, the native Indian woman who usually sat next to Nadifo on the bus, joined them at Sunshine and Washington Road. Her long graying tresses were pulled into the usual braid. She twisted her mouth of decaying teeth into a smile, greeting Nadifo. Her homely, faded rags sagged around her knees, covering part of her scabby, dusty legs. Many of the people who rode the bus appeared as though they had been run over, soiled with circumstance, robbed of the dreams that supposedly line American streets. There was plenty of hard life and struggle in the faces of the bus riders. She wondered how these people had inherited such lives.

The black homeless man Mr. Stan Tunstel dragged himself and his filthy, weathered "Linens & Things" paper bags onto the bus. No one knew exactly where he came from; he appeared every morning smiling and singing. The paper bags and a bunch of multi-colored plastic sacks contained all his earthly belongings. Nadifo could see through the translucent plastic label-less bottles of salad dressing tucked neatly amongst a few old newspapers and some aluminum foil, rolls of Saran wrap, paperback books with the covers ripped off, receipts, old soda bottles filled with pebbles, and many other unidentifiable objects.

He coughed a deep, wet-sounding cough that seemed to sap all of his energy. He leaned heavily on a chipped wooden cane. Nadifo brought him food and occasionally gave him money. He praised her profusely, although he knew she did not speak much English,

"Kunta Kinte, African queen, thank you, my Nubian sista! You are from the motherland aren't you, yeah; I hear it is real pretty over there! Where is your Kinte today?"

"Where to this morning, Stan?" Martha chuckled at his comments.

"Picking up my check! Hallelujah it is Friday!" He beamed widely.

Pale and chalky, Martha Clayton moved her false teeth from side to side while stroking her long greasy gray hair. Where the bobby pins failed, an aging rubber band kept her hair in place. Her energetic, sunny disposition did not reflect her true situation. Nadifo gazed at her with sympathy, thinking where were her children, relatives, siblings?

Martha called Nadifo "Scarves"—they shared an unspoken familiarity and a mutual admiration. Martha's massive home sat at the end of Indian Creek, not too far from Nadifo's apartment. It was the only American home Nadifo had ever entered. The cruelty of old age in America shocked Nadifo, wondering aloud sometimes if that is how she would end up. Martha's house was messy and altogether dirty, in dire need of deep cleaning, although she insisted that she did not need help, mainly out of embarrassment. Nadifo started to come by anyway to help and sometimes just to listen to Martha recount interesting stories about her life, although Nadifo rarely understood a word the women said.

Photos of Martha's stylish, more glamorous days adorned the living room end tables. Three children and a man appeared in the pictures. The pictures revealed a comfortable, happy life and a petite, elegant woman.

Nadifo's visits increased as she realized she was the only person who had entered Martha's house in years. Nadifo enjoyed her usefulness, knowing that company was all Martha needed. The easiness she felt in Martha's house surprised even her. Nadifo admired Martha's energy. The sickly Martha, who appeared much older than Nadifo, was at the bus stop every morning to run errands. She brought a large, dirty canvas bag with her, which she filled with things she collected on her errands. Things she bought and sometimes things she found around the neighborhood. Martha did not eat for days on end; her teeth were missing and she drank heavily.

An African-American man in his early thirties had joined the bus gang lately. He wore a large gold earring, long, untidy, drooping dreadlocks, and colorful African attire. He purposefully removed his headphones to lecture them.

Everyone looked forward to his arrival. He uplifted the gloomy bus ride. He talked about the *story* of the black man, talking to no one in particular but preaching to the whole bus, or anyone who seemed even slightly interested. The *story* of the black man was an ongoing tale of injustices such as police brutality, black men's gloomy disposition in America and how the politicians did not care. He seemed to know his topic well and would start where he left off the day before. He had equal dislike for all politicians, including African Americans:

"You know who Jesse Jackson benefits, that's right bro', that's right—himself. Where is Al Sharpton when all these brothers are being put in jail for no apparent reason? That's right bro, he is in his fat house enjoying the wealth he created in the name of civil rights!"

Sometimes it seemed they were all walking the line of sanity. Nadifo, Mrs. Bailey, Mr. Tunstel, Martha, all of them, had more in common than a bus stop. They were survivors.

A somber Somali woman hauling several children waited with them. Balance seemed impossible as she attempted to quiet the child riding her hips and soothe the other two who threw fits in their double stroller. Three older children took advantage of her distracted state and started squirting juice from their bottles at the people waiting for the bus. She did her best to maintain order, every so often striking one of the misbehaving older children. When greeted, she did not return the greeting and did not engage in conversation with anyone. Fatigue had lined her pretty face.

A fair-complexioned stylish girl got on the bus just before it pulled away from the stop. She stalked her way to the back of the bus, her glowing, near-naked form shimmying to an unheard song. She blew a large, fragrant pink bubble while she murmured the words of the song, "humm, humm, love...me...oh yeah" Shirwac's enormous eyes almost popped from its place, "Ayeeyo, she is Somali, right?" he asked confused.

"Yes Shirwac. Now shush! Keep your voice down. Don't you see? She can understand you," Nadifo scolded him.

"But why is she naked? Her stomach, it is naked isn't it haram?" he exclaimed, glaring at the stud on her belly with disgust.

"Shirwac, shut your mouth. Don't embarrass me."

"Shame on her and whoever brought her to this world! Are they not afraid of Allah? How can they let their children behave this way?" Nadifo said loudly enough for the girl to hear. "Bismillahi Raxmaani Raxiim, Allah shield us from such dishonor, May Allah burn her in hell" she continued.

An African-American man in his early twenties got on the bus. He looked around searching for someone. Then the girl called from the back,

"Hey, Derrick, here, come back here!" Nadifo looked up. The lanky brawny man walked to the back of the bus where the girl sat.

"Wasup, Saafi? Hey sexy," he said, slumping next to her.

"W'sup baby," she replied. They cuddled and began hugging.

"Girl, you are hot, I like that outfit!" he said, pressing against her.

"Ayeeyo, that girl is stupid! Is she not Muslim? Why is she doing that stuff with that American guy, she is *akhas*?" Nadifo looked very uncomfortable.

"God forgive our sins," she sighed. "Shirwac, stop showing me sinful acts, shush, don't talk anymore, you are a troublemaker, hush your mouth!"

"Do you know this naked girl?" Nadifo turned to the women hauling children.

"This is Xalimo's daughter" she replied casually, looking in the girl's direction while forcing her children in their seats.

"Which Xalimo, not Xalimo Abdi Sulub"

"Yes," replied the woman. "That Xalimo!" Nadifo pitied Xalimo to have birthed such a vulgar girl. Poor Xalimo would pay for the scandal of her daughter, her ways would disgrace the whole family. Somali women dreaded the birth of such a girl, promiscuous and disgraceful. Honor is the only true treasure and credit family posses. A good reputation means great marriage proposals and prosperity for a family. Honor allowed some women to walk tall while others slouched in embarrassment because of their daughters. In order to spare a poor mother the agonizing shame a girl like this could bring, women like Nadifo stepped in to scold straying girls. It was their responsibly to keep these girls in line; after all they were in an alien country where these girls drifted from culture and customs.

Shirwac stared at the girl and the American guy with a constant, intense gaze, but he reserved his comments. Rage collected in Nadifo's entire body, causing her lower lip to tremble. She felt a rise in her stomach, churning acid, and a knot in her throat as the bus rattled with vigor. *How could this girl do that in front of God? She is as unholy as the one taking advantage of her,* Nadifo mulled over, and then quickly rose from her seat and moved to the back of the bus where the girl sat. She quivered with stored anger and shame.

"Does your mother know what you are doing? Why are you disgracing poor Xalimo?" Saafi looked up, shocked; she put her hand over her parted mouth.

"Oh my God, what the—" Nadifo's face came uncomfortably close as she bent to level with her.

"Look at me," Nadifo demanded, shaking the girl's thin shoulders. Saafi turned her face in the opposite direction, avoiding any contact, shrugging. Nadifo's belligerence mortified her. Saafi pretended not to understand the language the woman spoke; she continued looking through the side window of the bus, ignoring Nadifo and busying her fingers with her cell phone.

Saafi quivered with anxiety, her mind raced as she looked at her nude outfit. The pink wife beater with a playboy bunny on the back and black mini skirt with a split on the left side was not the outfit she wore when she left home for school. She left home that morning with a full garb, long skirt, long sleeved shirt and a heavy scarf that covered her upper body. The bare outfit she wore hid under the heavy garb she wore to leave home. She peeled the long skirt and scarf off in a MacDonald's bathroom, planning to put it back on when she returned home. Now her charade would be discovered. She covered the tattoo on her arm with her purse, shaking and her mind in disarray. The bus's trembling coincided with a shiver down her spine as she thought of her mother. She knew this woman whom she did not know would out her, telling her mother what she wore and what she did with Derrick.

"Yo, Saafi, who is this lady all in your business?" Nadifo oblivious to him; kept shaking Saafi, shrieking in Somali. Saafi closed her eyes in panic.

"Why you letting her disrespect you like that?" Derrick stood up to push Nadifo.

"Hey, just shut up!" Saafi said pulling him back to his seat so that Nadifo would stop humiliating her.

"She can't be talkin' to us like that—we grown folks," he insisted. Nadifo began attempting to shame and guilt Saafi with stories of how her poor mother had sacrificed everything to raise them alone after their father had fled abruptly to pursue other interests. Saafi looked down the entire time.

"For real, you need to go somewhere with that, lady!" Derrick stood up, pointing his finger in her face. Everyone on the bus chuckled. Some eagerly watched the clamor. They did not understand what Nadifo said, but it was clear that Saafi was being reprimanded.

"Ma'am you need to return to your seat; please do not move around the bus while it is in motion," the bus driver said through the intercom.

"What is she saying? Is that her daughter? Oh my God, she is hitting her?" the patrons inquired.

"Ma'am, please return to your seat immediately!"

"Give her some elbow room! Why you all up in her face?" Derrick attempted to get up and push Nadifo again, but Saafi pinned him to the seat once more.

"Shut up!" Nadifo said unexpectedly and in perfect English, no less.

"I know you ain't gonna let her talk shit to me!" Derrick was up now, ready to strike Nadifo.

"Let's just get off this bus, babe," Saafi said, shaken.

"No, we will not get off this bus! Who is she to make us get off the bus? Yo, lady, why you all in her face? Go back to wherever the hell you came from, you trippin'!" Nadifo dashed back into her seat. The sweat of frustration formed a slick on her forehead.

"Come on, just get off, Derrick!" The couple snuck off the bus, but not before Derrick had flipped Nadifo the finger—not that she had any idea what this hand gesture meant.

"Why did you say that to her, you don't need to disrespect her like that?" Saafi said sniffing.

"Babe, she was rude and disrespectful; I was only trying to protect you, know what I'm sayin'?"

"But you don't need to say 'go back'; that means you have no respect for me, I am, after all, one of them."

"No, babe, for real, it ain't like that! I was hella mad cause she was hella aggressive, that's all."

"I don't appreciate you calling her names; it means you diss people like my mom, that ain't cool—it just ain't," Saafi said carefully.

"Come on, babe, its cool, don't be like that."

"These are my peeps..." she began to cry. "I will be in a whole lotta trouble when I get home; my mom probably already knows about this," Saafi sobbed.

"It ain't right; it just ain't right."

"Calm down, Saafi, it's okay..."

"I don't know what to do; she'll kick me out again." Derrick wiped the streaming tears from her soft cheeks. "She will send me back home this time, I know I am done, I am so done! I'm not supposed to be wearing this, oh my God, what I am going to do?!" Saafi said, pointing to her clothes. The slim girl took baffled steps as she reflected on the ramifications of her outfit. Her name, Saafi, meant 'pure and clean'—yet everything about her life in America was the opposite. The name was no longer befitting. With meandering reflections, she staggered with Derrick, who marveled at the very sight that created distress in her mind.

OCTOBER 17, 2002. MINNEAPOLIS.

I was apprehensive at first to witness the variety, availability, and ease at which these items existed; a web of guilt would overtake me, my dear Hawo. How could I easily reach and touch polished bottles of drinks, massive butter containers that could feed a whole village, extra large containers of rice, oil, and water, row after row of juices, cakes, chocolate, and stuff I have yet to figure out. How could I reach the end of the checkout line where a rouged girl with long black nails and blue hair lounges with a smile that escapes through a silvery pierced tongue, ready to bag the massive items while she pops pink bubble gum? How could I carry these items and store them in a massive refrigerator already overflowing with uneaten food? How could I take them out to prepare a perfect meal, on the electric stove that comes on with a mere switch, instant gratification? My dear Hawo, I starved myself for months, fasting to overcome this onus.

In this country people eat at all hours of the day. Food has replaced everything else. My children now eat constantly, at whim: while watching the noisy machine called 'television', while they drive cars from place to place, even while in bed at night. Imagine taking food to bed! This abundance of food has created diseases of which we have never heard. Imagine dying from too much food! I know it is hard for you to digest.

This is our reality, while yours is daily hunger. You go to great lengths to provide one meal a day for your entire family. As you go to sleep hungry, we overfeed ourselves.

I remember the tale you told of our cousin Hadiyo. She hid her frail, disappearing body for months before passing away from starvation. Every time I see wasted food, Hadiyo comes in front of me. Even the trash here looks too precious and valuable to discard. I wish I could send the wasted food to you. It would the entire town for months. In fact we are in the season when Americans indulge, eating, giving each other gifts and eating even more!

In mid-sentence Nadifo is interrupted by Bile. She does not turn the tape recorder off. The On, Off, Rew and FF buttons are still too complex for her. The confusion often results in Hawo receiving tapes that contain conversations between family members not intended for her.

"*Waryaa*, don't come in here, get out!"

"*Hooyo*, your weird friend, the homeless woman is here."

"Who is my homeless friend?"

"You know, the white woman."

"Oh, Marta, tell her to come in."

Nadifo continued taping the message which was ongoing throughout her conversation with Bile.

Sister this poor woman is my friend—she has no family, this country is not good for old people.

"Hi, Marta, how you are?"

"Hi, Nady. You busy?"

"No, me talk to sitter."

"What do you need a sitter for? Where is she?"

"No sitter, Marta, S.I.S.T.E.R," Nadifo spells out the word.

"Oh, sister! You have a sister? I didn't know you had a sister here!"

"No me talk here, me tape message for *sister* in Somalia."

"Oh you are taping a message, ok."

"You want say hi?"

"Hi! What is her name?"

"Hawo."

"What?"

"How do you spell that?"

"H. A. W. O., you know, like Eve"

"Oh, her name is Eve, oh Hi, Eve, Hawo whatever your name is! My name is Martha. Your sister is my good friend. Come and visit us here sometime."

"Yes, Marta. Tank you. Me cousin go Somalia, take tape."

"Oh, ok. Could I borrow some orange juice? I have a friend over and…."

"Yes, Marta of course, you want give orange to you friend."

"No actually we went to the liquor store and—oh never mind."

"Yes, you give friend orange juice, right?"

"Yes, yes, exactly! I want to give my friend some orange juice."

" Henna! Henna come here. Marta you ok? You sick."

"No, a little hangover."

"What?"

"Oh, never mind nothing, I am ok."

"Henna, give Marta what she needs."

"Oh, Marta, what this?"

"Ouch! Nady that hurts, I just shaved my mustache. Why did you pull that hair, gee whiz it hurts!"

"Oh me though something else."

"Ok, Nady see you tomorrow. Ouch…bye, Hawo!"

"Henna, the crazy white lady needs you."

"Who you callin' crazy, little idiot?"

"Hooyo, your crazy friend is hitting me! Ouch,—get off me, homeless lady!"

WORD LINK

Martha and Nadifo are an unlikely pair. They did not speak the same language, were from different ends of the spectrum, and according to the climate in America the women should be sworn enemies for the simple reason that their respective religions were on a collision course. One Muslim, the other a Christian of sorts (a rather secular one); the odds were against them, when their relationship was at its best. Not even the ambush against Martha in Nadifo's apartment after a Somali man was killed after September eleventh could shake their odd but endearing friendship.

Yet Nadifo and Martha defied the odds of what society has set as the norm. They did have one thing in common: they were both tough and willful. And maybe for that reason they chose each other's company even if society frowned upon it. They met at the bus stop and Nadifo would often come to Martha's house to simply vent. Martha's house was a safe venting place. She knew Martha would not repeat her problems like her Somali friends would, and the advice she gave, although often disoriented, was sometimes useful.

It was a chore to complain to Martha though. Nadifo used whatever English she could remember, but mostly reverted to Somali. And Martha, whether she knew what was going on or not, came along with her, sometimes changing the course of the conversation altogether.

Glistening with fresh tears, Nadifo banged on Martha's door as a winter chill hit her nose. The cheerless clouds hid any hint of the sun, adding to the gloom of the day. These are the days Nadifo wished for the blazing sun of home, anything to escape the harshness of Minnesotan winter. She was distracted, briefly forgetting the reason she was banging on Martha's door, when Martha's door sprang open ever so vigorously. But it was not the ferocity of the door that agitated her so much as the boozy odor and Martha's disoriented tipsy nature. Martha swung the door open and went back to her favorite spot. She drank from something in a brown bag. Nadifo had no knowledge what Martha kept in that brown bag. She was not privy to the fact that Martha's tipsy nature was due to the content inside the bag. Martha had started using the brown bag to conceal her drink only since Nadifo came into her life. She fondly remembers the day a year earlier Nadifo absentmindedly drank out of a cup containing a mixture of something she should not drink. She spit it out quickly and when she found out what it was she accidently swallowed, she prayed several prostrations and washed her tongue out more than twenty times. She was hysterical, asking Allah to forgive her. That is the day Martha decided to hide her alcoholic drinks in a brown bag.

Back in the day when they were the ruling elite in Somalia, Cartan drank alcoholic drinks. Actually back then all the men and some women drank alcohol, it was the elite thing to do to show off one's western values. Somehow there was something alluring about acting as a Westerner—that is how one knew one had arrived. She had never had alcohol herself; the odor had bothered her, and there was something taboo about alcohol. She was past those days when she viewed everything her husband did as sophisticated: now she frowned on anyone rumored to drink alcohol—anyone who is rumored to drink alcohol is an outcast.

Martha kept quiet for a while, observing Nadifo, then tersely asked "What the hell is the matter with you, are you crying?" That was Martha, crude when she needed to be compassionate. "Who the hell made you cry?" she continued, barely looking at Nadifo and busying herself with the brown bag.

Nadifo wiped her eyes with the edges of her shawl. "What you drink, Marta you drink *khamri?*" she said, curious about the brown bag.

Martha took a sip, swallowing hard, and then turned to her, noticing the inflamed redness of her eyes. "What is k…what are you saying you know I don't speak that weird language of yours," she said, fidgeting with the brown bag.

"You know *khamri*, the thing that make you crazy, you drink that," Nadifo wanted to snatch the brown bag and find out for herself.

"Scarves, have you been crying?" Martha repeated, attempting to change the topic.

"You drink *khamri?*" Nadifo would not relent.

"No, Nady, I am drinking rum," Martha chuckled, taking an enjoyable gulp.

"What rum?" Nadifo appeared at ease now.

"Rum is like coke, wanna try some?" Martha giggled again, passing the brown bag to Nadifo.

"Oh coca cola, okay that good."

"Want some?"

"No, no I ok," Nadifo refused, she vowed never to drink from Martha again ever since the incident. Then she sat quietly searching for a way to tell Martha what she came to discuss.

"Marta—Marta, Cartan, he wife pregnant another baby," she said in a frail voice, as if she were tired of repeating the line. She wiped fresh tears from her face.

"Jesus, are you pregnant?"

"No me no pregnant, Cartan he wife she pregnant," Martha kept silent for a minute, took a long slurp from the brown bag then turned to Nadifo, who was hysterical by now.

"I am sorry are you upset because you are pregnant, how did that happen you are my age?"

"No, not me pregnant Cartan his young wife pregnant."

"What the hell do you mean young wife?"

"Marta, listen me, Cartan me *L & R* husband he new wife yesterday, now I find she pregnant."

"How can that skinny dude get married to another woman? Isn't he married to you?"

"Yes but me religion four wives."

"Well, it's against the law to have more than one wife in this country. Gee whiz, how did he get four wives?"

"No not he four wives, religion four wives—he one another wife and me."

"Ok, I think you are saying your asshole husband has another wife, but I am not sure how, the dope head can go to jail for that!"

'But he no jail, he only marry for religion."

"What does religion has to do with any of this? Look, I'm confused where the hell is Shirwaa, call him—you're playing with my mind!" But Nadifo insisted on telling the story herself. She attempted to tell Martha about Cartan's new wife, but Martha conducted a whole separate conversation in her head. She was fixated on why Nadifo put up with him in the first place. Her final response surprised Nadifo, who was searching for some sympathy from Martha.

"You know, you could find yourself a boyfriend if you took those things off and showed your pretty figure. As a matter of fact, I have a friend who would be just perfect for you."

And so like many times before, Martha and Nadifo had a unique discussion and each took something from the conversation—maybe not exactly what each intended, but something nonetheless. Nadifo left Martha feeling better and Martha bid her friend goodbye feeling sorry for her, feeling responsible for liberating her. The confusion with Martha reminded Nadifo of the humiliating conversation she had with Dr. Osborne her internist earlier in the week:

"Dakhtar I am horny!" Nadifo said as she attempted to explain the pain in her back.

"Ok, I am not sure I can help with that, Mrs. Cafi!"

"Yes Dakhtar me horny so much."

"Ok, mmm, is your husband around, I mean I am not sure what I can do for you—"

"No, no me no husband now."

"I really don't know what to tell you, then, knowing you are a devout woman and all."

"Yes, but me very hard every night no sleep and I need medicine for that."

"Ok, I am not sure if we are talking about the same thing but the problem you are complaining about does not have any medication, but to make sure we are talking about the same thing let me see if I can bring someone to help with the translation."

The woman interpreter on the phone clarified that horny and hernia were not the same thing. Nadifo left the doctor's office humiliated and vowed to never see him again. Hernia, horny, hermaphrodite, hemorrhoids—they all sounded the same to her and frankly she did not see the difference, "H, H that is all I hear," she said to the woman, "All I hear is the h I do not know what any of them mean, but the dictionary I used assured me that word which starts with H stood for back pain!"

THE MERCILESS ABANDONMENT

Nadifo was getting ready for class the next morning when Martha knocked on the door. She walked in, putting out her cigarette before entering the apartment. She poured *shaah* from the flask in the dining room table and sat comfortably on the sofa as Nadifo got ready. Tupac's "Dear Mama" was coming from Bile's room. Martha still reeked of alcohol and looked tired. Nadifo worried about Martha, who was either not sleeping enough or eating good nutritious meals. No one could ever explain to Nadifo that Martha had a drinking problem that kept her up all night. Her bad eating habits did not help her situation either, but Nadifo could never put the finger on what ailed Martha. Martha wanted to get a new dress for Stan's funeral. Stan had been found dead a week earlier in a shelter he was staying in. Nadfio agreed to skip class and go along with Martha. As they walked to the bus stop, Martha explained in great detail how Stan's body had been found. She told Nadifo about his life, and how successful his daughter was in Atlanta. Nadifo understood only a little about Stan's life, but she understood Martha's fondness of him.

As they approached Phyllis' Place, Martha's favorite consignment store at the mall, Martha was overcome with emotion. She kept speaking in a low tone voice, saying something to Nadifo, who was not quite paying attention as her eyes were glued to the lights that hovered above them. The sheer number of people at the mall scared Nadifo. She was glad Martha was close by, not noticing that Martha was crying. The colorful Christmas decorations, jolly Santa and his elves, and the loud Christmas music overwhelmed Nadifo. Eventually, however, she settled into the rhythmic crowd, watching children cry and women swing large shopping bags filled with toys, looking for lost little ones. This was the first time she had allowed herself to enjoy such a scene. A few years earlier, shopping at glamorous stores around the world was not a scary situation but an expected one; but since the calamity that had befallen her life, something as simple as shopping at an American mall engulfed her with awe.

Suddenly, she had lost Martha, and assumed that she had walked into one of the stores. When she retraced her steps, however, she found Martha on the floor surrounded by people. Martha was crying frantically. Making her way through the crowd, Nadifo squatted down, trying to comfort her.

"Marta, what happen? Who did—?"

"Excuse me ma'am, we need to take her inside," said a man in a in a navy blue uniform. Martha was hiding her eyes. The security guard tried to clear the ring of people around her.

"Get these shitty people out of here!" she shrieked. "Where the hell is James!" she attempted to get up from the floor, but was overcome with fatigue. "Nady, call James, tell him to get over here right this minute!" Nadifo was confused. Which James was Martha referring to?

"Ma'am could you please get out of the way?" the security guard pulled Nadifo away from Martha. Nadifo was distressed and pushed back at the security guard, but she was no match for his weight. "Ma'am what are you doing? You need to get out of the way, this is an emergency situation," he said, pushing Nadifo out so that she was out of the crowd where Martha lay.

"Stupid man, no hurt me!" Nadifo equally nudged him, and scratching his arm.

"What the heck did you do that for?" he said touching the scratched area.

"Where is James?! Call my kids!" The security guard took Martha to the office, ignoring his scratch. He sat down and gave her some cold water; Nadifo followed them cursing the security guard.

"*Bahalyahow budhuq budhuqsani*," she said forcing herself inside the small crammed office.

'Ma'am you need to get back or else I will lock you up!" the man said, his over-baked freckles expanding with the anger in his face.

"She my friend, stupid man," Nadifo said, trying to force herself inside. He stood there blocking her, peering down at her

"Scarves, Nady, where are you?" Martha said from inside. Nadifo struggled, looking for ways to make herself seen by Martha who was sitting inside the office, oblivious. The man closed the door behind him with a lock and took Nadifo by the collar, lifting her slightly from the floor.

"I am not sure if you are deaf or stupid!" he said the massiveness of his hand blocking Nadifo's air. She did not struggle with him. She simply lingered motionless.

"I am going to lock you up if your dumb terrorist ass does not leave now!" he said letting the 'now' linger on his tongue to make a point. Releasing her to the floor with a thud, he turned back abruptly, letting her fall. Nadifo turned around and kept walking ahead. Fresh tears wetted her face, not because of pain but because she felt helpless. People stood around watching.

She sat outside the office, anxious. Where was Martha? Why was that mean enormous mean fat man with the baked face keeping her away from Martha?

An hour latter Martha emerged from the office in a wheelchair. The massive guy pushed the wheel chair while Martha protested.

"I don't need to be pushed in a wheelchair fatso," Matha said, attempting to get up. "Let me down, you idiot, do I look crippled, fatso!" she reached behind her to strike the guy with a fist, landing a weak punch in his stomach which was parallel to her.

"Look, lady you need a cab or something to get home—you sure as hell can't walk."

"Nady, call James! Where is he, anyway?" Martha was disoriented and frail. Nadifo hastened towards her. She wanted to hug her, or touch her or something. Instead she just said "Marta, you ok?" Martha said nothing.

They left the mall without purchasing the dress for which they had come. While on the bus Martha cried and Nadifo read verses from the Quran to calm her down.

"Stop reading that voodoo stuff to me," Martha said "What are you saying anyway, you crazy woman?" Nadifo continued blessing Martha, even as she protested. "I am not one of your damn people, stop it!"

Empty beer cans lined the walls of the living room as they walked into Martha's house. An old horn, a saxophone, and two violins clung to each other in one corner of the living room next to the *Kaban* Nadifo had brought back from Somalia. The rest of the house was scattered with furniture and other items Martha had collected from trashcans around the neighborhood. Nadifo noticed a mahogany nightstand that she had thrown away a month earlier in one corner. Orange drapes that had turned a rusty color with a coating of grease and dust lined the large living room window. The house was dark, cold, and somber. No matter how much Nadifo cleaned Martha's house, the clutter kept coming back.

Martha did not talk about her family much. From what Nadifo understood James played the saxophone and the horn, and was learning how to play the violin. He was a talented musician and a lieutenant in the army. He went to Vietnam and two years later came back a suspicious and sad man. His happy-go-lucky, music-loving nature was replaced with an irate hallucinating one. He was unable to keep a job and began drinking heavily. He beat Martha viciously, giving her several concussions and a broken leg from which she still limped. He took all of their savings to gamble and buy alcohol. He became obsessive with endless hours of cleaning his musical instruments, going over the edges of his violin over and over. The violin had been a gift from his best friend and music buddy Peter Lightner. They were college roommates and went to Vietnam together, but Peter never made it back alive. Martha had to work since James was unable to hold a job. She started working at the local animal shelter. They had three kids, Ella, Miles, and Scarlet, named after James's favorite entertainers. After he came back from the war James stayed home with them, until one day Martha came home to find Miles in his crib covered in his own feces and the girls in the kitchen trying to cook for themselves. Ella was four and Scarlet three. Ella had broken eggs into a mug, including the eggshells. Scarlet was pulling a chair towards the stove and James was passed out in the living room floor, swimming in a pool of his own urine, a few broken beer bottles floated around him while the front door of the house was wide open. From then on, Martha took the kids to Mrs. Pitman, her neighbor, to babysit. One day Ella inserted a small piece of chalk into her ear. Mrs. Pittman took her to the emergency room, leaving the other two kids with their father. By the time Martha came back from work she found Miles and Scarlet dead. They were shot by James, who also took his own life.

JANUARY 10, 2003.

I can't erase the images out of my mind, the images of old people thrown together to die? Mrs. Strickland was a surgeon by training, but you would never know that today. The frequent urination and constant trembling of her body, you would never know her shaky hands ever performed surgery on anyone. Why, my dear Hawo, are American kids so cruel to their parents? Why do they send them to a place where they await death? And why did I volunteer in Paradise Hill, a place where death and despair loom? It is the only thing in America that ever reminded me of the refugee camp. Both places are filled with people who wait for something to happen in their life. In the refugee camp it was people waiting to better their lives; in the Nursing Home, as they call it, it is people waiting for death to arrive to relieve them of their loneliness. Both await relief. Mrs. Strickland's kids come when it is convenient for them: they are busy raising kids of their own who will eventually put them here. It saddens me. It is a society that does not admire the wisdom of the old. Imagine how much they are missing when their wisdom is taken away and thrown in a sad somber place?

Mrs. Strickland passed away. Now I am helping Mr. Brice. He is a former astronaut; they are the people who go to the sun or moon or somewhere up there. He does not seem to be reaching for the stars these days. When he came here, he was confused because his wife of thirty years kicked him out. He has four children, but no one ever visits him. He is often sad, and sometimes I find him crying. He never tires of telling me how he ended up here, at Paradise Hill. He said his wife and kids kicked him out, when his wife found a new man, I am sorry sister I know I am sharing sinful story but it's what the man told me. He is older than her, so she is in her sixties, while he is now in his eighties. She took the house and all his money and kicked him out. I sometimes try to call his only son, but he is rude and abusive to his father. It's really difficult for me to understand what is happening to this man, but it's how old people are treated in America. Sometimes I feel sorry for him, and other times he amazes me how he is preoccupied on his wife's beauty, his money, and his wife's new man. Even elders with dementia are impressed by material stuff, sex and beauty. Mr. Brice enjoys talking about himself when he was in the army. He loves showing me his muscles and old pictures of how robust he used to look. He repeats the same story three or four times a day, each time I pretend not to have heard it before, that brings him a little comfort and a smile on his face. May Allah help these old people.

CULTURE CLASH

Shirwac sat across from three middle-aged women. The first woman, Mrs. Robby, was large with bulky spectacles and a polka-dotted brown sweater. She was the one tasked with the job of calling the meeting to order. The woman to her left was a heavy-set, light-skinned African-American woman in a very stylish black suit, bright pink shirt and tiger eye jewelry set with large silver hook earning and a large necklace that rested below her neck. To her right sat an older petite white woman with a typical middle-aged white woman look— she looked either bored or sick throughout the entire hearing. On one side of the table sat a burly Mexican man with stubbornly coarse short afro. The principal at Glenn Park Elementary, he appeared ready to spill the beans. He wore a blue shirt with a red tie that clumsily opened at the neck. His blue shirt was marked with perspiration at both arm pits, and he looked nervous. His forehead dripped with sweat as he shoveled through a stack of papers. Opposite the principal sat Haybe and Shirwac.

"Hello, everyone, thank you for coming to this hearing," said Mrs. Robby. "Shirac Gedi has been recommended for expulsion from Glenn Park Elementary School. The school will present it is case against Shirac. Honey, say your name for me again one more time, did I pronounce it correctly?"

"It is Shirwac Gedi."

"Yes, that's what I thought, Shirac. Okay, please hold all your questions until the end of the hearing. Now please raise your right hand and repeat after me."

"I solemnly swear that I will tell the truth, the whole truth and nothing but the truth, so help me god. Say 'I do' one by one," her pale face flushed crimson as everyone repeated "I do" after her. After every one took the solemn oath to tell the truth, the school principal explained the reason he was recommending expulsion for Shirwac. He explained how Shirwac had chased a cat on school premises a week earlier, throwing rocks at it and trying to hurt it. The school principal said Shirwac would be harmful to other kids around him if he was capable of hurting a cat, and recommended that Shirwac be transferred to the school for troubled children.

"Oh no, now why would you do that, honey?" asked the large Caucasian woman. "Is there something we need to know, what is going on in your life? She turned to Haybe. "Is Shirac facing any new challenges in his life? We all know when a child is cruel to animals, there's an underlying emotion he or she is trying to express. We recommend that you take him for some serious counseling ASAP." She turned back to Shirwac. "You've been a model student; I hope we can get to the bottom of what is going on in that little mind of yours. Okay, honey, you need to talk to a counselor; he will probably prescribe something to calm you down."

"But I did not harm that cat! Roberto Perez made it all up to get me into trouble!" Shirwac said, enraged.

"Calm down, Shirwac, ma'am. Shirwac assures me he had nothing to do with that incident, Mr. Gonzales here seems ready to expel the kid for no apparent reason," Haybe said, looking calm but angry.

"I am sorry, sir, and you are…." said Mrs. Robby, looking confused and peering down her nose on the notes.

"I am Haybe Gedi, Shirwac's guardian," Haybe said frustrated at the woman's unreadiness.

"Sir, Mr. Gonzales, did you witness this child chasing after a cat?" Mrs. Robby asked the questions while the other two women seemed to observe.

"No ma'am, but according to—" Mr. Gonzales sweat now dripped over his entire face, but he remained quiet.

"Yes, according to your favorite student Roberto, right, Mr. Gonzales?" Shirwac said, losing his usual cool. "Well, I did not do anything, you just hate me coz I am Somali, you hate all Somali kids, we know!" Shirwac was now crying.

"Young man, please control your anger!" Mrs. Robey said, hitting the pen she held in her hand on the table.

"Shirwac, take it easy, *abti*," Haybe said, rubbing Shirwac's back. "Ma'am, I have had these conversations with Mr. Gonzales before; every week he concocts a new story to get rid of Shirwac. I really don't appreciate the lies."

"Now, Mr. Giddy, Getty is it, you all need to calm down," Mrs. Robby said, unsure how to pronounce the name in front of her, staring at it as if that might make it easier.

After that incident, Haybe brought Shirwac to live with him and Ceebla. They enrolled him in the same school Idil attended. Haybe wanted to get close to Shirwac to mentor him; but Shirwac was no longer the little boy with a protruding belly in the refugee camp. He began asking questions, mostly about himself: he wanted to know who his father was. No one ever told him how he was conceived, how he came to be. He has known there was some controversy about his conception and birth. But he has never really cared about it until now; at fourteen Shirwac began to look for answers about his life. Once he moved in with Haybe his curiosity grew. He knew he could not ask Nadifo or other elder's direct questions—after all, the Somali culture is one where children never ask questions—so he began eavesdropping on conversations, but answers did not come easy. He heard nothing new. No matter how much he tried to piece things together, no new information emerged, and that frustrated him. So he decided to ask Haybe, the only man in his life he'd ever trusted who his father was. One day Shirwac walked into Kayd's room and found Haybe engrossed in changing Kayd. With Kayd, Haybe was soft, giggly, and childlike.

Shirwac sat on the chair near the window and watched them. Haybe continued playing with Kayd after he changed him; several minutes later Haybe turned around to find Shirwac sitting still, observing them. Haybe offered one of his blithe manly smiles.

"Did you finish your homework?" Haybe asked in a serious tone, still immersed in Kayd.

"No, not yet," Shirwac said, busying himself with the gameboy in his hand, not knowing exactly where to begin his questioning. He was not ready and felt apprehensive about asking Haybe who his father was. Every night in bed he rehearsed the questions he wanted to ask Haybe, but when the opportunity presented itself, he found himself speechless.

"Well, why the hell not man, what you waiting for?"

"*Abti*, who is my father?" the question came out of nowhere and surprised Haybe.

"Shirwac, go do your home work now."

"*Abti*, I am serious. Where is my father?"

"Why are you asking?"

"What do you mean, why I am asking? I need to know who I am!" Haybe put Kayd down and faced an intense Shirwac.

"Look, Shirwac, there is no reason for you to worry about such things in your life now. I—" Haybe felt awkward, not knowing exactly what to tell Shirwac, who stood erect, staring back at him.

"I don't like it when you say that! Please, *abti*, tell me!" Shirwac fought back tears, but no amount of convincing worked. Shirwac kept probing Haybe and Haybe continued dodging the question, promising to give him the answers he sought when he was old enough to handle it. But that was a lie, and Haybe knew it. He could never bring himself to reveal the situation which had brought Shirwac to life.

On several occasions Haybe attempted to ask Nadifo if she would give the boy the answers he sought. But she made it clear she did not want to think about it, let alone discuss the episode that had changed her entire life with Shirwac. She preferred to remain in denial about the

whole thing rather than let Shirwac know the details: in her opinion he was better off not knowing the unusual circumstances that had led to his birth. Maybe his own mother Henna was the best person to explain things, if she could ever muster up her life in a way that could be helpful to the boy—but Nadifo and Haybe remained skeptical of Henna ever taking such initiative.

Haybe felt stuck. Shirwac's constant questioning and his bold attitude ever since he decided to go on a fact-finding mission about his life had become tiresome. He felt bad for the boy, but his relentless curiosity had created tension between them. For the first time since Shirwac came into their lives, Haybe noticed Shirwac's demeanor changing. He'd been a well behaved, obedient and respectful kid. The shy boy who would never directly look any adult in the eye has now began having problems at home and school. His questions would sometimes border belligerence, and although Haybe understood the difficulty Shirwac faced in not knowing who his father was, the aggressive manner in which he sought answers did not help the situation.

UNTRENDY CURTAINS

Idil's loathing for people in Cedar Springs was never silent or subtle; it was boisterous and to the point. She did not respect authority, elders or anyone else who tried to impose their morals on her. "Try it on yourself first before you preach it to me," she would say to anyone who hinted she change her ways. Idil was every Somali mother's nightmare. She was hard-headed, outspoken and blatantly truthful to a point. Some women in the neighborhood would scorn her others would spatter the spit of evil when they passed her. Idil was their consciousness, the echo to their facade lives. She outed their secrets and dirty linens in ways they did not approve. The pressure society imposed on the mothers of Cedar Springs was downright cruel. Their misfit foreign life inflicted plenty of pressures. But they could only boast about two things since the rest of their lives were not at their helm: their home furniture, which they spent every last penny on, and their children.

Every mother bragged about the piety that existed in her household alongside the latest furnishings from abroad. They could not control their fate, but at least they would not be rumored to have raised indecent children, just as they would not allow anyone to gossip about their untrendy curtains. The cruelty and scrutiny of hearsay made mothers resort to dressing their daughters and windows lavishly, and so Cedar Springs held in its midst girls with double lives, forced by this new milieu. Heavy *jilbaabs* were a must now, no longer were women seen in the flimsy see-through dirics they'd worn for centuries, just as heavy burgundy color draperies were a must for every window at Cedar Springs. The youthful girls obeyed the sudden religious adherence their parents imposed on them; they were obedient, god-fearing and overall well-behaved in view of the elders. But the pressures their new Americanisms imposed on them were doubly coercive. They were expected to have a certain beauty, appeal, suggestive clothing and ever-lasting happiness. An eyeshot away from their parents and all the obedi-ence, and good girl righteousness flew out the window to be replaced by smoking, promiscuity and nakedness in the privacy of their own kind. Idil found their actions repugnant, but she found the mothers of these girls appalling as they flaunted their daughter's good religiosity when in fact they knew otherwise. The entire community lived on hypocrisy. Mothers who swore to have memorized the Quran and who paraded their knowledge of the religion would feed fictitious stories about their families. They would lie about their illicit daughters, doped-up sons and their cheating husbands.

These girls woke to a new devotion where their femaleness was pro-nounced, brutally inspected, cursed and seen as evil that could befall the family. Closely scrutinized and cruelly restricted daughters who have heard tales about the beauty of their culture which has freed it is females, resisted to lose their identity to the new culture their elders pasted on them. Their parents picked up this forceful culture from refu-gee camps when they stumbled on sacred devotion in the daunting life of warfare and poverty.

Why would they have to be the guinea pigs that received the sever-ity of a culture not of their making? Not only did they reject this new culture which their mothers were adamant about, they desired a typical America teen life. The constant buzz of happy teens on every glossy magazine inspired in them the desire to follow suit. They wanted what-ever that made silly American girls laugh with that vacant immaturity which apparently made them cheerful—wasn't that the epitome of the pursuit happiness?

They wanted to stay out late, go to parties, the prom, to the mall, and be like everyone else. But their mothers would not hear of it, so they got creative. They were bombarded with sex, looking sexy, dressing suggestively and being promiscuous. To achieve their goals they created their own culture with a pinch of Americana to the oblivion of their refugee mothers. They watched Gossip Girl, the Hills and America's Next Top Model. American teens appeared free, happy, spoiled and yet sad, and ungrateful. They wanted to act spoiled although they knew they were not. They wanted their priority to be their happiness, even though that kind of happiness was a borrowed term in their households. They wanted to reject the refugee status that separated them from achieving the ultimate teen status of self-obsession. At school they acted spoiled, as though they were only children, although they were one of many; they bragged about their lives although there was really nothing to brag about and they temporarily shelved the endless chores that waited them in their crammed apartments, the constant cooking, cleaning, babysitting and interpreting for their illiterate parents.

For a few hours a day at school they could be Fay, Sam, Nina, and Katy instead of Fatima, Samia, Amina, and Khadra. With their peers they could act their desire to be a typical American teen. Theirs was not a life filled with extracurricular activities where fretting mothers obsessed about their daily activity: they did not go to soccer practice, did not have music lessons or ballet, neither did they go to summer camp or swimming lessons. They were poor immigrant children who busied their creative minds with imagination to escape their own.

Even their walk vibrated with awe, their hips quaked with desire, destined for the life that eluded them.

Idil rejected the hypocrisy that existed at Cedar Springs. She was the voice of candor amid them, but she was detested by all because she went about her life in her own way, different from the rest. Difference was not welcome at Cedar Springs, where refugees from Somalia kept to themselves to reminisce about their decaying lives. She never wore the *jilbaab*; her favorite outfit was her tight jeans and hooded sweater, but at Cedar Springs girls her age wore long skirts and a jilbaab to cover their bodies, and so she invited spiteful gazes laden with insults and unflattering remarks. She did whatever she pleased, even if it were taboo, in clear view of others; being insincere and pretending to be someone else was not part of Idil's character.

She tossed a small ball around as she waited for Nadifo in the foyer of the building where she lingered every day until her grandmother came home from ESL classes. Like the day before when an older woman she had never seen before heaved big hips to throw venom at Idil for not covering her hair, the foyer was where Idil cussed or got cussed—it never failed. She was not bothered by these women, though; if they said one foul word she repeated twenty. Her snappish tongue would witness their flight. Her defenses were up and her tongue ready to lay malice on anyone entering her ocean. Xalimo Abdi Sulub stumbled through the lobby carrying several heavy grocery bags: the woman put the heavy plastic bags on the floor and came back to where Idil tossed the ball back and forth to busy her mind. The hood on her pink sweater concealed her eyes. She did this purposefully to avoid things that would get her into trouble. Idil pretended not to see the woman, although the woman's large frame and the kitcheny aroma coming from her clothes could hardly go unnoticed. Idil gazed at the ceiling fan that hovered over them, as if calculating the fan spin for a science project. She began to hum loudly; each hum coincided with a fan spin which created a slight echo in the large foyer. She turned away from the woman as if wishing the hum and spin would make the woman disappear. Idil knew Xalimo, who lived three doors from Nadifo's apartment, well. She also knew the woman was not coming to engage in some pleasant exchange: the day before she'd hurled a brown dusty sandal at her when she saw Idil on Josh's bike.

"May *Allah* burn you and your parents who allowed you to be naked in hell!" The woman said. Idil pretended not to hear, increasing the volume of the hum.

"*Naayaa*, I am talking to you," the sudden pull on Idil's hood tightened on her throat.

"I swear I will call the police on you, stinky old lady!" Idil roared, dropping her backpack to the floor.

261

"What the hell do you want from me? Why don't you find out where your daughter is before you even talk about my clothes!" coming face to face with the woman, Idil said viciously.

"Is Saafi at the library, or at the parking garage getting her freak on?" stunned by Idil's reaction, Xalimo looked around the lobby to see if anyone she knew was in the lobby to witness the vicious words.

"And where is your dope-head son Rasheed, the apple of your eye? That little sucker is either drunk or high!" the woman was shocked the mouth on such the adolescent girl could be so abrasive.

"*Naayaa*, shut your mouth! Xalimo don't you know not to talk to this filthy girl, she fears neither Allah nor her elders!" a woman said back from the safety of the elevator. Xalimo appeared staggered.

"*Acuudu Billaah Mina Shaytaani rajiim,* Idil *eeddo* come here, stop telling that poor woman's business to the world," *Hajiya* Shukri said, coming from behind Idil. She was a graceful elderly woman and the only one who had ever attempted to understand the girl's predicament; *Hajiya* took Idil by the hand and led her away. Idil doggedly followed *Hajiya,* but not without spitting more insults at Xalimo.

"How about your welfare collecting lazy husband, the respectable elder! Do you even know he has three other wives in this building?!" the woman toiled to pick the hefty grocery bags, causing one overfilled bag to spill. She fretfully attempted to collect the straying items while Idil continued the offensive.

"Idil, my daughter, be mindful of the evil eye, you have distressed this poor woman—look at her, she is shaking like a leaf!" Hajiya said as she dragged Idil towards the hallway to her apartment.

"You know your daughter is a mess! Your husband a crook and your son a dope-head!" Idil continued, not listening to Hajiya, frothing at the mouth she pulled away from Hajiya to return to where Xalimo stood aghast.

A toy truck being chased by a toddler landed under Idil's feet as she chased after the woman. Without any hesitation, she crushed the truck with the force of an angry adolescent. The little frantic boy ran back to his mother, who charged towards Idil with a fist.

"May Allah bring bad luck to you and whoever brought you to life!"

"And you, you are nothing more than a hypocrite!" Idil continued her attack on Xalimo, ignoring the little boy's mother, but Xalimo was nowhere to be found. She abandoned two of the grocery bags and rushed to the stairs to escape the stares of lobby traffic.

"Stop lying to yourself, coz you ain't lying to Allah, he sees the truth!" Idil continued even though the woman was nowhere to be found.

Idil's mind drifted to the previous night when she saw Saafi, Xalimo's daughter with a boy, holding hands. She wore baby blue jogging pants with matching hooded sweater; there was nothing beneath the sweater except a bra. Saafi had a name tattooed on her left wrist. Idil could not make out the name, but she heard the rumor that Safi's tattoo said "Derrick", her last boy friend's name. She also heard the rumor that Derrick dumped her for her best friend.

The diamond stud on her belly button accentuated a delicate midriff in great shape. Idil took a mental note of Safi; she swore the next time Xalimo ran her mouth about her she would use this scandalous scene against her.

A few minutes later Nadifo, dragging a backpack, surfaced in the lobby. She never occupied herself with lobby bustle, knowing well there often was a scuffle or two at any given hour. Her eyes did not lift from the black and white marble floors, the zigzags of it blurring her sight. She prayed silently, her right hand caressing against the rosary. Idil froze, abruptly stopping the cussing that overtook the busy lobby. By the time Nadifo noticed Hajiya Shukri's summons towards her, Idil was gone. In the lobby, news about Idil's sharp mouth and her attack on the woman added to the jaded day. Idil hid behind the stairwell, contemplating the bruises that were destined her way.

DECEMBER 25, 2004.

Sister, I ask myself who am I? Really! Canjeero-eating, hijab-wearing, broken English speaking, and stressed like most Americans. Am I American? Does that make one American? I never reasoned I would call myself American. The dark blue passport I hold does not confirm my belonging to this country. Who am I when my own grandkids cannot speak my language? When they detest what I want them to embrace? Who am I when America suspects my religion, and yet asks me to belong? Where do I belong? I dream of a home away, and yet I have had a home here for eleven years. So where is home? How can I ease my mind that America has given me literacy and driving skills, freed me so that I can do things for myself. Yet America rejects me in some ways. It makes me feel as if I am an alien, as if I don't belong. I have rights now, under the laws of this country: I can vote—I had never voted before I came to America, for in Africa we were never allowed an opportunity to choose a president, one was always chosen for us. Yet I am suspicious and they are suspicious. There is no trust between us. They mistrust my loyalty, assuming I am ready to blow up this country which has given me choices, safety, stability and Oprah. How am I supposed to assure them I will defend this country, that it's my Islamic duty to safeguard it? I can wear all the flags in the world—an act Americans have suddenly found patriotic—but I am still a Muslim, still under suspicion, still not patriotic enough.

I am happy when watching Oprah; she makes me think the kids have a chance here. Yet when I see racism it makes me think they should be among their own kind. Again Oprah, reminds me to believe.

Dear sister, I asked myself that question today, not because I was sitting around thinking where is home; in fact the question would never occur in my mind. I have never pondered it, because it was naturally clear home is Hamar, the place I long to be more than anywhere else on this earth. But I was watching Oprah, as I do every day at 4:00 on channel 7, to get the day's lesson, when an elegant young black woman was asked the same question by Oprah. The young woman, who is an American, an African-American, as they are called here, was talking in detail about an encounter she had had with a neighbor. The neighbor, a white woman of advanced age, asked the young woman where she was from. To which the young black women answered, here, I am an African-American. Then the white woman asked I know, but what part of Africa are you from? The young woman was tongue-tied—how would she know what part of Africa her slave ancestors came from? The question was insensitive and cruel, and so the young woman complained that she does not feel this is truly home, although her ancestors came over here two hundred years ago. Now if America does not welcome this young woman whose ancestors were enslaved in this country, could this be home for me? That is when the question occurred to me.

I should believe because the possibilities are so plentiful, despite the let downs. Shirley Chisholm was a woman who dared to dream: a black woman who ran for the presidency of this country when the idea was daring, and, to some, impossible, Amy told me about Shirley, to encourage me. To assure me that Asli, a gift from Cartan, and Hajir, a gift from Henna, can both dream and believe in the rights given to them by their country of birth. I do see a day when my hijab is not tarnished, a day I can say proudly without any hesitation, yes, I am an American, a Muslim American.

I could lie to myself all I want, to say I will go home one day and sit under a *mirimiri* tree in *Hamar Jajab* where I will sip tea with you and other relatives to catch up on the past. But I have been saying that long and it has no chance of becoming a reality now or any time soon. So should I accept my reality that I am a homeless woman whose home is unknown? Or should I join people like the young African American woman who are constantly asked where is home, only to become tongue-tied, and not know what to answer?

MIXING MADNESS

She was not even sure why she was enrolled in Political Science 101. College and Henna were ill-matched and she knew it from the first day of class. The whole roster call, reading, home work, group projects and endless papers of no innovative philosophy was something she was not willing to embark on. Nadifo had often reminded her that she was not the learning type, and college was an enigma to be figured out, and yet she was expected to attend college. And then there was the whole race and ethnic separation thing on campus which she did not see a point to. At U of M the Asian kids congregated in one corner of the student union, every one called them Chinatown, the Caucasians in another corner known as 'lala land', the Hispanic areas was 'south of the border'—nothing original there—and the African-American area was called the charcoal dump. There was so much hate and division among the groups it reminded her of the hate and division that existed in her own community. She was too new to care about race problems in America. She personally did not care to be labeled, she was not really black enough, and of course she had nothing in common with Hispanics or Asians, let alone Caucasians. While everyone fought for turf, she was an African in America, which meant she was unsure where she fit. Her plate was full trying to figure this American college life with its class schedule, class locations, a professor or two or three called TBA to pay attention to the nitty gritty nonsense of student hate and group association. She must have had the words "dazed and confused" on her forehead when Brian spotted her, baffled, across the hall. He was a senior and was auditing the same class. It was Brian who decoded college for her, and right there and then they became best friends. A year into their relationship after many nights of all nighters, papers and projects Henna would rather forget she was ready to marry him. Henna remembers it as if it were yesterday. How she was so eager to marry him and had defied her family to do so. A month before the wedding, she had asked her father to prepare for Brian's family. She informed him that they were coming to ask for her hand. She went to her father for things she knew Nadifo would not allow. He was reluctant, but he accepted it, thinking that at the very least he would give her away in the traditional way. He requested that she ask Brian to bring his male kinfolk. Brian was unsure what that meant—who was his kinfolk? He did not know, but in order for Cartan to give away his daughter, the men in Brian's family would have to ask for her hand, Henna explained. They would have to pay enough *gabbaati* to equal a hundred camels.

When they came, Brian and his father Kirk, cousin Matt, brother Dominic, and best friends Bobby and Sean were asked to sit with Cartan and the other men from his tribe. Nadifo left the apartment, finding the whole thing insulting. Why would Cartan waste his time with this appalling encounter? Everything about this marriage was wrong, she said. Why would Cartan expose his lost honor to the men in his family by bringing a gaal to sit with honorable cousins? How would they explain giving away their daughter, their cousin, their niece to a gaal? They knew it was unacceptable, but were complicit in the disgrace of their culture by their women. She decided not to have any part in the debacle.

Cartan and his tribesmen sat anxiously, chatting distractedly about politics as they waited for the Shields to arrive. No one knew how to handle the situation that was about to present itself. In Somali culture, the two families came together, and the daughter is given away to the groom's family, recognizing that although she would be a wife to her husband, she would still be a member of the original family, retaining her family name. How could they explain this to the suitor and his family when they expected Henna to change her name and become one of them? They would soon call her Mrs. Brian Shield. That was unnatural, argued Nadifo. Why would Henna swap her precious name given to her at birth through her father's proud lineage, for some name she hardly knew? A name which did not have any significance in her history? The day she changed her name, she would begin a new history, discarding her past, her family and her proud heritage.

The men from Cartan's side were nervous, each hoping he would not be the one asked to give away the cultureless girl. They abhorred Henna, pitying Cartan. Those who could not stomach the exchange did not show up. Cartan found himself on the defensive as the issue of giving his daughter to a gaal, was finally raised aloud. He even punched a cousin in the face after he insinuated that Cartan was allowing this to happen because he was a weak man.

Brian did his best to follow the direction at hand. He naively agreed to a tradition he knew nothing about, to make Henna happy. His father was appointed to give the *gabbaati*, the official gift, from one man group to the other. Mr. Shield had been briefed a few days earlier on how to approach his new in-laws: he was instructed to purchase a brand new men's shawl. He was then told to place inside it an amount of money that his family would give to the men in Henna's family as a gift.

Mr. Shield and his men arrived in full Somali garb. They wore sarongs that shifted about a bit uncomfortably and the customary hat and a shawl across their shoulders. Their movement was sluggish under the unfamiliar layers of clothing. Brian looked handsome, though relatively awkward. It was his idea to wear Somali clothing. His brother and friends could not wait to be free from the sheets of clothing that entangled them. They joined the other men in the room sitting on the Divan that lined the walls, cushions elaborately decorated with colors of Islamic embroidery. Mr. Shield tried endlessly to collect his feet under him like the Somali men. It appeared easy for the Somali men to sit on the floor and conduct this serious discussion. All Mr. Shield could think about the entire time was "how will I ever get up from this awkward position!" He wished for a sofa, or even a stool.

After Henna's side of the family accepted the gift and gave away their daughter to Brian's family, Mr. Shield was told that the couple can prepare for the religious ceremony performed by a sheikh, preferably in the mosque. Cartan asked his daughter to do that part of the ritual on her own, knowing full well that he could not marry his daughter to a non-Muslim in the holy mosque. His responsibility ended with the giving away ritual.

Henna picked an elegant ivory-colored gown that fit her slim figure perfectly. Her hair was twisted into a French bun and a tiara was nestled in her silken curls. After much preparation, argumentation, and conflict, Henna found bliss with her American husband Brian. She felt safe around him, describing him as generous, handsome, kind, and fun. She insisted that she would never find these qualities in a man from her country; she argued viciously when Nadifo had lined up all the eligible suitors from which she was permitted to pick, starting with her own cousin Qarshe. He was her type, wasn't he, they had liked each other, Nadifo insisted.

Henna's life began to resemble the mythical characters in the romance books she read. She often desired for someone to sweep her off her feet, that was her long-life dream, and when Brian came along he did exactly that. He was attentive and romantic, playful and ambitious. She was whole in his presence he never made her feel inadequate or imperfect. When her past was too painful, he offered open arms and a listening ear, constantly reminding her that he loved her. When she met his family, they welcomed her immediately, accepting her as one of them. The acceptance she longed for was finally here.

The band played Somali music. Everyone danced blissfully until the dawn hours, at which point the bride and groom left for their honeymoon in Morocco. It bewildered Shirwac, but he began to accept his new mother's new life. It seemed as if the newness of things would never cease. Here she was about to leave him again with a man he could only associate with people at the refugee camp who gave out food rations, arranged emigration plans and doctors visits, and yet they all laughed and danced through it.

Henna's annoyance with her community created an intimacy between her and Brian. Mothers withdrew their sons from the scene when they received word she was dating with the intention of marriage. No one wanted to have their son married to a girl with a murky past. That distressed her. When Brian proposed to her after a year of courtship, she accepted.

No one expected Nadifo to accept the union; she made her distaste for the union clear from the beginning. She would argue the transgression of her daughter's marriage to a non-Somali and a non-Muslim. She cried over it for months, prayed about it and prayed some more. She believed Henna's actions were a deliberate scheme to destroy her reputation. From the day of the onslaught until the present, Nadifo tried to control Henna's life. When she did not succeed, she was outraged. Her daughter was a failure, and often Nadifo felt that she herself was to blame.

This was one more blow to her soul; she was convinced it was all punishment from God. This was castigation for the sins she had committed: the attack, Shirwac's birth, and now this. She filled her sullen days with weeping and praying.

And so Henna sailed in her new American life with her American husband, doing American things. And Brian's nana gave Henna a chihuahua as a birthday gift when they first got married; she pretended to love it, patting the little dog and squealing delightedly. She named the dog Ursi which means sniff in Somali because the dog would forever sniff everything around it.

No one had instructed her on how to care for the dog, though. If she was not pretending, and fronting a love for the dog, the truth would reveal itself that in her childhood she chased innocent dogs and threw pebbles at them. She had never understood the obsession with dogs in this country, but it was part of the pretense she put on to love her new life with Brian. She wanted to desperately love the things Americans loved, and dogs she figured occupied a large part of American hearts. Henna did whatever it took to fit Brian's life, even taking in a little dog she had no business taking.

She knew better than to touch the dog, but she ignored the religious obligation that forbade dogs. She had no notion of how to care for it: the dog was often found whimpering, apparently from hunger, and it didn't occur to her it needed water. She never walked the dog and for the three months the dog lasted she never bathed it. By no stretch of the imagination were Ursi and Henna a good match. Henna found the dog too demanding, often ignoring the dog's needs. When Brian found the dog in the back yard one day, he was hysterical; it turned out a cousin of Henna's whom she had not seen for a while had found out that she was in the Devon Woods area married to an American. He drove all the way from Tucson to help her reconnect with religious obligations. Little Ursi, being the curious little chihuahua she was, had ran toward Damal, scaring him as he waited for the gates to open. When Ursi began its sniff around Damal, he kicked her slightly, injuring her. Henna had not remembered the last time she had seen the dog. Ursi died two weeks later.

Nana never spoke to her again, which was just fine with Henna. Her relationship with Brian had soured because she would not go to events with him. She found his friends boring and everything that appeared exciting at the beginning gradually became mundane. She could no longer fit into the life her husband had mapped out for them. She drove to LA every weekend to meet friends and escape a life she all of a sudden found boring.

One Saturday evening after her Bikram Yoga class, Brian asked that they go shopping. All he had to say was they were going shopping for her to jump at the idea. He rushed her. After taking a quick shower, she stepped into a pair of citizen of humanity jeans and headed out to meet him. Henna hated being rushed this way. She loved taking her time when showering after a hard workout. That was precisely the reason she escaped the gym showers: she felt uncomfortable being naked in front of other women at the gym. Her first time in the woman's locker room was a shocker. No one had prepared her for all the nakedness in the gym locker room! Although she saw herself as an open-minded person, she was traumatized by the amount of bare skin around her. Women felt comfortable toweling dry their privates while conversing about family, friends, and current events. She found it impossible to hold a decent conversation with someone whose breasts pointed her way and whose skin, flabby or not, exposed all its blemishes. From then on, she came home to take a long private shower after her workouts. She no longer wanted to converse with Jan, who was proud of her recent weight loss and found it necessary to stalk people with flabby arms and a sagging tummy around the locker room—or those like Olivia, who, with her severely thin body and stick-like bones, appeared obsessed with nakedness.

She met Brian at the Hollywood Mist boutique on Holly Hope Road. She found out the reason he had dragged her away from her luxurious bath was to purchase a gift for his nana.

"What does that old woman need gifts for anyway?" Henna asked disrespectfully. "She seems to have everything under the sun, doesn't she?" she continued, inspecting some colorful tank tops. "I mean, every few months, here you go again with another gift," she said while nodding at the store clerk.

"Hey, that's my nana, she practically raised me!" Brian exclaimed, trailing behind her.

"But you don't even like it when she visits," Henna snapped.

"It's only because we need our privacy; I don't like anyone interrupting our lives. Other than that nana is great." He reached for her waist and placed a peck on her cheek.

"But she is your nana, she practically raised you, there should be no privacy between you," she taunted. "In my family, we may not send flowers and cards with empty slogans once a year, but at least we take good care of each other. If there is a person down and out in our family we all pitch in to take care of him; you, on the other hand have some family members who are living on the edge in some trailer park somewhere, how come you don't send them gifts?"

"Hey, I don't even know that side of my family!" He looked slightly red in the face.

"But that is your father's family!"

"I have never met them, though." Brian squirmed uncomfortably.

"How many of them share that trailer in Missouri anyway? Is it fifteen of them?"

"Don't know," he said with rancor.

"The messages in your gifts are loud and clear—stay away! You are as good as the package this came in," she chided him, pointing to a green pastel pashmina.

"It is amazing how much she loves life, even at eighty; it is true what people say about you guys," she continued unfazed by his silence.

"Should I even ask what they say?" he asked afraid to hear the response.

"That you all love life so much you never, ever want to leave this earth!" she said it with a snide tone.

"I am sure we are not the only people who love life, don't you? Hey look," he said, changing the subject, "here are some Kate Spades, mom said nana wanted a Kate Spade."

"I can't believe she wants a Kate Spade at her age. Here is a cute tan one with zippers and a cell phone pocket, does she like tan?" she asked inspecting the purse.

"I think she'll love that. Let's take it."

"What else should we send her? It is her eightieth birthday, after all." Brian was relieved they had found something.

"How about a gift certificate from Bliss Bath?"

"That is a good idea, a day spa. I will tell her you picked it out." He grabbed her and placed a long deep kiss on the lips while she tried to balance the stuff in her hands.

"How about my gift?" Henna pouted.

"Do you want a Kate Spade too?" Brian was still holding her close to him. The clerk looked up from the cash register and smiled at them.

"No, of course not, you know that is not my style. I'm a Marc Jacobs girl; you promised me a Marc Jacobs bag, remember?" she asked, placing the stuff on the counter to free her hands. "Please honey, can I?" Henna stroked his hair while she drew his face close to hers.

"Are you sure you want it today?" he asked hesitantly. They left the store, gifts in tow.

When she escaped her life in Minneapolis, she judged she would never look back; but she began to think it might have been a mistake to pretend that she liked her life with Brian. The first year, it was fun and new. She pretended Christmas was cool, that hanging out with his buddies was fine, that spending weekends in the mountain was alright. But then it dawned on her that she came from a country where being in the outdoors was done to put food on the table. Africans went to the outdoors because they had to, not because they loved it. People avoided the sun because the sun was grueling, and people wanted to keep their dark skin a hue lighter. But there she was on some beach, laying next to people who strived to tan their skin: she lay there worried she would be pitch black while they baked their skin, barely reaching the hue they desired.

Christmas was not a tradition she was used to. And hanging out with the guys to watch sports was a stretch. She had put on a front, diving into his culture, thinking it was cool. Then she began to long for her own way of life. It became very clear to her that being away from her family and culture made her appreciate it more. She began participating in fewer and fewer events and stopped pretending she liked things that were alien to her. When she met Brian in college everything about him appeared interesting; back then everything about America appeared intoxicating. She immersed herself in everything American. She perfected the American accent, enjoying her new-found life, expressing herself through her fashion, music and friends, but somehow she felt empty.

CONCERNED OR CURIOUS

Henna had wanted to get involved in some organization that worked with immigrant women. When Barb Tyler, whom she met at the Y, suggested that she join Concerned Sisters, Henna jumped at the chance. She joined the organization thinking the women at Concerned Sisters would do activities that contributed to the betterment of immigrant women around Devon Woods. The idea behind the program was to partner immigrant women with little means with American women. The American women would mentor and empower them while helping them start their own businesses.

Concerned Sisters had started in Barbara Tyler's home, a socialite who made herself believe she just wanted other women around the globe to be free like American women. After four months Henna found the meetings to be nothing more than self-congratulatory social affair where women who had empty lives and full pockets could compare their ill treatment of the illegal immigrant women who raised their children, cleaned their houses, and cooked their food.

"I made it clear to Clara that if she had another baby, we would just have to let her go. It is enough that she already has three?" complained one pompous woman.

"I found my maid watching her soaps one day, just laying on my couch as if there was nothing else in the world she was supposed to be doing!" shared another.

"Hey, Hen, is Miriam still with you?" asked Barbara, taking the liberty to shorten Henna's name.

"No, *Barb*, Miriam moved back to L.A.," Henna said, rudely.

275

"So who is helping you around the house these days?" asked another—the shock of a wife living in Camino County without a maid straining her botoxed forehead.

"I don't have anyone; I can handle the work on my own," Henna replied, sensing the group's alarm.

"Hey, Hanna," Barb, with her thinking cap on, interrupted the other woman, "Hanna dear, how about if we—"

"My name is not Hanna; it is Henna."

"Hanna, Henna, hey what is the difference?" Henna's face jerked with annoyance, but she said nothing. "I think it's about time you picked yourself a familiar American name young lady, I think Hanna sounds so much nicer than Henna, what does that mean any way?" she said without a care in the world.

"You remember Karen's daughter-in-law, you know, the Chinese girl, her name escapes me?" She was talking about a Japanese-American who was married to one of the member's sons, a Caucasian man. "Well, you know she had one of these foreign names, and now she is Stacy Brown." Henna listened closely for the point that this woman was trying to make. "She took Jack's last name and replaced that two-letter last name from China. Well now she is Stacy Brown, isn't that nice?"

Celeste, who had been listening, covered Henna's stunned silence with, "Yes, indeed, simpler!"

"Now, Hanna," Barb continued, "surely it is time to take Brian's name; it will make things so much easier, right? It has a nice ring to it, Hanna Shield!"

Despite the ignorance of the women, Henna liked her involvement with Marshell Agwe, a Haitian widower with five children who ran a small food stand. Henna not only helped Marshell with her business, raising capital, she mentored her children taking them to the library, and sometimes taking Marshell's daughters shopping. Henna was amazed she could have such joy with Marshell and her children, despite her misgivings of the ignorant women who run the organization.

CEMENTING SOUR
EXPRESSIONS

As she drove to the Concerned Sisters headquarters, Henna inhaled the Southern California Pacific breeze in delight. She zigzagged through the rolling valleys of Pacific Road, which pulled the clear turquoise sky towards the distant horizon, melting into the rugged hills of Laguna Ranch Golf course. To her left she would see the Flower Fields in full bloom with their bursts of giant Tecolote Ranunculus flowers, minutes from the stunning ocean fronts. She chose this route for the tranquil moments of calm, which paled any issues she may have to confront. It is the moments she cherishes when outdoors enjoying every bit of the scenic view. From the first moment she set foot on this soil, Henna got the impression that Devon Woods was home to happy-go-lucky people unconcerned with much else except their looks and the size of their pockets.

The women at Concerned Sisters—mostly emotion-starved, perky wives—were similarly unconcerned with anything except their diamonds, the latest designer fashions, and the mention of their married names. These women, whom Henna found vacant and narcissistic at best, sought approval by arranging events they called "charity" that were more like extravagant fashion shows where they extended fake hugs and smiles while checking out each other's outfits and social calendars with envy. What deemed them valuable—their material worth and the charities they undertook—were polar opposites. They cared more about the seating order at charity events than the women they promised to help. That they managed to throw her off balance, forcing her to expose the most intimate issues of her life, was not the violating part of their rude inquisitiveness: it was the intrigue, or more correctly the captivation of what they supposed she may represent. Everything about Henna was a curiosity for these women. If she wore an outfit from the neighborhood mall they would show deep admiration for it, certain that it must have travelled some unconventional distance to make it to the shores of Devon Woods. In their minds, maybe the outfit has witnessed some scandalous ritual the tale of which they would be privy to. If she brought a dish for pot luck they wanted to know the ingredients, even if it were a simple dish. They craved exotic details and were awestruck by everything about her. Her presence added something to their lives. But there was something condescending about their fascination and awe. Their admiration was limited to their curiosity of her experiences. If she could share something of herself it may confirm all the barbaric things they associate with her.

The women took a keen interest in the dreadfulness of female genital mutilation, sometimes obsessing about the topic. The work detailed in the Concerned Sister's handbook and Mission Statement— to empower local immigrant women to establish their own businesses in Devon Woods —was sometimes discarded for the most intimate details about Henna's experience with FGM (Female Genital Mutilation). Suddenly she became their charity case and only fascination.

Of all the issues they could have taken up, the one that hurt Henna the most occupied their minds with unforgiving frankness. Their quest to supposedly create awareness alienated her. Henna found their approach revolting. They wanted to know how Henna felt about the ritual, but there was nothing genuine about their concern; Henna reckoned they wanted to appear worldly, and found her culture bizarre— FGM is after all the most bizarre issue to undertake these days. She was nothing more than an episode in their lives they could repeat. She would add to the excitements of dinner parties, family gatherings and casual conversation.

She found their approach snobbish and their curiosity strange. Henna did not hide her disapproval and she made it perfectly clear that the matter was not one for public debate. The more she refused to discuss the issue, the more fanatical they became. They asked eagerly if she had been abused by her father, brothers, or male relatives. They wanted her to own up to abuse she had never suffered.

"Aren't all Muslim women abused on some level or another?" said Barb, whose face this particular day was unwavering due to a Botox gone bad episode. "Were you allowed to get an education? Did you have to get married at an early age to some old man? Poor child, I bet you are happy to be here, lucky you, you made it out!" Their conversations were dull and predictable. She found them arrogantly uninformed. A four-year-old could ask better questions! They were simple, except they did not know how humdrum and ignorant they were.

They simply judged her without knowing anything about her. They did not take the time to know her personal experience; it was easy for them to just assume who she was. She regretted joining the group, spotting immediately their lack of compassion for the woman they were supposed to help and their shallow attitude towards other cultures. Besides a zip code, she realized she had nothing in common with them.

With their tight, expressionless faces, they formulated ways to "free" her. Henna chuckled at the picture. They actually wanted to reach out to her, to help her—but weren't they the ones who lead empty lives, when the only thing that lifted them was their husbands' money and the status that money gave them?

The very same women who cut away body parts willingly and braved unnecessary injections for society wanted to free Henna. Women who starved their already skinny bodies, and who viewed themselves as nothing unless they were Mrs.-so-and-so, wanted to free her. She found the entire episode ironic.

Barb, who kept referring to herself as a "liberal social do-gooder," as if Henna was supposed to celebrate that, took a keen interest on the matter—more so than the other women. She referred to FGM as "carving little girls' parts." Barb probed Henna constantly about the ritual. She was not necessarily interested in the cruelty of it and the pain these girls went through, as much as exposing the savage people behind it. She would ask very private questions.

"So how did it feel when they sliced you, huh?" You could almost feel the condescending curiosity emanate from her raw, shiny, post-op face. "Does sex hurt? I bet it does." Henna swore the woman was more interested in her sex life than in the pain, cruelty, and disgrace involved in the ritual she abruptly found interesting. "Does Brian know? How does he feel about it? Did they do you in groups? Oh, the horrible women who did this to you!" Her pouted, Botoxed lips seemed to be stuck on the word "Who".

How paradoxical, the very same woman who halved her nose three times willingly until the doctors could not find enough cartilage for yet another surgery, the same woman who had had three face lifts, a body lift, several breast implants, constant Botox injections to smooth a wrinkle here and a flab there, as well as numerous other surgeries which Henna could not pronounce, found the ritual barbaric. Somehow the body parts she willingly carved were not barbaric. No, the body parts Barb willingly discarded to undo what nature gave her was not barbaric. No of course not, the surgeries she went under were required by beauty standards. It was a must-have in order to appeal to her husband and be praised by society's norms—but FMG was an African ritual done by ignorant, barbaric people. Barb, with her very liberal, lipo-sucked, starving body, distorted fish lips and motionless forehead, never saw the similarities. She never internalized the cruelty and gracelessness of her missing nose and carved-up body. You could never convince the woman she was equally brutalized by society. Barb failed to understand the lifelong trauma going under the knife had on these girls. Unlike her, the girls who went through the cruelty of FGM would prefer to keep all of their natural body parts; unlike her, these young girls would never go under the knife if they had a choice. Unlike her, they were stigmatized and would recall the episode with agony; unlike her without the part that was cut they felt less whole.

She did not see the brutality of both societies; one that based its purity on unsuspecting little girls and Barb's, which celebrated her tight, injected face and sucked out fat, a society which cemented a lifetime of sour expression on her forehead.

THE GIFT OF PAIN

At Concerned Sisters, things were going on in their usual mundane way when Henna unexpectedly grabbed Delilah Simmons, shocking the rest of the women. Whether the ideas simmered in her mind for a while or whether she acted on impulse was not clear in Henna's demeanor. She grabbed Delilah Simmons' breasts, saying "when was the last time you fed your baby girl? Do you feel this?" As she squeezed her left breast; the women appeared too shocked to react. Next she pulled a compact from her purse and shoved it in Audrey Hancock's face, screeching "look what you have done to your face!" And then in a cold, calm voice she said, "what a shame, such a beautiful complexion, bleached to death. Hey Audrey, when you look in the mirror, who is that woman staring back at you? Huh? That fair white-skinned woman! Were you born light-skinned, Audrey? Is that your hair, your nose? Can I see a baby picture of you, Audrey? Or is that little black girl dead?" Audrey gasped, sitting back heavily in her chair. Barb quickly called security. Within a few minutes the meeting had come to an end and Henna was escorted to her car, panting.

Things did not begin as chaotically as they ended—the gathering only went awry when Barb, fresh from a Botox party, flew into the room where Concerned Sisters were having their weekly meeting, with her Prada nylon tote in one hand and a venti latte in the other. She brimmed with news, pulling out a long official-looking letter and announcing to the room that a women's organization had agreed to sponsor a benefit to help Henna educate her community about Female Genital Mutilation. She read the letter aloud excitedly.

"Our sisters in the Somali community are not enlightened, they don't know better. They may not understand the severity of cutting their body parts, they may not even be aware of the lasting psychological trauma such cutting may have. This is where an organization like ours can help educate and enlighten." Henna was lost in deep fury, repeating the words "enlighten" and "educate" in her mind. Barb and the other women started talking excitedly, planning a fundraiser to sponsor the event. Something in Henna broke. Before she grabbed the unsuspecting Delilah, she started talking, simply angry:

"You know what? I am offended that women like you, who suffer from addiction to plastic surgery, want to help anyone. Why don't you help yourselves first? Isn't that a good idea, Barb? Go tackle what is making you cut your face so much that you'll soon be giving Michael Jackson a run for his money."

"I am not going to take these insults from you, Hanna. You are crossing the line and I'll be damned if I'm going to stand here and listen to your insults."

"I am sorry, Barb—and it's Henna, by the way, not Hanna—I know you mean well. But look at you—it is a shame what you have done to yourself. Please go seek help."

"Young lady, I don't need help, and you need to take your opinion elsewhere." Then she flew out of the room as she had flown into it earlier. The others watched, horrified, as Henna finished her tirade against them; then they began leaving one by one as the security guard arrived to escort Henna out.

A few days later, Henna received a letter from Concerned Sisters claiming concern, despite declaring Henna's actions deplorable and barring her from attending any further meetings. They suggested that Henna seek therapy and wished her well for the future. Henna had never seen women who so happily swapped stories of how they endured all types of pain to have bleaching in places that should not even be touched, liposuction in places that do not even have fat to begin with, and cutting body parts to appear skinny and more refined. It is as if they wanted to outdo each other.

Women like Barb and others who lived in the affluent neighborhood she called home were happy to be the property of their husbands, yet somehow they never quite categorized their lives as not free. They downplayed their accomplishments, boasting of their husband's successes. They flaunted their "kept woman" aura. Henna expected to find women who were self-reliant and independent in Devon Woods: instead she encountered women who would not make a move without the approval of their men. Every aspect of their lives was consumed by how they wanted to appear for their husbands and how they could flaunt the material possessions these men gave them. They were their own worst enemies. Women who were accomplished and intelligent clipped away their vivid minds much as they had their bodies nipped and tucked to suit fashion. Henna didn't understand how it made them better women: how free were they when they couldn't even get a haircut without the consent of their men? Henna had an unsettling feeling she would turn into one of them soon, seeking Brian's approval to do anything, and soon enough feeling she was nothing without him. Is this the life she had strived to have? The culture she found suffocating at home with her family was beginning to look more freeing. She missed the women-only gatherings, she wanted to be alone once in a while without Brian on her tail all the time. She felt exhausted accompanying him everywhere.

ECHO AND RAIN

ady, sue him for everything he's got!" Amy said, taking the liberty to Americanize her name with an unauthorized shorter version. "Take the polygamist to the cleaner—that's what I did with Hunter." She would not allow Nadifo to get a word in, answering her own questions. Nadifo had never realized Amy could talk so much. "I sued Hunter for millions, and then he left everything to me and the kids when he kicked the bucket." She sounded cold and matter-of-fact.

The "kids" are Echo and Rain. Amy was serious in her advice to Nadifo after Cartan left her for another woman, but no matter how much she interacted with them, Amy failed to understand the emptiness of their lives. She could not fathom in this poor refugee community all you could sue one for was some shame and name-calling: Somalis did not sue each other for money, they just humiliated each other.

"Well, couldn't you sue him for the houses he left in Somalia?" *Yes, but they are all in ruins*, Nadifo reflected, still silent. "Mmm, I am sure you can get him some way or another. Damn. Does he have a job, so you can get his wages garnished?" Amy prattled on, oblivious to Nadifo's distraction.

"No, he on welfare."

"You could sue him for the apartment—isn't the apartment his?"

"No, it section eight."

"It is what?"

"Section eight."

"I don't know what that is. Is it some sort of a payment plan? Never mind—tell the authorities he is married to another woman, that ought to get him cut off from whatever you call that thing...," *No*, Nadifo wanted to say; she would never stoop that low; she couldn't bring herself to cut off the only means of survival Cartan had, any more than she could bear inviting the brutal, nosy authorities to meddle in their already ugly lives.

It was easy for Amy to switch the conversation from Cartan to Hunter Harington, Echo and Rain's father. Meeting Hunter was a fluke, she said: she was leaving the gym one day and he was coming in. It was love at first sight, to say the least, she said. Hunter was forty-two and the owner of "Harington Communications", a huge communications conglomerate; he was the father of three girls and in the process of divorcing his third wife. A self-made millionaire from humble beginnings, he pursued Amy like she had never been pursued. She played hard to get for the first time in her life. It was six months after she left rehab. She had had a devastating breakdown and was forcefully admitted to rehab for addiction to prescription drugs. From the way she told the story she was beginning to get back into the swing of things when she met Hunter: she said it was perfect timing, but her parents were not amused. They knew her weakness for men and they were afraid this was another one of her hard falls. But Amy was a changed woman, or at least she believed she was. Three years and two kids later it was she who was in divorce court suing Hunter for everything he had. It was messy and time-consuming, until he dropped dead at forty-five from a massive heart attack. He couldn't handle the pain of leaving all his hard earned millions to Amy. People whispered that she was the cause of his death.

Nadifo was surprised to see Amy at her door. She was now Amy Sky Harrington: where did Sky come from, and where had her family name Tucker disappeared to? Nadifo was afraid to ask. This new Amy with different middle and last names, a new life and brand new children—the whitest children Nadifo had ever seen seemed content.

Amy had disappeared from their lives abruptly four years earlier. The last time Nadifo saw Amy, she stormed out of a library classroom, enraged. Amy never looked back. The women got an ESL teacher called

Lourdes; Lourdes would never teach them ESL with the same enthusiasm as Amy. Nadifo kept the stuff Amy threw on the floor that day, she is sure it's still somewhere in the apartment. Here she was, knocking on Nadifo's door, a changed woman. She looked mature and somewhat settled, but Amy happy? That was a stretch. The words happy and content were not words one would use to describe Amy.

Nadifo was in an insolent mood; she was still struggling with Cartan's second marriage. He'd been gone from their lives for only four months; whatever had survived from what was once a carefree persona disappeared with Cartan's marriage. She was now a somber woman, with little to look forward to. She was almost sixty, no longer hopeful about life and it is offerings; just waiting for death to arrive, not caring if it were here today. She felt her problems were becoming insurmountable.

In the nonchalant innocent but at times cruel way Nadifo had come to know Amy, while she ached for a lost marriage, Amy left out no detail of her own marriage bliss. She said her wedding cost seven hundred and fifty thousand dollars and that it was featured in some famous wedding show. Was that somewhere near a million, Nadifo could not imagine, so she purposefully mistook, a third of a million for seven thousand dollars and some change.

"Amy, your wedding seven thousand dollars?" she would repetitively ask.

"No Nadifo, seven hundred thou—"

Nadifo would interrupt tenaciously, "Oh, yeah seven thousand."

Amy's daughter Rain was lovable and independent, but the boy Echo was grouchy and clingy. He either cried or snuggled close to Amy the entire time they were there. While Rain explored the immigrant home, he whined and pouted. Rain roamed around, touching everything, and halting to feel things she found odd. She let her little feet dance on top of a leopard-skin rug, aiming for the rough edges of raw leather and spilling dark ashes from an incense burner onto it. She then wandered back into the living room where the women were sitting, draped in a black and gold scarf with grey ash and a distinct *uunsi* smell all over her little hands and face.

The women laughed at the mess; Echo felt left out. Rain managed to let the women have one on her. They laughed the loudest, most free and exhilarating laugh for the first time since they had met. Nadifo shook compulsively until she dropped to the ground. Her hysterical laugh scared Echo, but Rain was on the floor laughing alongside the two women who kept falling on top of each other. It was relief Nadifo needed.

Rain managed to cover her hair with the hijab in a way Amy was never able to. As much as Amy was open to Nadifo's culture and as many times as she tried, she was never able to innocently wear a hijab the way Rain did. No matter how much she tried to shake it, the preoccupation with the hijab could never transcend the wearing of it.

Going back to her exuberant wedding, Amy said Hunter did not care how much she spent in the wedding; he just wanted her to have the best day of her life. "Nadifo, he did not care about money until I filed for divorce; then he obsessed about it." The huge rock in her finger was his first gift to her. "This one was seventy thousand dollars. I sold my wedding band and engagement ring for—" Nadifo interrupted again before Amy could divulge the amount. All and all Amy was extremely well off, she had fared well in life, finally encountering some happiness. "I reasoned I had the perfect marriage until he began an affair with a college student." *He had an affair too.* Nadifo offered a cold nod. "Yes, I caught him with a twenty-one-year-old intern in his office." *What was he doing with the intern?* Again Nadifo reckoned the questions in her head. Amy answered as if she could read what Nadifo was thinking. "What do you think? He was—"

"Okay, okay Amy" Nadifo cut her off, not wanting to hear the details Amy was ready to reveal.

"Then I began digging, only to find he'd had affairs ever since I got pregnant with Echo. He did everyone from the barista at Starbucks to the security guard at his office. I'm not sorry he's dead Nadifo, I really am not." Amy appeared at ease, not as apprehensive as the days she imposed on Nadifo her new identity as "Nady". Not as unsure of herself as when she detailed how Nadifo needed to spell her name to ease it on the American ear (Nadifo, N like Nancy, A like Apple, D like David, I like India, F like Frank, and O like Orange) except of course Nadifo could not say half the names the letters represented, making the ordeal of spelling her name much more difficult.

The way a majestic snow storm changes the landscape of Minneapolis, Amy Sky Harington changed the landscape of Nadifo's muddled mind. Nadifo and Amy breathed the same air, but inhaled different realties. How could two people be so different and yet present in each other's moments? The moon had been kind to Amy delivering a man, children, money and happiness. The same moon dealt Nadifo a life so bitterly cruel the temperament in her became as ridged as the hauling winter storm. Her thunderous criticism of Amy, that she sought impossible happiness echoed back to her now. While Amy planned a wedding, birthed children, and inherited millions, Nadifo clung to an empty nest, an anguished soul and doubtful aged sorrow. While Amy danced with the abundance of life, Nadifo clutched the bosom of despair.

Each drop of rain that fell after Amy left strangled Nadifo like an enemy's garotte. Each drip reminded her of that pitiful life that lazed around her and the sweetness of life that slipped from her hands. The smell of rain, fresh and smooth like a pine tree, sweet like slow background music, sounded harsh and violently loud. It polluted Nadifo's ears.

Amy came to greet her, but her visit sunk Nadifo in dejection. What made Amy come and splash Nadifo with her twinkle of life? Why did Amy choose this particular day, when Nadifo's sour rage racked her entire body? The body that throbbed with the reality of life! She gawked at her once beautiful hands, the long limbs she once was famous for. No longer were they elongated and shapely; they now twinge from years of plucking chickens, paper cuts they received when Nadifo faintly asked customers "Paper or Plastic", the vigor of industrial vacuum cleaners and the endless smell of chlorine, bleach and soap scum. Every job she has ever had in America left a permanent mark on the once delicate, alluring hands.

THREE-LEGGED WHEELBARROW

Tired, bleak, backward and rundown was not only the way Nadifo felt but the state of the city she had returned to. The modern city of white villas, sandy beaches and bustling streets had given way to warlords and militia who have turned the city into a dark place full of bloody alleys and brutal people. Hamar resembled a scene out of a bad horror movie where people dragged out bleak existences and anyone who had any scanty belonging was killed for it—except this was no movie but the reality of what has become of Hamar. She was met with dust as she entered Hamar city quarters where a ruined house sat at a dirty graveled road. Blue, white and red shiny paint camouflaged the brick cement. The left side of the roof was caved in, and the green paint covering the hole had been chipped away every time rain dripped off it. As she entered the house, the front door appeared sunken into the dusty crooked front edge of the entrance step that held it in place. Nadifo's feet hit a cold muddy earth foyer that broke dangerously into scattered pieces of cement gravel. A three-legged wheelbarrow sat at one corner of the roofless corridor. On the other side, four massive ashy rocks held the fireplace firmly on the dusty floor. Multiple yellow jerry cans adorned another corner. Black, orange and purple plastic buckets lined behind each other to collect water from the rain that has not fallen for months. The smell of kerosene pervaded the dim, cluttered house. This is what had become of the mansion she had built before the war. Sometime after Nadifo and her family fled the city, a prominent warlord took over the mansion and made it his headquarters. Between heavy artillery and mortar attacks, half of the mansion was destroyed and the other half severely damaged. By the time Nadifo's sister Hawo took over the now half-destroyed house, it was a disaster area the average person would flee from. But the maverick Hawo rebuilt the house as best she could to safeguard the fifty or so family members who had no other shelter.

There was no functioning bathroom, and part of the once massive kitchen was now a makeshift sleeping area for a family of five. The ruin of the house had been transformed into a shelter; children roamed throughout, unable to escape their grim and soggy lives. Their sad eyes searched for answers in hers; she was overcome with grief as she compared their meager existence to the kids she left behind—the ones who ate themselves to death and disease.

Nadifo's relatives had sold their meager belongings to accommodate her. Countless rugs from days of glory adorned the walls and floors: this was their way of recreating comfort in the ruined house. They collected the best house wares, plates, cups and utensils to create a comfortable environment for her, and bought a generator to provide electricity.

She wished they had not gone to such lengths to re-create happiness for her; she is satisfied to be among them, without an imitation of her "comfortable" life in America. No one could comprehend her desire to return to such an empty, somber place, a life of poverty and awesome daily casualties. Their accusatory gazes spoke volume. Why did she choose to return to this empty, somber place? Why would she leave heaven for hell, Minneapolis for Hamar? The creepy feeling of death and destruction was apparent all over the house; there was something ghastly about the place, apart from the numerous lively barefoot children it ejected into the street.

The entire neighborhood collected in front of the house to cheer her arrival. The girls wore baggy capes that covered their whole bodies; everyone looked thin, hollow, aged and tired. Nadifo lay awake that night, staring into the darkness and reminiscing. The Hamar she had waited to reclaim had delivered a disappointing reality of rust. Ironically she sought the life her relatives detested, a simple live, un-cumbersome and un-layered, no systems to follow—an amenable and austere natural existence. Her content stemmed from her familiar land, faces and language, even if it resembled something from the dark ages. She could not explain to them that she left behind a life blanketed with vagueness and confusion.

Nadifo felt welcome and calm in Hamar, despite its grief and stagnation; its unhurried way of life relaxed her. The hum of nature replaced that of agitation—refrigerators, screeching cars, and television that hummed with constant noise. This was the reality of life at the brink; she was no longer sheltered from what had become of her country. No part of her longed for the stress and the constant human noise of hurry. She didn't have to constantly learn, memorize and remember foreign things. Instead she is forced to deal with the needs of real people. She felt useful for the first time in a long while.

Wild cats, dogs and other animals wandered around the city by day and disappeared altogether by night, vacating the city for the dangerous humans that dwell in it. The journey began all over again in the morning when they again made their way across the city limits, adding their animal aroma and feces.

Nadifo found no signs to guide and warn her, asking her to watch out for pedestrians, to be alert and careful of animals on the road. Here it was all left for her mind to decipher. People and animals alike roam the streets: she may unintentionally step into a puddle of dirty water or a gap of open earth, or maybe even hit by a fast-moving vehicle or animal. She learned quickly not to be in the way of things.

The six hastily-packed bags of stuff, a reflection of the life she has left behind, became a feast the people had gladly received. People came from across town and took whatever they could get their hands on; she sat in a corner, fighting the guilt of not bringing more. They hurried through the stuff as if they were looters afraid of getting caught. People grabbed lotion, clothes, cereal, batteries, bottled water, toys, cookies, shoes, and even her personal belongings.

Markah Street, a few blocks from the house, had once been a bustling market; now it hosted haphazardly re-built houses that were erected without any planning. Sewage and trash lined the streets where children played, unknowingly luring the youngsters to lethal diseases. Blue houses with pink rooms and green roofs sprouted up uncontrollably. In the midst of—despite—all the tragedy in Hamar, Nadifo felt the evil of not belonging seep away. In the streets of Minneapolis, under the immense stadium, in view of the massive mall, around the countless food places, it lingered in the shadows; it slid along and rambled behind. But amid the chaotic city, it disappeared altogether: she no longer felt she did not belong. Indeed she came to know her feelings had been ego ridden, and bratty. She now realized she had acted like a child, throwing a tantrum because she did not get her way. She is forced to transcend her saga of conditioning, the continuous sadness of self-antagonism and doubt—many moons of intolerance and judgment of others. Who is she to judge, when she and Cartan had a hand in what has become of Hamar? She had convinced herself that the horrendous situation in Somalia had been created exclusively by others. That Hamar was taken away from her violently, just as Geele was. But the Hamar she returned to was a rude awakening; the Hamar she sought was nothing but a figment of her imagination—it no longer existed. The constant reminder of poverty began to weigh heavy on her. How could she not know the conditions under which her own family existed? How could she seek bliss when others clamored for mere survival?

She came to Hamar running away from Haybe's choices, Cartan's ways, and Henna's shameful lifestyle—not to mention Warsan's peculiar disappearance. Somehow their life choices were about her; they all conspired against her.

She was grateful for her American passport, the only valuable thing that came with her from America. She felt as if she had sacrificed her entire life to get it; now she was glad she had it, guarding it like one would a delicate infant. She had studied American history, memorized the Star Spangled Banner, the lives of the founding fathers Washington,

Lincoln, Hamilton, the Declaration of Independence, and the United States Constitution. And she had read the Bill of Rights over and over again.

She knew more American history than the average born and raised American. She had studied hard, because no one had ever expected her to know anything about history or intellectual matters. She passed the naturalization exam on the first try, shocking her family. Cartan, the one she had looked up to for answers, had failed the exam three times. He never bothered to study and had neglected his American citizenship as he did everything else. She was an American citizen and he was not. It gave her the validation she had desired, and was her ticket out of the ambiguity that had become her life in Minneapolis.

She realized that her happiness was within reach when she embraced her reality and accepted all aspect of refugee life. She felt guilty for the feelings she had harbored for so many years as the life she had cherished disappeared. It was much easier to exquisitely elude the self that situations around her were created by those around her. Her happiness was tied to a life she can no longer reclaim, a life tied to a past that had vanished with everything else. Being in America, she believed all her happiness resided here, but Hamar ended up being a hard bitter pill to swallow.

RUTHLESS AND EYELESS

By all measures there was a lot broken in Xamar Jajab borough where Nadifo's family resided, but the warlord Cali Cawar was not only exploiting the people; he was also causing their end. He had a strong militia presence, turned entire plots of fertile land to growing qat and marijuana, cut down trees to profit from charcoal, polluted marine life and caused degradation to the soil. He was the warlord of the borough. Cali *Cawar* (Cali the eyeless) wore a pirate like eye patch to conceal his eye, which according to Hawo, he had lost to shrapnel. Ships came and went bearing German, French, Thai, Malaysian, Italian, Korean, Japanese and American flags. They sailed to contaminate the shore and eventually cause harm to the locals. Cali the eyeless earned millions of dollars from the dumping. Nadifo remembered the famous Somali proverb "evil is either eyeless or legless": this evil was certainly eyeless.

The sandy sparkling beach that nestled between the pointed peaks of Mount Laacdo vomited its marine life. The seas ejected the kingfish, swordfish, lobster, and crab, killed by the hazardous illegal dumping of rusting barrels along the long lonely shores of the Indian Ocean. Radioactive uranium, lead, cadmium, and industrial hospital and chemical waste were dumped; Cali the eyeless pocketed the money. International companies as well as foreign government vessels sailed along the shores, inflicting cancers of the stomach, blood and throat. Hamar's residents were dying not just from hunger but from lethal radiation that led to severe illnesses no one could explain. Cali knew he was causing all these fatalities, but was profiting and did not care.

In the Bakaraha market, Nadifo found herself circled by aggressive market women selling everything from charcoal to live goats. She was examining some odd-looking mangoes, when a man she had seen before greeted her warmly.

"Who is that?" she asked Bahsan, a cousin's daughter who had accompanied her to the market to shield off aggressive market women.

"Cali *Cawar*," Bahsan said, "the one who is killing the land." She said nonchalantly.

"He looks nothing like I have imagined," Nadifo said, studying his demeanor, not comprehending how anyone could cause so many deaths for gain. He was a plump, round man with fine features, brawny where everyone else was thin, malnourished and sickly. His patch matched the traditional garb he wore. He looked handsome and respectable: no one would ever imagine this rosary-holding, apparently gentle and personable man capable of such vile acts. They exchanged stares, he studying her face and Nadifo his. She wanted to ask him how he could be holding a rosary, going to the mosque and pretending to be a religious elder when he brought death to so many in Hamar.

Later in the day Nadifo was resting in the backyard enjoying the mangoes with a neighbor who detailed the misery of her fifteen-year-old son who has been bleeding profusely from his mouth for the past six months while his body was inflicted with lesions the size of tennis balls. Kids from the neighborhood played on streets dusty with gravel. Nadifo was dazed, staring vacantly at a gangly man in a black t-shirt that read "Just Do It" who led a lanky, lean donkey that slouched from side to side with the heftiness of the wood it carried as the woman told one story after another of people falling to their deaths.

Hibo came running out of the house, interrupting the women, to announce a visitor waiting in the living room. When she entered the dimly-lit room with its massive cushions, she saw the eye-patched man she had encountered earlier in the marketplace standing in the middle of the room. She was lost for words, and he took notice of her anxious bearing.

"*Salaamu calaykum*," he saluted before she could catch her breath from the shock of seeing him in the living room.

"Salaam," she said, almost reluctant to greet him.

"Nadifo Cafi, I was a good friend of your late brother Kaahin, may Allah bless his soul, and your husband Cartan is a distant cousin," he announced, catching her by surprise. Shock widened her gaze. *How can such a killer share lineage with anyone close to me?* She thought.

"How can you do it? No—why do you do it?" She asked him in a chiding tone, not wanting to speak with this beast but forced to do so. Holding a cane in his beefy hand and a cup for his tobacco spit in the other, he seemed apprehensive at her accusatory words.

"Nadifo, I came here to greet you peacefully, since you are a relative and new to town, and to ask about my cousin Cartan." Spitting foul chewed tobacco, he sat himself down on the floor where silky red and bright green crocheted pillows adorned Persian rugs, with wooden carved decorations of camels, bowls, combs and other traditional items scattered about on the table. He moved the decorations aside to make room for his spit cup.

"I know about your plot but I promise I will be your much-detested shadow until I expose your ugly scheme" she said, affronted that anyone could camouflage ugly deeds with religion. "How could you single-handedly cause such killings? Please do not bother visiting again." Nadifo continued, standing erect at the door next to some wooden boxes, which she used for support, shakier than she wished to look.

"Indeed, you are a bold woman; I suppose that is what you have brought from afar." He roared like a hungry hyena. Oblivious to his roaring, she prepared her next attack.

"How can you do this under the charade of religion?"

"But you are wrong—" he snapped, leaving his cane on the floor to free his hands for explanation.

"You are a shame to our town and religion." She interrupted, emotional and with a lump constricting her throat. She pressed on, barely fighting back tears.

"Does your husband know you are this rude to his relatives?" He burst out, getting personal. "Why are you angry with me? Are you channeling your anger at your husband? Isn't that the reason you are back—he took a younger wife, didn't he?" He paused, looking for words to personally scorn her. "Now you are trying to find a cause to feel good about." He continued sneering under his patch with a smirk.

"You are indeed despicable, of course, with your kids away in America at the best universities and your multiple wives adorning cities all over the world." She barked, still trying hard to hide her emotions. "You have nothing to lose, so you turned to the victims of war to destroy them further."

"Respect yourself. You are an aged woman; act as such!" He said, gathering his legs to stand up.

"Please don't come here again." She said, a calm erasing the lump and tears, inwardly amazed at her will to stand to him. His one eye penetrated her; clearly, no one had ever addressed him in this manner.

"You are a rejected woman. I came here to greet you. Shame on you for not welcoming your guest! Foreign living has affected your manners." Nadifo walked away from him, still upright. With traces of anger in his face, he collected his cane and rosary and dashed out, causing a disturbing wind and leaving the spit cup behind. His entourage, which had waited outside the room, followed him with their weapons visible.

Nadifo had never been boorish to an elder, let alone not offering alms; it was as well, for as far as she was concerned he was no elder but a criminal. His first wife resides among the rich in Southern California, in a million-dollar home with her American educated children. His second wife refused to reside where the first is, opting instead for a lavish life in Dubai: shopping sprees and vacations to Europe is how she makes him pay for the sin of a third, more attractive and younger wife, all at the expense of blood money that has brought many Hamar residents to shallow graves.

WAYWARD WAYS

Hamar was no longer the modern city it once was; war had returned it to the dark ages. Animals and people roamed around the dangerous city. Nadifo tried to extract memories of the city as she knew it, but it was impossible to see any familiar landmarks. Villagers roamed with their animals, warlords rode with militia high on qat and other narcotics in their dangerous, roofless trucks, armed to the teeth. A red-shirted camel herder wandered past her. His camels were very lean and weak-looking. The herder rested his cane on his shoulders, using both hands to balance the cane in place. Nadifo looked up from the clothes she was pegging to the multi-colored lines hanging from a bare tree trunk. She jumped as the camel herder whistled to alert her to his presence.

"*Salaamu calaykum eeddo*," the camel herder, said letting his camels graze on barren polluted land, occasionally extending their long necks to tree trunks that had little or no vegetation.

"*Wa calaykum asalaam*," Nadifo said, distressed by the sordid scene of the hungry animals in search of sustenance in a city that had not had rain for months.

"Eeddo, my camels and I have been walking for many hours, I am taking them to the market and—" he said, hesitant to spell out his needs.

"I may not have water for the camels, but I can offer you some." Nadifo said reading between the lines. She went inside to bring water and some food for the youngster. He waited with the camels away from the house out of respect, whistling to keep the camels from straying.

Nadifo came back with a jug of water and a plate full of rice and camel meat. "Here, my son, feed yourself," she said, hoping he would not refuse the food out of pride.

"Eeddo, I only need water, thank you. I do not need food," he said, hiding his hunger and trying not to appear greedy.

"It is rude not to accept food from your host! Where are your manners, my son? Eat and be on your way, I will look after the camels," Nadifo went to join the camels, reminiscing on the days she accompanied her brothers to camel caravans when she was a young girl. The herder sat under a tree gathering his legs to an upright position. He then tied the white sheet that dangled from his shoulders to both legs at the knees. He put the plate to his right side, the cane and a cell phone to the left side, and began eating the food with his bare hands, taking quick amounts hurriedly, while his eyes followed the camels.

Nadifo walked close to the camels and recalled camel serenades from memory, songs she had lost in her cluttered mind. She retrieved them with ease. Elated to remember those sweet serenades, it reminded her of peaceful greener days. The camel herder interrupted her thoughts.

"Thank you, eeddo," he said. "That was good food, may Allah bestow more of it on you and your family," he said hastily, then ran after his camels calling them together after they had wandered to wider vicinity. Nadifo did not have to say anything; she admired his efficiency and dedication. Legend defined camel herders as sturdy men who endure hardship: she saw in the youngster the reason such impressive descriptions have been bestowed on them.

He stroked his tummy, satisfied, and sang to the camels while he chipping away a piece of thin pick from a leafless tree branch instantly picking his teeth. She was momentarily thrown into a web of memory about camels. When she accompanied her brothers on camel caravans, she would try to outdo them. Camels are mostly male territory, but she was allowed to go with them, and proved to be every bit as good as they were with camel care. She would load and un-load them and take them for long water journeys. But she sometimes broke the rules when the males mistreated the camels: she was caught feeding the camels too much, or letting them drink much more water than they were allowed. They once returned her home in the middle of a journey complaining she was a nuisance, and she was eventually banned from accompanying them altogether when she was caught sneaking a weaning calf to its mother.

A group of men arrived at the house as she stood mesmerized by the scenery. The elder of the kin, a man in his seventies, began explaining his aggression and disappointment in Nadifo. He accused her of being uncultured, shameful, and disgracing the family by standing up to a respectable elder in the community.

"Nadifo, you are our cousin, but you are a woman, you must respect your position."

"But all I—"

"Don't interrupt an elder, where are your manners?"

"Talo walaal diide tagoogta ayuu ka jaba, ogow taas gabadhyahay"

She reluctantly welcomed their comments while struggling to be given a chance to defend her position. She was scolded, reprimanded and the elder alluded to having her kicked out of town if she continued her errant accusations. *"Naagi ama guri hakaaga jirto ama god,"* he said, shocking her by the use of the proverb.

This led to more backlash from her family and others in Hamar. Rumors that she came to spread western values reached everywhere; people began to mistrust her. She could not get the support she needed from any of her family members, least of all from male members. Even women who earlier sought her help began to castigate her, staring at her with doubtful gazes in the marketplace. These were women who lost their kids from mysterious illnesses, women whose husbands and sons lost their lives to Cali Cawar. Cali Cawar had a fleet of boats that transported people from Hamar to Yemen: women flocked to him, borrowing the exorbitant fee he charged urging their sons and husbands to go to Yemen to find a better future for them. Most of the boats capsized, killing many from the borough; but these same women were now shunning Nadifo.

She knew it was a long shot for her to overcome Cali Cawar, but she was shocked when women who urged her to go after him suddenly turned against her. She was temporarily elated when she was able to convince women to stand up for their rights and chase Cali Cawar out of Hamar, by shaming him. She began holding secret meetings in various houses, proud she was teaching women community organizing, all the while excited that Amy would be proud of her. Amy had said in one class called Grass Roots Activism that "you ladies can bring change in your community, community activism starts with one person, don't be afraid to express yourself and organize yourselves, there is so much you can do if you come together." But surprisingly it was she whom they wanted out—she had worsened things for them, they said. They wanted her to go back to wherever she came from. She was no longer welcome to pollute their minds with western thinking. Even her sister Hawo advised against her activities. Nasri began to detest her, looking for a way to move her family from the house, away from Nadifo. Nadifo tried hopelessly to explain herself, pointing to brothers who died in the high seas, children who fell to spells of unexplainable lethal death, grandmothers who were shot for protecting their land—all to no avail.

Each dawn, Hibo, at the tender age of nine, awakes to nourish the lives that loom in the house. Her rusty cinnamon complexion would win prize in any beauty pageant in America, but here each dawn she wipes her eyes, forcing them open.

She gathers firewood, lights the wood with kerosene, then clumsily and unnaturally squats on the floor, her bare dusty feet tucked under her tattered dress. She leans forward, reaching her childish hands, delicate for anything harsher than toys and books, over the massively blackened prickly kettle. She pours water she collected earlier from the yellow jerry can, adds whatever spices are available—usually cloves and ginger—and a little sugar, and brings it to the burning flames, settling the kettle between three sturdy rocks which she uses to support the kettle.

She dusts away the chalky white ash that begins to settle on her short pointy nose and dry, chapped lips, all the while chasing whirling heavy black smoke from her teary eyes. Her nose drips, so she wipes it with the edges of the bulky defiled bright orange *jilbaab*. While the tea boils, she beats the batter for the *laxoox* crepes she must prepare before the others awake. She uses the base of her feet to hold the silvery bowl that is too cumbersome for her dwarf hands. She beats the batter by hand, taking small intervals to rest her tired, flour-covered hands and wipe away the flour that escapes from her face with her wrist, avoiding the flour-covered areas of her hand. She hunches on her knees on the floor and scoops cupfuls to splatter on the heating pan which is sizzling on the blazing fire. She stands over the fire so as not to burn herself while she bakes the crepes one by one. She repeats the process for each individual crepe, enough for a herd of refugees in the shelter they call home.

She milks the goats, chanting familiar friendly songs to trap them in her embrace. Once again, her tiny fingers gently wrap around the goats' teats, milking the contents into a bowl beneath. Warm foamy milk collects in the bowl, which she uses as a creamer for the tea and milk for the children; she sometimes goes through two or three goats to get enough. She accomplishes all that before the task is presented all over again for the lunch and dinner periods. Her diminutive frame endures so much. She has never set foot in a classroom, yet she prepares her younger three brothers for school each morning, ironing their uniforms, helping them dress and walking them to school. Her little fingers perform the task from memory each day; she neither fusses nor smiles. There is sadness in her eyes, and she is often deeply lost in thought when she sifts through the many duties conferred upon her as an eldest daughter, the first girl of ten.

The toys Nadifo brought her she never used; instead she jumped on the necessities missing from her childhood. Hibo grabbed a blue dress with pink trimmings and flowery bow and gleaming matching white shoes. She tossed aside Sasha the luminous Bratz doll with it is hip pink-and-purple outfit, and high heels. She quickly put on the crisp new dress: she has never owned anything new in her life. Her brothers, who still have some childhood in them, play with the trucks and speedy cars. When Nadifo attempted to discuss the matter of little Hibo with her mother Nasri, she was shunned for shamefully brining Western ideas to pollute their pure culture. Nadifo was overcome with emotion as she witnessed the dire state of this child. She pled with Nasri to allow her to attend school; she even offered to hire a helper to do the daily house-work and to pay the three dollars it cost to attend the school. That was what separated Hibo from her brother—three dollars.

Nadifo's niece didn't take the offer well: she shouted accusatory words, "you see how your children ended up, mixing with Americans and freeing themselves in an un-Islamic manner, you want my daughter to follow suit." The shadows of illiteracy loomed over little Hibo, remind-ing Nadifo of her own struggle with literacy. She didn't want to see this child lead a dark life of illiteracy like she did. Occasionally—when Nasri and Hawo were not looking—Hibo's face shone as she played with other kids. She temporarily indulged her child-self, attending to child-like things; this only time her striking face cracked into a happy smile, revealing her *dabar*-stained teeth. She never smiled around her mother and grandmother afraid she would be reprimanded for it.

Her name is called more often than any other in the house, to per-form more tasks. She has shouldered a mantle of adult responsibility handed to her by a broken society, a life void of childish activities but filled with adult ones—a practice Nadifo noticed all over Hamar, inno-cent young females pushed into adulthood responsibilities to take care of their families' needs.

A few days after she discussed Hibo's education with Nasri Nadifo came upon some commotion in front of the house. She had left the house only an hour earlier to fetch camel milk to heal a recurring pain she kept having in her knees. Women milk vendors whose stalls sweltered on the scorching Barawe Street sat under huge umbrellas to avoid the heat. They sold camel milk in silver containers by the cup. She did not anticipate the task to take an hour, but Nadifo, who by now was known to all as "Gaal is mood", had to fight exploitive vendors who charged high prices for everything they sold. She also had to assure she was purchasing pure camel milk, as she was tricked many times before with contaminated milk that contained everything from water to expired old formula. She was exhausted by the ordeal and was looking forward to rest. She walked faster, craning her neck to catch glimpses of the crowd that congregated in front of the house. Unable to see, she attempted to walk faster, spilling most of the milk on the dusty street below. Her heart beat piteously against her chest. As she advanced closer, she saw furniture scattered all over the front yard. Porters were moving items, and the children rejoiced in the clamor.

"What is going on here?" She asked as she came across her sister Hawo's sloppy, diminutive form on the floor, covering her head with her hands and crying.

"She is moving. Nasri is taking her kids to a horrible place," She said loudly waling. Nasri appeared with one child strapped on her back and the baby a few days old on her chest. She looked away motioning the porters to move the stuff faster onto the donkeys and wheelbarrows that lingered in front of the house as soon as she saw Nadifo.

"Where are you taking the kids?" Nadifo asked, confused and worried, but no answer came from Nasri: she later found out that little Hibo had been promised as a fourth bride for Cali Cawar. He offered the family a cement house and a monthly stipend to marry the nine-year-old. He would take her to his house to help his third wife. She would herd the sheep and help with chores until she became a marriageable age. She would be living under the same roof with a man who killed her uncle, a brother and other relatives. She would remain with him for five years until she is fourteen, at which time she will become his fourth bride. Hibo's life became grimmer. She was now a slave bride to a rich warlord.

Nasri's modest, destitute state and fear gave into his pressures. Hibo's father Dalmar has been mute for a long time; his sordid reality has silenced him. Flaky thin, Dalmar does not say much, nor does he contribute much to his family's situation. He sulks in a self-pitying ambiance of missed opportunities. His wife recently gave birth to their tenth child. She often complains all he adds to the family is its number. Dalmar had a rare lucky break to help his family's condition. He had immigrated to America five years earlier but after only a three-year stay, he was deported back to Hamar, back to despair, back to misery. He has never accepted the mishap and has languished in his sorrow for the duration. Rumor has it he found himself in an unmarked plane for a destination he did not know. He was let out by American military personnel in the middle of the Kalahari Desert, far from any city. He walked for days, delirious from the ordeal and finally found a village. He stayed with a family in the village for a month before making contact to come back to Hamar. Nasri had to send him money to join them. Whatever they did to him on that plane, he has been unable to speak ever since.

He has bitten into the forbidden fruit and has been ejected from paradise everlasting. People like Dalmar are nicknamed Adam and Eve, for causing their own expulsion from the paradise of America.

Nasri is a vegetable vendor, selling whatever she can to feed her children. She accomplishes everything in silence, hardly engaging in self-pity or blame. Except for the loonies and the qat-chewers, Hamar shields muted people who almost never discuss their fate. They watch as their city deteriorates; warlords exploit them and residents fall limply one by one. They come together to bury their dead, salvaging whatever they can of the city, and move about in silence. Cali Cawar's greed has silenced everyone. Nadifo began to ponder the sadness of the situation. The feeling of failure had begun to sprout unintentionally into her daily musings. Why had she and the others survived the war, only to remain at war with what remained? Who was better off, those who vanished or those who witnessed the destruction until today? Was Hibo lucky to live her grim and hopeless life? Was it valuable just to live? *Maybe*, Nadifo reflected, *I need to celebrate Hibo's every breath, at least she is alive.*

KEPT SECRET

Fifteen months after Nadifo fled to Hamar, Haybe flipped tender beef cubes so that they browned evenly. Adding onions, green paper, and mixed vegetables rhythmically, he held a spatula in one hand and a cordless phone in the other. He was finalizing some cases on the phone while he prepared dinner before Ceebla got home from work. Haybe found the task somewhat overwhelming, but he tried to help his wife on occasion, particularly if he arrived home before she did. This was very new to him. Housework had usually been woman's turf; the female members of his family had performed it perfectly. Even in college and law school, he looked forward to going home to eat exquisite home-cooked meals. Hot Somali food often entered his dreams at college. It had appeared so easy to him then; it was certainly not so now. The challenge presented itself at least once a week when Ceebla worked late.

He seemed completely engrossed with the conversation, and except for occasional "Aha", "huh" or "I am sorry!" he did not say a word. He had met the woman on the phone earlier in the evening at the money transfer store where both sent money to relatives back home, a monthly bill-paying obligation customary for most Somalis. Haybe had been out of law school for three years now; his clients consisted mostly of young Africans in trouble with the law. It was the sole reason he pursued law. He found the predominately white justice system was not just at all. He stared at stark vulnerable faces that resembled his own anxious teenage face only years earlier. Scared faces marred for life by racist police whom he had referred to as "pigs". He often wondered why the police constantly harassed these youngsters, never finding an answer beyond race. Many of his clients had been slammed into jail for minor violations leaving a slanderous stain on their records and launching a vicious cycle with the law.

Current issues of the *New Yorker*, the *Independent* and the *Economist* littered a mahogany-hued round table with a gleaming glass top. Toys filled the corridor from front door to the kitchen. A small voice squealed from a back room, "Aabo!" It yelped for attention.

Haybe promised the person on the other end of the phone a call back and turned the handset off. He waded gingerly through the toys, an apron still wrapped over his office clothes. He picked up the sleepy toddler, who was rubbing his eyes and whining. Hugging and caressing the child, Haybe began singing his favorite lullaby.

Huuwa ya Huuwa, hooyo ma joogto
Kabax kabax aadday
Kabahaheeday qaadatay
Geel jire helyaa mooyi
Geedkii habaasweyne
Ku habowdayaa mooyi

He handed a SpongeBob cup filled with milk to Kayd who refused it, throwing the cup onto the floor and opting for his thumb instead. Haybe swung him up in the air, covering him with kisses as he descended.

"How long are you going to hide this child from his grandma?" his wife often asked. "You need to tell her sooner or later." The whole issue ached like an open sore. He detested even thinking about the way Nadifo had shunned his family. But he assured Ceebla that Nadifo knew about Kayd and that she often sent hugs and kisses when she called. In reality, the only reason Nadifo ever called from Hamar was to attempt to shame him. She never acknowledged his son's existence or his marriage to Ceebla. It was another of Nadifo's attention-seeking acts, he reasoned. Haybe promised himself that he would never beg her to recognize his son; she had wronged him, and for once he was going to stand to her for what was right. He remembered how she promised to disown him if he married Ceebla—he had never shared that with Ceebla, wishing to spare her. Perhaps Nadifo would use the words she reserved for Shirwac on Kayd, calling him a child of sin. He would not let such words pollute his son's ears.

Ceebla interrupted Haybe's reminiscences, wobbling in with multiple shopping bags from Vivi's Keepsakes, Perfections, and Harmony; the crackle of the bags stirred him from his reverie. She let out a sigh of relief upon entering the house; it emanated warmth, love, and the delicious scent of green peppers and onion.

"Shopping again, Ceebla?" Haybe asked, wondering how she could carry such a load as she neared her fourth month of pregnancy with their second child.

"I need these things; I had to go shopping after work," she replied, removing her hijab from her throbbing head and thumping onto the sofa. "I am expanding by the day; nothing fits!" she exclaimed as if disappointed. "Hi, baby." She motioned for the ornery little boy to join her while she slouched onto the floor to remove her boots. Kayd was busy with his thumb and burrowed deeper into his father's chest, ignoring her. "Is he hungry?" she asked, missing her son's cat jumps, which were the usual welcome.

"No, I just fed him." Haybe handed Kayd to her. "Maybe he's coming down with something."

"Shirwac, hurry it up or we are going to miss the prayers!" Ceebla said, with Kayd riding on her hip. She was dressed in a midnight-blue *cabaaya* that covered her body from neck to toe. A chic silk scarf covered her hair. Her face gleamed with the smoothness of caramel and softness of whey. Poised, Ceebla appeared settled in family life.

Haybe was already in the car, waiting impatiently and sounding the horn. This had become their ritual. Every Saturday morning they spent the better part of the day worshipping at the local mosque. They wanted to introduce Islamic practices and studies to their little boy and Shirwac.

Their marriage contract stipulated that Shirwac and Haybe take Islamic studies on weekends. Haybe's wedding night had marked his first experience in the local mosque: he was raised in a Muslim country but had never been well-versed in Islam—he associated Islam with Arabs, whom he detested. Like most Somalis, he disliked Arabs who for centuries mistreated Somalis in their land. Some deserted the religion for that reason. Now Ceebla was introducing the truth of Islam to him. He finally understood that Islam was a religion for all people, not for Arabs only. He was humiliated by his lack of Islamic knowledge. When he met her he was unable to recite a complete *suura*, except the opening *suura* which even little children could recite from memory. With Ceebla's help he began attending classes every weekend. He tiptoed into class like a thief. His elementary knowledge had forced him to study with boys half his age: he sat in the same class room with Shirwac.

The mosque was in an old warehouse donated by the owner of various local businesses. Every Saturday and Sunday morning, Greenery Lane witnessed the overflow of people seeking spiritual connection; Muslim women with their elaborate attire hauled their less-than-enthusiastic children.

Since the Muslim community in St. Louis Grove was scarce, the warehouse was not renovated to function as a mosque: it was divided into four sections which functioned as classrooms. The more advanced students, mostly Arabs well versed in Arabic, occupied the better part of these classes. Haybe's remedial class was filled with kids and non-Arab adults like him. He fared better than the Pakistani, Indonesian and African-American gentleman in his class: the Pakistani, a medical doctor, spoke little English and no Arabic. The Indonesian, a businessman with ties to the ruling elite, seemed reluctant to be in class. He hardly spoke in class but remained apprehensive. The African-American spoke some Arabic and energized the class with his eagerness to show off his little knowledge. They were lucky and had a patient iimaam whose sense of obligation to teach adults rudimentary Arabic and Quran seemed unwavering. Haybe improved rapidly, and when he changed to an advanced Arabic class he had a pompous Lebanese teacher whose pronunciation he did not understand. He could swear the man—who once referred to a Somali kid as an *cabd*—was intolerant of the non-Arabic speakers

He purchased an English translation of the Quran to ease the study. His ignorance of his religion ripped through him: he had busied himself with formal studies going to the best schools, and yet ignored his own rich traditions. His suspicion of being "colonized in the mind" rang true. He was able to commit to memory the law of the land, business news and world politics, but not a single verse from the Quran. Nadifo's pleas for him to attend religious events when he was an adolescent had met with mute refusal. He now regretted it.

Ceebla and Haybe had been leading secular American lives, but September 11th changed everything for them. The backlash was enormous, but had it not been for all the negative publicity Islam got from Western media, Ceebla and Haybe would have probably remained secular. Their reintroduction to their faith was an unexpected silver lining in the personal backlash against them. She decided to live a life that exemplified a true Muslim woman, wearing Islamic garb: she turned heads at work, some of her co-workers asking if she was in mourning—otherwise why had she hidden her lustrous hair? Why hide all that beauty? Some responses were quite negative. Others were mesmerized and desired a more comprehensive understanding of her boldness amid such backlash. She embraced the Muslim garb when others were pealing it off.

She welcomed the questions, taking colleagues to Muslim events and explaining the true meaning of Islam. She was encouraged by the conviction of other strong Muslim women surrounding her. Her co-workers were surprised that the same woman resided under the veil: they surprised her in turn with their questions. Some seemed innocent enough, and yet others judged her according to the latest media cant. She found herself defending Islam, and lost her closest colleague when he began making fun of her prayers. He joked more than once that she looked odd when she bowed down that way. It amazed her that even a garbed woman of her caliber could not escape his advances.

Shirwac's tardiness and rebellious tendencies became excessive. He stayed out more, and stopped doing chores around the house. His schoolwork suffered and his teachers called Haybe frequently. No matter how much Haybe disciplined him, Shirwac would rebel and do the very things he'd been asked not to.

Haybe was in the office finishing some cases one evening when he heard Shirwac on his cell phone. It was ten p.m.; Haybe had stayed up to wait for Shirwac, who had taken to coming home late.

"Hey, Shirwac, come here," Haybe called from behind the glass doors of his office; but Shirwac ignored him, continuing the conversation. "Hey, did you hear me?" Haybe came out of the office to find Shirwac still on his cell phone, laughing. Haybe grabbed the cell phone and threw it across the room, and then took Shirwac by the neck and threw him on the floor.

"Waryaa, is your name not Shirwac!" Haybe surprised Shirwac with a tight choker grip.

"Ouch, leave me alone!" freeing himself from his uncle's grip, he ran down the hallway to his room, trying to swallow the humiliation he felt. Haybe followed him holding a belt in his hand.

"Waryaa, where the hell are you?" He found him behind the door, hiding his face and sobbing.

"Don't touch me!" he said. "You don't have the right to touch me!" by now he was gathering things to throw at Haybe.

"Oh yeah and what right is that?" Haybe saw a hamper headed his way, and ducked; the two men struggled, Shirwac being almost as tall as his uncle by now. Haybe never liked resorting to violence, but Shirwac's tardiness had become excessive. "Waryaa, still, stay still waryaa!" Shirwac continued to throw things at Haybe—the hamper was followed by his heavy algebra book, and finally a ten pound weight which landed on Haybe's left foot. He then ran out of the room, slamming the bathroom door across the way shut. Haybe realized Shirwac was much quicker than he was, but ignored his injuries and followed him. "Waryaa, come out this minute! Right now!"

"Why should I come out? So you can abuse me? You better stop hitting me, or I am going to call the police on you!"

"Oh really? And where did you learn that, you little bastard?!"

Ceebla's due date was nearing. In three weeks, their second baby was to arrive. It was a miracle that she was able to live a normal life, let alone have children. The doctors had warned her that she would be infertile because of the damage she had endured from the attack: every part of her body had been opened up and stitched closed to repair the damage from the shooting. Doctors had advised against any pregnancy, but she had gotten pregnant immediately. Now that her second baby was on the way, Haybe was considering names. He wanted to name the baby after his grandmother Hagarla if it was a girl and after his deceased brother Geele if a boy.

"I am not naming my kids after anyone," Ceebla repeated for the umpteenth time. "Let them have their own unique identities. Must we repeat family names?"

"Go ahead; name them something hip and easy so Americans do not stumble on their names, then! Isn't that the reason you picked Kayd?"

"Excuse me for not wishing my child's name to be mutilated like mine on a daily basis. If I had a choice I would pick something simple for myself as well."

"Simple for who, Ceebla? Simple for your colleagues? Your American friends? Your doctor? The DMV? Who? Remind me what they call you. Don't they call you "Kiblah" because they pronounce the first letter of your name as a 'K'? Right? They don't care what your name is. It's foreign so who cares, right?! Do they call you 'Keeb' or, oh, maybe just 'La'?" The snide smirk on Haybe's face infuriated Ceebla.

"I correct them every time! I will not change my name for anyone. I correct them every single time!" He continued.

"You know what they call me, 'Hey-babe.' And when I correct them, you know what they hear, 'May-bee'!"

"Well, I do not care to see my children teased because their names are different," Ceebla tried to sound calm. "They already have many obstacles; their names do not need to be one more barrier against them."

"Ok, then that must be why all Somali kids are now named Adam, Sophia, Sarah, Jasmine, and Sam!" Haybe leered angrily. "And of course, God forbid if the name sounds too Islamic! So what is the solution, Kiblah?" he looked satisfied with his sarcasm.

"Kayd, 'my kept secret,' is totally adorable and uncomplicated," she kissed the child while tickling him. "His siblings will have equally mean-ingful and adorable traditional yet easily pronounceable names. Really, Hay-babe, take a chill pill." Ceebla leaned on the desk where Haybe cleared scattered papers which almost hid the laptop he pounded.

"Shirwac was called 'Chirac' by his teacher for two years until he corrected her; then she began to call him 'Shirwaa', altogether changing the meaning of his name. Kayd's doctor calls him Kay. Haybe, honey, it'll be okay. They aren't doing it maliciously." She leaned closer, bringing her face close to his bearded face. She gazed into his tired red eyes, slightly kissing him.

"Chill, bro," she said before she picked up Kayd, who was oblivious to the entire discussion.

"I am tired of altering my culture to simplify things for Americans." Haybe said embracing her from behind while she juggled Kayd and his toys.

SWEET JUICE

Bastard, that is what Haybe called him. Of all people, Haybe, whom he adored and looked up to, called him a bastard? Although Shirwac knew name calling in the Somali culture was nothing serious, it stung him. Shirwac was as cold as ice when he heard the labeling from his own uncle. Since he came to America no one has ever called him a bastard. The refugee camp was another story altogether, a rough place to grow up; he was called every insulting word in the book. He was called thief, ugly, bastard, dumb and hideous. He never took any of the insults seriously because insults were just part of life. But the word bastard was a hurtful word, more so than the other insults and people said it with conviction. He figured early in his life that being a bastard was something most Somalis frowned upon, so it stung him when it was destined for him. Shirwac never missed hearing the word; he heard it so often in the camp that when he came to America he tuned it out and dismissed it from his life.

He recounted the different versions of the same word that was often destined to label only him in the camp. He wondered, even before he obsessed about the word, why were there so many terms for the word? Why was it so despised?

Deep down inside he knew his birth marked something ugly for the Gedi family. That word had a close association with who he was. He escaped the word, but it followed him everywhere. He listened and searched for clues as to why people were eager to label him bastard, coming to the conclusion that Henna had him at a very tender age. But he never knew how. Did she get married young? Why had Henna had him when she was the age he is now? He never knew who his father was or why the marriage ended—why he was left at the refugee camp by himself without his family. All these questions puzzled him, but when Haybe called him "bastard", it all came roaring back. Like a wave his mind began to race. He searched for clues, thinking back to events at the camp. Could he remember anything from the camp that could give him a hint? Why did Haybe call him a bastard?

Ever since their first encounter, Shirwac and Haybe had been close. Shirwac was fond of Haybe and Haybe was tough but loving. But since Haybe uttered the word bastard an unbearable silence rose between them. Haybe wanted to reach for Shirwac, hug him and take back the word, but it was too late. Haybe was consumed by remorse. One single word changed everything he had worked so hard to reverse in Shirwac's mind. In a moment of needless anger, Haybe spit bane that would forever shape Shirwac's life. Neither of them slept that night.

Shirwac began to think deeply about the word. He lay in bed, glazed with agony, wanting to know about this bastard life that everyone was so judgmental and yet silent about.

<hr/>

Shirwac had some very strong and uneasy feelings about Idil when he first came to America. She was constantly running the streets like a boy—tomboy, they called her. He liked Hilac better. She was a bit quieter, and ladylike. Idil would answer Nadifo back; she was a stubborn girl who got whipped all the time. One day Shirwac was playing soccer with some Somali boys in a run down, drug-infested parking lot near Nadifo's apartment. He has only been in America for a year and still struggled with English and American pop culture, overdoing things a little sometimes. He would wear his cap backward and walk with what he deemed was a cool walk which ended up being homely and lopsided. He spoke slang with a heavy accent, sometimes misusing words.

He had never been to school in the refugee camp, but was put into fifth grade in his new school: he had to sit in a classroom full of kids his age who had been in school since kindergarten. There were no remedial courses he could take. He could not read, write or follow instructions, so he sat in class until the end of the year, never understanding a word. He stopped going to ESL class because he was called dumb and stupid. Shirwac with his athletic build was good in soccer—in fact he was the best in the neighborhood. He was competitive, even a bit aggressive, because the soccer field was his turf. He had the ball, and was about to get a goal when a boy from the other team shouted "you stupid *flight 13*, you are so dumb you don't even speak English." Shirwac let go of the ball and headed for the boy. He started to beat the boy, but a crowd of boys from the boy's team came upon him. They began taking turns, violently beating Shirwac. Shirwac was struggling to free himself when Idil showed up unexpectedly with Nadifo. She immediately took off her earrings and shoes and started hitting the boy who was on top of Shirwac with her shoe.

"Dense-head, get off of him, dumptz!"

"You little dumtard, stop hitting me with your shoes!" the boy growled.

"Why you flashin', stupid!" she kept beating him hard.

"You nuttin' but a stupid fugee yourself!"

"I will bust yo' grill!" she continued. The little boy deserted the scene in a hurry, bleeding all over. She was the toughest girl in the neighborhood and everyone feared her. Shirwac developed a friendship with Idil ever since that incident. She showed him the ropes, how to talk, walk and look tough in the streets, even what lingo to use. "No, Shirwac, it is "ballin'", not "powling". When he said "flossing" she corrected him to say "flossin". The first person he wanted to talk to after the incident with Haybe was Idil. He waited for her in the usual spot where they met after school, but she was not there; he found out that she and some other Somali kids had been sent to detention.

Immigrant kids by all accounts had an advantage over their American counterpart when it came to issues concerning school. Since Somali parents at Spring Valley High could not communicate with their kid's teachers directly, and since the school did not have an onsite interpreter to help the parents, the kids became the sole interpreters between teachers and parents. It would not be a stretch to suggest in most cases the kids tilted scenarios to their favor. So when a girl called Miido (sweet juice) in Idil's class got into trouble one fateful day, she appealed to Idil to come to the rescue. Mrs. Bowden, Idil's language arts teacher, asked Idil to interpret for her when Miido's grades declined and she began showing signs of destructive behavior; Idil was only happy to oblige. Mrs. Bowden was not aware that the Somali kids at Spring Valley High had in place a code of conduct of their own making. It was understood that whoever interpreted for a parent would translate exactly the opposite of what the teacher complained about. And so when Idil spoke to Mrs. Dirir, Miido's mother on the phone, she reported Miido's successes in school and her impressive grades. It never occurred to her that the entire group would pay a dear price for the lie. Mrs. Dirir's sudden appearance at school the next day raised Mrs. Bowden's suspicion. Idil along with Miido and six other students were sent to detention after Mrs. Dirir brought an elaborate array of deserts to celebrate the achievements of her daughter. Little did Idil know that the cover of a system they had put in place for quite some time would be blown by one renegade parent who was overjoyed with the success of her daughter and decided to break the cycle by showing up in her daughter's classroom unexpectedly. After detention that day, Idil, who regretted the blown cover, began one of her rants. Shirwac was looking for answers, he was uneasy about Haybe's labeling of him, but what he got was more than he ever bargained for.

"Look, Shirwac, all them are fake—ayeeyo is whacked, abti Haybe M&M sometimes he a'ight, but they all hypocrites, yo! Look, I heard them sayin' sometin about you, that your mom had some messed-up stuff done to her! Did you know that? I mean, Shirwac, I am not trying to hurt you or nuttin' but that's what happened, yo. Ayeeyo is messed-up! They all fake. They tell you not to do sumtin' and then they go ahead and do it themselves. None of them care; they just care about their image. Idil don't do this, Idil don't do that, it is *ceeb* for a girl to be wearing pants. Whatever, man—where the hell are they when I am fetching for myself every day? Where is my mom when I go to bed hungry at night? She rottin'in some crazy people house, if what they tell us is true, 'coz she weak. Couldn't handle life, poor Warsan—whatever, man! Why did she bring us into this world any way if she can't take care of us? I hate her. And ayeeyo, all she cares about is did we do the dirty or not. She only cares if I am cuttin', and my dad, and awoowe Cartan, they are high on that qat drug thing. But they go crazy telling us not to smoke weed. They freaking qat heads, nuttin' but qat heads or whatever the hell that leafy junk they eat is called. Don't trust any of them. Why do you think Henna ran away? She left the freaking fake life! She ain't better either, marrying that white dude and all. But at least she ballin'! Why ayeeyo flippin' all the time?" Idil would go off, making him question everyone around him. He began to believe her. She sounded bitter, but what she said made sense.

"I am so sorry, I know this probably confuses you, I don't mean to hurt you or nuttin', but I wanna be honest with you." Whenever Idil went on one of her outbursts she revealed something. So it was true. He was a child of sin, a bastard as Haybe called him. Idil was in her own world, hating family members, but Shirwac was not in the same world. The news struck him like a ton of bricks. His worst nightmare had come true. He came to the world in a scandalous way. Like Josh, he had no known father. He was indeed Allahkeen, a child of God like Tusmo used to call him at the camp. A *wecel* like little Ali called him; a *farakh* like old man Nur called him once. He was a child without a father, a nobody! Immediately the sympathetic stares he received made sense.

WRINKLED AND ROUGH

Ella's feeling for Martha could be summed up in three little words: resentment, revulsion and detachment. As soon as she had the opportunity, she left home and never looked back. She married her high school sweetheart who turned one small fast food restaurant into a multi-million dollar business. With him she had three children, but would never return to the tragedy that had befallen her family. The years passed, each erasing Ella a little more from Martha's memory, while Scarlet, James and little Miles captured more and more of it.

She simply stopped living when her children died. Their photos were all over the house. James' lyric books, music notes, and musical instruments were the only neat things in the house. She listened to his old records and decorated the house with framed music notes. She collected records by his favorite artists—Frank Sinatra, Nat King Cole, Louis Armstrong. He had shot the kids first, laying them next to each other in a perfect straight row. He put Scarlet's favorite book, *The Cat in the Hat*, on top of her lifeless body.

He then put one bullet in his mouth. Blood splashed across the bedroom wall, splattering an unfinished glass of ice tea which sat on the dressing table. The death coincided with that of Pete Lighter, a year to the day.

Martha stroked the edges of the violin, like James did, every day before she left the house. For twenty-five years she cleaned and polished his musical instruments, massaging the same edges he had polished. She was never the same after the mall incident: she no longer left her house and her health deteriorated. She became frail and confused, and lay in bed for days. When Nadifo came by to feed and bathe her, she would find her curled up in a fetal position; if Nadifo attempted to move her, she became incensed, demanding to be left alone. She refused to eat, and sometimes would assault Nadifo.

"Where are the kids? How is James doing? Did he finish his dinner? Call him in here!" Nadifo lied to Martha to tell Martha that all of her family members were okay. She noticed that Martha's whole body relaxed when she lied to her.

"Yes, Marta, James good, the kids okay," she said to ease her agony, although it bothered her to do so. Martha was very sick. It seemed as though she were slowly traveling backward through time.

"Did Jimmy get back yet from Nora's house? I will bake a chocolate cake for you, Scarlet when daddy gets back; you can take it to your class tomorrow."

Nadifo bathed Martha in the bathtub as Martha's health deteriorated, singing Somali lullabies like she did when she had bathed her own kids. She had noticed the years of hardship had finally taken their toll on Martha's face. It was a few months since she'd returned from Somalia, and was still struck with the devastation she had witnessed.

She poured a cupful of warm water over her wrinkly face; the bags under her eyes turned charcoal black. The water dribbled over her cracked lips. Nadifo gathered her thinning hair in one hand; it felt light like feathers. Her body had become hollow, that of a living skeleton. She must have lost forty pounds in the space of three weeks. She was lost in the raspberry chamomile suds, when Martha swiftly opened her delirious eyes, clasping Nadifo's hand with strength and taking Nadifo's hand to her lips, kissing it repeatedly.

"I love you, Nady," she said slowly. "You're the sister I never had. Remember that always," Nadifo was astounded. Martha had never displayed such affection before; she did not even know Martha was capable of such feelings.

"Me love too," Nadifo said, quickly embracing Martha's frail naked upper body tightly and soaking her cloths in the process. She has loved plenty in her life, although she had never said "I love you" to anyone. She was uneasy about people who constantly said "I love you", as if their love could not be authentic without announcing it. She noticed her kids would say the phrase to each other or to their friends or even to Cartan, but never to her. It is as if she did not deserve the words, and to Nadifo it did not really matter. But of course in this case she felt obliged to say it; Martha needed to hear those words, even if she felt awkward saying them.

That night she had decided to move in with Martha the coming weekend. She arranged for Hajiya to stay with the kids while she cared for Martha.

Martha's feistiness did not surprise Nadifo. That is who she was, a crude, rude and at times aggressive woman, but to Nadifo Martha was like a sister. Nadifo remembered an incident at the corner fast food place a couple of years earlier.

They were walking home when Shirwac, who was beginning to enjoy his new-found food variety, decided he wanted a cheeseburger for dinner. It was before Nadifo found out the food at the restaurant was not halal, and before she forbade Shirwac to ever eat out again. She never liked the smell of fast food restaurants, so she waited outside. She stood there, thinking of the call she had received earlier that day. She needed to send two hundred dollars to Hawo, who needed to take her sick husband to Dubai so that his throat cancer could be treated. She heard an uproar coming from the restaurant: she looked inside, expecting to see Shirwac involved in a fight or some other mischief. The noise, however, was not coming from Shirwac but Martha, who was sitting inside the restaurant with two men. Martha looked sick and unclean. Her hands moved as she talked to the two men, who listened attentively. One of the men was in his twenties, the other an older gentleman in a wheelchair. Hurriedly Martha excused herself and dashed after some trash that a customer had just tossed into the trash can. She took out a large coffee cup from the trash bin and proceeded to the bathroom. A few minutes later, she emerged with a wet cup, shaking excess water off the lid. She walked confidently toward the cashier, standing straight and tall to discourage suspicion. She waited patiently as the cashier helped other customers, picking at her cuticle, biting her nails. When her turn came she acted surprised, and then handed the cup to the cashier. The cashier inspected the cup hesitantly while Martha waited for the refill.

"Ma'am, how can I help you?" asked the cashier with the wet cup in her hand.

"A refill please," Martha said looking up at the ceiling and biting her middle finger nail.

"Ma'am you can only get two refills a day; you have to pay fifty cents for any refills after that."

"Well, then, refill it!" Martha said in a raspy, throaty voice.

"You have already had your second refill, ma'am! You have to pay fifty cents for this one," the cashier said, tossing the cup to the side.

"It is none of your business how many refills I get, hear? Just fill the damn thing!"

"Ma'am, watch your language!" The cashier said, exasperated; she signaled for the man behind Martha to come forward. The line got long. Martha would not yield to other customers.

"You stupid cashier! Where are you from anyway?"

"Ma'am, please, I need to help the other customers. Please step aside."

"Other customers? What am I, chopped liver? What are you, Mexican?" The cashier then bolted to the back of the restaurant, throwing her hands in the air frustrated. A black man in his twenties surfaced with the cup in his hand.

"Ma'am, what can I do for you?"

"Nothing, just a refill that is all I asked for!"

"Okay, ma'am, but our policy is two refills—" She did not let him finish his sentence. She threw the lid at him and began calling him names. She managed to bring the restaurant to a standstill, refusing to move.

She calmed down only after the policeman arrived some twenty minutes later. The policeman took her aside, threatening to take her down to the station if she did not leave the restaurant. She was let go with a warning never to return to the restaurant again.

Nadifo spent the rest of the next morning grocery shopping and cooking. After she finished cooking she wrapped up the food and headed for Martha's home. Nadifo let herself in, taking the key out of the box that sat next an acacia tree that she had brought back for Martha.

Martha was lying on the floor. Frank Sinatra's "Under My Skin" was blasting inside. Martha looked up, and immediately turned her face away, mumbling, "How can I get along without you? You got the part that used to be my heart; so why not take all of me?"

"Marta, you sick—Marta what happen yesterday?!"

"Leave me alone. What are you doing here?" she mumbled and then continued with Sinatra. "Take my lips. Take my arms. I will never use them."

"Mrs. Martha, are you okay?" Shirwac came up behind Nadifo.

"I got you under my skin…" She sat up irritated and said "Tell this woman to leave me the hell alone, what is she doing here?" Martha got up and began yelling at Nadifo, but Nadifo ignored her like she would an irate relative. Martha picked up the song where she had left off, "Can't you see I am no good without you?"

"Shirwac, ask her if she needs to go to the hospital," Nadifo said hurriedly reaching for the volume on the record player.

"Mrs. Martha—"

"Is she still here? Tell her to leave me alone. I am not in the mood for her nonsense tonight."

"Yeah, but do you—"

YASMEEN MAXAMUUD

"Leave me alone! Go away, the both of you!" She ran into the bathroom and slammed the door. "Tell her not to touch my record player again, okay!"

"Ayeeyo, let's go; she does not want you here."

"Shirwac, it is okay, she is sick; ask her if she needs to go to the hospital." Martha was shouting through the bathroom door, crying and shouting, demanding that they leave. Nadifo finally agreed to go; she left the food on the table and walked out, her eyes lowered in sadness.

By the time she returned, the next morning, the house had been surrounded by yellow tape. As she approached the house, one of Martha's neighbors, an angry-looking stocky man who stayed in his pajamas all day, met her at the gate as she attempted to open it.

"She is dead," he said.

"What? Died? No me no understand who dead? Me…?" She stared at him, squinting and twisting her mouth from side to side, *Bismillaahi Raxmaani Raxiim* she murmured in a calm but concerned voice.

"She is not here anymore; you don't have to come by anymore!" he muttered disdainfully. He opened his mailbox, sorting through a stack of new mail on his front porch. She waited until he had finished sorting through the mail. He wore a red-and-white polka-dot robe that stopped at his ankles. She looked down at his feet while she waited. His feet were calloused, his toenails dark. There was a patch of discolored skin on each of his ankles, ashy and white. When he had finished sorting the mail she began asking him again.

"Marta where, Sir? Where she?" She flipped her left hand upside down to indicate a question. He glared at her. She pulled her diric down and straightened her jilbaab, looking down at her covered upper body to see if anything had shifted out of place.

"Are you still here? You don't speak English; how do you work for her if you don't even speak the same freaking language?" his words were

327

implacable, exposing yellow teeth, and wrinkling his wide freckled forehead. "Why don't you learn? You've been here long enough," he said, walking away rudely.

"Please, Mister, where Marta?" She followed him, almost running into the screen door, which he had closed behind him as soon as he entered his house. He stood there, sneering at her offhandedly from behind the fleshy folds of his face, raw and red from rubbing. His long, graying hair with hints of attempted bottled blond fell haphazardly from a receding hairline. The entire outer ring of his ear lobes were pierced with rings and his left ear lobe was opened by a large black stone of some kind.

He threw his mail onto a brown couch that sat in the middle of the living room behind him. The living room was not what Nadifo had expected—it was immaculate. That man who inhabited the room looked as though he had not showered for days—a layer of grease covered the red blemishes that blighted every exposed surface of skin—but his home was spotless. She stood there, waiting, holding her right hand to her cheek, troubled.

"She is dead," he said again in a matter-of-fact voice as he patted a big German shepherd, which had been snarling at Nadifo the entire time they were talking.

"She died last night, at the bus stop, on the bench." Nadifo did not react; she did not understand what he said, or, perhaps she did not want to understand what he was saying, although she had a pretty good idea.

"She go to bus stop?" she asked.

"No, idiot, she died at the bus stop!" he replied, attempting to close the door. As she watched him close the door in her face, something snapped inside Nadifo. She pushed the door open with astonishing strength.

"You kill Marta!" The words came out easily somehow. "You stubid man, you kill kill kill Marta!" Her tongue dragged the word "kill" as if to glue it into his ears, and then she did something even more surprising.

She grabbed his robe, throwing weak untimed punches that mostly hung in the air. She was hysterical like a cornered animal.

"You crazy imbecile! I'll call the police on you!" he threatened, holding both of her slim hands in one of his massive ones. She froze the minute she heard the word "police." His hands felt soft and human, which surprised her. She freed her hands, struggling with him. He gathered her up and pushed her down the front stairs to the sidewalk, and then he shut the door.

"*Allah hoogay, wuu dilay, bahalku, waxan foosha xun oo urayaa ayaa dilay Marta waan garanayey!*" she exclaimed, still accusing him of killing Martha. The yellow police tape was everywhere, but there were no policemen present, so Nadifo ran home and asked Shirwac to go with her to the police station.

At the police station, she found out that Martha had been wandering the streets the night before and her neighbor, the same man Nadifo encountered earlier, had called the police on Martha, claiming she had disturbed him. The police came to her house to quiet things down, but she began assaulting one of them. The policemen called for more help and when she saw more police sirens she ran toward the bus stop. At the bus stop, she tried to hide from the police. She resisted arrest and started throwing empty soda bottles and other trash at one of them. In her mind they could not see her when she hid under the bench. When she brandished a broken bottle at them, the police apparently found the old woman threatening: they drew their guns, but she would not back down, so they shot her. She died at the bus stop, the only place she'd felt alive ever since she lost her family. Nadifo believed somewhat ironically that maybe Martha had chosen the place where her life would finally conclude.

Nadifo cried that day. She cried for all the people who had vanished from her life since the war. Each death reminded her of the others. She did not know how she would handle yet another death, but, of course, she did. Prayer times got longer, as the list of dead people she must pray for grew. Sometimes she forgot some of the names; she might leave out

Ahmed, the eight-year-old nephew who died on their way to Kenya, or Haaji Isniino, the seventy-year-old aunt who was dismembered, or Nabaad, her best friend's daughter who died in her sleep the day after both her parents were shot. Nadifo counted the years to envision what so-and-so would look like now, imagining what this person would be doing, how many kids one would have. When she looked at children of the deceased, she saw their dead parents in their image. Her eyes moistened when she saw Samatar's son Harbi, named "fighter" for the tragedies that brought him to life. Or Haaji Isniino's daughter Basra, named after a once bright, beautiful city. They hated the sad eyes obtruding from Nadifo's craggy face. And now Martha, old, wrinkled, rough and funny, is added to the list of sorrow and images of the dead that haunt Nadifo.

UNINVITED GUESTS

Brian's obsession with Little Hamar, the area populated by Somalis in Devon Woods, had become a bit excessive for Henna. Indeed, on Kenilworth Blvd between Fiftieth Street and Monroe Ave, women, comfortably hijabed, walked leisurely with strollers or grocery bags or shuffled hurriedly to catch prayers at Masjid Makkah. Brian came home early every Friday to ask Henna to accompany him to the mosque for Friday prayers. Mosque congregants spilled over to the busy street, lingering to catch up on news and exchange greetings. News passed from one person to the next and within hours spread to the rest of the globe. Everyone knew the latest scandal, news, celebration or rumor. Henna accompanied him sometimes, but she often refused, making him go alone. He would sit in Subkane, an all-male restaurant on Kenilworth Blvd. The patrons at Subkane were suspicious of him at first, wondering if he were a CIA operative or an FBI agent; they did not see any other reason a white man would be among them.

But then they found out Brian was a *seeddi*. Their natural animated chatter of politics soon resumed, surrounding Brian. They named him Cilmi *Cadde*, expecting him to be privy to the most confidential immigration information. They would ask him to help them sponsor their families to join them. His frequent visits to the Somalis became a bone of contention between him and Henna.

Any healthy affiliation Henna desired with the community was dissuaded by her past. The Somalis had a way of outing people's business without permission; she felt vulnerable, considering her past. She approached the community with caution, knowing full well she did not want them to pass judgment on her.

That was precisely the reason she did not want Brian to associate with them as much as he did: she knew Brian's naiveté would expose something about their lives. The evil-doers would only need a small piece of information to concoct a story about her. The more she insisted he stay away, the more Brian got fixated on little Hamar.

He was the one who knew of community events, gatherings and the most current news. He became politically inclined and simply wanted to hang around Somalis. Sometimes she went along just to shut him up. On one such occasion, he said that they were invited to a wedding ceremony. He did not personally know the bride or groom, but a cousin of a cousin of the bride had invited him while he drank tea one day in Subkane. Brian, who would usually wait for an invitation and promptly RSVP an event before attending it, began showing up at Somali wedding celebrations uninvited. Henna knew they were in trouble when he began acting like a Somali, attending events he was not personally invited to.

They arrived at Marriot Vista Beach, the hotel ballroom where the wedding party they were not invited to was taking place. Henna wore a traditional *baacweyne,* a sleek beige diric with brown sequins and a pair of beige stilettos with diamond squares. She looked stylish, like the slew of women who wore similar outfits. Brian wore a long *khamiss* robe with a Moroccan fez. They stood at the doorway for a while attempting to locate a seat in the heaving ballroom. A polite youthful man with dark shades and a hat, looking more like a presenter at the BET awards, took them to a table they inherited from a group of young men dressed in the latest hip-hop attire who suddenly found themselves at the doorway. It was not the first time they inherited a table not intended for them. Henna was embarrassed. The dance floor brimmed with men and women, young and old, dancing to Somali remixes of old tunes. Henna avoided gatherings of this sort; wedding ceremonies forced images she had fought hard to forget. She often wondered if her attackers were present in the same room. While Brian danced jovially amid the Somalis, Henna fidgeted with her cell phone to avoid the stares of those around her. She was aloof among them, unsure of what to say. When did she loose her Somali etiquette, becoming suspicious, mistaking a greeting for a rude inquiry and a simple smile as hateful?

She decided to go to the bathroom to waste time, but the line in front of it was impossible. Women and girls sporting different colors of the same baacweyne she wore filled the areas around the bathroom. She then decided to go to the lobby.

The ballroom was filled with at least three hundred people, but the lobby equally filled with people who escaped the ear-piercing music to catch up. Women zigzagged through the crowd, stealing glances at each other's outfits and gathering ammo for vicious gossip.

The bride and her family spent all their savings on the wedding. They did this not necessarily to pave their marriage path with happiness, but to create jealousy, set a trend, and provoke envious gossip. It was understood that every Somali was a possible enemy who would not want your happiness, so families went all out to create the envy they internalized. Women tried to outdo each other, whether they were invited or not.

In the lobby people of all ages sat on chairs, tables, stairs and whatever space that would hold a body. Henna found a hidden corner and made a phone call to Ramallah. There was nothing new to report except the usual complaint of how she was dragged into yet another unoriginal and dull wedding ceremony. She wanted to keep Ramallah on the line for as long as she could to escape the evil stares that seemed destined for her.

As she chatted away with Ramallah, she saw a face she thought she recognized from the corner of her eye. The face brought back distressing memories; her heart began to sprint. She hung up the phone and walked slowly behind the man. He wore a beige suit and a purple tie. He was a small-built man with a dark brown complexion. He walked, bouncing from person to person, horse-playing with other men on his way to his seat. He took a seat next to a fully-garbed woman, one of the few in the room. Next to the woman sat three small children, all under five. The man put one of the kids on his lap. He swung the little girl from side to side and then he sat her next to him. He began feeding her by hand, shoving small amounts of food in her mouth while he chatted with the woman and other very elaborately-dressed teenage girls at the table. Henna searched for Brian, who seemed lost in the middle of a circle where he danced wildly while the crowd cheered.

She wanted his attention but Brian was engrossed in shaking his body every which way, sending his hands above him and shuddering his torso to please the crowd. He was too immersed in his activity to even offer a look her way. The man took the garbed woman's hand and headed for the bride and groom's table. He shook hands with the groom and kissed the bride, introducing the woman, and then he invited the couple to dance with them. They danced next to Brian, who cheered them on. The man and Brian took turns dancing with the bride and groom.

A few weeks later Henna needed to purchase a pair of stilettos to match a dress she had bought earlier in the week for an Aids benefit she would attend with Ramallah. She ended up in the mall after a lazy Sunday of slouching, feeling sluggish and bored and. She decided to force Brian to come with her instead of attending some luncheon at his Nana's house. As she checked out a pair of Jimmy Choo snakeskin heels, she spotted Brian with a pair of garbed Somali women outside the store.

"*Naayaa, adiga walaal?*" Brain said excitedly, in the loudest voice. The women looked at each other and chuckled; bewildered that he was bold enough to demean them through the use of the word "naayaa".

"*Haa, haa walaal*" said one woman while the other walked swiftly past him. Henna hid behind the store mirror, shaking with embarrassment. She ducked unsuccessfully moving from one aisle to the next, until she was in full view of the women.

"Honey, look here—I found some of your relatives! They were walking by," he shouted excitedly pointing to them as if they were some exotic animals. She ignored him, and extended her hand to greet the women. Jittery, she felt self-conscious, aware her tight jeans and tank top were not pleasing to the women, who abruptly lowered their gaze as if they were in full view of a sinful act. She kept pulling her tank top down tensely, trying to hide her bare pierced bellybutton. She cursed Brain under her breath, promising to put him in the dog house. The women were ferociously curious to know whose daughter she was.

"Say, eeddo, what is your father's name?" one woman asked as she looked Henna up and down.

"His name is Mursal Sagal," she said convincingly. She was glad they were speaking in Somali, or else Brian would reveal her bluff.

"Which part of Somalia are you from, eeddo?" the other woman asked, visibly searching her head for familiarity in the name.

"We are from Beldweyn," Henna continued her fib.

"And your mother's name?" the women were taking successive turns with the questions as if they'd rehearsed.

"Ugaaso Haji Cisman," Henna prided herself in the rapidity of the responses.

"Ummm?" said the more eager of the women. "Where does Ugaaso live now?" she asked, somehow unable to pair Henna with anyone she knows.

"May Allah bless her soul, hooyo is deceased." Her insensitivity stunned her.

"*Innaa Lillaahi wa innaa Ilayhi raajicuun*," murmured the quieter of the two.

"Where do you live, eeddo?" continued the inquisitive woman.

"We are from San Francisco; we are only visiting family in Devon Woods," she said, signaling Brian to rescue her.

"You are married to him?" Henna was unsure if it was a question or a harshly stated fact; she frowned at Brian, who understood the cue not to approach them. The woman twitched her mouth from side to side to reveal her disapproval.

"Yes, he is my husband." Henna said decisively, bidding the women who stood there for more questioning goodbye. After the women tossed some superficial blessings at her, they walked away fast, smiling nervously, grateful to leave the sinner behind.

The women would instantly search for information about her exclusively for the purpose of condemnation. They would publicly condemn her mother for birthing such a disgraceful daughter and the entire episode would be repeated on the phone, in gatherings and in any scenario where the women could gather more info on Henna and her family.

"Look, you need to stop this ignorant B.S., Brian! I am not related to every freaking Somali person in the world, you know!" she said, dropping the shoes into the pretty pink box forcefully. "I'm tired of this—I told you not to do this after you dragged that poor old man over to me the last time we were down here."

"But I thought you like meeting your folks, whatever you call them, your cousins?" Brian said, knowing full well he was in big trouble.

"They are not my cousins, stop acting ignorant and stupid!" She kept running her hand through her hair, messing the stylish long hair in the process, then bit her lower lip in rage and then held both hands up, as if to make a point. "I am so shocked at your behavior, Brian!"

Feeling irritated she dashed out of the store without buying the shoes she had come to purchase.

SANTA ANA DRAMA

No one would claim things were settled in the Shield/Gedi household—at least nothing was settled with Henna, who at any moment felt she would lash out at Brian. The hot, arid Santa Ana winds that restricted her breathing had something to do with her mood change: the same ferocious winds that caused her to pour with annoying sweat all over her body. The Santa Anna also caused her infamous, rather obtruding Somali forehead to break out with three unbecoming pimples on top of each other. It would be easy to underestimate the effects the Santa Ana winds could have on the mood of an already-bickering couple. The hot winds which could distort an otherwise pleasant, sweat-free Southern Californian would bring ashes of homes engulfed by vicious fires into Henna's nose, mouth and taste buds, altering any cozy feeling she may have had about the beauty of Southern California which she'd fallen in love with.

She suddenly grew distant, and felt stuck in the marriage. And so when Ramallah suggested that she move to New York City to pursue a career in modeling with her, she jumped at the idea. In reality, she was running away from a life that ceased to exist for her. She just was not the trophy wife Brian needed anymore.

Other than frustration and boredom she received no revelations as to why she was no longer interested in her life with Brian. She pondered upon the question endlessly. She reasoned it was not a flaw in her personality to lose interest in the life she chose with Brian, knowing the astonished protests of her mother. When she had first met Brian she made him the center of her world. Every word that left his lips conveyed something meaningful. He appeared so educated, intelligent and kind. He had opinions about everything, opinions she welcomed at the time. Every project received his undivided attention and was painstakingly completed. He never took anything lightly and would deliberate over minute projects. But five years into their marriage and his world gradually collapsed into boredom. His elaborate descriptions of things, no matter how mundane oozed with dullness. "Must you give the history of every freaking machine!" she once said to him, annoyed. His meticulous habits got in the way: she wanted him to act normal, like her, without showing off all the details of every topic. How quickly she noticed that he had no traditions or customs, or anything that made him unique. The sudden monotony of her life with Brian would excite an escape with anyone, going anywhere. Ramallah, whom she'd met at a friend's party when she was fermenting in her excruciatingly boring life, was a savior. She would have gone to the most dreadful of places at that point to elude the boredom she felt. Moving to New York City did come with some reservations, though—she was afraid the city would swallow her with it is glitz and glamour. She felt somewhat safe and stable with Brian. Adventuring on her own to a big city like New York kept her awake at night. Brian slept next to her, innocently unaware she planned to leave him while he was busy planning a celebration here and a milestone there. She tossed and turned with guilt. He has been an ideal mate; he showered her with undivided attention, was generous and he loved her. So what more did she want? She wanted to leave yet she craved the stability and security he gave her. It was the only stability she had known since her move to the U.S. She argued with herself, scolding her self-centered side, the side of her that wanted to discard their life. She asked herself hard questions. "This man has saved you, what the hell are you looking for?" Then the irrational side of her would reason the distance the differences of culture had created was too hard to deal with. "Would you love Brian or even feel comfortable with him if it were not for the affluent life he has provided you?" She looked around the house. The massive walk-in closets, her custom-made Mercedes

Benz, all the diamond jewelry, the personal trainer, yearly skiing trips, and shopping sprees in LA, Paris and London. What else could she want in a man? But she hated his bad habits—funny how his bad habits conveniently became apparent. The way he shoved food into his mouth, his appearance, which was edging towards shabby, his bad breath and the balding, receding hair did not help in the argument against leaving.

If it were not for what he was giving her, would she be attracted to him? What was it about him that suddenly made him annoying? She was ready to walk away from it all, to regain her sanity. That was the logic she provided. Her sanity was in jeopardy! Now that she was living among people whose pursuit of happiness was inscribed into the constitution of the land, she figured she had a right to be happy. And so the search had begun to attract happiness into her life.

And so Henna fell into a trap, the same trap that every Somali woman falls into, that she too can become the next runway model that the world falls in love with. She had received enough compliments that she was pretty and model material, and so she began her pursuit to model and make a life for herself in New York City. She imagined the streets of New York would be lined with modeling contracts and agents willing to book her for the best jobs, but after four months, she could no longer lie to herself that she would hit it big in NYC. When the money Brian gave her dried up, she had to move in with Ramallah to pay for the bare necessities. They worked in the garment district for an apparel company run by a cruel Chinese women, Lara Wu. On rare occasions minor modeling assignments came their way.

Life in New York City became so unbearable that Henna actually contemplated returning to California. She missed the material comforts of her life with Brian, although she did not miss the emptiness of it. But she could never return to him, he was still angry and called her selfish and spoiled when she asked for divorce. Any chance they may have had to reconcile their already rocky marriage was marred by Brain's refusal to investigate the mysterious man he had casually enjoyed a very animated dance with in that wedding. Henna thought the guy with the nice family who was amusing himself in that wedding was none other than her old neighbor Liban Culusow. She remembers him to be one of the cruelest of her attackers, now in the safety of his American life he looked mellowed and a respectable community member.

But by the time Brain inquired about him, he found out the man's name was Cumar Bakayle. Henna insisted his name was Liban and that he was one of the men who attacked her family that fateful day in Hamar. But Brian was insistent that the man was innocent until proven guilty by a court of law and that he was not the man she thought he was. With a little digging she found out Cumar Bakayle was indeed an alias and that Liban Culusow had changed his identity as soon as he crossed from the Mexican border some seven years earlier. Now he owned a number of small grocery stores and was married with five children. Brain dismissed her concerns as aggressive and unbearable. That must have been a sign for her to move on to a new life.

In New York City a man she had been noticing for a couple of weeks followed her one day after she had left an assignment with a perfume company. He ran after her, shouting in Khuzayman.

"*Inti min feen!*" he said as she passed the waterfall where he sat with a group of Middle Eastern looking men. She'd noticed that the Pulitzer fountain on Fifty-ninth and Fifth Avenue was a hangout place for Khuzayman men. She had had an assignment for four weeks and had avoided walking past the north side of the fountain where these Khuzayman men in white robes and head scarves seemed to congregate. Tall with a compact body the man who was in his late twenties kept following her, insisting that she speak to him.

But Henna walked quickly, ignoring his comments. By the time she had reached the edge of the water fountain he was standing right in front of her. She had forgotten the belligerence of Khuzayman men; it was a culture she did not miss. Whenever she visited Khuzaymah Saqr Island she began to appreciate America, where men did not announce women's arrival with whistling to make their desires known. She crossed over to Fifth Avenue to evade him. He crossed the road behind her, and this time he followed her closely as she walked faster to avoid him. He was tall and broad-shouldered, unlike the others she saw him with, who looked obese and clumsy. He looked neat, even handsome, and from his bearing and attire, far from destitute.

"Hey! Where are you from?" he asked, finally speaking in English as he walked beside her. She did not detect an accent.

"What does it matter where I'm from?" She sped up a bit.

"Please slow down, I need to talk to you," he begged.

"Look, I'm tired—no! I am exhausted, and obviously you have time on your hands, so how about you leave me alone so I can get home and take a nice, much-needed hot bath." She was still walking, peeking at her blackberry from time to time. She did not look tired: her sleek, straightened brown hair, fresh makeup, and long cream slacks made her look ready for a photo shoot.

"Look, I know you probably think I'm trouble, but you are so striking. I was waiting to talk to you all day; I have to get to know you. Please let me put my number in your blackberry, and you will be on your way to take that sweet hot bath."

"Really? That easy, huh?" She finally turned to face him.

"No, seriously, I have been seeing you for a week now and—"

"Look, please leave me alone. I am in no mood to waste my time, just let me be on my way."

"I don't mean to bother you—seriously, just give me your number." He stared at her, embarrassed. "What's your name?"

"Look, why don't you go bother someone else? Just leave me alone, ok?" She turned around to attempt to cross the street again.

The old Henna would jump at the opportunity to talk to a man like this—handsome, and apparently rich and sophisticated. The new Henna, after a failed marriage, knew herself better. She knew dating was no longer part of who she wanted to be as a Muslim woman. She was a secular Muslim: she did not veil, or dress modest like a practicing Muslim woman, but she practiced Islam in her own spiritual way. She vowed to obey the covenants of the religion that forbade promiscuity.

This continued for weeks. He was so persistent—she could ignore him if she wanted to, but she instead agreed to have coffee with him one afternoon. They met in the lobby of the Ritz Carlton, which appeared to be a haven for Arab families.

"You must have some Arab blood," he said earnestly as he nibbled at a piece of baklava.

"What makes you say that?" She asked distracted by some Arab children who were chasing each other close to their table.

"Are they bothering you? Do you want to go somewhere more quiet?"

"No, no, they are not bothering me. I'm ok," she replied, trying to sound convincing.

"So you don't seem to like Arabs much—why is that, refusing your people?"

"Look, I am not an Arab; being a Muslim does not make one an Arab."

"Somalis are Arabs, even if Somalia is in Africa."

"Why do you want to group us in with the Arabs so badly? Must all Muslims belong to you? Somalis are not Arabs." She pushed her coffee aside to make room for her hands. "There are more non-Arab Muslims around the world, and yet somehow you guys make the world think every Muslim is an Arab. Look at Indonesia, Malaysia, China, and India— I could go on and on."

"Why do you Somalia detest Arabs anyway? Every Somali I meet seems to hate Arabs," he said casually.

"It is a bad habit I find in most Arabs that I meet—they try to converse by first assuring you are one of them. It is rather rude to take away one's identity that way; I think Arabs do not know who they are, so they claim others to belong to them."

"Wow, we don't know who we are, huh?" He chuckled.

"Plus, people despise you because of the way your treat them in your country."

"And how do we treat people in my country?"

"Are you kidding me, you must be aware of all the inhumane things you guys do to people in your country."

"I mean you guys are so inhumane with laborers, maids and basically anyone in your country that is not from the west."

"Look, I don't want to waste time on these stupid issues. Let's talk about you."

"You claim we are Arabs, and yet you never accept refugees into your country, those who are unfortunate to find themselves in your country find their heads or arms chopped off."

"You seem angry, please let's drop it and talk about you."

"Well, I'm sorry, but it amazes me that such a rich country like yours never takes in Muslim refugees with dignity, but non Muslim countries around the world are taking in Muslim refugees, sheltering them form wars and chaos and educating their children, so what have you done for us lately?"

"Well, I'm sure we are not as bad as you say we are."

His name is Naif al Ali, a prince from Khuzaymah Saqr Island, who was spending his summer holiday in New York City. She began spending more and more time with him. He was so convinced they should get married before he traveled back to Khala, although they'd only known each other for two months. But Henna's divorce from Brian was still not final and she did not want to jump from one relationship to another.

"Hey, did you get the message from Rachel, she has been stalking me hoping I will lead her to you," Ramallah said as she entered the tiny apartment they shared in the upper Westside.

"Yeah, yeah uhmmm," Henna seemed distracted.

"Hey did you hear me?" Ramallah said, looking Henna's way to get her attention.

"I am sorry, it is Naif, he just texted me. What?" she responded to Ramallah's bewildered expression.

"My God, how many times do you guys talk and text each other? It's insane," Ramallah started to straighten the shoe closet.

"Hey, did you pick up that letter from the property manager?" Henna peeked from the blanket she hid under on the sofa.

"Yeah, it was for me, the grant is approved. Anyway, gotta run—some of us have real jobs, you know." Ramallah teased.

"Hmmm, I am so sleepy. I'll call Rachel back later—could you pick the kabob special from the Lebanese House on your way back please?" Henna said lazily.

"Okay, but I'm not coming back until late."

"I know, I am just too lazy to go out today."

"You need to snap out of it, girl, you've been slacking."

"I will, *Insha Allah* Naif keeps calling at odd hours, that is all."

"Whatever!"

Naif and Henna married when he visited the following winter. She was hesitant at first, especially when she found out he was already married to two women in Khuzaymah Saqr Island. But she desired him, and his lifestyle. Once again, she could not handle her new life in New York City. That unsettling feeling, the itch she got once in a while, the same one that lead her to marry Brian presented itself again, with urgency. Naif's proposal seemed like a good way to scratch it off, so she agreed to marry him, reasoning it beat being his mistress.

She moved into the Fifth Ave penthouse he shared with his brother. She had finally married a Muslim man, she reasoned, who at least shared some familiarity with her culture. This next chapter of Henna's life was one of luxury and travel, although it came at a price. She had to keep the marriage a secret, since the prince already had two wives in Khuzaymah Saqr. She had to remain in New York City, he came and went as he pleased, and there were to be no children in the marriage.

He would visit her once every two months. Her new lifestyle made it easy to shop, travel, and have fun with her friends. But when he came, she abandoned everything to answer to his demands. She was happy, although he was very persistent, and difficult. She actually grew to love him. He was classy, romantic, and extremely generous. He was different from his brothers and cousins who also kept wives and mistresses in

New York City; he was a bit worldlier, and much more loving than they were.

He amazed her when he accompanied her to Goma's Angels, a charity that supported rape victims around the world. It had been started by Ramallah, whose three sisters had died in the Rwandan genocide. Henna helped start the organization when Naif donated fifty thousand dollars of his own money to the charity. That gesture alone was enough to convince her he was a good man.

He accompanied her to visit the children who came to New York City with their mothers for counseling. He played with them, brought them all kinds of toys and gifts, and simply spent time there as Henna worked with their mothers. She usually condemned rich Arabs like him, whom she identified as heartless and spoiled; but Naif was neither.

LOUD AND PROUD

Cedar Avenue was Idil's turf: it is where she is known for her business savvy and where she sold everything worth selling, sometimes resorting to selling anything at all. Idil created a market for everything from sambuusa to illegal merchandise, selling to anyone who would buy. She reinvented herself, calling her business "The Whole Nine", as in the whole nine yards. Her street name was "Idol", a name she had adopted at school after everyone mistakenly mispronounced her name as Idol. Idil was perhaps the only one in the entire Gedi clan who took after her grandmother. She was forced to deal with the changes in her life, and, like Nadifo, she refused to be broken by her situation.

Idil found herself reluctantly living with Nadifo after her mother Warsan disappeared. There are varying stories as to where Warsan disappeared to. Some speculate she vanished into the world of Zandakan criminal life after she followed Femi Obiageli, the founder of Softer Communications, a multimillion-dollar software company, to Harey; others speculated that the family admitted her to an unknown psychiatric ward after she became mentally ill. Wherever Warsan was, she was not with her three children. Hannad, the father who could not handle taking care of all three kids on his own, discharged all three of them to various family members. Hilac, the eldest, went to stay with one maternal aunt in Virginia; Hogad, the second child, was sent to Columbus, Ohio, to stay with another. And Idil was left to stay with Nadifo at the notorious Cedar Springs, where Hannad visited occasionally. Idil lived a middle-class life with her parents until the sudden change in family

346

structure. She went from being a spoiled little girl in a family of five who pretty much had everything she wanted, to living with her grandmother in a fixed-income household where she went to bed hungry most nights. The unbroken Idil resorted to doing whatever she could to survive. Her brother Hogad got involved in a street gang in Columbus at age thirteen. He survived two shootouts, both times walking away, although with injuries. Hilac was subdued by the situation; she hardly called or talked to anyone anymore.

By age thirteen Idil was running a fully-fledged business from Nadifo's apartment. She wore t-shirts that announced her business slogan "The Best In Town, by Idol". She handled most of the transactions on her cell phone, and would use kids all over the neighborhood to deal. Idil came home one day to conduct her business from Nadifo's house as usual, wearing a t-shirt that said "Don't hate we the same!" and tight skinny jeans that accentuated her shapely figure.

She was annoyed when she saw the house bustling with Somali women from the neighborhood. She could never escape them without either commenting on her clothes or saying something hurtful. Provocative and loud, the messages on Idil's t-shirts often announced her state of mind. It was her means of freedom of expression; after all, Nadifo and the other elders in the community could not read or understand these slogans. She seemed to have a shirt for all occasions, making a lucrative business out of t-shirts with messages such as "Ducking the sandal", "Coffee shop: Not your personal living space" and "We are loud and proud!".

Idil had been around Somali women enough to know they gathered either to gossip, deliver bad news or to gang up on someone. She ignored them as she passed through the living room. Their eyes conveyed their judgment and so she looked down as she passed them. She was headed for Nadifo's bedroom to handle her business, when Nadifo's rude words intruded over the iPod earphones.

"Naayaa, make tea, don't pour all the sugar at once like you usually do, and bake a cake!" the orders were not bashful or modest; rather they were direct and egotistic, without one pleasant word for the tired student. The curious lot kept staring rudely, and she caught two of them elbowing each other without saying a word.

Idil hated making tea for these women; they were never satisfied with her tea. They complained that there was too much sugar, not enough sugar, too much cream, not enough cream or spice or whatever else they could find wrong with it—or her.

"Okay, ayeeyo, I will," she said unenthusiastically restless that this task would cut into plans for the afternoon.

"Naayaa don't forget the halwa and cookies, if you need more go to Haweeya's house to get some!" Naayaa may as well be her pet name; it was the only way Nadifo ever addressed her.

"Okay, okay, ayeeyo," Idil said ignoring the vibrating cell phone which had been going off the entire time. She did not even change from her school clothes but began boiling water for the tea when she finally answered the phone and was ranting about some money that someone owed, when she heard the words "Devon Woods" and "Henna" coming from the loud women in the living room. She hung the phone up quickly, taking her time to make the best tea she had ever made. She served the tea, cookies and halwa, and just made herself available the entire afternoon, clearing the table, washing dishes and tidying up the kitchen, a chore Idil was known to despise. Her phone kept ringing but she ignored it, turning the ringer off. She started straightening the food pantry, piling spaghetti boxes on top of each other behind the tomato paste and onions, when Nadifo interrupted her eavesdropping and snapped in Somali:

"Naayaa" she yelled that horrendous word naayaa again, which readied Idil for trouble. "Why are you in the kitchen—are you listening to our conversation?"

"No, ayeeyo, I am doing a school project," Idil said searching her mind for what to say next.

"A school project to do what?"

"My teacher Mrs. Loewen asked me to list the kind of food you keep in your house."

"Which class, naayaa?" Nadifo said insolently.

"Ayeeyo, it is for my nutrition class."

"What does your teacher want with my food?"

"She wants to know how we eat, like what kinda food we eat."

"Why, why is that important to her?"

"It is for nutrition, like vegetables, meat, pasta, you know, she wants to know what kinda food we eat."

"Okay, finish quickly and go to the room, naayaa, instead of getting involved with adult conversation!"

"Okay, ayeeyo, I promise, I love ya," she agreed grudgingly kissing her on the cheek surprising them both with the gesture. Who knew such futile backbiting gatherings could serve a purpose? Idil had no idea the information she gathered from an evening of painful snooping where she spent hours decoding Somali words she did not understand would help Shirwac. One woman who came from Devon Woods announced that Henna had left Brian; the woman clarified she did not know where Henna was living now. But Idil found out that a man in Devon Woods whom the woman referred to as "one of the men" may have been one of the reasons Henna left town.

Idil emerged from the eavesdropping incident with information she deemed necessary for Shirwac, whom she'd had began to influence recently. They were having another chaos -filled afternoon in Cedar Springs where, instead of doing homework, Idil and Shirwac hung around the neighborhood park where they either got into a fight or some hair-raising incident involving Idil's business. Without the watchful eyes of Haybe and Nadifo these two got into all kinds of trouble— usually at Idil's instigation.

"Hey, yo Shirwac! I know it is federal for us to go to California but we got no choice!" When Idil resorted to slang, Shirwac knew she was up to some troubling scheme.

"Idil, I don't want to break no laws and I don't wanna to get in trouble with Haybe. Anyway, how the heck are we going to go to Devon Woods —we don't even know anyone there!"

"Hey, how about Brian, he'll hook us up, right!"

"Idil, I haven't seen him for five years, he probably doesn't even remember me!"

"Come on, dude, of course he do! We might find your daddy there if we go."

"He ain't my daddy!"

"Who knows? Maybe he is." Idil's snoopy ways came away with information concerning a man who could possibly be Shirwac's father. His name is Liban Culusow, a thirty-five-year-old guy with a wife and five kids. Shirwac was conflicted to meet this man, but then the urges inside of him played with his head. *Maybe he is my father. Maybe I even look like him, but will he even recognize me as his son?* He wondered, terrified of rejection. Idil had an idea. She found Brian's telephone number and address in Camino County, California. She called him and told him who she was, that she wanted to know if he knew where Henna was and if he knew anything about this Liban guy. All the years Henna had lived with him, Brian has never heard from her family, and even after she left no one had called to find out why. He had moved on with his life, married one Jessica Brooks and had two little boys. It has been two years since Henna left. He has not heard from her for the past two years, and now out of nowhere her niece and son were looking for her. Brian found the whole thing odd. Why were these teenagers interested in Henna now? Where was Haybe, the only person who seemed the least bit interested in Henna's affairs and well being when they were married? Idil had somehow convinced Brian that she and Shirwac would be coming to see him with Haybe. She said they had some business with this Liban guy and that they needed his help. Brian did not object. He wanted to help Henna's family any way he could—after all, he was familiar with the Somali community in Devon Woods; he still had some ties with them.

About a week later on a Saturday evening, Jessica came home to finish some work she brought home after dropping her husband and two boys off at Dave and Buster's. She was on the phone as she pushed through the front gate, and had not noticed them at first. She got out of the car, picked a package from the front seat and proceeded to walk to the front of the house when she noticed Idil and Shirwac sitting on the front porch bench. Jessica froze. She removed the phone from her ear, but did not hang it up entirely, tip-toeing slowly back to her car. Idil came up to her.

"Hey, how are you? Are you—"

"Please, here is my purse, please don't hurt me I—" Jessica threw the package and her purse to the ground and started crying. Idil picked up the stuff; by this time Shirwac joined them. Jessica looked scared—terrified, actually.

"Hey, we are not here to rob you," Idil said with a silly giggle.

"Okay, okay, please don't kill me, I beg you! I have two little boys and a husband and—"

"But I just told you, we ain't thieves!"

"Hey, Idil, let's go, I think we're at the wrong house."

"Shirwac, just shut the hell up, let me handle this! Is this 245 Laguna Drive?"

"Yes, it is. Who are you? What do you want?" In her head Jessica planed to get back into her car quickly, but stood there frozen.

"Where is Mr. Shield—I mean Brian?"

"Uhmm, he is not here—who are you?" She slowly slipped out of her Via Spiga ankle-strap sandals so she would not trip on the pointed heels.

"This is Shirwac, do you know him?" Jessica's terror was very apparent to Idil. She was still convinced they intended to kill her. Her flushed face drizzled with sweat and her lips trembled as she stood stock-still.

"You think black people came to your crib to kill you?" Idil sniggered, pointing her finger toward the terrified woman and joking with

Shirwac, "yo, she whack, crazy white people! I ain't mad at you though, you gettin ya' roll on."

"I beg your pardon?"

"I mean I like yo car, what is it, an Escalade, you ballin'?"

"Yes, it is an Escalade," she was busy planning to open the door of the truck and speed away. She had not paid attention to what Idil said.

"Yeah, I like that—it's fly, I like that color too."

"I am sorry, we came here to see Brian," Shirwac said in a light wispy voice, almost embarrassed by the misunderstanding.

"Of course. I'm sorry, I thought you—"

"Yeah, you thought we was going to rob you, huh!" Idil cut her off. "Do we look like robbers? Is it our clothes?" Idil said rudely, pointing to her baggy jeans and black hooded sweater which hugged her petite frame firmly.

"No. I am sorry, I really was not expecting anyone and I thought—"

"You know, your husband's ex, Henna, this is her son," Her voice sounded shrewd, rough, and husky, belying her small physique.

"Oh, Shirac—wait, Henna's son? What are you doing here?" Jessica pretended to acknowledge him, and then she opened the door to her Escalade and disappeared behind the locked doors, frightened and tearful. She quickly maneuvered through the wide opened gates avoiding, Idil who was banging on the window. Her purse, wallet, and cell phone lay scattered around the lawn with other items from her purse.

"What the—hey, come back here!" Idil sped to the driver's side of the car and tugged at the handle, but she could not stop Jessica, whose eyes secreted tears; she fled as if to catch up with the life that flashed right in front of her.

"Now what? She's going to call the popo on us, dang," Shirwac shouted, sounding mad.

"Dumb blond—what the heck do we look like, criminals?"

"Hey, let's bounce, dawg, she probably calling the 5-0 on us. Snap, I knew this was going to happen!"

"Shut up, Shirwac, this ain't time to panic. Let's go around the back!"

"Go where? We don't have any money."

"Man, let's just dip!" Idil went around the back of the house, expecting Shirwac to follow. "Hey, what the hell you doin'? Leave that alone, man!" Idil shouted, throwing her bag down to try and pull him away from the stuff.

"I wanted to put her things in the purse, and...."

"Look, leave it alone dude, let's just dip!"

"I just wanted to put it on the bench for her; it is her cell phone and stuff."

"Let' just dip, man; we don't have time for that mess!"

Idil's big idea to take the back route to the main street did not work. They were running on North Promenade Ridge Blvd when they heard police sirens.

"Yo, just walk, okay? Don't run," Idil said, attempting to look calm; she appeared nervous instead. It was the first time Shirwac has seen her apprehensive about anything: he often trusted her quick thinking. When he heard the sirens he knew they were in trouble. They stopped running and began walking. Two police cars cut them off as they were about to cross to the other side of the road.

"Hello. May I see your IDs, please?" asked one officer while the other remained in the car.

"We didn't do nuttin," Idil said, keeping both of her hands in her pockets.

"Young lady I need to see your ID. You too, sir!"

"I didn't bring my school ID with me," Shirwac said, terrified.

"What the hell do you need ID for, I told you we didn't do nuttin," Idil said, taking both hands out of her pockets.

"Where do you live, miss?" The officer asked, looking directly at her. "Are you hard of hearing? I asked you to give me your address."

"What business is that of yours?" She wanted to sound convincing, but was too nervous to pull it off.

"Okay, I guess you will not answer my questions. I'll just have to arrest you then."

"Officer, we live at 2046 Cedar Springs Road," Shirwac said unexpectedly.

"Where is that?"

"Minneapolis, Minnesota."

"Minneapolis? What are you doing here then?"

"We are looking for my Uncle Brian Shield's house."

"Brian who?"

"He's our uncle—I mean he white and everything, but he our uncle."

"Okay, the both of you get in the car; you have no business being here!"

"It's a free country," Idil said as she was being shoved into the police car. "We just have to call Brian—he white like you, I am sure you all understand each other's lingo right."

"In the car, motor mouth."

As they sat in the police station, Shirwac's admiration for her was wearing thin. Sometimes he wished she would just shut her mouth. The danger of loving someone who is daring and outspoken stunned him: he contemplated the entire trip as he watched Idil bad mouth the police man who picked them up.

"What, one can't walk the streets of America freely unless they's white?" He wanted to shut her up, but instead remained quiet, awaiting his fate. Shirwac felt a knot in his lower abdomen. The reality of what they had done scared him. His mind began to race with anxiety: What would he tell Haybe and Nadifo? How would he explain this one?

But Idil was too engrossed with making her case to muscular and insolent officer McBride to notice his worry. She wanted to know why he'd brought them to the Police Station. The officer was not interested in the attacks she'd laid on him continuously for the past two hours; instead he rolled a stress-relieving, shiny pink ball in his hand while he conversed with the receptionist. There were some unsavory looking people in the lock-up who were enjoying the verbal onslaught against

Officer McBride: he would sporadically reply "You need to keep it down, miss," and that would infuriate her even further.

"What! Now you want to control my free speech? Hell, no!"

"Idil naga aamus, yaan nala xidhin'e" Shirwac said in Somali to try and calm her down.

"I can't believe this freaking racist crap!" she continued.

Shirwac kept apologizing to the officer while she went on and on. Finally the officer booked her and put her in a cell to quiet her down. To Shirwac it seemed too surreal that they were sitting in a police station in a city where they knew no one; but Idil seemed to enjoy the thug aura she presented. This was the second time she had gotten him in trouble with the police. Now she was in a holding cell awaiting her destiny from the white police officer who showed his annoyance with his refusal to allow them use of the phone.

Three hours after they were picked up, they were taken to a hotel where they would spend the night. Shirwac kept calling Brian two hours after they were brought to the police station, at which point officer McBride had had enough of Idil's mouth. In the holding cell she found another angry, self-expressive vulgar woman, who added her unflattering descriptions of police in America. Her vulgar behavior matched that of Idil's.

Brian would not answer the phone. When he finally did after seven attempts, he came to get them. Brain was furious with them; he explained that Jessica had gone to the emergency room for a panic attack, and had been admitted for stress. Shirwac did not understand what that meant; he just knew stress was something most Americans enjoyed talking about, and were very sensitive to. He felt responsible, knowing he added to Jessica's stress. He was resolved never to trust Idil again, and felt responsible for the inconvenience he caused Brian. Idil curled herself in the back seat, sulking in anger. Shirwac enjoyed the quiet; he preferred it that way, instead of getting into some elaborate discussion of racism that would condemn all white people—or worse say something unpleasant about Jessica. She was better off curled up and mute. He was glad her anger and disappointment with their trip shut her up for the rest of the evening.

⁂

Shirwac had noticed how it was cool to say "I hate my mom", "my dad is the most annoying person on earth" and "my mom is so weird". Kids in America enjoyed belittling their parents. Josh had once said he hated his step-dad so much he was going to kill him one day. It shocked Shirwac, upsetting him. Idil hated both her parents; Jibari hated his dad. Shirwac felt left out, as usual. He didn't have the luxury of hating his parents. All that remained of Henna was a picture she sent when she was on some vacation; he simply did not know her well enough to hate her, although he wished he did. Neither did he have a father to hate, but he fantasized about the phrase "I hate my dad." He craved the luxury to hate his dad, to dislike him so he could brag to other kids that he also hated his dad even if he did not. He supposed kids hating their parents was a direct result of having unlimited parental love. As if a kid could not have hate for parents if those same parents did not give them so much love. So how could he hate his parents when he has never received parental love from them? He despised them when they said it, he felt as if the words were designed to crush his ego. For that reason Shirwac become obsessed with things he could not have. He secretly wanted to rejoin the man who would have answers to his life problems.

All of a sudden, Shirwac felt nothing in his present life belonged to him: it was all the making of his new family. They claimed him when they thought appropriate; and ignored him when they did not want their lives interrupted. Now he wanted none of it. He was eager to find the truth. Why was it so hard for him to know how he came to the world? That should not be a very difficult question, but it proved impossible. He wanted to meet Liban in Devon Woods. The trip to find Liban with Idil had been disastrous—after the mishap with the police officer they were sent right back to Minneapolis. Idil developed an attitude throughout their return trip. She wanted to stay in California—she actually had concocted a plan, but never shared it with him. Her plans included moving to L.A., to never return to the place she referred to as the "dump". She never wanted to see her rotten family again. Shirwac and Idil's disappearance from Minneapolis was not felt until two days after they left. Haybe thought Shirwac was with Nadifo for the weekend; Nadifo did not call Haybe's house unless there was a reason. There usually was no reason to track or look for Shirwac, but Idil was a different story. She was often missing in action and her father rarely looked for her; he was busy being trampled by life's mishaps. And Nadifo hardly looked for the teenage trouble-maker unless she was given a reason to, reasons that often surfaced for one mischief or another.

Brian sent them back to Minneapolis, but Idil refused to come with Shirwac. Her refusal caused them to travel as "unaccompanied minors." They were not left alone one minute until they were handed to Haybe, who received them with contempt. She had few unpleasant exchanges with an airline hostess when she tried to go off on her own in Chicago's O'Hare Airport while in transit.

When they returned to Minneapolis, Shirwac was forbidden to see Idil: Haybe complained that she was the one distracting him from school, and the one who encorged him to be inquisitive. She influenced his thinking, causing him to ask too many questions. His punishment was severe: TV and phone privileges were taken away, and his iPod and most of his clothes and gameboy were auctioned off on eBay. The proceeds were donated to an orphanage in Hamar, along with six pairs of sneakers. Shirwac's mind was not on the lost privileges, but more on Idil. He missed her, more than he could handle. Without her, life was dull. Her ways inspired him, moved something within him. He was bold around her, ready to meet Liban, the man who could be his father. Nadifo had referred to Idil as a hurricane ready to attack with vengeance; to Shirwac she was a breeze of freshness that gave his life purpose. There often was something up her slippery sleeves. Without Idil there was no news from Henna, and news about Liban halted, and without her life became a long boring chore.

Shirwac did not see his purpose in life before he got close to Idil. He did not care much about his birth, parents or anything else around him; he was just happy having found his family. But change came quick as he and Idil got closer: he became bold, curious and he was no longer willing to accept things at face value from anyone.

She encouraged him to question his identity, to expect more from his life and discard his naïve, trusting attitude. He began to dream, but his dreams mainly consisted of her. *Idil.* the more he pictured her in his mind, the more he began to have feelings he thought he could never have. He began to imagine her. All that beauty Idil hid from the world by wearing baggy hip-hop clothes. The bulky shirts hid her slim hour-glass figure; the hooded sweaters, which she seemed to have every color of, concealed her silky brown hair. Her anger and demeanor hid her soft face, her natural honey-glazed skin, and her striking pointy nose, which she twisted to show annoyance, typified her beauty. That long neck that seemed to elegantly stretch from her shoulders ever so high into the air, as if her head was independent of her body. Her long arms dangled from her shoulders, ending in meticulously shaped fingers that appeared elegant in the oddly-shaped large rings on them. Her beauty transcended her demeanor, which immediately announced hostility. Idil appeared vibrant with beauty without trying to achieve it. The never-ending long legs that kept stretching to her delicate and yet fast feet, with their high arches off the ground as if tip-toeing. Milk white teeth inside a mouth graced with full plum lips. *Idil is striking,* he reflected. She was coarse, brash, vulgar, straightforward, unpretentious and gorgeous.

Shirwac remembered the day Idil explained to him what the concept of beauty meant to her. They were leisurely walking home after she bought ice cream for the pair of them from Mr. Floyd, the owner of The Sweet Melt Creamery, as she has done so many times before. An African-American woman passed them, pleasantly surprising Shirwac with her comment.

"What a beautiful attractive girl you are," the lady said. "Please use all that beauty wisely," she continued with the unsolicited advice. "I hope I don't see you in one of these nasty videos shaking your butt," she chuckled a little and kept on walking. Idil was stunned, but she kept quiet as if absorbing the women's comments. It was the rarest of moments to witness Idil not offended, and lashing out. She actually smiled and said "Thank you ma'am," ever so loudly, as if she were elated to receive the advice.

"Hey, that was nice," Shirwac said licking spoonfuls of the melting chocolate latte ice cream. "Did you mean that?" he continued licking stray drops of ice cream from the spoon.

"Well, she was nice. I wanted her to know I appreciate her concern," Idil said confidently.

"But you usually insult people, even when they mean well."

"Yeah, but they really don't mean well; but this lady, she do," Idil bit into the softening ice cream bar. "I could tell she was genuine."

She was quiet for a long introspective moment as if to digest what the woman had just said, then said, "I'm annoyed by people's standard of beauty. All they see is my exterior, they react when they see me, not knowing what makes me tick. I hate that. This so-called beauty takes away from my intellect, sense of humor, kind heart. I don't want to be beautiful; I want to be helpful, I want to contribute something to the world. God made me this way, I am grateful but I hate how people react to it."

"But you should be happy you look like this, Idil, you are so beautiful." Finally he said it, the words that would often surface in his mind but never make it to his tongue.

"Happy for what? Beauty will take me nowhere if I am thick and stupid. It's unfair that I am limited, that people expect me to be stupid because they consider me beautiful. I need something more than beauty in my life."

Shirwac wanted to say out loud, *I love your beauty. Flaunt it.* But instead he said "I am sure you will make your mark one day, and it won't be just for your beauty."

"I am not some shell people can peek at to admire."

"I am sure you are not," he said observing her gestures, not admitting he was one of those that admired her shell.

"Anyway, beauty is overrated in this country." For the first time since he met Idil he noticed her calm. She swapped tranquil words for the rough slang that usually dangled from her mouth. She was even more attractive when calm. Why did the words from this stranger touch her in such a remarkable way? Who was this girl, stunning and polite one moment, vulgar and arduous the next? He was in awe.

WOMB OF TERROR

A bang is how Henna's life with Naif began. Bad luck seemed something Henna could not outrun, and her life with Naif was no exception. The beatings started almost immediately. There wasn't even a honeymoon period where she could enjoy him a little. Five months after their marriage Naif began banging on her as if she were his punching bag. The man she fell for disappeared almost immediately into an aloof, abusive one.

The man who encouraged her involvement with the charity, who appeared compassionate about causes she cared about, vanished. He actually wanted her to stop hanging around Ramallah and limit her association with the charity. Naif became controlling and obsessive. He would push and shove her, using demeaning vulgar language. His mental abuse transformed her into a meek vulnerable woman almost from the start. It was easy to attack her using information she willingly shared with him. His cruel language would turn her into a defenseless victim, unable to defend herself against his beastly actions.

As they ate dinner one night at café Chanterelle, his favorite French restaurant, Naif abruptly got up from their table to chase after a fly. He chased the fly all over the restaurant. Henna was embarrassed. He returned with excitement in his eyes. "If I had caught that sucker I would have crushed it to nothingness," he said. That night he beat her, breaking her nose and jaw.

She fought him hard, kicking like a wild horse. She was hospitalized for two days. He had come from Khala three days earlier and was in such a nasty mood that she had to walk on eggshells around him. He criticized everything she did. He fired the chef and asked her to cook all his meals; when the food did not please him he threw it against the wall. Then he broke all the crystal glasses in the china. He went on a rampage. She ran into the bedroom to evade the shattering glass but he caught up to her.

"You are nothing but a cheap whore! Who the hell do you think you are? *Sharmuta, bintal kelb!*" He grabbed her by the hair, dragging her out to the dining room forcing smashed clumps of food that had mixed with shards of broken china and crystal into her mouth. "Eat this shit you call food, you bitch!" When he was done beating her he forced himself on her. After he was done with her he burst into a wild laughter, mocking her moan and cries. He then poured whisky down his throat straight from the bottle, collapsing next to her, drunk.

Every time he came back from Khala, he came back with rage and unbearable abuse. His media empire was in Khala, but he was in New York City every opportunity he got—New York relaxed him he said. She would tolerate him for the first few days after his return. Then he would disappear for days, bar-hopping and bouncing from one mistress to another and then he would show up days later to pick up the beating where he left off. For the first time in their eighteen months of marriage, she was actually afraid of him. His belligerence and abuse had escalated, but Henna made excuses for his nasty moods, she thought maybe he was stressed out. Sometimes he appeared puzzled, taking out his frustrations on her; she once again dismissed his abuse to stress. She would finally come to the conclusion that Naif was not stressed, crazy, or sick from any apparent illness, but was egotistical and controlling. When he could not control her the way he wanted, he beat her, sometimes so severely she thought she would die from the injuries. She moved back with Ramallah.

"Henna, don't go back to him, girl, I am afraid this man is going to kill you!"

"I'm not, Ramallah. I am not moving back with Naif."

"That is what you said the last time. This time please mean it."

"Have you seen my medication? I thought I put it here?" Groggy and delirious she searched on top of the entertainment mantelpiece, next to the DVD player.

"Are you still taking that Vicodin?" Ramallah shot her a surprised look.

"My back is killing me, I can't stand it."

"You need to sue his ass, girl—imagine all the money you could sue him for."

"God, please leave it alone, I need to sleep, I don't want his money."

"You better go to your family; you are so messed up in here, that man is playing with your head!"

"Ramallah, stop it, I can't handle it anymore! Please leave me alone!"

"Why the hell are you running away from your problems Henna?"

"Leave me alone, Ramallah, please!"

"If you don't leave now, he will kill you!"

"I am sick and tired of you lecturing me!" She curled up in fetal position, hiding her cut lip and black eye under the covers. The sofa had become a permanent place where Ramallah would find her time and time again, sometimes passed out.

Her face at its brightest reveals anxiousness and vulnerability. All that beauty hides the pain and torture she feels. Her glaring smile erases people's suspicions of her state. No one will ever know she is dead inside. No one will ever know, the very person she clutches to has been killing her, a slow murder. She offers her wide smile, hiding her agony and angst well. She pities her circumstances, forging energy to enjoy the party, although her movements are languorous. Every bone in her body throbbed from the massive blow of his fist only hours earlier; the various objects that indiscriminately competed for her body have caused pain she has never imagined could exist. The strike of a hammer, the burst of a bottle, the bang of a chair, the crumble of a lap top, the pound of a kick, the crack of a wall. Not to mention techniques she has picked up to survive a throttle, a blow to the head, kicks and slaps. Each came with a preceding warning that gave her enough time to strategically put her defense up. Cover her face with her hands to avoid a black eye or cut lip that would invite suspicion. Never mind the abusive language. She could almost predict how many times he would repeat each word— stupid, ten times, whore, fifteen times, heifer, sixteen times, cheap bitch, twenty times. Heavily emphasized words destined to damage her psyche, to destroy what is left of it. His favorite term is cheap bitch. Every inch of her body ached from his forceful intimacy. How could he enjoy himself after he almost sent her to the grave? Maybe that was his intrigue? He wanted to further kill what was left of her.

She resents him and everything that he has brought into her life. The beatings, the wealth, his family and his unpredictable violence— all she wants to do is kill him, to spill his blood. But for the moment she smiles, mutilating her psyche further, wearing an invisible cabbaya to hide what has been given to her by nature, a curse of beauty. The wounds she sustained days earlier are camouflaged with professional make up and elegant clothing.

They are approached by an elegantly American woman who takes him to the side, whispering something in her ear. She suspects it is one of his mistresses or call girls. The place is buzzing with festive mood. She looks around to see if she recognizes anyone. The only people she knows are his obese brother and rowdy cousins and their imported Asian male partners. Of course no one is privy to the fact that the hard-working male servants of this family are also tasked with duties that have little to do with making *qaxwe*—they are exploited. She sees Marco, Fahad's servant, from the corner of her eye. Marco is a Filipino man in his twenties who has been tossed from brother to brother to cousin, and was forced into his current life style. He wears a low-cut, tight silky black shirt that reveals his small but muscular frame. It is apparent he chooses his clothes for a purpose: it how he has made his fortune, albeit with a hefty price.

She spotted Fahad at the bar, downing fully loaded drinks while his massive hand massaged the curvy back of a tall, slender blond. Dressed in a black strapless silky-chiffon gown, the blond nailed a vogue pose with toned legs and long straight hair. She looks too tanned and totally manufactured.

Then she saw Salim, the son of a prominent *clerk*, the religious authority whose department is the sole defender of virtue to prevent acts of vice in Khuzaymah Saqr. He also travels with an entourage of men whom he takes turns with. He almost attacked her one night after she found him in their foyer, passed out. She kicked him in his groin. Come to think of it, there is not one friend, cousin or brother she has not had to defend herself against.

Marco sat on the other side of the room with a drink in his hand, oblivious to Fahad and his advances on the female, probably relieved. Marco and the other Filipino companions accompany their bosses to America only to witness temporary rejection for American women. Since some parts of his task are forced, Marco is never jealous; and he rarely ever protests. He enjoys his multiple travels, lush life with royalty and his sudden abundance. Henna and Marco struck up a close friendship after they were both beaten by their drunken partners one evening. At first she detested him— perceiving his promiscuous walks, and flamboyant outfits as lewd. She ignored him when she saw him in gatherings, reminded that he was selling himself cheaply, and allowing the crude al Ali family to use him as they saw fit.

But as time had passed she got to know his kind nature. She was reminded how alike they were, both lost into a mirage lifestyle that lured them as a result of their conditions. How different was she from Marco? Wasn't she also being used for her beauty? They both offered pleasure to the royal family, and in return they were compensated.

Marco had constant traces of worry on his face that word would get back to his wife and six children who have swiftly gained an opulent life in Manila.

The party lingered with glamorous, beautiful women and plenty of booze, which is how Naif preferred his parties. He pulled Henna out of her hell-hole closet where she had been hiding for two days after he violently attacked her about some papers she had misplaced in his study. A lame excuse to once again lay his filthy, bloody hands on her. She vowed to reverse his obsession with her. She shaved her head, and began mutilating her face and body. Then she became terrified of what she did to herself. *He surely will kill me this time*, she said to herself as she hid inside the guest room closet. The sole reason Naif wanted Henna in his life was to flaunt her beauty, the rare beauty he'd become obsessed with. Her honey nutmeg complexion, large almond brown eyes and long silky hair resembled the rarest beauty Khuzayman men fixated on. She was not a Khuzayman, and yet in his prejudiced, merciless eyes she looked like one. To him she was a sophisticated, Americanized version of the women he'd marginalized all his life. She was never an equal; somehow she remained beneath him. He dragged her out of her safety to flaunt her at the party he'd organized to show off Ithar, his new yacht. He had a jazz band, a group of belly dancers and several musicians to entertain the A-list millionaires, celebrities and politicians. He lugged her from floor to floor, when he was not busy flirting or doing acts that did not require her presence. She followed him around, mute with horror and pity at the range of expressions crossing his face: vividness, surprise, anxiety and then resolve as he bounces from one side of the room to the next.

She remained below the radar feeling awful, sick, and woozy. She did not see Hajir for days, being consumed by her condition; she left the child to be cared for by a nanny. Hajir, the baby she had with Naif. The baby that Allah saved from his murderous rage, the gift she has been given, Hajir whose conception caused his ugliest savagery yet. She came from the womb of a terrified woman, and arrived in the world equally terrified. She is mild-mannered, her gazes puzzled by his hatred. Her playfulness languid, as if she does not want to bring attention to herself, as if aware she came to the world unwanted from the belly of a woman buried in terror.

Henna's bony body stores memories she would rather forget; it is crisscrossed with marks of love and malice. People are attracted to it and then repel from it as soon as they begin to know it. She has come to view her body as the sack that housed her turmoil.

⸎

Henna was now the meekest of women, having assumed victim-hood. Ramallah was conflicted, unable to help Henna who became sub-missive with Naif. Only two years after she moved away from Brian and the women she called passive and weak, Henna became exactly that. She became the women she was so sure she could never be. How many times had she frowned on women who were beaten? *Why didn't they fight harder*, she would remark. *They are weak, and stupid.* What hap-pened to Henna, with the strong and self assured persona? The woman who went out of her way to spot abused women, calling them all kinds of names?

He lured her back again and again, this time with a new four mil-lion dollar mansion in Westchester County. The new mansion was her refuge from his wild male relatives. Every time they visited, it was an opportunity for them to corner and grab her. When she complained of their behavior; he beat her, accusing her of inviting their attention. He forced her to wear a cabbaya around the house, especially when his male relatives were around.

The next time he called from Khala, he ordered her to move into the new place; one of his other wives wanted to stay in the penthouse for the summer, so the move was abrupt. He gave her three weeks to pack and move. He arranged the whole thing from Khala, sending assistants run-ning around like scared children. He assigned her a personal assistant who would make the entire move smooth, the same assistant was tasked to give her a daily birth control pill, unless he was present, at which time he would force the pill on her. He did not want more surprise pregnancies, he said. The fretting presence of the movers and assistant made her on edge. She wanted to unpack her own boxes and take her time with the new home. After the movers left she decided to give the assistant and the housekeeper the afternoon off. She wanted to go shopping, and would unpack when she returned, so she left the boxes all over the new house. Henna appeared thin, she had lost weight and her skin appeared patchy and dull. She could no longer fit into any of her clothes, which began to hang on her. The phone rang while she was getting ready.

"*Habibti, keefik?*" Naif said, oblivious that she'd sent the assistant home.

"Hi honey, hmm, why are you calling again?" she rinsed the tooth paste that foamed around her lips.

"*Habibti*, I miss you! Can't I call my darling to tell her I miss her?"

"No, I mean, it is late over there, right? What time is it?"

"It's three-thirty. How is the move, did the movers unpack the stuff?" she dismissed the question.

"No, hmmm, yes actually they have," she looked around to sound convincing.

"Good, I don't want you to do anything, darling."

"When are you coming?"

"What are you wearing, honey?"

"Naif, I am going shopping. Can we talk later?"

"No!" he shouted.

"Why are you mad, I need to go—"

"Can't you go shopping later? I want to talk to you."

"Naif, you know I would love to talk to you, but I need to go shopping, Ramallah is waiting."

"Didn't I tell you not to see her again?"

"Calm down, what is wrong with you?"

"Look I don't want to argue with you, but you know how I feel about her!"

"Naif, she is my friend, please chill."

"Okay, then. Call me later when you come back?"

"Okay, *habibi*, bye."

"Bye."

By the time Henna drove to Ramallah's place, there was a change of plan. Ramallah had promised to introduce Henna to a nearby spa which specialized in herbal facials, and made an appointment without letting her know. Henna agreed to get a facial and a message and if they still had time they would go shopping. And so while Hajir remained with Ruqiya the nanny, Henna, in the middle of moving, began a day of pampering with Ramallah.

The two women sat comfortably in their beauty chairs at Chick Chic Day Spa. Henna nibbled on fresh fruits and sipped a strawberry and kiwi smoothie, while Chavon, the herbalist aesthetician, smoothed green clay-and-cucumber mix over her face to tighten her skin. Moments after Chavon placed fresh cucumber patches on her eyes she heard him squeal and struggle with someone at the reception area. She quickly removed the cucumber eye soothers, dripping liquid eye gel into her eyes: Ramallah was already up and running towards the front door when Chavon, who was out of breath, bumped into her.

"Tell your friend to get out of here," he bellowed.

"Chavon, what is going on?" Ramallah had not finished her question when she spotted Naif fuming behind Chavon.

"Henna! Where is Henna?" he was irate. As soon as Henna appeared in front of him he slapped her masked face.

"Ohmgod, what are you doing here?" was all she could say.

"Liar, you are nothing but a cheap lying bi—! Why did you lie to me?! Why didn't you answer your phone?"

She got away from him, hiding behind a stall with a masked woman whose surprise was hidden behind the gooey clay on her face. She started throwing bottles of soap, gel, a CD player and mask mix, whatever she could get her hands on, at him.

"Burn in hell, Naif! I am not going down easy this time!"

"Come with me, you liar, sharmuta!"

"Someone call 911!"

"Call the police; he is going to kill me!"

"Okay, okay, Henna, calm down honey, I wanted to surprise you, that's all."

"Call the police!" the panic on her face showed even with the gooey green facial hiding her expression.

"Sir, please leave."

"Henna, come on, let's go home."

"No! I am not coming with you!" Naif kept surprising her in this manner, and beating her when he did not find her where he expected her to be. Something as simple as a change of plan would set him off. He was suspicious of her, accusing her of having affairs. He would make up elaborate stories of how he heard about her activities when he was not around. Apparently when he called earlier in the day he was not calling from Khala but from a restaurant across the street from the new home. He came all the way from Khala to check on her and see what she was up to.

He went in the house after she left, and was not happy with the mess, and clutter he found everywhere. He followed her from Ramallah's apartment to the spa. Since she told him she was going shopping, he expected her to go shopping.

BONFIRE BELLIES

Seven months after Hajir and Henna rejoined Naif, Henna made arrangements to move back with her family in Minneapolis. She was ready to walk away from her life of tortured material abundance. She wanted to ask for Nadifo's forgiveness, and try to be a mother to Shirwac. Once and for all Henna came to the realization that running away from the past, pretending that it didn't matter was destructive. She was tired of running, was ready to embrace her past, and erase the illusion that had become her life. She was ready to meet her past, to make sense of her present. There was a little hidden hope which lay with Nadifo. Maybe Nadifo would clarify the reason she was attacked at age fourteen, they have never talked about it, and finally Henna was ready to talk.

Naif, however, had other plans. He wanted to move her and Hajir to Khala with him. He no longer wanted them to be apart, he said; he loved her and wanted her near him at all times. He wanted more kids; he wanted Hajir to grow up in his family's mansion where all the al Ali children grew up, with her other siblings.

She had a nightmare that night. For the first time since the assault on her body at age fourteen, she dreamt about the shack that had hid her pregnant body for months. It overwhelmed her like a wave. Was she in danger again?

Henna was so terrified she had to confront the past. She had avoided thinking about the attack her entire life. How could she have been happy when she had walked around for years as a victim? She wanted to hear the details of that day, who had assaulted her, and why.

In the dream women clothed in male attire with shaved heads stood on a hill as onlookers. A large bleeding woman with parts of her body severed summoned all the pregnant girls. She was tall and stiff, and wore a simple old orange rag to cover her bloody mutilated body. Her wounds were fresh with blood.

She ordered all that the secret shacks be emptied of pregnant girls. In the pitch-dark night a bonfire burnt especially for the occasion on the outskirts of the camp. The flames awoke the whole town to the disorder of events.

She had asked the girls to sit around the flames. She ordered them to bare their swollen bellies, cutting through their cloths. The luminous flames hit their frightened faces and inflated bellies with a flaring fiery orange color giving way to a dusty aura, as if they were all about to die. The faces had grime on them, as if mud was smudged onto them.

There were at least twenty girls around the fire. The bleeding woman charged each male relative, who were now completely garbed in women's clothing, to pick his closest pregnant female relative. Discomfited cousins, brothers, uncles and fathers stood to identify their kin. They were instructed to disappear into the dark jungle that loomed behind them, with the females in tow. The growls and howls of predators in the jungle were heard in the distance.

They did this in progression. Each male emerged from the jungle alone, without the pregnant girl. Excruciating cries were heard coupled with wild happy animal roar, and a crackling noise. The male-attired females on the hill barked with protests. Some threw their bodies down the hill to stop the men from taking the pregnant girls into the jungle. When the men emerged, they handed the bloody woman something. Most were crying, others sad-looking.

The bloody woman drew the thing to her mouth and murmured something into it. Then she handed it back to the men. Each male clumsily walked in the direction of the now rolling women. Laangadhe was among the men. Henna kept signaling him not to come for her, bawling to stop him.

But he never looked her way. He avoided her. When her turn came, as they walked into the jungle, she begged him not to take her in. She assured him it was not her fault to shame the family. She even asked him to marry her to correct the shame, to restore the family honor. But it was as if he were hard of hearing. He ignored her request. Together, they disappeared into the jungle; he dragged her along the entire way.

Henna woke up drenched from sweat, on the floor, flinching and frightened.

THE RELUCTANT MOURNER

Guests who had come to pay their respects and sympathy were discharged into the street as Nadifo's living room overflowed with people. On the living room floor a large round dish full of dates sat next to a large glazed clay bowl brimming with popcorn and another filled with a traditional red bean *cambuulo*. Nadifo and Saxarla sat next to each other, fresh sesame oil dripped from their heads. They were both dressed in traditional white mourning clothes. The room was quiet except for the Quran that emanated from a small CD player and the continuous beating of rosary beads. Women occupied every space on the floor and along the walls of the living room. The room was free of furniture to make room for the guest. Some of the women sat on the bare floor, while others sat on the few cushions that lined the living room floor.

As they arrived at the mourning, every woman announced her shock: those that never knew Cartan went into elaborate detail of how the news of his death had caused them not only anguish but afflictions of unknown sudden ailments unique to the bad news. The mourning ultimately would become calculatedly about them. When not recapping the invention of their shock they would recite Quran verses and pray quietly while nibbling on popcorn and dates which are the traditional mourning food.

It was around six in the morning when Nadifo's bell rang belligerently, three days earlier. She had just dozed off after morning prayers. She rushed to open the door, forgetting to cover herself, startled. She was usually vigilant with the door but it sounded urgent.

"Sorry to disturb you so early, Nadifo," the woman standing at the door way said, holding a sleeping child against her bosom. The woman appeared disturbed.

"What is the matter?" Nadifo asked rubbing her eyes from sleep. "Who are you?"

"I had to come and talk to you."

"Who are you?"

"Saxarla." It took Nadifo a short minute to realize who the woman standing in front of her was. She opened the door widely to let her in.

"Come in," Nadifo said puzzled. The woman sat down on the couch. Nadifo had almost closed the door when she saw two little kids, a boy and a girl, standing on the other side of the door, hidden from view.

"What happened, why are you here?" Nadifo sounded cold. Saxarla roared uncontrollably as soon as she entered the apartment. She put the child on the sofa and took out a bottle. She shoved it down the sleeping baby's mouth, wiping her eyes with the tip of the black cabbaya she wore.

"Sahal, sit down, hooyo, where is your sister?" The boy shrugged, sucking his thumb. Nadifo entered the bedroom to find the little girl on her bed, fast asleep. She took the little girl's shoes off and tucked her under the blankets. She came back to the living room where the woman was still wailing, the baby was on her lap now sleeping with the bottle in his mouth. Nadifo was hanging a pink jacket that said "the Bratz" on the back when the woman began bad mouthing Cartan.

"He ruined my life and left me," Nadifo appeared busy with the closet, removing shoes and other stuff from the foyer.

"He left me with three of his kids, then took a new wife in Somalia!" there was a hint of rage in her voice. Nadifo did not want to hear what she was saying; she went into the kitchen and filled up the kettle with water. *Cartan went back home? He married again?* "I hate what he did to me!" Saxarla continued. Nadifo threw cardamom and cloves in the kettle. "He died before I told him how much I hated him!" She added sugar, a lot of sugar, and then she could not move. "Nadifo, he died—Cartan is dead, and he ruined both of our lives!" Nadifo stood in the middle of the kitchen, stunned. Putting the tea kettle on the stove proved difficult. All that came out of her mouth was *"Innaa Lillahi wa innaa Illayhi raa-jicuun"* She repeated it several times. She did not respond to Saxarla; instead she went into the bathroom to perform ablution, read Quran, and then prayed two processions methodically. By the time she came out of the room, Saxarla was asleep on the coach, next to her Sahal. Nadifo tapped the woman on the shoulder, alerting her to come to the bedroom. She took the older son first and laid him next to his sister. Then she took the baby out of Saxarla's lap. He began to cry, so she lulled him on her shoulder, rubbing his back to sooth him.

"Go inside and sleep with the kids," Nadifo commanded.

The announcement of her husband's death came from a rival wife. The very first day she met her co-wife she announced the death of Cartan. For so long Nadifo wanted to see her, to eavesdrop on their lives together. But this woman, the one who stole her husband walked leisurely into her life, to announce he was dead. *Whatever gave her the right?* Nadifo felt as if the thoughts in her head throbbed with pain.

How was she supposed to feel about this person who destroyed whatever that was left of her life? She now slept on the very same bed Nadifo had shared with Cartan. And he is dead! Nadifo searched for odious feelings but was left with the task at hand; she pushed away whatever feelings she felt, to prep for the mourning. Unfortunately, whether she liked it or not, her co-wife was here and they needed to do their duty as Cartan's wives. They needed to go through the mourning period together.

Little Sahal's eyes met Nadifo's with fury. He didn't just look at her; he stared sternly, as if he knew something about her even she didn't know. He frightened her. His walk, talk, and gestures were a replica of his father's. She avoided the three-year-old, wary of him. Was she afraid he would disappoint her as Cartan had, if she got too close? What kind of magic did this little boy possess?

Saxarla moved in with Nadifo for the four months and ten days they mourned as Cartan's wives. They performed the rituals together. Outside of that, Nadifo mostly avoided Saxarla. She held no feelings of love or hate, but took her in small doses, knowing she had to.

She showed Saxarla the precise steps she needed to follow as a mourning wife: "Take only simple showers, no lotion on your body, or oil in your hair, nothing luxurious for the entire time, pray for forgiveness from God, pray for Allah to forgive Cartan, take away all your gold and new clothes, no perfume, eat white rice and yogurt only, no sauces, or sweets, only basic black tea, no music or movies or TV, remain indoors for the full mourning term, and wear only a basic white diric with a matching white shawl for the entire time. No colorful joyous clothes and no unnecessary phone conversations." She tended to the three kids as if they were her own, but she felt weird around them. The baby, Zakaria whom everyone called Zaki, mystified her; he reminded her of Geele. Although he looked nothing like him, he had a warm smile and Geele's mannerisms. The middle one, the girl Asli, she felt drawn to. Asli closely resembled Saxarla, and Nadifo felt obliged to protect the girl from her mother's ways and the curse that often befell beautiful Gedi women.

In mourning she was just as dutiful a wife as she had been when her husband was alive. She shed no tears for Cartan, yet his death brought her a deep unsettled feeling. Perhaps she wished to have had a few departing words with him, not words of anger or chiding but a moment to tell him how she felt, to tell him that his departure was a welcome change that she could never have imagined. She discovered so much about herself in his absence. She was grateful to him for giving her an opportunity to discover her inner self. She no longer felt discarded but validated. His walking away from her life had brought a sense of peace and acceptance. She mourned twice for him, but this time she mourned the missed opportunity to tell him she was alright. She wanted to person-ally beg him farewell, to exchange forgiving words, to tell him that she did not hold him responsible for their life's outcome. She was alright.

Saxarla had difficulty with the mourning period. She appeared limited, she wanted to shed her clothes and move on with her life. She appeared unready, and forced to the process. Saxarla's demeanor reeked with impatience. Why did she have to mourn for four months and ten days for Cartan? She did not even love the man.

Nadifo scolded her harshly when she found her on the phone gossiping. She would snatch the phone out of her hand as if she were one of the kids: "there should be no gossip in a mourning house," she would say. She tried to explain that they needed to respect Cartan, even if he was not an ideal husband to either one of them. She did not particularly scrutinize her actions, but she found it peculiar that Saxarla rejected the rituals. Nadifo would pull a straying headscarf into place, or she would cover Saxarla's legs if she saw the mourning clothes wandering off. She would close the door tight when she found Saxarla changing so the kids would not to see her naked.

One day, as Nadifo bathed Zaki, she saw a figure in green colored clothes from the corner of her eye. She rushed to garb herself, thinking Saxarla must have opened the door for someone, although she did not hear the bell ring. People often wandered in and out of the apartment to pay their respects.

As she finished drying Zaki, Saxarla entered the bathroom, looking for a hairbrush. She wore a green silk diric without a petticoat or bra, her hair dripping wet. She smelled fresh, as if she had just showered. They were two months into the mourning period.

"What are you doing?" Nadifo asked, stunned, as she let go off Zaki.

"I am not doing anything. I need to brush my hair; I just washed it," replied Saxarla, smiling as if she were teasing Nadifo.

"Who told you to take the mourning garb off?" Her voice was slightly pitched as if to make her disapproval clear.

"I am not keeping this stinking white garb on anymore!" She was brushing her hair now, gathering a knotted strand in her hand.

"Do you think it's up to you? Who forced you to marry him in the first place? Where you forced?" Nadifo was now squealing, causing Saxarla to look up apprehensively from the cabinet she was rummaging through. "Did you think about the consequences of marriage when you were flaunting yourself at him?" Nadifo drew close to her, almost consuming her breathing air, she was shaking violently. Saxarla took her son and went into the living room. She released the child to play with his brother and sister and then proceeded to the bedroom. "Are you listening? Why are you disrespecting Allah's covenants?" Nadifo followed Saxarla to the bed room, tears streaming down her cheeks. "You forced your way in here, and now you think you can have your way!" She looked around for the mourning clothes and found them tangled on the edge of the bed. She gathered them up. "Here, put these back on!" She proceeded to snatch the brush, forcing it out of Saxarla's hand.

"I have had enough of those stinking clothes! For two months I forced myself. I am not putting them back on!"

"Enough of them! Do you think it is up to you? What will people say—do you want to invite gossip?!"

"Let go of me, you crazy woman, people are already talking, but who cares!" Nadifo attempted to peel the diric off.

"Crazy? You are the crazy one, snatching people's husbands and then disrespecting them in their death, who asked you to force yourself into our lives in the first place? Did we invite you in?" The women struggled with each other. Nadfio tried to rip Saxarla's clothes off to put back the white cloths. Saxarla resisted while trying to avoid hurting the older woman. "Stupid lady, this is what you inherited for marrying him! Wear it, you destroyer!"

"Let that poor man rest in peace, why do you want to bring scandal to his house?"

"Nadifo, leave me alone. I don't want to hurt you!" Saxarla pushed Nadifo off. "Scandal—as if there is any more scandal about your family to talk about!" Saxarla repeated this snide remark, only to heighten Nadifo's suspicion. Sahal giggled, but the baby cried, extending his arms for Nadifo to hold him. She picked him up, throwing the clothes on the floor. She muttered something under her breath, ignoring Saxarla's last comment, and spitting on her as she left the room. Asli sat observantly, quiet, in a corner.

And just like that Saxarla moved on to her next life. She left her three kids with Nadifo. She never looked back. Her other children were scattered with various relatives. At the tender age of thirty-four she had left behind three marriages and eight children.

Saxarla was not aware of it but her body was a diversion ground for men. Her voluptuous body invited their hungry eyes. She has been rumored to have never gone through the compulsory three months of abstinence between divorces obliged by religion; she married the next man without being divorced from the previous. She was not sure which child was fathered by which man, using guess work to match fathers with children. If she were pregnant when she parted with a partner, the next husband naively assumed fatherhood for a child that was not his. The confusion that surrounded Saxarla and her children created worry for Nadifo. She grew wary of the children. Were Sahal, Asli and Zaki Cartan's biological children? She searched for familiar signs in the children.

Nadifo inherited three children from Saxarla and Cartan. Sometimes the unapologetic manner in which he brought children he cared nothing about into the world enraged her; other times the kids made her forget her rage.

She never noticed his discontent with life, she just though he was spoiled and irresponsible. His kids grew around him, and he never interacted with them. He did not know what they did or who they were. He was oblivious to them, just as they were to him. He, like everyone else, existed temporarily in his present life hoping that his real life would one day resume. When it didn't he became reckless, hurting everyone around him. He had mapped out his political life when the first war bullets sounded. He was obsessed with that dream, the dream that emptied houses and crushed lives, the dream that every Somali wife and child detested, the mirage that every Somali man chased after. In his dream Cartan was head of state, and powerful. Cartan died in quest of the dream. In his head at seventy-eight he still had a chance. Most Somali born males die before they realize the dream—a dream of wasted lives and broken families.

MAY 19, 2005.

Sister, I took my entire savings out of People Bank, all $8,633.44 of it. My aim was to spare my entire savings on a useful transportation for the family, for the kids really. I never thought I would ever drive in my life. I was content with public transportation or whoever offered to drive me.

It all began when I saw a commercial a week ago: it claimed that if one bought a car that week, there would be 0% APR. I was not sure what that meant; when I asked Idil she assured me that if I bought the car and put down all my savings, there would be no one coming after me for anything else. That day I planned to get my driver's license, which is the permit one needs to legally drive a car here. It took me six months to get my license. I failed four times: one lady who gave me the driving test kicked me out of the car I brought to take the test, saying I was too dangerous. Another time, two men I went with lost their opportunity to take the test because the instructor told them to take me home, and never to trust me with a car until I went through a driving class. They had to go back the next day to take the test.

After six months with a driving instructor, I got my license. The next day I took the money out of my bank account, took my new license with my picture, and gave the guy the entire amount. He gave me a nice-looking car in exchange: it was shiny and black, with four doors and automatic windows. Its glossiness and the new car aroma made me trust my entire savings in this strange man's hands. Why then, dear Hawo, did they take away my car and my entire savings after seven months? They said that I did not pay my monthly payment of two hundred and fifty dollars. But why did they take all my savings if I was expected to pay so much money every month? I never know why sister. They explained 0% APR does not mean you put down all your money and walk away with a glossy black car. I still don't know what it means, but it surely does not mean what I thought it did. They came and mercilessly took away my car, leaving me and the kids without transportation. When I asked for my money back, they refused to give it back to me. Now I have no car, no money and the children are sad. They are no longer car riders, they are now bus riders and they are not happy about it.

GUITAR LESSONS

I dil sat at the top of the steps in front of the building entrance, waiting for Nadifo. Next to her was Josh, a boy she had befriended at
a train station last year; they had become very close, and this was
where they usually met every afternoon after school. Josh looked anxious; he sat on his skateboard with a backpack on his back and earphones
plugged in his ears. Idil said he lived on the other side of town—the side
where people looked happy, and their lives looked manicured just like
their lawns. The side of town where mothers looked like they stepped
out of a happy story book, children looked so clean they appeared never
to have touched dirt and fathers appeared as if they were either going to
or coming from golf. Josh, whose name confused Shirwac because his
real name was Joshua and yet people called him Josh, came every day for
two hours to give Idil guitar lessons. He was habitually timely, and very
committed to the schedule. Josh was an aloof boy, with a lopsided freckled face and a mouth full of braces. Josh's face sparkled when he talked
about music; he looked elated when he held the guitar. He didn't know
anything about Idil and he didn't care; he was only interested in teaching her how to play the guitar in the middle of a destitute neighborhood
where people sat around all day, and where grey-and-red bricked buildings ejected caped little girls, energetic boys, and old men with cayenne
pepper beards in colorful sarongs holding multihued African canes.
The women who wore umbrella-shaped cloaks with matching thick
long skirts glued their eyes on Josh. To Josh the people who resided in
this building looked odd, bizarre and loud. He would get ready to call
the police, thinking a fight was ensuing when these odd-looking people

communicated with their hands, pointing fingers at each other, yelling and never listening to one another, until he was informed that's how they talked. They were so drastically different from the controlled environment he was used to. He did not give it much concern as long as he was teaching Idil the guitar, although he could not help but notice their oddness. They intimidated him, except for Idil, who made him feel tranquil and joyful. For her he would even risk his life, being in the midst of these weird-looking people in one of the most dangerous neighborhoods in Minneapolis. Josh, who appeared vigilant at all times, wondered how this place got to be the way it is. It was shocking for him to witness the dire poverty that surrounded him; yet the people he called weird looked happy in their destitute environs.

Shirwac disliked this boy. In his resentful mind the boy came to sniff their miserable lives only to return to his happy life where everything was perfect; but he was also intrigued by him nonetheless. Josh was a donor kid; Shirwac didn't understand what that meant. Josh had informed Shirwac that neither he nor his mother had met his biological father, whom he referred to as #936 SPH (Six-Pack Hunk). He talked endlessly as he detailed his inception and how he came to the world. *Could humans be born this way?* Josh's situation would make his mind swirl with questions: *Was he some sort of a magical child, is that why he was weird-looking,* because none of the SPH (Six-Pack Hunk) part transferred to him. Shirwac contemplated, imagining maybe he was a donor kid too. Maybe he also had a father with some weird number code: possibly that was the reason people talked in mysterious whispers around him. It annoyed Shirwac that Idil gave so much attention to this boy who searched for something in their poor neighborhood only he knew of. Shirwac hid behind a tree where he could just catch a glimpse of them. He stood there for good ten minutes, to gather enough courage to talk to Idil. He was afraid Idil would dismiss him, or say something brash and rude. Playing the guitar made her content, and serene; she did not like to be intruded upon when Josh was there. She was spanked, or more realistically beaten severely, for bringing this odd boy to the

neighborhood. She was belted, locked indoors, kicked in many hurtful places, threatened with arranged marriage with some unknown
dude called geel jire, but she found a way to defy Nadifo and her father.
For guitar lessons Idil would risk everything. She looked goofy walking around the neighborhood with her guitar case, inviting stares and
insults. He did not want to be a nuisance, but he had to see her—he
simply missed her. They no longer attended the same school; Idil was
kicked out of Spring Valley, and was now attending the school for bad
kids.

Idil sat with the guitar on her lap, playing. Josh sat very close to her,
going over music notes. She sang a sweet melody, one of her favorite
songs, "Motherless". She said it reminded her of an old song Warsan sang
for her when she was a baby. Warsan sang many old songs from her past
happy life. That was one of them. She wrote "Motherless" after Warsan
disappeared. She wore a blue hooded sweater. Her hair was scattered
today; Shirwac had never seen Idil's hair like that. Over the wild hair she
wore a dark green cap with the words "Nomad Nation". She wore tight
black capri pants and pink-and-black flip-flops. He did not like her look
today. Although she never wore a scarf on her head like other Somali
girls her age, her hooded sweater hid most of her hair which she usually wore in a pony tail. What happened to the baggy sweat pants, the
over-sized t-shirt, her signature? Her clothes appeared too tight today.
As he enviously marveled at them from behind the tree, the two turned
around, oblivious to the constant traffic of the building and Shirwac's
close scrutiny, their backs to him as they searched for something in the
small, sticker-covered old vintage suitcase where Josh kept all his music
books.

"Idil." Shirwac said excitedly, startling her. She jerked vigorously,
and in turn Josh jumped. She looked annoyed, not at all pleased to see
him. She closed the suitcase and pushed it away from her; Josh got up
promptly as if he'd been caught doing something illegal. He picked up
his suitcase and started getting down from the steps instinctively. "Josh,
wait!" Idil said irritably. "Shirwac, what are you doing here, you scared

me!" She put down the guitar and waited for Shirwac to respond, but he was tongue-tied. He was not expecting her to be this boorish. Josh turned the music on his iPod loud, as if he did not want to hear their conversation. He immediately got lost in it, standing next to Idil. She did not get up, or look at Shirwac; she waited for him to talk. He found himself looking at her closely. Before he found out he felt something for her, he would jump into her world without feeling self-conscious: now all of a sudden he stood in front of his best friend, his cousin, small, as if he was naked and she was ashamed to stare at him.

"How is your new school?"

"You came all the way down here to ask me about my bad-ass school?" she asked, getting up and shoving her guitar into its case. She looked furious.

"No, no, that's not why I came," he sounded defensive and self-conscious.

"What, then, Shirwac? You in trouble or sumtin'?" she put her backpack on.

"I just came to say hi," Shirwac was trembling; he hoped she would not see it.

"Hey, Josh, hold this," she handed the guitar to Josh who was still waiting like an obedient student next to her. With her wild curly blond, red and burgundy colored hair falling on her face, she looked extremely thin in her tight clothes, somewhat vibrant; she jumped from the top step and joined Josh, who was now on the floor. "W'sup, Shirwac?" she said, still waiting for him to say something new.

"Nothing. I am sorry," he turned around and started walking, embarrassed. She surprised him when she said "Hey, wanna come? We gonna get some ice cream," she said in a slightly friendlier tone. He felt like an afterthought. Every bit of the anger she felt was apparent from her demeanor. He knew he shouldn't have interrupted her lesson, but he could not help his eagerness to see her. He was crushed. Refusing to go with them he started walking back in the direction he came from, trying not to show his defeat. Idil walked with Josh, who carried her guitar in the opposite direction. She was animated and happy beside him.

Shirwac walked for a long time before looking back. In his optimism he wished if she would come after him, to undo the humiliation she caused him. He continued walking and when he was far enough he looked back to see where they were. He could see them side by side, disappearing into Cedar Street, appearing minute amid the massive zigzagging bridges and bullying buildings.

Three days later a knock vibrated the still house. Shirwac was in the living room doing homework alone. Without Idil's adventures and faced with life's confusions, he turned to studying, not out of obligation or want but out of boredom. He sat there long enough to stare at an algebra problem which stubbornly refused to admit an answer. It stared back at him for the last hour, unsolved. He ignored the door, not out of obedience under Haybe's direction to never open the door when he was home alone, but because he longed to solve the problem in front of him. But the person at the door was impatient and persistent; he wished whoever it was would leave so he could tend to the problem at hand. Evenings like these vomited door-to-door sales people and bizarrely-dressed women who preached what they called "the word". He usually ignored them, and soon they left. Whatever they were selling, this person did not want to leave.

When he opened the door, there she was, waiting with Josh. Shirwac was astounded. He wanted to forget her, so he stopped thinking about her, or at least he tried ever since the humiliating incident a few days earlier. He tried to replace his obsession of her with the obsession of figuring out who he was. He preoccupied himself with Henna, Liban and anything that would reveal his identity. He looked around the house he shared with Haybe, Ceebla and little Kayd. Nothing in the place belonged to him. The family belonged to each other; the house belonged to them and their son. The rules were their rules. The order in which things ran was their creation. He noticed how he was a temporary addition to their lives. As if they waited for him to finish school at their order, with their rules, and their orderly way of life and after that someone else would claim him, may be a university or either one of his parents if they decided to reclaim him. It was strange how he felt temporary all of a sudden. Then he noticed how his addition to the family was more pronounced than he paid attention to. The room he stayed in was an addition: the furniture was borrowed from various people. Nadifo brought the mattress, Raaxo the twin bed her son had outgrown, Tusmo the chest of drawers he kept his stuff in. But the family who inhabited the house had their things permanently there. Even little Kayd had a permanent aura about him. Doubts about his permanence anywhere or with anybody enveloped him. *Was he also temporary in Idil's life?* He wondered.

Shirwac did not say anything. The donor kid, Josh, was a permanent fixture with Idil now, or so it seemed. Shirwac was not surprised to see him there, standing behind her, saying nothing and yet loudly announcing his secure position with her. Shirwac loathed his assured attitude. He acted as if he had one over him. She twitched her nose purposefully, the way she usually did when something was wrong. "Hey, w'sup?" she said, waiting for Shirwac to ask them to come inside, which he did not. "W'sup?" he replied, remaining still, acting unfazed by her closeness. "Nadifo needs you to come," she looked away to Josh, as if she wanted him to help finish the sentence. "Sumtin' happened to Cartan." she craned her long neck to check if someone else was inside.

"What happened to him?" Shirwac did not move, or allow her to enter.

"He dead!" he found her words stunningly cold.

"When?" he was shocked but still wanted to remain in control.

"Don't know, somewhere in Somalia, or wherever the hell he flee to!" the words flew out of her mouth with no emotion or concern.

"How is ayeeyo, is she okay?" His heart began to jolt, maybe because of the news he just received or possibly because of his eagerness to touch the hand that rested on the door. He noticed her nails were neat and clipped, with melon-colored nail polish, not their usual bloody and bitten-down condition.

"For real, I think she is not feeling well," he was staring at her face, which looked lighter than he remembered and her hair, which seemed as disorderly as his psyche. She had changed the way she dressed, revealing her beauty more.

"What the hell are you staring at? Are you coming or not?!" Once again Idil managed to shake his core.

And so when Idil and Shirwac were tasked to pick up the mourning food from Cadceed restaurant in Fifty-Fifty Mall, neither prepared for the embarrassing episode that followed. People who visit the mall for the sole purpose of shopping may not find parking, or may be harassed by men of all ages who come to the place to run away from their realities. They come to the mall to claim their share of the day's gossip, political news, and all the food, tea and clothes they can bear. Women in full garb walk between stores, losing their bearing under the sheer number of eyes on them. Other women come to the mall precisely for the gazing hungry eyes, roaming around the parking lot eager to be noticed. The scene of women in revealing Somali apparel, all made up, attractive and luscious, create comfort and lust for the men. Idil crossed the flooded parking lot, lost in her pink iPod; she looked down to ignore their grubby stares. She has been pestered by men as old as Cartan. She is often defensive around them, using whatever means she can to shame them. The men transported age-old customs where they could marry whomever they desired, usually very young girls, ignoring State laws which stipulates underage marriage as a crime. She was elated when one old man in their building was sentenced to fifteen years for marrying a sixteen-year-old girl. The same old man eyed her whenever he saw her in the lobby.

As she entered the restaurant, a middle-aged man brushed against her vigorously, the way men in this mall do to pick their prey for the day.

"Fresh, and pretty, good enough for a third wife!" he said, licking his dark dry, chipped lips, hiding a very unattractive overbite with severe red gums through a forced smile which revealed unsightly stained and cracked front teeth. Idil ignored him, as she had done so many before. She waited next to an incensed-looking man who piled up numerous large carry-out trays of food. The man, sweating and worn out, took trips to and from his car to load up the trays. Shirwac stood next to her as she tried to remove food particles that stuck to the bottom of her shoes. The floor was soiled with rice and grease. The restaurant smelled not of fresh food but old, soggy dirt. She looked around, amazed how people even bothered to eat in a filthy place like this. She refused to come to the restaurant earlier, but was forced by Nadifo. The tables were slimy with dirt, and some waiters chewed qat in broad day light, looking unclean. She avoided touching anything while at the restaurant, afraid she would pick up some plague from all the filth around her.

The man with the unattractive overbite came back and stood next to her. She ignored his foul cigarette and sweaty smell, and began asking the cashier for the food they had come to pick up.

"Hey, what's your name, pretty girl?" he asked, rubbing his hands and smiling desperately. He spoke in a low tone voice, as if cautious not to raise suspicion with other patrons in the restaurant.

"What the hell do you want, pervert?" Idil exclaimed, alarming the cashier and other customers in the restaurant.

"Is this how you pick up women? Hey Shirwac, this moron wants to pick me up in the middle of the suuq!" Shirwac and the man whom the comments were meant for vanished quickly out of the restaurant. A large, elderly woman exchanged evil looks with Idil between breaks from the food she tossed into her mouth with a greasy hand, in front of her sat a massive plate brimming to the top with lamb, rice, spaghetti and sauce. The woman said something that made three other women with loud chewing and greasy mouths to look Idil's way with disdain.

"Take it easy, adeer, don't be so angry," The man with the food trays said, losing his serious, and angry demeanor.

"He has no shame, talking to a child like you." He said as he sipped tea from a Styrofoam cup next to the cashier, resting the trays of food on the floor beneath Idil.

"I am sorry, adeer, I am so shamed for him, shame on him," he wiped his sweaty forehead and resumed carrying the trays of food to his car. Idil felt unwanted attention on her from the patrons. Incidents like these never bothered her, but the man who consoled her made her feel remorseful. He was kind and concerned. No one has ever addressed her in that manner: people usually scolded her with repugnance like the woman with the greasy hands. She did not know how to respond to kind people, no one around her was ever kind.

"Adeer, look out for yourself, there are hungry hyenas like this one everywhere!" the man called before he vanished into his small beaten-up Mazda to deliver the trays of food.

Shirwac said nothing, busying himself with the waiter to ensure the order was correct, something he usually would not bother with, but being around Idil had lately become agonizing. They took the food home quietly. Idil sat in the back seat of the taxi cab digesting what had just transpired, Shirwac sat quietly next to the cab driver, a man neither knew who came to pay his respects before he found himself picking up food for the mourning family.

AN UN-CEREMONIAL GIFT

Ceebla changed the baby while Kayd amused himself running after a lizard toy. He chased the lizard with his car toys, throwing them against the lizard as it sped away. Ceebla did not look up but would occasionally summon Kayd to stop running around. He continued chasing the lizard. Shirwac walked in looking distressed. He managed a weak "Hi" that appeared forced from his diaphragm. He didn't even smile at the kids or play with Kayd as he habitually did; he headed for his room when he heard Ceebla call after him rather loudly.

"Hey, don't walk in the house with your shoes on, what is wrong with you?" she sounded aggressive today, or it could be that he no longer tolerated their rules. How could he forget not to take his shoes off? Stooped and rather languid he headed for the foyer to remove the shoes. Kayd, abandoning the lizard, came towards him as he removed the first shoe. The toddler took the shoe and started to kick it towards the living room.

"Kayd, stop that!" Shirwac said in an acidic, irritated voice and then grabbed the shoe forcefully from Kayd. The toddler started crying. Ceebla ignored them, fussing with the infant on her lap who was glued to the purple dinosaur and his colorful friends on TV. Shirwac watched them as he removed the other shoe. She laid the baby on her stomach across her lap, gently stroking the baby's back. "Give mama that delicious burp, one two three! Oh you smart, pretty little girl," she had her on her shoulder now. "Where is that burp? Give mama some of that delicious burp," the baby's unstable head wiggled. She watched Shirwac, her milk-pink lips stained with a little escaped baby puke. Ceebla placed the baby in the bassinet, satisfied with the loud drawn-out burp only a mother's ears can appreciate. She was surprised to find Shirwac marveling at her and the baby.

"You still here? I thought you went upstairs," she said tidying up and putting away scattered toys.

"Eeddo Ceebla, who is my father?" the words left his mouth unplanned. Ceebla kept moving about the living room, snubbing the question, alarmed by it. "Did you hear what I said?" he stood next to her, holding up Kayd against his chest. He gave her no space to ignore him and he came face to face with her as she picked up a fire truck under the coffee table.

"I'm sorry, what did you say, Shirwac?" the unconvincing surprise in her voice sounded insincere even to her.

"Eeddo, you heard me," he put Kayd, who was eager to claim the fire truck, down. "Who is my father, where is my father?" he repeated, this time boldly claiming her space.

"Honey, are you okay?" she touched his shoulder and attempted to sit him down.

"I'm fine, I just need to know who my father is," he said loudly, upsetting the baby who began crying.

"I think you should ask your uncle that question," Ceebla picked up the baby, soothing her on her shoulder.

"I never had that," he sat on the couch and began crying. "My mother never put me on her shoulder, I never had a mother place me on a sleeping mat, I never had a mother feed me and burp me!" he paused, wiping his eyes. "All I ask is to know where I came from," he continued rubbing his eyes, which surged with more tears. "Why do you guys deny me that?"

Ceebla sat next to him, quieting the fretting baby. "Honey, I understand your frustration, please don't distress yourself." Not knowing what to say, she rubbed his back.

"I don't even know where my name comes from, or who named me or why. No one took days to figure out what my name should be, like you did with Daryeel, assuring her name was just right. Daryeel, Safeguard," he repeated the name, looking heartbroken. " Ceebla, you should understand me more than anyone else in this family." A new wave of tears stormed out.

"I wish I could help you, Shirwac, I honestly do, but I know nothing about—" she stopped herself short of saying something damaging.

"About what?! What is it that is so horribly secret about my birth?!" he got up, throwing the little truck he'd cupped in his hands to the floor. "What the hell are you all hiding? Who am I?!" he stormed off the room, causing little Kayd to cry after him. Ceebla did not summon either one of them. She was stunned, and speechless.

In his room he stood in front of the mirror, going over the scar on his face. He touched his nose, widened his eyes. Shirwac began to notice the ugliness about him. He hated his name; his features which people admired but to him seemed unfamiliar and odd. He could never say whose eyes he had, or if his height was like his father's or how his voice fared against the unknown parent who gave him life. He lay on his bed with a worried face, which aged him. He was condemned by the fury of silence. The sadness inside him seeped through his body, turning into revulsion. A knot of emotion originated in his stomach, gagging him as he let out a harrowing yelp. He felt an excruciating pain, and a yellowish-red puke surge from his mouth and rush to the bed sheets. He moaned with pain, his body unable to stop the gush that narrated his history, the pain, the un-ceremonial birth, the discarding of his life. The pain spelled years of neglect, confusion and desire to belong. He vomited his reality, the mysterious history that weaved the edges of his life. His mind swirled, the smells of the camp came back to him—Tusmo, death, Sulekha's murdered in front of him. He searched for clues in the faces of the people who took care of him in the camp. Tusmo's voice haunted him. She relayed the story of his life when she thought he was not in earshot, he listened closely for clues to his saga, hoping she would reveal a thing or two about him, but all he heard was the reason he was named after a dead man:

"He was nameless for two and half years until he found the dead body of the camp shop keeper, his name was Shirwac Madoobe. Shirwac was his first word, so we gave him the name." Even his name was as tragic—as incidental, as unplanned—as his life. He heard the slow movement of careful steps towards his room. He was lead from the mess by gentle hands that cupped his head with a gentle touch of love. He was undressed and lead to the bathtub. Lucid water touched his body, gently massaging away remnants of puke. A fresh warm towel dried the wetness away, gently stroking the neglected arid skin. The smell of freshness, through lavender and mint suds, relaxed his clogged nose. He was led back into a clean bed. He lay erect, his ordeal halted with warm lentil soup. He drifted into peaceful sleep, snoring with a gentle whimper. The doubt of his future blanketed his trembling body. When he awoke, Shirwac was wobbly in a hospital bed, shivering in the midst of a cold room, humming with loud machines and fretful nurses.

"What did they say is wrong with him?" Ceebla jumped from her seat, dabbing her puffy eyes.

"They are doing more tests on him," Haybe said, matter-of-factly. The waiting room reeked of stale sickness. He stared at the large TV hovering over him: "three more terrorists have been picked up by the FBI today. Mr. Steve Morgan, a thirty-year veteran with the FBI, said for a year the perpetrators attended a mosque in……" Haybe looked away from the overly excited reporter. Instead he glimpsed at the beefy, pink-faced man sitting across from him with his hands crossed in apparent apprehension. The man's concrete attentiveness on the TV missed his wife's summons that their daughter had just been wheeled out of the OR. Haybe shook his head and got up, to pace the room.

Idil sat next to Nadifo, whose eyes ejected fresh, raw tears. Idil sobbed quietly. She recalled the fierce struggle she had with Nadifo only an hour earlier after the frantic call from Ceebla came. Ceebla informed them that she found Shirwac in his room unconscious. Idil flew into a rage.

"It's all your fault, especially you!" she shouted between wails, while she got dressed. "You are evil, ayeeyo! You all are evil, even Haybe!" Nadifo did not respond. She was distraught, fearing something serious happened to Shirwac. She'd grown fond of him; he was her favorite now. He never disrespected people the way Idil did. He still had some culture left in him; she depended on him for that reason. A kind and respectable boy who managed to keep the impatient American ways Idil and others picked up at bay. He remained calm with her even as he stumbled into trying times. That is the Shirwac she came to love and respect—and Nadifo did not respect too many youngsters. *He is a gift*, she thought, *a gift Allah returned to her.*

"Naayaa, shut up and take care of these kids while I go to the hospital!" To interrupt her rant.

"I am not staying here; I am going to see Shirwac! I am not going to babysit these unwanted children! How unlucky they are, another generation of messed up Gedi kids!"

"Shut your mouth, naayaa!"

"He probably doesn't want to see any of you anyway, especially you!"

"*Naayaa* shut your mouth, may the jins take you, you stupid girl!"

"There are no other jins, you are the jin in disguise!"

"You better be glad I have my hands tied, otherwise your ugly little face would be telling different story!"

"Try it, I dare you!"

"These are the times I wish I was in Hamar where I could show how many shades of blue your body could have for a filthy mouth like yours!"

"I dare you, try it, I would love to see that, confused old lady! Look around you; you drove all your kids away! You managed to kill your husband, and Geele! Geele died because of you and Cartan's corruption! You let your little girl be attacked in front of you, because of greed. You sent Bile to jail, and Haybe is about to lose it because of your tribalism! Oh yeah, and my selfish mother, where is she, ayeeyo, huh? Why did she

396

up and leave us like that? Because you spoiled her so much with corrupt money she could not cope with life! So what did she do, she run away with that ugly dude! Did you think I did not know all this, huh? I know everything, even Shirwac and how he came to this ugly world! I will tell him everything when he feels better! You know, Warsan is just like you, a selfish witch! I can't believe she left us for that man, and why? Because he is rich! Rich, rich, rich, is all I ever heard from her! We use to have this and that, we lived in a mansion, and we had servants! So what, you don't anymore, so deal with it, idiot! Be grateful for what Allah gave you! But no, she used to drag me with her when she was having an affair with the ugly man! Eleven years old and I had seen it all! I used to come home with all sorts of stuff to shut me up! But I tried to tell dad about the man, except he was busy chasing that crap he chews! He never listened to me! And then one day we got up and found out our mother had left us, for a rich Zandakan! You lied to us, saying she is in a crazy people's house, oh I wish she was! I hope she is rotting in hell like the rest of us!" Idil wiped her nose, visibly exhausted from her own tirade. But she was not done.

"I hope that crook sells her body parts to the highest bidder! Now Hogad is a gang leader, Hilac will probably bring you another bastard child! You deserve it too, to witness our sorry lives so you know you are the cause of it! Look around you, the mess you and Cartan created, and the lives you have destroyed! It is your fault! You sent Henna to an early grave—hell if I let you do that to Shirwac! He's the only decent person here, I will protect him from you with my life! Image, image, image that is all you ever cared about! You are so pathetic, raising more unwanted children! They are going to be a mess like all of us, poor kids!"

Nadifo sat on the couch with Zaki on her lap aghast. She could not believe what came out Idil's mouth. *Who has been talking to her, telling her about family secrets? How did she know so much?* Nadifo thought, stunned and silent.

"Naayaa get out, now!" The children cried through the uproar. Hajir cried "Ayeeyo I want to go with you!" Idil dashed out of the apartment.

"I hate you; I hate my life!"

Nadifo called her neighbor Madino to look after the kids. The short ride between her apartment and the hospital felt long. When she got to the hospital Haybe, Idil and Ceebla were sitting next to each other, each appeared consumed with thought. It was the first time she saw Ceebla since her marriage to Haybe. The two women exchanged silent greetings, each momentarily forgetting the discomfort between them. Now, they both wept for Shirwac. It was not time to unravel the ugliness of their lives; it was time to come together as a family for the boy they all came to love. Nadifo appeared old, not with age but apprehension. The last time the two women met, Nadifo used unflattering descriptions on Ceebla, a few days before she went to Somalia to escape their marriage. Nadifo took a seat next to Ceebla, avoiding Idil, who now sobbed loudly

The hospital waiting area served as a reunion spot for a family who had for years avoided the reality of their lives. They were confronted with the specter of yet another death. Pain after pain of burying family members piled on top of Nadifo's heart. She felt heavy with responsibility. Here he lay, the little boy she'd abandoned years ago at a lonely refugee camp. Now he lay in a hospital room, barely clinging to his short troubled life. She grew tired of him lately though, his questioning became ruthless, and irritating. She could not give him the answers he sought: could not offer him the basic genetic makeup of his life, how could she tell him who his father was? Maybe she should have told him the truth about his conception, but she kept that away from him thinking she was doing him a favor by not sharing the details of that day.

"Sir, we need to talk to you in private," the loudness of the doctor's voice cut through her thoughts. She jumped towards the doctor. "Are you his mother?" The doctor asked Nadifo, she looked at him with confusion. Haybe spoke.

"Yes she is—no, I mean, I am his uncle, his guardian."

"Very well, sir could you come with us."

"What did he say, did he say Shirwac is ok, what did the doctor say?" Nadifo asked anxiously, avoiding Ceebla who held Kayd on her lap.

"I ain't tellin' you nuttin'!" Ceebla looked at Idil in shock.

"Naayaa, don't talk to ayeeyo that way! Haybe will tell us what is going on with Shirwac when he returns, hooyo" Ceebla responded to Nadifo's question. Nadifo was calmed by Ceebla's respect.

"Insha Allah," her voice shrieked.

Their lives flashed in front of her. The part of her family she had tried to avoid for so long sat with her in that waiting room. It was quiet, but the musty air tightened around her, smothering her. She felt heavy with blame. Was what Idil said true? Did she cause all that harm in her family? The words kept banging in her ears. *You know Warsan is just like you, a selfish witch! You managed to kill your husband, and Geele! Geele died because of you and Cartan's corruption! You let your little girl be attacked in front of you, because of greed.*

No one has ever said those things to her. Was it true? Haybe came back; he'd obviously been crying. Nadifo's heart missed a beat. Tears she did not shed for Cartan or Henna stormed out of her. She could not move from her seat.

"Both of his kidneys failed. He needs a transplant, or he will be in dialysis for the rest of his life."

"He needs a kidney? Why—what happened to him?"

"They said it is probably something he caught in the refugee camp; both of his kidneys are malfunctioning."

"What does that mean, I mean what....?"

"See, I told you, it is all your fault! You are going to kill Shirwac too!"

"Shut up Idil, get out of here, I don't need your ranting now!" Haybe said.

"I hate you all; it is your fault if my cousin dies!"

"Naayaa, get the hell out of here!"

"Haybe, just leave her alone, come on, Idil, come with me eeddo."

"Ceebla, you better leave before they kill you too!"

"What is going on with her today?"

"Haybe, what can we do for him?"

"Well, they are not sure yet, it may be an infection that's caused his kidneys to fail, they are doing more tests." Haybe choked on the words.

"A kidney? Allah forgive me, it is serious, isn't it?"

"Yes, hooyo, it's serious."

"Can I go and see him?"

"Not now, they are still doing more tests on him."

Idil sat at a bench outside the hospital. She looked anxious and angry. The loud ring of her slim pink cell phone interrupted her thoughts. The name "Josh" flashed in a red neon color.

"Hi, Josh," she said. "Sorry, what? Oh, yes, I am with my demented family. Yeah, Shirwac is in the hospital. I am not sure, I am sorry you had to come all that way. Okay, bye. Sorry—no I will call you; you don't need to come. Okay, I will see you tomorrow. Bye." Before she returned to the room she heard Nadifo say something about a kidney.

"I will give him my kidney—I am old and have few years left anyway; I owe him at least that!" Nadifo was saying when Idil barged into their conversation.

"No don't give him your rotten kidney, it will probably kill him!" Nadifo did not realize Idil was behind the door, listening to them. "I will give him mine, he is my best friend!" she collapsed onto the floor, sobbing hysterically.

"Me too! I will give him mine!" said little Kayd desperately trying to join in the turmoil.

Nadifo recalled many fine memories with Shirwac. When Henna left, Haybe got busy with his law school, Cartan was running after that woman, it was Shirwac who made her life worthwhile. She was the first to boast her knowledge of America to him. She introduced many things to him, the mega-shopping centers, McDonald's, gameboy games, the library. It was the first time she felt useful. She spoke some English before he did. She was able to brag about that too, mis-pronouncing words, giving him the wrong meaning of things. Showing him how the microwave worked, the bus schedule.

Later it was he who perfected the language and would translate things, filling out application forms, accompanying her to appointments. Even if he was bothered by her, he never complained like the other kids. He was kind and useful. She sat with sweaty palms, her once-graceful neck now creased with anxious wrinkles. Her eyes, once almond, now pinched with folds, her face ridden with unpredictable worry. Losing her last attempted silky smile to life and it is cruel gifts of family drama and never ending sadness, she felt utter despair, and looked around only to find the causes to all the wrinkles, folds and sagging in her life. Her family.

A SEAMLESS HARM

A broken promise has its sad consequences: it can shatter dreams of a lifetime. On the other hand dreams that come in the middle of the night for no apparent reason, with a shady ex one despises, could be the announcement of trouble. Ceebla lay down next to teething Daryeel, falling into a semi-conscious reverie. In her dream Colaad looked fat, clumsy, and beaten up by life: she was satisfied to see him in that condition. They were in a situation together, and Ceebla was reluctant to participate. The loud ringing of the phone coincided with Colaad's reaching for her with extended arms. She was startled, not only by the sharp noise of the phone, but also by the strange dream of despised Colaad. Dreams confused her: she'd been brought up to believe that dreams of a horrendous event foretold good fortune, but if one dreamt of some happy occurrence, then bad luck was around the corner.

She fell into fearful silence, keeping her eyes on her children as Istaahil *CNN* bellowed incessantly on the other end of the phone, without giving Ceebla an opportunity to respond. That was Istaahil's style—to never give anyone an opportunity to speak.

Ceebla's life was calm now. She felt an inner peace she had not known for a long time—she had begun to trust again, and settled into her life with Haybe. Their life together was itself a dream. She would often read Suura al Falaq to ward off the evil jealous eye from their happiness. People in the community, war-ravaged and poor, were envious of the slightest accomplishments: they too were once prosperous and well-to-do, but ever since the war a cloud of jealousy and suspicion

402

had fallen on people who were once light-hearted, full of potential and hope.

They envied her husband's success; his firm had quadrupled in size and was now lucrative. She did not have to work full time, and cut her work week to three days. The kids were healthy and growing fast. But she was reluctant to mention the blessings in her life, afraid that announcing her good fortune would jinx it. Melancholy had no place in her life now: she even considered herself an optimist, thanks to Haybe's positive outlook on life. They were planning to have a third baby when Daryeel turned two and Kayd three.

She was sorting through some boxes earlier in the day, going through mementos of the old house, the one she'd reluctantly agreed to sell after much arm twisting from Haybe. She had been meaning to tend to the boxes for a while, but a year after they moved to the new house the boxes still lingered in an empty room, holding pictures, books, toys and clothes. Ceebla had convinced herself she was short on time to tend to them. Their lives were busy, and quiet times when she could drift into pleasant day-dreaming next to a toddler were rare. She actually looked forward to nap time; it was the only time she could find serenity and the only time she carefully re-evaluated her life. She was still sentimental about the old house, fond of the memories she'd built there and saddened to abandon it: her freedom from Colaad, her marriage to Haybe, her children's births—although there were also had a few bad memories, like her near-fatal attack.

Haybe had continuously complained the home was too small for them, but the reality was that when his income started to grow, he wanted a bigger, and newer house. The new house had seven bedrooms, four bathrooms, two living rooms and a family room, but it was far from anything that mattered to her: its vibrancy was lost in its sheer size. She did not yet feel any harmony with it: it was so distant from the Mosque and the community members she had come to value in her life. An old, pristine forest surrounded them: The pleasant scents of pine, tamarack and northern hardwoods wafted through the elegant home.

Scenic lake byways and a grand state park were a stone's throw away. The gated community of Willow Brook and all its trappings was now part of who they were: this is how success was measured in America. Taking long walks with the kids and Haybe on breezy summer nights along the byway on Willow Crest Lake, a feeling of surrender unknown to her would wash over her. Their next-door neighbors were from Ukraine, two doors down were the Chins; further down Willow Way were a Moroccan doctor, Dr. Faiza Alim, her American husband, Jared "Scooter" Taft, a professor of Anthropology, and their three kids. The diversity mattered to her: she wanted the kids to grow up in a mixed neighborhood. They had a meet-and-greet dinner for their neighbors the night before and she was still tired, although Hoodo- Qalanjo, the part-time help, had cooked everything.

Istaahil wasted no time on getting to the point; she talked so fast her words overlapped in Ceebla's ears. "Raaxo has been arrested," she said. "She is the one who tried to kill you—she paid those guys to kill you so she could end up with Haybe. Haybe is Cusayb's father." The speed at which she spoke made it clear she wanted to be the one to deliver the bad news. Daryeel, woken by the phone, was now fussing so loudly it was hard to hear Istaahil's words. Kayd was also awoken, and crying. It was all too much to take in. The kids did not allow her to digest the news, and Istaahil began shouting.

But Istaahil's words contradicted the life Ceebla shared with Haybe. How could any of it make sense—why should these comments delivered over the phone shatter her peace? The threat of Istaahil's words was in complete contrast to the stability and calm she found in the life that this news endangered. *Raaxo was the one trying to kill you, but Haybe was in on it too?* Her thoughts were jumbled. Shirwac walked in, tossing around a basketball as he chattered on his cell phone. Ceebla handed Daryeel to him, and Kayd enthusiastically followed the pair as they headed to the living room. No one would ever guess only six months earlier he lay on a hospital bed with a sudden illness. His recovery from the kidney infection that almost took his life was not swift, but gradual.

By the time they moved into the new house Shirwac was recovering well, and he was back in school full time.

Making quick succinct decisions was something Ceebla thought she would be incapable of, but after her experience with Colaad she has learned to be ready to walk away for sanity's sake. She didn't even think of calling Haybe: instinct told her to take the kids and leave. How could she live with a man who was aware of her shooter? How could anyone keep such a serious secret that long? And then he has had an affair— her best friend Raaxo and her husband Haybe, the man she called her confidante, and love tricked her. Haybe and Raaxo. She could not take it in, her head throbbed and her heart raced. It was inconceivable. *They are nothing alike, yet they played me? Little Cusayb is his son.* Her head whirled with thought.

She was shaken but calm, much calmer than she expected to be. She prepared two bags, one for the kids and one for herself. She was quiet but alarmed. She collected everything she would need for the kids, but a task that would normally be quick and concise took over an hour. She trembled, and her head seemed to spin. It was almost as if she'd waited for this moment to arrive, as if she knew the best life she'd ever known would be snatched from her—she had sometimes felt as if she did not deserve all the abundance and happiness, the loving husband, the beautiful kids and the great life.

Haybe, Raaxo and Cusayb. The litany clamored in her mind. Shirwac helped her get the kids ready, thinking she was putting them to bed: he had no way of knowing what Ceebla planned. He was in his room as she headed for the door, she could hear the music blasting; normally she would ask him to keep it down. But not tonight—she didn't even say goodbye, he would ask too many questions and alert Haybe. She did not scream, although she wanted to: tears streamed down her cheeks. She collected herself as she buckled the kids into their seats. More tears came as she loaded the truck.

It was sheer luck that the hotel down the road from her work had rooms available. She stayed there for two nights and began looking for an apartment. Ceebla had not spoken to anyone about the incident; she was alone with it, in an empty hotel room with two small children. Who could she share this with? She absentmindedly found herself thinking of calling Raaxo to tell her what Haybe had done, only to remember bitterly that it was with her Haybe had betrayed her. In her mind, she was done with him.

Haybe found out the news when a friend called him to tell him what he had heard about Raaxo's arrest. Such news had a way of being repeated on phone lines only minutes after it occurred. Somalis worked the phones when there was bad news: a community that had known nothing but tragedy had made reporting bad news part of their being. He rushed home, knowing full well that any number of people would have called Ceebla—not a single detail would have been left unreported. But she was already gone when he arrived. He left twenty messages throughout the night, she ignored all his calls. Insomniac and distraught, she lay in bed with the children while listening to his messages. Maybe she sought a different answer in his message: she wanted him to say it's all wrong, everything Istaahil said is a lie, but he didn't; in a way he confirmed it.

"I am so sorry, honey; I am not sure what they told you. I hope you'll give me an opportunity to explain things. I am worried—you should not be alone with the kids. Please go to Nadifo's place if you don't want to see me, but please don't be by yourself."

"I am so sorry, Ceebla; I never meant to hurt you, I didn't know she was behind it, I just found out too."

"Please answer the phone!" she could hear his sobbing "Don't leave me, baby, I can explain everything, please don't leave me, they will succeed, Ceebla, they will win, don't let them win, honey, I love you!"

It's what he both loved and disliked about her: Ceebla was strong, she dealt with bad news differently from him. He couldn't concentrate on work, could hardly eat and was disoriented the entire time she was away. For two days no one knew where Ceebla was, only disheartening him further.

Like everyone else in Cedar Springs Nadifo found out the details of Raaxo's arrest, and her intentions with Haybe. Apparently she'd blackmailed him, threatening to reveal the child to Ceebla if he did not leave her. Raaxo's interest in Haybe peaked once she introduced him to Ceebla: women's wisdom says if you have a good thing going with your man, don't share it with your best friend.

Ceebla's constant praise of Haybe had made Raaxo want him for herself, and she regretted introducing them. She wanted Ceebla out of the way so that she could have her way with Haybe. Since she'd had a one night stand with him—even though that one night was a year before Haybe and Ceebla had met—she blackmailed him, thinking that if she got rid of Ceebla he would marry her. Ceebla began to remember incidents with Raaxo: Raaxo made crude comments when Ceebla was pregnant with Kayd, and often shared stories of pregnant women who lost their babies for one reason or another. One particular woman lost her baby when the man's ex-wife attacked her. Ceebla thought the stories were tasteless, but she did not think Raaxo was being malicious.

One time Raaxo suggested they visit a traditional healer: Raaxo said she was worried about the injuries Ceebla had suffered in the attack, and wanted the healer to give her some herbs and roots to keep away the evil eye. Ceebla refused, but Raaxo continued with her bizarre behavior. After Ceebla gave birth to Kayd, Raaxo didn't visit for a week; when she finally came, she looked angry and then sad. On another occasion Raaxo insisted on cleaning Ceebla's house, saying she wanted to help out after the birth, although Ceebla had a cleaning lady. Once she asked for the house keys, when Ceebla had a doctor's appointment. Looking back over the seemingly trivial incidents, Ceebla recognized that Raaxo had been trying to put bad luck charms in her house from the traditional healer—trying to ruin her happiness.

Ashamed and apprehensive, Nadifo approached the two-bedroom apartment Ceebla had moved into. She recalled all too sharply how she despised the woman she is about to beg to come back to her son: she found it unnatural to hate one person so much. And hate Ceebla she did, for a long time, although those feelings had somehow subsided since.

The apartment looked small and bare. The kids played in the living room, oblivious to Nadifo. Ceebla was formal with her; she was surprised to agree to see Nadifo at all, when she was almost sure Nadifo was in on the plan to get rid of her. Ceebla did not wait for the older woman to sit down, she started attacking her, leveling all sorts of accusations at her.

"She wanted me out of the way to take Haybe! Did you know Cusayb was Haybe's son? I know she is your relative, I am sure you arranged for her to marry Haybe when you were griping about me!" The older woman was stunned by the accusations, but she understood Ceebla's anger.

"My best friend, the only woman I ever trusted betrayed me—and Mr. nice guy to all people—what was she, a charity case?!" Nadifo was silent.

"He was having an affair with the woman who tried to kill me! Weren't you behind the plan to kill me too? I know you to be a good, devout woman, why would you want me dead?! I mean, you could have your son back, but why would you want me dead? Well, Haybe can go to her now. You can all have each other."

"Did you know Haybe was Cusayb's father?" Ceebla was crying—the kids were crying, even Nadifo was crying. She wanted to hug Ceebla, but she'd never been the emotionally demonstrative type.

"Of course not." Nadifo reached for the little girl, who shied away.

"Haybe is not that boy's father. She is just saying that to break up your marriage."

"Why would she do that?! What did I do to her?"

"People are jealous, Ceebla, envious. Look, I don't blame you for being angry with me, after all I was not the most welcoming mother in law, but I had no part in any of this." Nothing Nadifo said would convince her.

"I know you are angry, but she is probably making it up, Raaxo is not a good person."

"Oh yes, go ahead and blame the woman, why don't you!"

"Haybe is not a man who would do that to a woman he loves."

"But he did not deny it! I mean he slept with her—he is an adulterer!"

"*Bismillaahi Raxmaani Raxiim*, my daughter don't say that, it is so sinful!"

"Well, your son is sinful, he is an adulterer!" Ceebla repeated the words to hurt Nadifo.

"I really don't know what I believe any more."

"All those phone calls between them, nothing makes sense, why did she introduce me to him if they had something going? Why couldn't he come forward and tell me what happened between them? The fool that I am, I though their cozy relationship and teasing was just friendship. Somehow I was sure you were the one who tried to kill me, but it was Raaxo—Woow, how am I to deal with that?!"

"Ceebla, please calm down, come and stay with us, the kids would love to meet Kayd and Daryeel..."

Desolate and dead, is how Ceebla felt inside, as if Haybe had taken a knife to her heart. He stabbed her and destroyed the safety he'd created. Fairy tales are just that—fairytales. The fairy tale that had become her life was now coming apart. She felt hopeless, miserable: feelings she no longer associated with her life crept back into her, crushing any hope she may have had with Haybe. Yes it was true: Haybe had had an affair with Raaxo, before he met Ceebla. Another person may brush that aside, but Ceebla could not forgive Haybe for having had an affair with Raaxo while she was married to Farah. That is adultery, and the punishment for adultery is severe. She remembers how he tried to explain it away:

"It was only one time, before you and I even knew each other. She ambushed me, and that kid is not mine. You are the most important person in my life. I made a mistake, I almost got you killed, but that was never my intention! This woman is unstable, all that stuff that happened to her when she was young and all—" As if she could forgive only one time. Adulterer. That is what she started calling him every opportunity she got.

Life-altering decisions pressed on Ceebla more often than she liked to admit. She'd had to accept a community that shunned her mere existence, and then she got involved with a wife-beater and a loser; when she had the courage to leave him she thought she would never make the same mistakes again. But here she was facing another life-altering decision to leave Haybe. Once she settled into her life with Haybe, she'd begun to believe she was immune to the bad luck that claimed other women—husbands leaving for younger wives, husbands just disappearing without a hint of warning, woman whose marriages were in disarray. *No, not me*, she often thought. *I am immune, because of Haybe. He is a gem of a man. That will never be me, worrying about another woman, never part of my life with my darling Haybe. He will never marry a younger woman; never will he find me too old. I will be forever precious to him.* But reality scars the soul and kills hope. Hope no longer existed with her. She felt vacant, like an empty, abandoned city, a desolate soul with no point to move on. But she refused to be a statistic, she refused to be one more woman whose life was altered by a fleeing husband, or a cheating husband, she refused to be one more woman who went insane because of the actions of a selfish, weak man who broke the sanctity of marriage for selfish gain: she was not going to allow statistics to speak for her.

SECOND CHANCES

T he deafening thud of a woman's wide behind on plain concrete on a clear Sunday afternoon coincided with Raaxo's clamoring fight with a woman who accused her of masterminding the hit against Ceebla. It was precisely the same moment Nadifo's head swirled due to news about Warsan's plight in Zandak in the West coast of Africa. The whirl in her head blinded her to the ground, where she found herself cemented next to Brenda Gayle. The two women tripped on top of each other on the sidewalk.

It all began innocently enough, as a woman Nadifo did not know but who looked familiar chased after Nadifo one Sunday afternoon. Sundays were a dressy day in the neighborhood where the mosque was located: she'd had not seen so many dressed up people the rest of the week. She never found out why they dressed up on Sundays, but they did. She walked to the mosque every Sunday morning: it was two miles away, and since the bus that usually took her did not run on Sundays, she had to walk. She would enjoy the serenity of the walk more, if the calm did not bring all types of worries in her mind. It is when she remembered incidents she did not wish to remember, and when she peeked into the past only to create more pain. There was nothing pleasant about Sunday afternoon walks, but they were a necessity.

Nadifo's walk back home from the mosque coincided with the dressed-up people. As she passed them, she secretly watched the women who congregated in front of a red brick building, wearing elaborate hats and colorful clothes. Even children dressed up on

411

Sundays. Nadifo was admiring a large woman who wore a green pastel hat with matching skirt and jacket. The woman was not particularly striking, but her hat and outfit were spruced with feathers and other fluffy things. It was a hot summer day, and Nadifo wondered how hot it must be inside the elaborate outfit, feeling the heat that soaked up by her own hijab, which was less elaborate and much thinner than the woman's outfit. She did not realize it at the time, but she had halted her walk to stare directly at the woman. She was large in frame, tall in height and the fat that hugged her skin was not hidden by the colorful clothing. She was taller and larger than everyone else, and yet she wore high heels. Nadifo did not realize how rudely she was staring at the woman until the woman turned around, having completed a round of greetings and that is when Nadifo's limbs became paralyzed. She wanted to walk, but her legs defied the attempt. The woman began walking her way, and that is when Nadifo's puny legs took off in an unexpected sprint. The large woman with the green pastel hat sprinted behind her, holding the large hat in one hand while clutching a handbag in the other. Her protruding belly jiggled while she called Nadifo's name. Nadifo kept running, and it was when she heard the thud of the woman who tripped and fell next to her that she realized the green outfit camouflaged Brenda Gayle. Brenda Gayle, what was she doing in Nadifo's neighborhood? There was no love lost between the two; Nadifo was moved to another social worker in an office downtown where a freckle faced woman treated her worse than Miss Gayle ever had. But the unpleasantness of the freckle -faced woman was a consolation for Nadifo: her dislike for Miss Gayle allowed her to tolerate the red-faced woman. The lazy freckle-faced social worker who inherited her case did not remind her of her unwanted refugee status as Ms. Gayle has done years past. Next to Brenda Gayle, Nadifo looked more attractive and youthful: the woman had aged and become obese, but she was not seething with unkindness like before. There was something serene about her now.

"Nadifo, it is me," she said, the words bounced of her tongue. She has never addressed Nadifo that way before. Nadifo's name sounded calming, the way Ms. Gayle pronounced it.

"Yes, Ms. Gayle," Nadifo said. "What you do here?" the extra vowels and the way she stretched the words created inquisitiveness in Ms. Gayle's sweaty face.

"Yes, I go to the Mount Zion Church over there," Ms. Gayle said, pointing to the church while attempting to leave the hot concrete. "There," she pointed to the church, allowing Nadifo to follow her forefinger.

"Oh you church there," Nadifo shook her head while using the concrete for support to get up.

Days later Nadifo would find out about the sad tale that made Brenda Gayle the bitter woman she'd been. Neither knew the tragedies of the other. They scuffled and grunted at each other, Nadifo feeling the supremacy Gayle exhibited, and Gayle rejecting the conceit that jumped from women like Nadifo, although they are refugees with nothing, refugees who reside at the bottom of American life, struggling to climb out of the wreck. She never waited for their snobbish behavior to emerge; she beat them to the punch with her American condescension. Although she resides somewhere not that far from them in the cocktail called America, the one thing she had going for her was the smugness that every American possesses, the smugness that assures they as Americans are better than the rest of the human race, no matter how grim their reality. Ms. Gayle's arrogance announced how much grander her life was compared to the heavily accented women she helped.

But their similarities were shockingly alike. Brenda Gayle lost not only one son to violence but two: a police shoot-out took her twenty-one year old son Trey, and exactly a year later her twenty-three year old son Orlando was gunned down three blocks from their home. And so the two women met every Sunday afternoon after Church and Mosque services, at the Korea Korner Café.

"It may not have been much, Nadifo, but it was my struggle; and now I realize I had so much. Before my sons died I was slaving to make ends meet, but their spirit and smiles kept me going even when I didn't think I could. Now this settlement makes life much easier, but for what? I have no one to share it with. Every time I overspend I feel as if I am drinking that pool of blood the police spilt. I feel guilty, but I am glad how the trial for Trey ended—three police men in jail for twenty years and a seven-million-dollar settlement from the city. How's that for justice?"

The conversations were mostly one-sided: Nadifo listened attentively, unsure when Brenda would emerge if she misspoke. She was still cautious, although she had witnessed the change in the woman, and the softness and kindness that radiated from her.

"Nadifo, she is not Chinese, she is Korean, and yes I feel her stares too, it is only a habit she picked up after she arrived here, to treat us like dog poop!" she looked up from a large plate for two of Seafood Jongol. Nadifo drank orange juice from a small Styrofoam cup. She stared at the manner in which Ms. Gayle devoured the spicy food. A plate of fried dumplings and another of kimchi pancakes hugged one corner of the table.

"Why she look us like that?"

"Maybe it is our outlandish outfits—your hijab, my hat and these gloves. Maybe we are freaking the poor Asian woman out"

"She rude every day we come here she no nice."

"I know she's rude, but what choices do we have in this part of town? Every store and restaurant is run by them, where else could we meet?" She pointed to the dry cleaner's, the ice cream parlor and the beauty supply store to make her point.

"Me don't like this Chinese woman."

"Nadifo, she is not Chinese I keep telling you, she is Korean—her last name is Choi."

"Me think all people like that Chinese, we call *indhayar*, like small eye!"

"That is demeaning. Who're you calling small eye?"

"No, that their name."

"Now why would you do that, calling people such ugly names?"

"No, it no bad, just name."

"Well you wouldn't like someone to call you some demeaning names because you are black, or Muslim so stop calling her names."

"How would you like to be called Ethiopian, or for that matter Nigerian—now I know you wouldn't like that, so stop calling this woman Chinese when she is not! You bring memories of how people from your country are so full of themselves, not wanting to even be called black, and now you want to call someone else what they are not."

"No, me black—who say we not black?"

"You all protested when I asked you to check the box that said BLACK NON-HISPANIC in the social services application forms, instead you all went for the box that said OTHER. What the hell is other anyway?"

"I don't know what you talk about, but we Somalian black."

"Funny how you used to call me the N-word every time you were angry with me—that does not sound like someone who is proud to be black!"

"Yes, you call to me terrorist, you remember me."

"Yes, how ironic—we sit across from each other when we used to detest each other. Anyhow, it is ignorance that makes us say these things, we used labels given to us by the white folk to hurt each other," she chuckled.

"Yes, that true."

'Honey child, don't even get me started on white folk's talk—I haven't got the energy nor the time. Now, let's go back to this menu and tweak it, I am tired of staring at it all day!"

And so the Korner Korean café became where they conducted their business grunted and shared while Mrs. Choi's unfriendly stares continued. Two grandmothers who met at the most challenging times of their lives, still at it with grandkids and extended family to care for.

It is where they came to appreciate each other and became business partners, opening a restaurant opposite the Korean Korner Café; they named Second Chances Café, an African-Caribbean Bistro.

HENNA LEAF

She lay, limply, sucking her thumb. Her delicate face showed signs of fatigue. Dried teardrops discolored the areas around diamond-shaped green eyes and drifted down to a perfectly positioned straight nose. She attempted a wail, but settled for a quiet sob. She circled the refrigerator again and again, unable to reach the door handle. She cried, exhausted, dividing her time between the fridge and the body that lay next to her.

"Mommy, mommy," she tapped on her mother's shoulder rather than attempting to open her sealed eyes.

"Juice, mommy, I want juice!" She whined continuously, dragging Hala, her favorite brown doll, all over the kitchen. Soaked and wet, the doll stained the golden Persian rug. Exhausted, the toddler lay down next to her mother and resumed to sucking her thumb. A Somali lullaby "Huuwa yaa Huwa" kept rewinding itself on the CD player—*Huwa yaa Huwa hooyo ma joogto kabax kabax adaay kebehidii qadatay...*

The hennaed flower pattern her mother had applied only a week earlier on her tiny hands and feet looked fresh. They were preparing to celebrate her birthday. A gold necklace with a protective blessing amulet which said "May Allah keep away the evil eye" in Arabic hung from her neck, resting just below the baby folds of her neck. Her cries, now mere whimpers, echoed off the grandiose ceiling, muffled slightly by the intricate Quran canvases covering the massive walls. She laid face-up, staring straight into the blinding light of the tiered chandelier that graced the ceiling. Finally, her mind relaxed and allowed her fatigued body to drift into deep sleep. Her pink sweater and white skirt remained

417

vibrant, even while stained and wet. Wet from the sprinklers that put out the fire, set to deliver their end.

By the time firefighters broke down the door to enter the house, the little girl lay asleep in the curve of her mother's elbow, all of the colors had blurred together in the light, creating a scene of brilliance. She opened her eyes and cried, but she did not resist the woman who lifted her from the mess. She clung to her; the warmth of the woman's body soothed her. She rubbed her eyes, peeking over the woman's shoulder between the long, wet fringe of her unraveled braids to witness the covering of her mother's body. She continued sucking her thumb as her mother's body disappeared from view into the waiting ambulance. She cried without noise. This is how the little girl's life crossed her grandmother's at age three.

Henna could be described by everyone as naïve, even unwise and indecisive. But one thing she had decided in life was to rejoin her family in Minneapolis. Perhaps she was tired of Naif, or tired of running away, maybe she missed her family. Whatever the reason she was ready to face her past head on. However naïve, Henna knew Naif would not allow her to relocate to Minneapolis to re-join her family. She somehow sensed her end would come quicker than she wanted if he ever came back and found her at home. He was a monster, moody, unhappy and very violent. It didn't help when his communications company, al Ali Communications, and its subsidiary American counterpart, Bedouin Entertainment, lost its biggest deal to date, the launching of Rihana and Niyaf, the first all-Middle-Eastern English entertainment channel in the US. At first she excused his behavior as stress-related, then she convinced herself he loved her so much that jealousy caused him to act erratically. But then Henna realized spousal abuse was nothing new to Naif. Whenever his brothers and cousins visited, she would hear bits and pieces about Naif and his other wives. She found out Nhur, his first wife and the mother of five of his children, died a mysterious death. No one would reveal the full story of the mysterious death, but she knew Naif had something to do with it. One cousin suggested he shot her accidently, another said she shot herself—that was enough to make Henna seek a change in her life.

She feared him, and was afraid of what he would do to Hajir. After all, he made his loathing for the child clear. She was in the midst of her escape when Naif arrived from Khala unexpectedly. He found all the packed suitcases in the living room and grew suspicious. She explained to him that she was only visiting her family in Minneapolis, that she wanted them to meet Hajir. But he convinced her not to go, and she agreed out of fear. When he found her talking to Haybe the next morning, and overhead the plans to escape, Naif accused her of having an affair. She tried to explain that it was only her brother Haybe she was talking to, that she wanted to visit Nadifo, but Naif was not a man who took no for an answer; he also did not take well to women who defied him. The use of force and violence was how he and his family tamed women in their lives. If killing them would discipline them, then they resorted to killing. Women in the al Ali monarchy were expected to be obedient; those who deviated from the norm saw their end very quickly. Henna fell into the category of disobedient women. He shot her with a pretty new gun he had purchased on his last trip: the handle was inlaid with delicate little mother-of-pearl designs. He shot her ten times without flinching once, in front of their daughter. He fled the country that evening after he set the entire house on fire.

The police found her, lying face-down on a gorgeously-woven Persian rug. The delicate, sparkling fabric of her dress swirled in the many brightly-colored pools that mixed together around her. Unfortunately she did not pass into the next life beautiful, happy and content, the manner in which she had envisioned her life: instead Henna was beaten so violently her face had sunken into her skull. Her body was covered in bruises and decomposed. It was as if he came back to New York to bring her end. He didn't want her to be alive if he was not going to have her as he wished.

Henna's body was found rotting in the mansion with her three-year-old daughter sleeping next to her. The police were alerted by Ramallah, who had become suspicious after Henna did not return her phone calls for two days. Unaware of the murder, Ramallah reported Henna and Hajir missing. She went to the mansion three days after Henna was killed, but could not find Henna's car where it was usually parked. Henna sought happiness in men, but it was the violence she had suffered at their hands that had created emptiness in her. In the end a man from whom she sought happiness took her life. Henna was not a match for the tragedies that hunted her: she chose to escape her problems, but in the end she died, embittered, frightened and still running.

Nadifo had unintentionally buried Henna the day she was raped. But the tragedies of that day haunted her. Why didn't she do more to help Henna? How come she was not bold enough to harm the men who ruined Henna's life? Why didn't she let Henna escape? She has lived with remorseful consciousness that she was partially responsible for Henna's confused life. She should have reached out to her, to save her from herself.

Nadifo could not reconcile with the reality that her daughter attempted to escape her past, that their life was a reminder of her lost innocence. Nadifo found out that Henna had changed her name and assumed a new identity more suited for her new life in New York City. As a model she used the name Kafia Kahin. She wanted to discard the past and be born anew. She wanted a name that was not soiled with family calamity and a horrid past. She tried more than once to shake the past off, to make sense of her fate, and assume a normal life. All her attempts failed. Kafia Kahin was as unlucky a name as Henna Cartan Gedi. Now Nadifo had to live knowing that fact for the rest of her life.

Hajir clung to the police woman who surrendered her to Nadifo a day after she was found. She fretfully sucked her thumb, her greasy messy hair hiding sad eyes: she looked dirty, as if she had not been washed for days. Nadifo reluctantly received her. Hajir soon joined the chaos of the apartment, chasing after Zaki, Asli and Sahal, oblivious to the yarn of her birth, glad to receive a sandwich, some fries and the touch of a caring relative.

Hajir's radiance and resemblance to Henna reminded Nadifo of Henna's birth: what a joyous time it was! She came at a happy time when her family prospered and Cartan was promoted to Foreign Minister, a prestigious and powerful position that had shocked everyone. She was born bright and red like the traces left from a beautiful Henna application. She was a blissful baby; her beauty attracted much attention. She was born on a bright Friday ciid morning when the entire country was in a celebratory mood. Nadifo gave birth to Henna in her home with Dr. Ignazio Raffaele Zaccaria, her OBGYN travelling from Rome to the Gedi home to deliver the baby. Every woman who visited Nadifo was radiant, flaunting unique henna designs. They brought gifts for the baby and placed their dark red flowery fingertips on her cheeks. They held the tiny baby to check her birthmark, a dark-red leaf-shaped mark at the base of her stomach. It was so beautifully placed; they said it resembled their designs. Nadifo named her Henna, purposefully rejecting all traditional names. She named her after the bright red-leaf birth mark she was born with.

CARDBOARD CHRONICLES

Nadifo was at work at Second Chances, the restaurant Brenda Gayle had financed. The restaurant had become a hot spot after other businesses mushroomed around it: a barber, a beauty shop, a grocery store, a pizza shop and a community center opened within a year, all African- and African-American-owned. Nadifo was busy at the restaurant; sometimes putting in a seven-day work week.

Engrossed on a game between the Lakers and the Rockets, Shirwac was annoyed when Zaki asked him to get his ball from under the bed. The ball had rolled over to Henna's old room which was now the children's room. He went to retrieve the ball, his attention still on the game, and that was when he found it: an old red suitcase belonging to Henna. He tossed the ball to Zaki and then pulled the suitcase from under the bed. He stared at it for a moment, wondering about its contents. Squatting on the floor, he pulled the suitcase towards him. His hands trembled and his heart shuddered as he flung open the top. Zaki and Hajir began to squabble with ear-piercing shrieks, but he ignored them as he dived into the dusty folds of the suitcase, revealing scattered photos, albums with mostly gleaming pictures taken during Henna's high school and college days, books, and dozens of CDs. He found romance novels and textbooks: one book was entitled Surviving Violence and another Chicken Soup for the Soul. He was fascinated by his late mother's music collection: Alanis Morissette's "Jagged Little Pill", Janet Jackson's, "That's the Way Love Goes", Maria Carey's "Hero" and TLC's "Creep". Then he found a stack of old sectioned cardboard boxes neatly cut and stacked like a book at the bottom of the suitcase, arranged and organized by date and held together by a thinning pink yarn. The cover said "Henna's Cardboard Chronicles". The TV blasted while he carefully took apart the stack of cardboards, going through the entire thing one piece at a time. His head felt heavy as he read the words detailing his birth.

The spectator's cheers and commentator's exhilarated bellows jostled with the written revelations inside his banging head:

"A monster dunk by Shaquille!"

Take this thing out of me.

"Another over time over the pack, oh wow!"

The beast.

"Shaq just brings that kinda energy—"

The thing.

"Right to left in the first period, wow, it's a FLAGRANT FOUL, you don't see too many times when Shaquille gives a high five!?

It was not even inspected for signs of life...

"—the Lakers had exploded it by seven, what a shot!"

...nor were the customary prayers whispered in its ears.

"I'm telling you, you don't play defense better, what a speed! Second overtime, Kobe, yeah its Kobe! It has to be reviewed, never seen an ending like that, two unbelievable shots scored at the buzzer!"

All I wanted to do was to expel the repulsive child.

"FREE-THROW AND IN THE PAINT, out of bounds!"

All the secrets that surrounded his life were right there in barely legible writing. He had searched high and low, in Naidfo's apartment, in all the rooms, closets, drawers, kitchen and bathroom cabinets, and every possible place that could hold a secret. He must have looked under all the beds in the house, but somehow his eyes never caught this particular suitcase.

Shirwac sought to unfold the mystery of his birth, from everyone around him. But the key to the mystery came to him unexpectedly one day as he babysat the kids. There it was right there under Henna's old bed, next to an old trunk where Nadifo stored African quilts and heavy acrylic faux-mink blankets.

There was nothing protecting him from the information that lurked amid the sectioned cardboards, which confirmed his suspicion: he was a child of rape, an illegitimate child, one with no rights.

After the illness that hospitalized him, Shirwac had become reserved and angry with everyone, even Henna. But now he was enraged —the new revelation saddened him. Imagine finding out you were born a hated child, under a tree in the middle of a jungle. According to the cardboard diaries that revealed his unsavory history, Nadifo kept him for exactly three days, unable to decide what to do with him. She then gave him to Tusmo when he was three days old. Henna refused to look at him, let alone breastfeed him, so Tusmo, who was breastfeeding her own five-month-old son while they were en route to the refugee camp in Kenya, agreed to breastfeed the new baby. That is how Tusmo came into his life.

They reached camp Iffo two days after Tusmo took him. Nadifo never claimed him back—she begged Tusmo to keep him. His care at that point was left to Tusmo and Sulekha. Sulekha, who had lost a baby boy at birth the same day Shirwac arrived at the camp, cared for him for a year and half as if he were her own, relieving Tusmo, who was over-whelmed with her own ten orphaned children. Through breastfeeding, Shirwac would ultimately become milk siblings to Sulekha's kids.

He could be the son of any man who violated Henna that day, any-one on the streets of Minneapolis, Hamar or anywhere in the world. For years the clues were in Henna's old room, they were all around him. And then there was that embarrassing search for a guy called Liban in Devon Woods —the poor man fled America thinking he was going to be charged with a crime he did not commit. He was killed in Hamar. He wasn't even in Hamar when Henna was attacked; the rumors that he was one of the attackers started when Henna mistook him for one of the attackers. He was hounded for a crime he did not commit, that mistake in identity eventually led to his death.

Shirwac became confused and withdrawn. He did less and less with the family. Unexpectedly Idil's words rang in his head. "Ayeeyo is evil"— that is how Idil described Nadifo. He never understood Idil's revulsion: now he reviled their grandmother as much as she did. In Iffo, whenever Nadifo came across him she'd pretend she didn't know him. She created a wall between him and Henna: she made sure the little boy born a bastard under a tree to her daughter at age fourteen would never follow them to America. She made sure he remained behind, alone, in a dirty refugee camp at the mercy of others. He remembers people struggling with what last name to give him: finally Tusmo settled on her kids' last name. He felt the oddness of the naming situation which made people fidget with unease. Tusmo gave him her children's last name, Jamac. Why didn't they just name him Shirwac "Nobody"—*since that is ultimately who I am*, he thought. He was Shirwac Jamac until Henna ordered him to change his last name to Gedi when she brought him to live with her family. A boy is named after his father: since they could not name him that way, they picked a name to suit him, but all the names in the world would not erase the reality that he was a fatherless child who would forever occupy an empty space in society's nest.

AUGUST 23, 2007.

I am cursed, dear sister, and why not? The country is cursing me. The people have been cursing us since the war, and I never understood why. But now I know. I wish I'd never left Gobwanaag—I wish I'd remained the innocent village girl that I once was, the one that did not know the ins and outs of the city. I am never to regret, my sister, for to do so is unholy, but I wish I could turn back the clock. I should have never left the village. Look at the curse on my family! Henna was killed by her millionaire husband. I taught her to seek wealth and when she did I got angry with her. I expected too much from her—I never told her how sorry I was for the violence against her.

Warsan could not stand her poor cab-driving husband, so she left behind three kids who are now confused. You remember how Warsan was spoiled and we always said her confidence erased any insecurity she may have had about her looks? She always thought she was better than everyone else and that the world owed her something. She was materialistic but then she became obsessed, and everything became about money. She had tried to live a life that was not meant for her. She wanted to prove to others that she was better than them by wearing what they call here "designer" clothes, clothes that are expensive and create a certain image. She thought she could dress up her emotional state. Her love for material possessions and love for herself ultimately destroyed her.

And Bile, that sweet little boy whom you loved so much, has turned into an angry teenager. He is now a silent child who only says "mom, leave me alone." Then I find out he is a gang leader and that he was part of a group of kids who killed a girl. Imagine—his gang name is "Warrior" and he is the head of a gang called the Rough Boyz. As if we need any more warriors. Did I bring him here to get into a gang or to better his life? He is in jail, sister, and every time I visit him I curse myself. The girl they killed left a six-year-old daughter. I see her sometimes in the community center. I feel guilty when I see the little girl my son has made an orphan.

For years I lied to you, sister. May Allah forgive me for the lies. I kept telling you they were all doing well, that they were successful and made good lives for themselves. But except for Haybe, they all turned out to be war tragedies. These days we blame everything on the war. Though they had plenty of choices, to become whatever they desired, they couldn't cope. The beauty of America is that your life depends on the path you choose to take: it is a country that gives opportunities to those who take the right path. Haybe is the only one that I can say I am proud of, the only one who did not turn out to be greedy or self-centered. He married a girl from the Gobaad people. At first I detested him for shaming the family by marrying such a girl; but now I regret what I have said to him. His wife is decent; they are the only two I can say make me proud. He is loved by all; even white and black people in this country like him for what he is doing. He is a lawyer and he helps people. He is my pride and joy, dear sister. I wish Bile had turned out to be like his brother.

Cartan and I created a fallacy for our children, teaching them to think they are important—we thought them to be entitled. They all strived to live the life we used to live. What they fail to understand is that their parents looted the country and that is why they were glorified, for Somalis glorify thieves, corrupt officials and thugs. I have found Allah's word now, and I pray to not take the sins I have committed with me to the hereafter. That is why I accept my punishment. Every time I hear a tragedy in my family, I try to feel relieved it is happening to me now rather than later when I die. I ask Allah for forgiveness, to put me in eternal heaven, for that I will endure the pain that my actions have brought me. May every tragedy in my life become one less sin for me in the hereafter, say aamiin. I accept my *hambo* life, for life has been nothing but hambo. This life feels as if it is temporary and that I will resume the real one soon, but the supposed real life never comes. This life is ultimately what has become of my leftover American life.

CAGE BATS

The end of high school marked a new path for Shirwac. Having found out about his birth and the circumstances surrounding it, he thought it best to begin anew. He started working hard in his junior year, taking his teachers by surprise. Mrs. Shaynack, the eccentric science teacher, insisted he apply to engineering schools, considering his high SAT scores and natural aptitude for science and math. All Shirwac wanted to do was to leave Minneapolis and start afresh. There were multiple reasons to escape. First of all, Hamar, where he thought he could search for a father, proved to be the murderous capital of the world—he wouldn't know where to begin. So he had to retreat to more realistic goals, like college. Another reason to escape to an unknown place, he reasoned, was to finally abandon his love for Idil. Idil was a reluctant participant, not that he ever let her know how he felt about her—his love for her may be unrequited, but it warmed his tender heart, making him forget other pressing issues such as the question that surrounded his birth; in fact his love may have been exacerbated by the rejection he felt. He could not love those who gave birth to him, could no longer love Nadifo for what she had done, so all the love in the world he could conjure up was transferred to Idil. The only person who ever acknowledged him, validated him, loved him, and the only person he felt he mattered to. So it could be said his was love by transference, not a real desire for intimacy: she was there at a drop of hat, on his side, getting angry on his behalf, saying all the words he could not summon up on his own. She defended him, worried for him, scolded people on his behalf, and used her nasty ways to shield him and look out for him. No one ever cared for him, the way she did. And for that he loved her and even at times obsessed about her.

But there was a huge obstacle to Shirwac's love, Idil herself. She would be floored if she ever found out he was yet another male impressed with her physique; she detested men who admired her just for her looks, and worked hard to never attract them in that way. But that was simply impossible; it is not as if men who liked her went for her brains, or humanity, or humility or cleverness. These were admired attributes, but their attraction was physical, and that made Idil angry. Take Josh, for example: Idil warned him to not stick around if he thought she would get mushy with him one day. "Please don't waste your time," she said when they first met. "I don't believe in all that useless stuff with boys, I hate boys and would never waste my time with them; I don't even want to get married." He knew to steer clear, although deep down he actually liked her. It was amazing how every boy her friends liked wanted Idil instead. She advised the girls to ignore the boys they liked, because ignoring them obviously worked. She had good example of women in her family who were destroyed by men and she was not going to repeat their mistakes. She associated ruined families and doomed Gedi women to the men in their lives. In her mind, men were there to do one thing and one thing only: ruin women, and she was not about to hand anyone the power to do that.

Idil would never know how Shirwac felt about her, and he was relieved that she didn't, for it could have severely impacted their relationship. She loved him so very much as her cousin—so even though he loved her so very much as a woman, he could never act on his love for her. Plus, she would frown on the idea of cousins loving each other that way, being western-minded; she would find the idea revolting. It was legal and lawful for cousins to marry in Islam—Nadifo and Cartan were cousins—but she pushed away the idea, determined that that would never become her. She referred to such things as primitive and transported culture, and viewed it as part of her extended family's life but not hers. Shirwac explained how it was normal in Islam to marry cousins, he even tried to drive the point home eagerly; but he never had the courage to tell her how he felt, and that the reason he often tried to find examples of married cousins she could relate to was so that she would warm to the idea. When he acted like a sick puppy around her so she would recognize his feelings, she would say "snap out of it Shirwac!" Whether she understood his intent or not, she ignored it—matters of the heart were always a waste of time in her opinion. She would marry one day if she felt pushed into it for practical reasons, maybe to procreate, or to find a companion not out of love but out of necessity.

And so when Shirwac found himself face-to-face with a long-legged young woman with vanilla cream complexion, small squinting eyes that made her look serious even when she was not, plump dark lips and full clear cheeks, he was ready for change. She, this new girl, was the kind of girl Nadifo often warned against: *they are fast and unyielding, stay away from them Shirwac, they will try to get their way with you!* The girl sat in the back of the stuffy classroom where he reluctantly attended Engineering 210 at North Western State University. Professor Taber, who could use a nice long frothy scrub, spent the better part of the two-hour class scraping his thinning hair to the back of his balding spot; for the entire semester, the Professor never realized he wasn't fooling anyone. Shirwac sat next to Gupta Duranjaya, a nerdy kid who slept throughout the entire class because he stayed up all night working on topics on the syllabus not yet covered. He wanted to be the one to answer every question, so that he'd win the bonus points the ever-so-boring Mr. Taber handed out for class participation, except he cheated himself by falling asleep.

One of three females in the class of mainly young men, Heaven appeared comfortable with the subject, which Shirwac thought was mainly male territory. The other two females—who also displayed equal mental agility in the class—were a Muslim girl, judging from the elegant hijab she wore, and a tall girl whose muscular, athletic build would have better suited a man. She was the captain of the crew team—not that Shirwac ever knew what crew was or why the girl's body appeared manly. So when Heaven, the quiet girl in the back of the class, started to show interest in him, it bewildered him as much as it would have Idil.

Their lives could not be more dissimilar. She was born to two professional Somali parents: her father was the Dean of the School of Engineering where they both attended, and her mother owned a successful architectural design firm. She was a child of faculty, and he was on a full scholastic scholarship. Heaven was born in America and sheltered from the likes of Shirwac—refugees devastated by war and considered unsuitable, unstable, lazy and dangerous by her father. She grew up in affluent Irwin County, in upper-class abundance. Her parents were educated, ideological, and secular in that order. Heaven, whose real name is Jano, spoke no Somali and had very limited interaction with the refugees her parents called dangerous, whose lives were marred by the collapse of their country and its aftermath. Bulxan and Geni did not want to expose their four kids to the trauma that engulfed the Somali refugee community in Minnesota; they worked hard to shield them. They left Somalia in the early eighties, met at the same university where Bulxan was now a Dean. From the start as struggling students in America, they had plans for their family, and when all four kids arrived theirs was a life of private schools, sports and after-school activities, to assure the highest success known to America. Heaven was the last of the three biological children; when Geni decided to adopt a little girl from China—that was in 1994 when Shirwac was a toddler in a destitute refugee camp, himself in need of rescue. Geni wanted a fourth child but did not want to take any more time away from her career, so instead of bothering with physically having a baby she decided to adopt one, after she watched a show about Chinese orphans. They named her Vivian, and she is now a freshman at Brown.

Everything about Heaven was odd to Shirwac. First of all, they, the biological children of Geni and Bulxan went by their translated American names: Victory, Dusty, and Heaven which are directly translated from Nasra, Awaare, and Jano. Victory, the eldest sister, was a corporate lawyer living in Hong Kong with her boyfriend. Dusty was in his last year of Yale medical school. Heaven, who oddly enough has never stepped foot in a dugsi (which almost all Somali kids must attend in order to learn Quran) was as ignorant on all things Somali as the average American. Her naiveté would emerge immediately as she shared family secrets and spoke honestly, outing family privacy like people on the morning talk shows he would guiltily find himself glued to, who let out family secrets that did not belong in the public arena. He was used to people who guarded their secrets with their lives, so those who spoke easily of them intrigued him. He grew up in a system where children were sworn to confidentiality in the womb, to never reveal family secrets; but with Heaven family privacy was something she shared easily. For example, apparently Heaven's father was living with an American woman with whom he had fathered a child, and her mother was in the process of marrying a young man from Tibet: the couple was divorced, but no one in their extended family knew it, and both the baby and the mother's marriage was a top secret, except Heaven shared the secret as if keeping it, would mar her psyche.

Heaven blabbered information he could do without, like the family secret she shared with him as she licked enchilada sauce from the corner of her mouth, guiltily muttering "so much for cutting carbs."

According to Heaven, her parent's marriage failed after Bulxan had had a fling with a younger Somali woman who made their lives a living hell. He met Tufaax at J.F.K Airport one fateful October: he was returning home after attending a conference in Germany and was using the waiting time productively to tweak the final manuscript of his sixth book *Engineering in the Technological Era* when he noticed a vivacious, voluptuous young woman chatting away on her cell phone. She wore a red dress which hugged her body in all the right places. She was drinking soda, Bulxan followed her every move with the bottle, from her lips to its resting place on the table. He must have been watching her for a good half an hour when she saw him; she then changed her seating to give herself more privacy. She later confessed she thought he was a pervert, watching her that way. He did not hesitate to move next to her and immediately strike up a conversation. The entire time he was talking with her his mind was on her body. He imagined intimacy with her as soon as he saw her. Tufaax, a strong Somali refugee, was single-minded and as hard as steel, and knew exactly what she wanted out of life. For Bulxan, Tufaax was a far cry from his wife Geni, who was diminutive, mild-mannered, hard-working, and altogether predictable—she never strayed from the straight and narrow. Tufaax, on the other hand, was adventurous, lively and fun-loving. Bulxan found himself drawn to this younger woman apparently for all the wrong reasons, in spite of his habitual distrust of Somalis. Before long Tufaax was travelling to various parts of the world to meet him. What Bulxan failed to realize is that she had her own agenda as well: her plan was to make him leave his wife and settle down with her. She was not really attracted to him as much as he was to her; after all he was a middle-aged man with a bulging belly and receding hair. But she saw an opportunity for stability with him, stability she could not find in a man her own age. She was approaching thirty-something, and all her friends were married with children. She was the last unmarried one and the pressure was mounting. Within a few weeks she planned it all out: three kids, a house in the suburbs, and in five years she will be in divorce court. She figured she would be left with at least a house and some alimony. He, on the other hand, planned to remain with her for as long as they could see each other at a whim. After a year of trekking from one state to another and from country to country, she had enough. It was she who popped the inevitable question of marriage: Bulxan tried to end the relationship and cut all contact when the fun girl made her intentions known. But he underestimated Tufaax, for Tufaax was not only interested in ruining his marriage after he dumped her—she was interested in ruining him. The FBI who was only too eager to receive informant information got a phone call from Tufaax which pointed to the distinguished professor's involvement in some underground organization. According to the informant, the organization with which Bulxan was involved was intent on destroying America. That he was in the business of teaching his Muslim students how to make explosives. That is all it took for Dr. Idris Bulxan, a respectable professor, engineer, and a prominent member of the city of Irwin, to be handcuffed in the middle of a peaceful night, ripped from his comfy American suburban life and thrown into jail like some criminal. Never mind his credentials and the multiple Board positions he held with prominent companies: he was stripped of all the accomplishments he'd worked so hard to attain. All that hard work was crushed by a tailspin of events that would not end. After he was bailed out, it took him a year to clear his name; the University gave him an unpaid sabbatical and then fired him after he was cleared of all charges. His wife divorced him and he found himself in a predicament he never thought he would be in. Six years and a few law suits later things are back to normal for Bulxan, who was reinstated albeit with a subordinate position. But the ugly episode created in him an unwavering suspicion.

Heaven, who was never bashful about sharing the most intimate details of her parents' lives, was odd, and yet honest and companionate: she was as naïve and giggly as any American girl, and would jog five miles every day, although Shirwac thought she could use some fat on her skinny bones. She volunteered at animal shelters, homeless shelters and group homes. There was a lot of honesty and humanity in Heaven, she was always busy with one volunteering project or another, trying to rescue people and animals alike. For a long time Shirwac thought maybe she was interested in him because he was another project to safe, but that was not the case. She loved him unconditionally, which was strange to him, because he did not comprehend why anyone would love him unconditionally.

There were some drawbacks with Heaven, though. She was needy, always wanting to please, annoyingly needing approval and clingy in a way Shirwac was not used to. Heaven was always bringing him gifts for one occasion or another, and he would set them aside, never valuing them quite the way she wanted him to: they got into endless fights because he never remembered to mention what she got him. She always wanted to be surprised for her birthday or some other important occasion he was unaware of: he didn't ignore these dates out of malice but simply forgot—there were entirely too many occasions to remember. Birthdays, and so many anniversaries: our very first day together, the first time we said yes to each other, the first day we promised to be exclusive, the first day you said I love you...days Shirwac could not remember. His birthday was Tusmo's creation; she'd made it up when they were accepted to immigrate to America. How could he celebrate a day and year that were fictitious like everything else in his life? Heaven was not equipped to understand that as refugees they did what they had to, even resorting to creating fake birthdays in order to survive.

The whole family tried too hard to mimic America: they were total assimilationists, from their soft tone to their spoiled way of talking to their accumulation of things. And the family drank what Shirwac for a long time though was wine but turned out to be sparkling cider. Her mother Geni often appeared indecent to him, she dressed in shorts and tight tee-shirts while in the house. He wondered what had happened to the decent long caftan most Somali women wore at home, and refused to go to their home, being embarrassed by Geni's indecent attire and her father's immature behavior with his girlfriend—companion, common-law something or other, everything under the sun except his legal Islamic wife. This certainly was a family with imposed cultural abandonment issues.

It must be true what they say: opposites attract. Shirwac was not used to needy, spoiled, clingy women; the women he has been around all his life were women who coped with situations without pity or nonsense. Women like Nadifo, Ceebla, and Idil never seemed stuck, even when they were, and they were strong, unyielding and never needy.

Unable to simply trust her, he played along, expecting for the game to end. Everything in his life eventually did. It was awkward at first she wanted to be everywhere with him. He remembers the first time she gave him a ride to run errands. After he was done, they sat in her Lexus SUV, separated by heavy breathing and stillness. He was about to get out and get his stuff from the trunk when she landed a shocking kiss on him. He didn't know what had prompted her to kiss him—maybe she thought it obligatory, or she must have seen too many movies where that was the expected outcome. Then she called him the entire night to apologize.

Again the girl was bizarre and daring, making her feelings known right from the start. He could not help but wonder why she paid so much attention to him. Shirwac could not help but think he was in some sort of bad made-for-TV teen movie, the kind where the pretty, rich girl falls for the poor shabby guy and she is happy, smiley and ever so generous.

"We are so different. Your parents will probably not be happy with your decision to fall in love with me, as you put it," he said one night as he sat across from her in an Italian bistro she picked.

"Oh my gosh, are you kidding? Daddy will love you! And mum— well she's aloof anyway."

"So, do you know what tribe you belong to?" He said to create tension.

"Tribe? What does that mean?" She asked as she stuffed fried calamari into her mouth.

"I mean what is your family lineage? Which ancestors you count your name back to?"

"My parents don't care about that stuff. They never told us, so I don't know—and frankly I don't care."

"How come you never went to dugsi school?" He asked, diving into the lasagna she picked.

"What's dugsi?" she asked with a full mouth.

"You know, Quran School," replied Shirwac in a judgmental tone.

"My parents were never particularly religious," Heaven appeared apprehensive.

"You mean they are not practicing Muslims."

"No."

"You mean they don't pray."

"No, not really."

"How come?"

"Look, we were raised with choices—religion was never a big part of who we are," she said defensively.

"It's weird to me, that is all," he said, feeling the tension.

"Victory and her boyfriend Sasha practice Taoism."

"What is that?"

"I don't know. Some Asian religion."

"You mean your sister is not a Muslim."

"I think she is—she is just exploring other spiritualities."

"And Dusty, is he Hindu?" he chuckled.

"That's not funny. He's actually the only one in my family who prays: some African-Americans at Yale introduced him to Islam in his freshman year."

"How about you, are you Muslim?" he said sheepishly.

"Yes, but I don't even know how to pray."

"I can teach you, if you like."

"No, thanks. I will learn on my own one day."

Heaven was kind and easy going where Somali girls were aggressive, calculated and manipulative. She wanted Shirwac and she would do whatever it took to win him over. He on the other hand immediately had thoughts of transformation. His ego wanted to allow her to love him enough so he could transform her: she needed to be rescued from the indecent clothing, unholy obsession with material stuff, her dead inner self which has been numbed by things, things her family gave her to avoid her soul. Maybe to Heaven Shirwac was a poor abandoned refugee who needed to be loved; but to him she was a lost soul who needed to be rescued with spiritual correctness.

For that reason, Heaven soon replaced Idil. Although he did not transfer his love for Idil to Heaven, he accepted Heaven, with all her intriguing, odd ways. He even tolerated her beagle Biscuit, although he obsessed about washing his hands afterwards. Heaven came at a time he needed a diversion. It was a nice distraction to be among people who called each other sugar, peaches, my little caterpillar, and munchkin all day long, a nice diversion to be in the presence of a mother who would endlessly repeat "pure joy" at every interval, to be among people with a different kind of drama. If he was not in class watching Dr. Taber cement his thinning hair with saliva, he was with Heaven, curiously welcoming her imperfect, American ways. Who knew he would be playing a game called rock, paper scissors? She was as baffled as he was when he informed her he was not aware of the game or its rules. For weeks after that weird encounter he searched for ways to outdo the game, thinking of other objects that could destroy all the objects.

Then there was the trip to the batting cage. When Heaven announced they would be visiting a batting cage one day, he was expecting to be taken to some cage filled with bats. He was anxious the entire ride to see how it would end, how this genius American girl would make a game out of caged bats. He was disappointed not to see any bats; and was further bewildered when she put on some weird attire and started hitting balls inside the cage. This is how she practiced for her softball game three times a week, when she was not watching back-to-back episodes of "Gilmore girls". Shirwac quickly became acquainted with Lorelai and Rory, given how often Heaven referred to them.

For almost an entire year his world contracted to the routes around campus between the cafeteria, library and his room, which he shared with Prescott Seely, a young man whose main purpose in college was to get as many girls as he could. He noticed colored blocks with Greek letters, but never cared to know what they were: he soon discovered the colored blocks belonged to Greek organizations called fraternities and sororities. He began attending football games, homecoming games, and whatever else Heaven thought they should participate in. He became part of her world; opening his eyes to the world that existed around him, one he never though he could be part of. Shirwac exiled himself to a new school, new people and new way of life, to give fate a new beginning.

COMPLETE AND LADYLIKE

Nadifo's apartment became where Haybe and Ceebla handed each other children back and forth. The place was always bursting with the thunderous noise of Sahal, now eight, Asli, seven, Zaki and Hajir both four-and-half. The same three-bedroom apartment where Cartan once claimed a corner, where Henna shunned her family in the confines of her room, where Bile escaped his family's situation through gang activity, has now become a nurturing place for four young children. Harmony was not something the Cartan family had worked hard for: but something they fell into it through tragedy. Idil who had once despised Nadifo, now visited frequently.

The leisurely lady-like manner in which she moseyed through the same corridors where she had attacked people and had been chastised by elders was a far cry from her younger days, but there was always someone to remind her of the past, which she appeared to take in stride. By all accounts Idil was doing well for herself. She seemed to have reconciled with life. She shared an apartment with her business partners, two girls she had met in college. And if one was to believe the rumors, Idil was already a millionaire at eighteen. The boutique she ran with her partners sold vintage clothes and awe-inspiring shoes and accessories from all over Europe, Asia, and Brazil, which college students paid a lot of money to purchase. Order did not come to Idil out of choice, but out of necessity. She had been on the path to destruction, with Warsan gone, Hogad in and out of jail and Hilac depressed, obese and running with some drop-out girls in Virginia: there weren't many choices, and the opportunity to fail was everywhere. She had no parents to lead her to the path of greatness, and there were too many boys in her neighborhood in trouble with the law, girls throwing their future away in marriages they were ill-equipped to handle to gain their independence. Idil was smart enough to know that was not the life she wanted.

She kept a mental list of the statistics she was not going to become: she was not going to become a pregnant teen, a doomed Gedi woman, a confused Somali girl with no other choice but marriage, and definitely not a young black woman without a future. She was adamant to change her future and began turning her life around at sixteen. She took school seriously, minded her tongue, and saved herself. She found solace in reading anything in print: books, magazines, literary magazines, and the classics. She would temporarily escape her situation by transporting her mind to places she never knew existed. She practically lived in the library: imitating Josh, she became disciplined and serious about hard work. This boy, hated by her whole community, was her savior. He introduced her to things she would otherwise not have been interested in: he was odd, did things teenagers normally disliked, such as going to the theater, and museums. She found going to the theater boring at first, but then she got hooked. They went to see a play called "Slice" about the AIDS epidemic among Muslim women, written and directed by Josh's cousin Briana. After seeing "Slice" she wrote a short story, then another. She enrolled in drama classes. Then she wrote "Hooyo", a play about her life, and sold it to Josh's cousin: that was the beginning of many more plays and scripts.

The one issue Idil could not come to terms with was Warsan's disappearance, which left a gaping hole in her life. She'd heard multiple stories of why Warsan disappeared, but none made sense. Parents abandoning kids in the care of relatives is nothing strange to her: she was surrounded by kids whose parents had dumped them for one reason or another, but it was not consolation for her, and she found it hard to cope with Warsan's mysterious disappearance.

INTRICATE ELEGANCE

In the middle of the *buraanbur* recitation was none other than Brenda Gayle—relaxed and joyous, although admittedly clumsy in her attempts to perform intricate traditional dance moves that should be done precisely and carefully. It looked easy to her when performed by women draped in their best Somali attire, heads and torsos covered elegantly with silky garbarsaars to create an artistic illusion of hidden mystique. It looked easy, the way the women swirled to the drum beats and the poetry recitation, making sure each drum beat coincided with the intricate steps of the dance. The women moved their feet, torsos and lower bodies artistically, trying to outdo each other by adding their own creative moves. Ululation and clapping from the circle of women surrounding them completed the performance. That is when Brenda got bold and threw her long arms up in the air, trying to mimic the dancers—but she was not elegant or intricate as the women before her. Nevertheless she enjoyed herself, almost tripping on the long, wide baacweyna that swathed her bulky body. She knew she would have trouble moving around in the bulky diric, but Nadifo insisted she wear it. Amy was also among the clapping women, in an olive drab diric with a pear garbasaar. She was sane enough not to simulate Brenda: she had been to enough buraanbur parties to know she was better off not swirling among master buranbur artists. The ballroom, elegantly decorated in shades of green, brimmed with many more than the two hundred guests invited. This was a fundraising event Idil had organized in honor of Warsan, who was jailed in a small country called Zandak in the west coast of Africa.

According to her family, Warsan's disappearance was deliberate. She was not kidnapped, tricked or forced to leave Minneapolis: she left willingly, in search of something grander than her life with Hannad. After three years of mystery, Warsan was finally located in Zandak. The millions she went after with Femi Obliageli were nothing more than a mirage. She met Femi Obiageli when she was assigned to his company Softer Communications as a financial analyst. He had found the mul-timillion-dollar software company ten years earlier. Femi was married at the time with four children. Warsan and Femi became close friends and began to spend time with each other, each complaining about the marriage they felt stuck in. He was ten years her senior. Warsan was not attracted to him—he was a froggy-looking man with bow legs and a huge gap between his front teeth. He was boorish and unrefined; his eyes peeked out from beneath folds of skin, red and continuously sunken; he seemed to look downward even when he was straight. He was frugal with words, and on the rare occasions when he spoke his voice was barely audible.

But he charmed her, paying attention to her when she felt most vul-nerable. There was nothing soft and sensual about Femi. He was a hard man, and life had not dealt kindly with him. From what she had gath-ered he'd served a stint in jail for fraudulent activity, there were grown children he'd abandoned back in Zandak, and perpetual accusations he was committing some crime or another to win federal contracts. He must have had friends in high places—how else would one explain away the many knots he had untied for himself? There were rumors that he was a CIA operative and as a result became a millionaire overnight.

None of this mattered to Warsan when she began to see him little more than casually. He dined her at the most expensive restaurants and bought her valuable gifts, including a brand new Mercedes. He made her forget her struggling husband and lonely life; he also made her leave the poverty-stricken Somali scene for a high life of travel to LA, New

York and London for movie premieres, Oscar after-parties, and charity events. She knew perfectly well he was luring her with his millions and grand life style. Femi liked new adventures, and this one was a challenge. She refused to be seen with him at first, rebuffing intimacy—she rejected him, too proud to be with a man with his uninviting looks, although she was attracted by his money. He set the perfect trap, knowing full well she wanted to escape the misery of her present life. Anyone could have created the mirage of life Warsan has been seeking, but Femi happened to be in the right place at the right time. She left with him to supposedly start a new company in Zandak—he promised her a partnership. Warsan left her husband and children, desperately hoping that a better life existed anywhere, even in a new country she'd never heard of or knew anything about. Her children's state of mind in her absence was the last thing in her mind.

THE DUNGEON

The awful stench of dirt never left your nose: it was the first thing one woke up to in the morning and the last thing one smelled at night. But it did not bother people; they became part of the smell, it was part of their fabric, they were part of the shitty city that swallowed their souls. And doesn't every city have its own funky smell, and don't people just get used to it? People in Harey City, the capital of Zandak, were no different; they simply went about their business, through the stench, a blend of rotten fish and sewage. But the city was not all that smelled bad to Warsan: the people in Zandak also had an entirely different smell which she was not used to. When she first arrived it was not just the stench of the city that got to her but the awful body odor that assailed her nose, from high government officials to lonely slum beggars. It was as if people had never heard of deodorant or personal hygiene, and the hot, humid weather only made things worse. She noticed people wore the same unwashed clothes for days. Daily showers were not the norm and perspiration dried on people, passing the stench from them to the noses of unsuspecting passersby. The over-spraying cologne added to the funk, and the whole thing became an unpleasant miasma that never dissipated. Streets were packed with people like sardines; there was no way of escaping the odor. The people were loud, aggressive, always looking to outdo each other. She might have gotten somewhat used to things if it was not for everyone trying to take advantage of her, even little kids. There was too much dishonesty: never knowing if the person begging was really crippled or just playing one for the day. People took turns to take advantage. One day she saw a man she had given money to a day earlier, whom she thought was crippled, climb out of his wheelchair to a perfect standing position. It was muggy, smelly, and dishonest, and even the air gripped her with its tightness. Fanning only transferred hot foul air, making her delirious.

In Zandak the sweltering surge of humanity disappeared into the massive foot traffic. In *giambara* slum where Warsan ended up after she fell from grace with Femi, the streets were at war with the massive traffic, including aggressive street traders who refused to make way for human passage unless one pushed through when meandering cars passed. The house where she was held against her will was dingy and uncompleted; it sat in uncomfortable proximity to the famous "If you don't want to see mess, don't look" rows of single rooms. There were no bathrooms: people did their business either early in the morning or late at night, out in the open.

Warsan's start in Zandak was not as horrific as it would end. She joined Femi in his ten-room mansion. He made her the CEO of his lucrative internet business Zandak I-Net, which generated three to four million dollars a year. She was at the helm of the company and split the profits with Femi. In order for her to keep her position, Warsan was required to accompany him to high level government meetings where her presence was important in gaining government contracts for the various companies he owned. She entertained government officials who were happy to have a beautiful Somali woman, but they were belligerent and sometimes abusive. For a while she ignored the fact that Femi was prostituting her: when she refused to accompany him to meetings, he threatened to demote her. So she went along: in her naïvete she would go along with him until she'd saved enough money to go back to the U.S.

She would never make it back with the two million dollars she had saved. The first year and half, things were good between them; she worked hard to earn his respect and trust. But a year after he promoted her to President and CEO of Zandak I-Net, her life changed drastically: her passport was confiscated, her account was closed, and her money transferred into Femi's personal account. She blamed the Senegalese girl Salimata Boubacar, who arrived just in time to take away her job. She was tossed aside to do the most gruesome things after Salimata arrived, the same way she had displaced Ezinne, who was one of Femi's executives until Warsan took her position. Ezinne would later die in the same slum Warsan now called home, selling drugs; she was killed by an addict who took her and the entire supply.

Soon after Salimata took over her job, she was forced to become part of Femi's criminal business. She was coerced into participating in everything, from arms deals and drug pushing to organ harvesting. Warsan was exposed to a world she had only seen in Hollywood movies. She was moved from the opulent mansion she shared with Femi, where servants and chauffeurs saw to all her needs, at last living the life she had imagined for herself, to a small-four room cement house with no running water in the worst slum. The fall was not gradual but swift and painful. She shared the jail house with twenty other women, who had all apparently fallen from grace with Femi. Femi functioned in two worlds: the crime-ridden underworld and the corrupt business of colluding with government officials. The underworld is where she found people tugging at her dress, pushing and shoving to steal the little food she was given. She never knew who was working for whom. The guards worked with street beggars, who stole the most mediocre things because "the dungeon", as the jail house was called, was bare of anything valuable. It did not make sense, since the house guards could do as they pleased. Warsan and the women would be transported to work for long grueling hours and then brought back to the dungeon. They left at five or six in the morning and were brought back at ten at night. They were never left alone and were not allowed to communicate with anyone outside the group.

Sometimes Femi would desire one of the women, and that is how Warsan learned to use her senses: her senses became her safeguard. She knew when they were coming to take her to him, so he could use her then whip her. Their rhythmic footsteps sounded loud when they were coming to take her to Femi, but when they walked unhurriedly she knew mercy came with them—that was when they brought food or gave her permission to shower, giving her an opportunity get out of the hell for an hour. At times her senses saved her, like the time Femi came to the dungeon and she hid in a kitchen closet amongst containers of kerosene, or the time he sent his brother to fetch her and she snuck out and hid in a neighbor's pig house. Sleep was impossible; she was always on guard. She went from eating the best Indian, French, Thai and Middle Eastern food to eating awful uncooked white dough with bland sauce that sometimes tasted as if it had rotten meat in it, and not enough spices to kill the horrid taste. She pushed it down her throat holding her nose to keep from throwing up, but she almost always did, unable to swallow her disgust.

There were other women confined with her: Omolara, Nnamdi and Jummai had taken risks to leave other poverty-stricken slums in Africa. They hadn't had any choice. She fell for the same scheme they fell for: she may not have known it then, but she had been tricked. She had lost her family and everything she had worked hard for in a few frivolous moments of greed and adventure, thinking she could outsmart a Zandakan. Idil raised more than one hundred and fifty thousand dollars for attorney's fees and bribe money to get Warsan out, but Warsan was still stuck in Zandak. The twin boys she gave birth to were taken away from her; Femi kept them in his mansion with other kidnapped children of the women he exploited.

Idil crowned herself savior of Gedi females trailed by bad luck. Her attempts to rescue Warsan and the boys were met with corruption, bureaucracy and mind games she was ill equipped for, but rescuing Warsan and her brothers became a mission that preoccupied Idil for years to come.

UNTAMED ROYALTY

Bitter, regretful and angry: that was the Nadifo of before. The Nadifo of now is busy running a household with four kids under ten and working full time. It's the reason her day begins at six. After dawn prayers and reading Quran, she gets the kids ready for school. With different schedules, Sahal is the first to leave at seven for an hour-long ride to third grade at Mercer Lake Charter Academy. Then it is time to tend to the two whining girls who refuse to wear the clothes she picks for them and who won't touch breakfast unless she shoves the food speedily down their throats. Morning is the most hectic time in the house because five-year-old Zaki is convinced he hates school, so it's a chore even to get him out of bed. He is the most annoying child, crying all morning till he hits the bus door steps, where Mrs. Sandoval, the driver, shouts "Come on, Zaki, I don't have all day!" It's the only way he wakes up. Fear works on him, and Mrs. Sandoval is scary. In Minnehaha Prairie Elementary, where Asli is too cool to attend first grade, the trio are not exactly ecstatic to attend before- and after-school programs. Every morning it is the same commotion: Asli not wanting to go with the babies, thinking it's time she went to Mercer with Sahal, where there is no space in second grade. She fusses most mornings, unhappy to go with Zaki and Hajir, whom she calls babies: "Why can't I go with Sahal? I hate these babies!" Then it's the long ride, punctuated with prayers and uneasiness, up the highway where Nadifo ties up rush hour with her dangerously slow driving, to Second Chances Café. Eight hours later, its back home where the kids do homework and Quran readings. Idil and Aragsan, the part-time babysitter, look after them when she is tied up at work, which is at least two times a week. Nadifo's attitude towards the kids' education has taken a tremendous shift: she has become hands-on, making sure everyone does their homework on time.

If nothing else, Nadifo has picked up the habit of order. Every evening the kids read Quran after they finish their homework: she makes them read Quran to bless Geele, Henna, Cartan and Warsan. They repeat the same prayer: *Oh Allah bless Cartan, Henna and Geele in the grave, take them to Jannatu fardows, and forgive their sins. Allah please bring Warsan back to us in peace. Bring her back to her family healthy and happy.*

The tragedies of the past have made her mellow, attentive and patient, which explains the three hours she spends every day helping the children with homework, although she is exhausted from a long day of cooking sambuusa, jerk chicken, rooti, beef suqaar, curry goat, and aloo dum. The energetic four have no inkling that she cannot make out the homework she checks: they do their work as if she knew what she was doing. There are consequences for not finishing their work: time outs, or confiscation of favorite toys. There are also rewards for good behavior.

She should have been overwhelmed with her responsibilities, but she isn't. She thinks the kids are a blessing; children are always a blessing in a household. The blessing that comes with them is not limited to the fact that Nadifo is now in a very good place in her life. Second Chances Cafe is doing very well; Hajir's family, the royal al Ali family, bought a five bedroom home for Hajir, which Nadifo and the kids moved into rent-free. Besides her income, Hajir's child support from her father's family is a blessing Nadifo humbly accepts. She has not seen this much money since her arrival in the U.S. When you do good deeds, Allah rewards you: that is how she explains what she considers an abundant life.

And so their new Minnesotan life began in Velvet Crest Cove, away from the commotion-filled hallways of Cedar Springs and the cramped apartment where they fought over space. A non-traditional family thrown together by circumstance, Nadifo and the four kids nestled in their bright, airy home accented by graciousness and warmth, rustic white oak floors and stone hearths in many of the rooms, surrounded by tranquility and wide-open expanses of rolling green hills and lakes, scarcely spoiled by human meddling. The Minneapolis suburb of Chelsea Wood boasts a prosperous downtown, where Nadifo in her sixties and the kids enjoy modern conveniences. She has become a soccer grandma, chauffeuring them to soccer and basketball games, swimming and hockey. She cannot get used to the home's exquisite design, impressive floors, arched windows facing the lake, and a double-sided stone fireplace that spilled warmth into the living room and kitchen. The kids like the family room where they do homework. The sloped, beaming ceiling graces the family room, complete with couches, HDTV and homework area with a large mahogany table. The detached three-car garage is mainly used for storage: Nadifo uses the attached two-car garage for the Sienna. Idil stays in the guest room when she is around, which was a lot more than Shirwac.

There would have been no connection between this thrown-together family and anyone from Khuzaymah Saqr Island if it were not for Naif al Ali bin Nassir. He brought tragedy and never-ending despair for Nadifo when he took Henna's life. The Gedi family, who never paid attention to the royal family of KSI, as it is known, became obsessed with everything KSI after Henna's death. The man who brought Henna's tragic, sad life to an end was born an Emir, but he was shunned by the royal family because he was the last son of King al Ali bin Nassir of Khuzaymah Saqr Island and Rahaf Nidal. The king fathered the boy, along with his nine siblings, when he went to Syria to treat what was thought to be the last stage of lung cancer. While in his death bed he married his cleaning lady, a stunning young peasant girl of twenty. While in a Syrian hospital, the king was overthrown and exiled by his son; he recovered from cancer and had ten kids with Rahaf, of which Naif was the youngest. The King passed away ten years after he married Rahaf, cut off from his millions and royal throne.

Naif grew up shunned by his twenty brothers from various mothers, particularly the four eldest, Jabbar, Adel, Saif, and Fadl, because his mother was a Syrian; the fact he and his full siblings were born in Damascus was also looked down upon. Naif and his brothers were only invited to be part of the royal family when he was fifteen, and only after the father had passed away. He grew up with insecurities, and his place in the royal family was somewhere near the bottom, alongside the women of the family who were not highly regarded. His brothers were not troubled by similar insecurities and embraced their mother's heritage, but Naif struggled with his identity, and that confusion had led to the tragedies in his life.

As a young man Naif proved himself by becoming overly ambitious. He created three companies, a communications company, a toy company and a construction company, using his family's influence and his royal stipend of twenty thousand dollars a month. His company Budur Communications became world-class and was bought by an American firm for twenty million dollars when he was only twenty-five years old. He created another communications company, al Ali Communications, which ran satellite TV channels all over the world.

Naif married five women. His first wife, who was also his first cousin Nhur Talal bin Nassir, died when he shot her at point-blank range after an argument about their first-born daughter, Amira Budur, whom he named his first company after. Nhur wanted Amira Budur to attend college in America when she graduated from high school, so that her daughter would have the opportunities she was denied. Naif was enraged when Nhur decided to take decisions concerning his children's education into her own hands. She pleaded with Naif to allow their daughter to travel to America, and it caused her death.

Naif married Henna, his fifth wife, a few months after Nhur's murder: Henna would not find out about the killing until a few months before Naif also took her life for reasons that had to do with his perception of her as a woman. Naif al Ali bin Nassir was a shy, complex man with deep psychological scars. He had delusions of persecution that his wives were cheating on him, and that everyone in his family was conspiring against him. His psychotic episodes were not limited to delusions; he also suffered from hallucinations where he heard voices. By the time Naif was hospitalized he had committed two murders and countless incidents of inappropriate or dangerous behavior.

He had married five women by the time he was twenty-seven years old, but he never loved any of them: Naif al Ali bin Nassir hated women, all women. He hated his mother for polluting his royal blood and for being a peasant; he despised his five sisters because they were products of their mother. All he wanted to do with his daughters—seven girls including Hajir—was marry them off to men from KSI who would treat them as he treated their mothers—badly, inhumanly and disgracefully.

All Naif al Ali ever wanted from life was to be accepted by his older brothers from noble blood lines. He wanted to have a Khuzayman mother like them, and he wanted to sit on the throne one day as a proud full blooded Khuzayman. But that was not to be: it was spoiled by his peasant mother Rahaf.

Naif called Badr al Ali Mental Hospital home nowadays. Two of his companies are run by his five sons. Emir Emad cleaned up his younger brother's mess, taking care of Naif's wives and children. Naif al Ali is the reason the Gedi family became obsessed with everything Khuzayman, and not in a flattering way. Hajir was shunned for her royal blood line, and even Idil, who had never paid attention to such things, took it upon herself to educate others about Khuzayman culture, once again not in a flattering manner. And so Hajir continued living with Henna's family, a family that did not hide their dislike for her Khuzayman roots. She enjoyed the trimmings of royalty on the rare occasions when she saw her extended family. But one thing remained solid in the Gedi household: Khuzaymans and their culture found only hostility in their home, and they were determined to dissuade Hajir from seeking out her royal connections.

OCTOBER 11, 2008.

Dear Sister, may Allah bring you my deepest salaams. May Allah give you and your family abundance in wisdom, patience, and prosperity. May Allah lessen your worries and bestow on you his blessings.

Today I saw a peculiar scene. A young woman on a bike was run over by an older gentleman in a car who almost killed her. I was walking home, with bags and bags of things I bought for the house. I usually don't pay attention to things that happen around me, but I saw how deliberate this man was when he pushed this young girl out of the way with his car, throwing her to the sidewalk. I dropped everything I had in my hands on the floor to help. Thank Allah there was a young man who called the police and she was taken to the hospital. Later on after I went home, the news said the man tried to kill the girl because she is black. He asked her to go back to where she came from, but this girl is American. The scene and the man's intentions scared me. I don't care about being white or black, I just want to be human. But every form I fill out demands that I spell out my color. It was one of the first things I noticed about America. The fact that I am black hit me like a ton of bricks as soon as I landed—it was announced immediately. Suddenly here I was seen only as a black woman. The fact that I am a Muslim woman adds to the discomfort.

But I don't let it bother me. I think it bothers my kids more than me. We took things for granted because we came from a country where everyone is black and we never thought of color, we didn't have to.

I always laugh when I remember the first time we saw a white person. We ran away as if we had seen a ghost. I was thirteen and you were eleven. The Russians were doing something with Mount Lacdo, and one of the Russian men happened to be passing us by as we watched the maqal on the outskirts of Gobwanaag. He stopped to greet us, but we sprinted away, ending up in our neighbor Cali Saleeban's house, crying the whole time. The man came after us to calm us down, but we refused to touch him, peeking at his white skin behind ayeeyo Cawo's diric. We kept peeking, wanting to touch that milky white skin. It looked like it would break off if we touched it. For days I could not sleep and could not be alone with the animals, afraid the ghost would come back. Now I have white people in my life. Amy and her kids are constantly coming here. The kids touch my skin; it is as if they want to see if it will rub off on them.

In this country people are divided. The whites and blacks seem to have some unfinished business that I am not sure I will ever understand. But there is one word that white people say to black people, and it usually gets them into trouble. I have no one to explain it, but if a white person uses the word black people are offended. I also don't understand why when white people say the word they have to apologize, and sometimes they lose their jobs; they are ashamed to have been caught using the word. It is one of the many things I don't understand in this country, like the names. I have been here so long and still American names confuse me. For example my Manger's name is Robert but everyone calls him Bob. How am I supposed to know Bob is another version of Robert? And then Americans confuse me with their pronunciation. Our pediatrician Dr. Whitley's first name Sean is pronounced with a "Sh" instead of S? Where is the "sh" sound in Sean? I will never know.

GLOSSARY

Aabo:	Dad.
Adeer:	Paternal uncle.
Aamiin:	Amen.
Abti:	Maternal uncle.
Agoon:	An orphan.
Akhas:	How disgusting.
Alle keen:	An illegitimate child.
Attar:	Concentrated oil perfume from Middle East.
Awoowe:	Grandfather.
Baacweyne:	A trendy bulky kaftan dress.
Baastar:	An illegitimate child, (Bastard).
Bajiye:	A popular snack made out of re-fried beans.
Beer:	A Somali delicacy of liver with onions and green paper.
Bukhuur:	The Arabic word for Incense.
Buraanbur:	Woman poetry recitation.
Cabaaya:	A black body covering garment women by Muslim women.
Cabd:	Slave.
Caday:	A traditional twig used to clean teeth.
Cambuulo:	A dish of beans, sesame oil and sugar used for special occasions.
Canjeero:	Somali pancake.
Ceeb:	A shameful act.
Cigaal Shiidaad:	A legendary character known for his cowardly acts.
Ciid:	Muslim Religious holiday and festival.
Cudurkii xumaa:	AIDS.

Dabar:	Stained teeth as a result of lack of chloride in water.
Dawaco:	Fox.
Dermo:	Rush mat.
Dhaandhaan:	Idiot.
Dhaqan celis:	Re-introducing Somali traditions to Diaspora born children.
Dhuxul Cad:	A fictitious refugee camp in Kenya.
Diric:	A woman's dress (kaftan-style of very light material).
Doqon:	A foolish person.
Dugsi:	Quran School.
Eeddo:	Fraternal aunt.
Eeyaa:	A rude term used to refer to older women.
Faal:	A spell put in a person for harm.
Fadhi ku dirir (FDK):	Somali men's arm chair politicking often seen in coffee houses, mainly in the Diaspora.
Fadhi Xun:	A fictitious IDP (Internally Displaced Persons) camp in the outskirts of Mogadishu.
Farakh:	An illegitimate child.
Flight 13:	A popular term to describe Somali refugees in the US. It refers to the last possible flight that came to the US with refugees from Kenya. It could also be used as a put down to highlight the backwardness of the group.
Foox:	Frankincense.
Fulay:	Coward.
Gaajooning:	An Americanized version of the Somali word gaajo which means hungry.
Gaalo:	A person of European origin or non-Muslim.
Gaari:	A clean and neat woman.

Gabbaati:	A gift of money given in marriage to a bride's family from the groom's family.
Garac:	An illegitimate child.
Garbasaar:	A shawl that goes on the shoulders, with a woman's traditional diric dress.
Gardaadis:	A blessing ritual done a few months after a baby is born.
Geel jire:	A camel herder.
Girgire:	Coal burner used mostly for cooking.
Gobaad:	Fictitious tribe.
Gobwanaag:	A made up town in the Northern part of Somalia
Guntiino:	Woman's body warp similar to a Sari.
Guulwadayaal:	Victory pioneers.
Habaryar:	Maternal aunt.
Habo:	Short for habaryar.
Halal:	Refers to food that is permissible according to Islamic law.
Halyey:	A hero.
Hamar Jajab:	A neighborhood in Mogadishu.
Hamar:	Another name for Mogadishu, the capital of Somalia.
Hamari Dialect:	A dialect unique for the people of Mogadishu.
Hambo:	Leftover food.
Haraam:	Refers to foods that are unlawful according to the Islamic law.
Henna:	A natural plant dye that makes the dyes area red-brown color. Used for celebrations and as a beauty tattoo.
Hijab:	Modest attire for Muslim woman to veil and cover their body.
Hooyo:	Mother.
Iimaam:	A spiritual leader in a mosque.
Indhayar:	Small eyes.

Isbarmuuto:	A sugary grapefruit drink.
	It is also used in other context such as when one is met with an unfortunate situation.
Jilbaab:	A heavy two piece garb that covers the entire body, usually worn my very devout Muslim women.
Jin:	Satan.
Kaban:	A native string instrument like a guitar also known as Oud.
Kacaan:	Revolution.
Khamiis:	Ankle length robe with long sleeves worn by men in the Arab Peninsula.
Khamri:	Alcoholic drinks.
Khansiir:	Any meat or by product of a pig.
L&R (Lisan iyo Rifan):	Refers to a wearily thin person.
Laan yar:	Fictitious tribe.
Laxoox:	Somali pancake, same as canjeero.
Libaax:	Lion.
Majlis:	Middle Eastern designed floor divans.
Masar:	Egypt.
Masayr:	Jealousy.
Masjid:	Mosque.
Meher:	Dowry.
Minyaro:	Junior wife.
Miridh:	A minute.
Mirimiri:	Acacia tree.
Mu'addin:	Prayer sommoner.
Muufo:	Oven baked flat bread.
Naayaa:	Somali word used to address a female in a rude manner, often offensive.
Nacas:	A foolish person.
Qaxwe:	Coffee.
Qudhac Dheer:	A fictitious refugee camp in Kenya.

Qumayo:	A woman with a loud mouth and hot temper.
Quran:	The Islam holy book.
Reer Hamar:	A person who hails from Hamar.
Sabaayad:	Fried bread similar to an Indian Paratha.
Salaamu Calaykum:	Arabic greeting meaning peace be upon you.
Sambuusa:	Meat or vegetable stuffed pastry.
Sangadhuudhi:	A derogatory word used to describe a person with African features.
Seeddi:	Brother in law.
Shaah:	Somali Tea made with spices and milk.
Sheydaan:	Satan.
Suqaar:	A beef stew dish.
Suuq (Souq):	A market place.
Taraara:	A blessing ceremony for a pregnant woman.
Tiireh:	Root from a special tree used by traditional healers for women.
Timir:	Dates.
Uunsi:	A special Somali incense.
Wa Calaykum Asalaam:	Response to the traditional Arabic/ Islamic greeting meaning and upon you be peace.
Walaal:	Brother or sister.
Wallaahi:	A word used to stress seriousness, similar to swearing to God.
Waryaa:	Term used to address an unknown male in Somali
Wecel:	An illegitimate child.
Xaaji:	One who has completed the pilgrimage to Mecca.
Xalwo:	Sweet delicacy similar to Halva.
Xanaf:	Pain sensation felt after a surgery.
Zamhariira:	The most severe hell in the afterlife.

DIALOGUE IN SOMALI

Aabihii la gub, ma anuu halkaa igaga dhaqaaqaa. Awalba jidh xun buu ahaa. Ilaahow maanta maan dalkaygii joogo, wallee waan dooxi lahaa: I always knew he was a bad person, but I can't believe he left me.

Adiga aniga ku jecel ayeeyo: Broken sentence meaning I love you.

Afweynaa maanta halkaa ka nacnac lahaa: Afweyna was spreading his propaganda today.

Afweyne ha dhaco: Doom to Afweyne.

Afweynaa maanta xidhay rag inagga ah: Afweyne has jailed some of our cousins (clan members).

Allah hoogay, wuu dilay, bahalku, waxan foosha xun oo urayaa ayaa dilay Marta waan garanayey: Oh my God, I think the ugly beast killed her.

Bahalyahow budhuq budhuqsani: Fatso.

Foolxumada waxaad ku darsatay fulaynimo, fulay yahay fulaydu dhasahy: Not only are you fat you are a coward as well.

Haa, haa walaal: Yes brother.

Idil naga aamus, yaan nala xidhin: Shut up Idil or else we are going to jail.

Ilaahay nabad iyo caano ha ka yeelo: May God bless them.

Ma wax lagu dhalay i daa iyo diiday baa khayr yeelanaya, wallee ilma Kaarshe ayaan dad noqon: How can children who came out of such a horrible father and marriage turn good.

Naa Nadifo tani xagay idiinka timid: Hey Nadifo, where did you get this one from (Referring to young Warsan as an unattractive child).

Naa way is caddeysaye sidaana uma qurux badna: She is not that light skinned she uses fade creams to lighten her complexion.

Naayaa, adiga walaal: Hey, you sister.

War magaciisa wax igama geline iga soo saar saan caddaalaha, haddii kale wallaahi waan ku gowracayaa: I don't care about his name, get him out of my house or else I will beat the crab out of you.

QURAN REFERENCES

Acuudu Billaah: Shorter version of the phrase Acuudu Billaahi Mina Shaydaani Rajiim.

Acuudu Billaahi Mina Shaydaani Rajiim: Supplication used to guard one from Satan.

Alif laa miim daalikal kitaabu: The beginning verse of Suura Al-Baqrah or the Calf. It's the longest chapter in the Quran.

Allah: The Arabic word for God

Allahu Akbar, Allahu Akbar: which translates into "God is great" is the first part of the call to prayer. It can also be used as an informal expression of faith.

Alxamdulillah: Arabic phrase which means "All praise belongs to Allah"

Bisinka: Shorter version of the phrase *Bismillaahi Raxmaani Raxiim*.

Bismillaahi Raxmaani Raxiim: In the name of God most gracious most merciful (Commonly used when one wants guidance from God)

Innaa Lillaahi wa Innaa Ilayhi raajicuun: This is the phrase that Muslims recite when a person loses anything in life. People usually recite it upon someone's death. It *means* Verily we belong to Allah and to Allah we return.

Insha Allah: Arabic phrase: Arabic phrase meaning "If God wills it". Muslims use the phrase whenever they commit to a plan of activity.

Jannah: Heaven.

Jannatu Fardows: The highest heaven of heavens.

Subxaana Allaah, Istaqfurulah: Supplication used when one is asking God for forgiveness.

Suura: A chapter from the Quran.

PROVERBS

Talo walaal diide taagoogta ayuu ka jabaa: One who refuses a sibling's advice shall break an arm.

Naagi ama guri hakaaga jirto ama god: A female is better in her father's home or in the grave.

ARABIC

Habibi: Darling, masculine.

Habibti: Darling, feminine.

Inti min feen: Where are you from?

Sharmuuta bintal kelb: a demeaning phrase to put down women

NICK NAMES

Somalis are famous for their nicknames. People may inherit nicknames for their physical features; or clever ways or for their wisdom. Sometimes nicknames are overt, other times they are covert. Covert nicknames are rarely used in front of the person.

Afweyne:	Big mouth: A name given to the late president of Somalia Mohamed Siyad Barre.
Amina Lugdheer:	Amina the long legged.
Arraweelo:	A mythical queen who neutered all the men under her reign.
Axmed wax ma diide:	Axmed the ever accepting.
Cali Cawar:	Ali the eyeless.
Cilmi Cadde:	Cilmi white.
Cumar Bakayle:	Cumar the rabbit.
Faadumo Dawaco:	Fatima Fox.
Faroole:	Fingerless.
Filsan Jiis:	Filsan the crippled.
Firqat Shaydaan:	A name given to a group of women, which means the Satan Group.
Gaal is mood:	An American wannabe.
Gacanlow:	The handless.
Guleed Dafle:	Guleed hyper.
Hoodo- Qalanjo:	Hoodo the attractive.
Istaahil CNN:	Istaahil chatty.
Laangadhe:	The limping one.
Liban Culusow:	Liban the heavy.
Lugbuur:	Fat legged.
Mire Jeenyo:	Long legged.
Shirwac Madoobe:	Shirwac darkie.

Shirwac Qahar:	Shirwac nuisance.
Shirwac Shar:	Shiwac the devil.
Shukri Buuro:	Shukri fatso.
Tiriig Belo:	Tirig the mischief.
Ugaas Faruur:	Ugaas the Harelip.
Warfaa Badhnaag:	Warfaa the feminine.
Yoonis Tuug:	Yonis the thief.

SOMALI LULLABY

Huuwa ya Huuwa, hooyo ma joogto *Huwaa oh Huwaa where has mother gone*

Kabax kabax aadday *She has gone taking her shoes with her*

Kabaheedi qaadatay *She may have met with the camel herder or*

Geel jire helyaa mooyi *She may have gotten lost in that dusty tree*

Geedkii habaasweyne *Huuwa oh Huuwa*
Ku habowdayaa mooyi

THE SOMALI ALPHABET

B	bah
T	tah
J	jah
X	xah (with a ha sound)
KH	kha
D	daa
R	rah
S	sah
SH	shaah
DH	dhah
C	Cah (with an A sound)
G	Gah
F	Fa
Q	Qa
K	Kah
L	Lah
M	Mah
N	Nah
W	Wah
H	Ha
Y	Ya

VOWELS

A	ah
E	eh
I	ih
O	oh
U	uh
Aa	aah
Ee	Eeh
Ii	Iih
Oo	Ooh
Uu	Uuh

LaVergne, TN USA
20 January 2010
170591LV00002B/51/P